COMBATING CHAOS

CHAOS

ALL SYSTEMS DOWN

Jill S. Flateland

ISBN 978-1-966012-00-9 (paperback)
ISBN 978-1-966012-01-6 (hardcover)
ISBN 978-1-966012-02-3 (digital)

First printing: February 2020
Revised and ©: July 2024

Website: JillSFlateland.com

Cover illustration by Kendra Petersen

Printed in the United States of America

10 9 8 7 6 5 4 3 2 1
First Edition
Second Edition

Dedication to My Family

I dedicate this book to my husband, Byron B. Flateland. I am grateful for his continued support. He is my greatest inspiration and the love of my life. I feel blessed knowing he loves me and will stand beside me always. For this, I am truly grateful.

Over the years, we've visited 86 countries, and we have barely touched the surface of the world. Wherever I go, I meet new people and learn about their culture. It's been thrilling to weave bits of their personalities, insights, and inspiration to create the soul of my characters.

My true blessings are our daughters, Kirsten Sielaff and Crystal Fletcher, and their husbands, Tim Sielaff and Jason Fletcher. Kirsten set aside time to edit my novels, making many corrections and patiently reviewing my rewrites. Her technology skills have bailed me out on many occasions. Thanks to Crystal for her great sense of humor, honest appraisal, and for supplying me with updated criminal, forensic, and pharmaceutical information I can use in many more novels.

Thank you to my sister, Cindy Williams, for all the help and wisdom you've shared with me in writing these novels. We share a special bond like no other, like a gem, you shine brightly and reflect your radiance on our world. You are truly gifted, and I love you dearly.

Special Acknowledgments

I am grateful for my dear friend Renee Bergeron, whom I've known and loved since grade school. She has years of experience as an attorney and public defender. Her insightful feedback on legal situations in this book has been invaluable. Thanks for letting me tap into your brilliant mind and bounce around ideas for plotting these scenes. It's like old times, and as usual, you keep me on the straight and narrow while having another great adventure.

I want to also thank Jeri Lou Maus and Mary Ann Fraser, friends who gave their time and effort to help produce a better, stronger manuscript. I'm amazed at their thorough feedback and rapid turnaround time. Jeri Lou has been on several trips with us, including visiting Vill-Angel Medical Clinic in Kitale, Kenya. Our trip to Africa was a wonderful adventure.

Regrettably, Mary Ann passed away on May 18, 2022, following a car accident. I miss her kind words, genuine insight, and talented music, as she was also our church organist—loving gratitude, always.

I am blessed to have a terrific graphic artist, Kendra Petersen, who creates the most wonderful book covers depicting the story within. I never know what I'll get, but I've never been disappointed.

Last but far from least, I give thanks to the 93rd Street Irregulars, my writer's group, who I'm privileged to call my sounding board for creating this novel. They helped to refine the chapters, bring my characters to life, and make the book flow.

Agent Joshtine Cordelia-Hastings Crisis Series
By Jill S. Flateland

Combating Chaos: All Systems Down is the fourth book in the Agent Dr. Joshtine Cordelia-Hastings Series. In the aftermath of taking down the New York power grid, Cordy discovers a far greater terrorist plot involving major international cities: London, Paris, Berlin, and Rome, plus an attack on the U.S.'s largest oil corporation near Wichita Falls, Texas, and discovers a Russian General Okueva is behind the plot. Cordy and her team unite with foreign agents racing to prevent further disaster as the clock ticks closer to destruction.

The third novel is Crashing The Grid where Cordy and her team race to reverse a cyber attack on Air Force One, which is the climax of the second novel, Rapid Response. In that book, Cordy fought against a bioterrorist attack. Cordy rushes to find a cure when U.S. President Spendorf, his key advisors, and many members of Congress become infected with the deadly Virus X. After landing in the U.S., Cordy and her team are faced with a major crisis. A terrorist organization has taken down New York City's power grid and water treatment plants all over the country. In a world of complex electronic puzzles, Cordy's skills as the leader of the FBI's Intelligence Analyst team are put to the test. Her past experience as an FBI research analyst has honed her abilities to analyze, decrypt, and decode information. Cordy's strategic thinking and ability to plan ahead like a chess game have helped her stay ahead of every move, always anticipating three steps ahead of the enemy.

If you read Sweet Revenge, the first novel in the series, you have already met Cordy. She is an adventurous, quick-witted, and energetic woman in the prime of her life. Despite being absolutely feminine, she is equal to any man. Her shoulder-length, strawberry-blonde hair is usually styled in a professional French braid, which shows off her heart-shaped face, ivory skin, and alert eyes, the color of a spring pond.

Her Irish-French heritage manifests itself in her contrasting personality traits. Her father's Irish ancestry instilled in her a strong sense of honesty, loyalty, and a slow-to-anger disposition, unlike her father, who was known for his short fuse. However, when she reaches her breaking point, she displays the heart of a French lion and can be fierce in standing up for what she believes is right, just like her mother. She never gives up and will fight for what is right, refusing to accept defeat.

Character Summaries

<u>**Major Characters:**</u>

Dr. Quint Altari, PhD – Former intelligence agent, MIT graduate with PhD in computer science, Cordy's lead IT intelligence analyst

Dr. Joshtine Cordelia-Hastings, PhD, DFS (Cordy) – Lead Cyber Threat and Research Analyst, Former FBI intelligence analyst, MIT graduate with dual PhDs in computer science and forensic criminology, recently promoted to Head of the FBI Cyber Team, Braun's wife

Vice President Thomas James Harris, JD (Tom) – VP under President Spendorf sworn in as acting president during Spendorf's recovery

Agent Braun Hastings – Commander for a Ghost Unit within the Joint Special Operations Command (JSOC), former FBI agent, negotiator, and SWAT commander, Cordy's husband, Usher's brother, Usher's younger brother

Special Agent Usher Hastings – Special agent foreign affairs, FBI agent, former SWAT, Braun's older older brother

Chief Jackson – Private Investigator, former FBI agent, previous boss of Cordy, Braun, and Usher

Agent Dr. Jacqueford Kelly, RN, DNP – Nurse Practitioner with Doctorate in Nursing, FBI, RR7 member

Lieutenant Roland Kildeer (codename risingstar) – Double agent for Bratva, Special Russian agent for General Okueva, installed 5th Dimension virus and the Big V, creating an NYC cyber attack, downed a plane, wiped out NY grid, contaminated water systems, etc.

Alexa Flinsh-Klinedorf – AK's half-sister who found AK after hit-and-run incident killing AK

Victor Klinedorf – Parking Garage Superintendent at OYZ Foundation, Alexa's husband

Alyosha Krackovitz, JD, nicknamed Cracker – IT specialist, Russian lawyer, member of 'The Team,' Floyd's cellmate at a supermax prison after being convicted of murdering FBI Agent Crueger Yates, serving a life sentence–not guilty, Rozalina's husband

Dr. Rozalina Krackovitz, MD – Russian medical doctor, member of 'The Team' as computer researcher and hacker after her husband flees Russia for the U.S., Cracker's wife

Agent Zina McLoughlin – FBI liaison officer from Dublin, Ireland, stationed in London, UK, sent on original assignment to hunt down Cracker in Russia, later partnered with Usher to track down General Okueva in Russia.

General Surko Okueva (code name Risingsickle, and the Journalist) – Leader of the Chechen mafia, rival to Bratva, joined General Rutoon to overthrow democratic governments in the U.S., Great Britain, France, Germany, and Italy; hires students to hack major financial systems

Captain Ahtoh (Anton) Orlov – Part of 'The Team,' 2nd in command, member of Russian Bratva, renowned hacker, Svetlana's Papa

Svetlana Orlov (also Ivanhoe) – Fifteen-year-old hacker, only surviving daughter of Anton, poses as her dead brother, Ivanhoe

General Rutoon – President Spendorf's trusted friend and past commanding officer in the U.S. Marine Corps, National Security Advisor, who betrayed all when he launched a deadly bioterrorist attack. The lethal Virus X infected Spendorf and killed Rutoon, but not before joining forces with Okueva, planning multiple cyberattacks across the democratic world

Emma Sloan, RN, MSN, CCRN – Registered nurse certified in critical care, kidnapped by Zahair, Loran's wife

Agent Loran Sloan – FBI Director and Braun's and Usher's boss, Emma's husband

Perry Smirnov – Eighteen-year-old hacker who created the Big V Virus that was stolen, enhanced, and wiped out NY grid, member of 'The Team,' worked for Russian government then was wooed away to Red Panda at South Africa, but soon was charged with embezzlement of Russian funds and sought asylum in U.S., Svetlana's best friend

U.S. President Isaac (Zac) Spendorf – Recovering from Virus X

Floyd Wecholtz, CFO, MBA – Former CFO of OYZ Foundation, convicted of murdering AK and embezzler of investment funds, serving a life sentence in a supermax–not guilty

<u>**Secondary Characters:**</u>

Zev Abadi – Student hacker from Israel breaking into American Express, last year at the University of Iowa studying computer engineering

Lieutenant Boris – Member of Russian Bratva, Anton's neighbor

Russ Bracken – SWAT Team Leader of Federal Forces in Colorado, former Navy Seal Special Ops Explosive Breacher, served in Afghanistan, Cordy's past boyfriend

Marshal Albert Chernyshevsky (Uncle Albert) – A Russian hero retired at the highest military rank as a Marshal, leader of the Rebel Army, Rozalina's uncle

Chico – SWAT Member under Bracken's command, served with Bracken in Afghanistan

Desmond – Bomb expert under Bracken's command, former Seal, newest team member

Colonel General Dimitri – Pilot, 2nd in command of Marshal Albert's Rebel Army

Colonel Denys Evanko – Head of the Ukraine mafia

Sergeant Foley – Bomb expert under Bracken's command, served with Bracken in Afghanistan

Governor Mo Hendrum, JD – Governor of New York, former attorney, judge who sentenced Floyd Wecholtz to life in a supermax prison

Sophia Hendrum, JD – Attorney, public defender for Floyd Wecholtz, Mo's wife

Agent Orin House – FBI negotiator

Seamore Hyde – MIT professor, expert witness reviewing parking garage camera feed (videotape)

Chief Ignacio – Moscow's chief of police, an oligarch, an underground leader of the Chechen mafia

Maude Ingram – AK's secretary at OYZ Foundation

Officer J.D. – Peggy Wyller's partner at Metropolitan Police Department 4th Division

Kayman – SWAT member under Bracken's command, served with Bracken in Afghanistan

Andrew Madeim Edwardo Flinsh-Kedderton (AK) – Founder, CEO of OYZ Foundation, world-renowned philanthropist, Floyd Wecholtz's partner

Alexa Flinsh-Klinedorf – AK's half-sister who found AK after a hit-and-run incident killing AK, Victor's wife

Victor Klinedorf – Parking Garage Superintendent at OYZ Foundation, Alexa's husband

Lieutenant Colonel Leo – Serves in Marshal Albert's Rebel Army, Vlad's military partner, and friend

Dr. Manaheim, MD (Manny) – Lead physician at Russian Medical Center who works as an undercover agent with Rozalina, brother of Feliks and Trey

Dr. Feliks Manaheim, MD – Russian Coroner, Medical Examiner, older brother of Manny and Trey

Trey Manaheim – Vnukovo International Airport tower's controller, youngest brother of Feliks and Trey

Ron Moore-Les, JD – DA for New York City in Floyd Wecholtz's trial

Jabril Pacaud – Student hacker from Israel breaking into the Pentagon, last year student at Wichita State University studying economics and business management, Zev's cousin

Dr. Nat Ping, MD, PhD in Internal Medicine – Recently promoted to National Security Advisor, retired Secretary of Health and Human Services (HHS), former Central Intelligence agent for counter-terrorism, former Senate Foreign Relations Committee member

Chief Amos Polack – New chief of Metropolitan Police Department in Washington, D.C.

Poncho – SWAT member under Bracken, 2nd in command, served with Bracken in Afghanistan

Agent Saul Reed – U.S. FBI agent also assigned to hunt down Cracker in Russia and returned to the U.S. after assuming Cracker died of a myocardial infarction

Rolo – Manny's pilot

Cadden Singh – Student hacker from Pakistan breaking into Wells Fargo, native language is Urdu, in final year of medical school, front-runner for Valedictorian of his class

Agent Lester Smirro – FBI agent who took over Kildeer's case from Cordy

Termine – Okueva's computer guru overseeing the Wichita students' hacker assignments

General Urk – Commander of the Russian mafia known as Bratva, Captain Anton Orlov's boss as leader of 'The Team'

Vlad – Usher's Russian contact for Special Operations, later joins Marshal Albert's Rebel Army

Guy Weimer – Secretary of Dept. of Homeland Security (DHS), RR7 member

Ashton Wellshire, JD – Floyd's ex-lawyer

Winston Willoughby – President's chief of staff

Carl Wyller – Secretary of Dept. of Defense (DoD), RR7 member, Peggy's husband

Officer Peggy Wyller – Police officer at Metropolitan Police Department 4th Division in Washington, D.C., Carl's wife

Xander – Student hacker from Pushkin, Russia, breaking into the New York Stock Exchange, senior at Wichita State University majoring in computer science

Abbreviations

AA – Alcoholics Anonymous

AC – Air conditioning

ADT – Atlantic Daylight Time

AFB – Air Force Base

ATC – Air Traffic Control

BATT – Ballistic Armored Tactical Transport

BBC – British Broadcasting Corporation

BST – British Summer Time

CDC – Centers for Disease Control and Prevention

CDT – Central Daylight Time

CEO – Chief Financial Officer

CFO – Chief Financial Officer

Chert – Crap in Russian

CNN – Cable News Network

CVG – Cincinnati-northern Kentucky International Airport

CET – Central European Time

CIA – Central Intelligence Agency

DA – District Attorney

Da – Yes, in Russian

D.C. – District of Columbia

DoD – Department of Defense

DHC – Department of Health Control

DHS – Department of Homeland Security

EDT – Eastern Daylight Time

EEST – Eastern European Summer Time

EMDR Training – Eye Movement Desensitization and Reprocessing training to determine if a person is lying or telling the truth

EMT – Emergency Medical Technician

EOD – Explosive Ordnance Disposal

ETA – Estimated Time of Arrival

FBI – Federal Bureau of Investigations

FDA – Food and Drug Administration

FEMA – Federal Emergency Management Agency

FHTI – Future Hub Transit, Inc

GA – Gamblers Anonymous

GPS – Global Positioning System

HUD – Housing and Urban Development

ICU – Intensive Care Unit

ID – Identification

IEDD – Improvised Explosive Device Disposal

ISIS – Islamic States of Iraq and Syria

IP address – Internet protocol address, a logical address assigned to each device to identify personal data

IV – Intravenous

IT – Information Technology

JD – Juris Doctor, graduate degree in law

JSOC – Joint Special Operations Command

KGB – Komitet Gosudarstvennoy Bezopasnosti (Soviet Union's primary internal security agency)

LYA – Love you always

MD/PhD – Doctor of Medicine/Doctor of Philosophy

MIT – Massachusetts Institute of Technology

MDT – Mountain Daylight Time

MSK – Moscow Standard Time

NASA – National Aeronautics and Space Administration

NBC – National Broadcasting Company

NSA – National Security Agency

Nyet – No in Russian

NYSE – New York Stock Exchange

Pen drive – Also known as thumb drive or flash drive

PDT – Pacific Daylight Time

RNAV – Area navigation

RN/DNP – Registered Nurse/Doctor of Nursing Practice (Nurse Practitioner)

Ser – Sir in Russian

Spasibo – Thank you in Russian

STAT – Medical term from the Latin word statim, meaning immediately

STRATCOM – U.S. Strategic Command is one of eleven unified commands under the Department of Defense

SUV – Sport Utility Vehicle

SVR – Sluzhba Vneshney Razvedki (Russian Foreign Intelligence Service)

SWAT – Special Weapons and Tactics

UAE – United Arab Emirates

U.S. – United States

Washington, D.C. – Washington, District of Columbia

WW – World War

Table of Contents

FESS UP!

Sept. 15, 20?? – 7:50 a.m. EDT,
Cincinnati, Ohio Police Station

Agent Joshtine Cordelia-Hastings, known as Cordy, bolted upright in the car seat, her eyes wide with disbelief as she exclaimed, "Oh, no! I can't believe you did that!"

"What did I do?" her husband, JSOC commander Braun Hastings, asked as he drove to Cincinnati's District 2 Police Station for an interview with a Russian terrorist, Roland Kildeer.

"Not you!" Cordy balanced her laptop on her knees, her fingers rapidly tapping her keyboard. Nervous energy poured through every cell as line after line of code became quarantined on her darknet. "Stop! You're killing my laptop!"

"Who's killing your laptop?" Braun asked.

"Kildeer's code!" Cordy exclaimed as she hit the power button twice, her voice trembling with emotion. "I just entered the equipment code I received from the William H. Zimmer Power Station that Kildeer delivered two days ago. It's a faulty software update causing power grids to go offline, much like CrowdStrike's latest outage, but that was global and caused a system-wide crash of banks, hospitals, airlines, and more. It took weeks to repair. Just think what this virus could do if populated just in the U.S. It can shut down every power grid in the nation."

"How can that be?" Braun asked. "CrowdStrike is cloud-based, and this is only on a thumb drive."

"Either way, the virus is devastating, and it's on my device!" Panicked, Cordy flipped the laptop over, removed the battery, and shut down her computer. "Why now? I'm too busy for this!"

"You'll figure it out," Braun said. "You always amaze me."

"This is far worse than I imagined." Cordy entered a text message to her lead analyst, "Quint. Warning: Don't enter Kildeer's code into your laptop. The 5th dimension worm self-destructs as each line is read and implemented. It took seconds to wipe out my code and will take hours, maybe even days, to repair my software."

Braun placed a hand over Cordy's trembling fingers. "I can tell you want to work on that, but first, we must find out what else Kildeer has planted. You've been up since 3 a.m., spending nearly every waking moment working to reverse the Big V virus and installing your malware detection program in systems across the U.S."

Cordy clasped his hand and gave it an affectionate squeeze. "Perry's reversal worked great for the Big V virus, but it's the 5th Dimension that's the problem. Perry can't arrive soon enough. We can use his help." She blew out a deep breath to calm herself. "My gut says there's more ahead, but what?"

Braun exited the highway and headed for the police station. "We're almost there."

"We must find the mastermind behind the attacks." She checked her watch. "It's nearly 8 a.m. Agent Smirro should be here by now. I can't wait to interview Kildeer."

Braun circled the block for a second time. "Don't be too anxious to meet Smirro. If I were in charge, Roland Kildeer's case would have been mine."

"Why did your boss give it to Smirro?" Cordy asked.

"He was the next FBI agent open for an assignment, but he's not the easiest person to get along with." Braun slowed the car as he got closer to the precinct building. "I can't find a place to park."

"Drop me off, and I'll meet you inside." Cordy threw open the passenger's door as soon as he pulled to the curb and dashed inside the station. She nearly collided with the cantankerous, gray-haired curmudgeon. "Agent Smirro, I'm glad I ran into you. I want to sit in during your interview with Roland Kildeer. I have a whole list of questions—"

"Nope, not happening. I don't want you in the interrogation room," Smirro said as he walked up to the counter and showed his credentials. "I'm here to interview Roland Kildeer."

The officer behind the desk called Detainment to bring Kildeer to Interrogation Room 2.

Cordy stepped behind Smirro. "Why can't I—"

"Kildeer knows you set him up." Smirro raised his voice. "Your presence will only create a negative outcome. I'm sure you found proof of his involvement on those thumb drives Braun confiscated."

Cordy crossed her arms over her chest and scowled. "You know he used that digital code to destroy New York's power grid. If that malware goes viral, it will wipe out our power stations. With no electricity, there are not enough generators to keep U.S. businesses, hospitals, or financial systems operational. Traffic lights, fuel pumps, heating, cooling, and water systems will shut down. Transportation will come to a halt once vehicles run out of gas. Food will spoil without refrigeration, and people could starve. Lack of phone and internet services will cut off communication—"

"Isn't it fortunate you stopped Kildeer before any of that happened?" Smirro walked down the hallway, still muttering.

"But what if we're too late, and he planted this into other power grids? Cordy snapped.

"If so, focus on trapping that code to prevent further damage. My job is to uncover who is behind the cyber warfare. He wasn't working alone; I doubt he even wrote a single line of that code."

Cordy was sure Kildeer hadn't written the code either and dashed after the agent to try again, "I have a list of questions a mile long and need answers. I'd be glad to share."

Smirro threw open the door to Observation Room 2. "I've been interrogating suspects since you were in diapers," Smirro said as he pulled his navy polyester suit jacket tighter around his rotund belly. "You can wait in here."

Braun stepped into Smirro's path and glared at the man. "That's unacceptable, Lester. She knows Kildeer didn't write the code. He only planted it, but he can help us find the ringleader."

Smirro shook his head. "She's not to meet with Kildeer."

Braun persisted, "We've discussed your past decisions to prohibit female interrogators."

Smirro remained unmoved. "You've heard my arguments, so let's drop it, or we'll waste our time getting our boss to reassign the case and wait another week. We all know this is urgent, so let's move on."

Anger tore through Cordy like a tornado, twisting and turning her gut. "Wait! I disagree." Seeing Smirro's determined expression, she seethed inside, "But if I have no say in the matter, I will watch you like a hawk through this two-way mirror, taking notes and recording every word you say."

The older man stiffened and cleared his throat. "Fine. Take all the notes you want."

Determined, Cordy tried again and handed him a list of questions for Kildeer. "I need answers to these—"

"You wasted your time." Smirro grabbed the list, wadded the paper, and threw it in the trash on his way to his interview with Kildeer. "I'll ask the questions."

Cordy stood her ground. "And I'll be watching."

Smirro made a gesture of disgust. His beady eyes shifted toward Cordy and narrowed into a glare. "This is my interview, and I'll do it my way. I don't want to hear another word from either of you." He gave Braun an abrupt nod of dismissal.

Braun blocked the interrogation room door. "I'm going with you."

Smirro looked as if he was ready to bolt and then sighed. "Let's get started."

Cordy heard a hint of fear in his voice. She clenched her fists as she moved toward Braun. "You can sit in, but I can't? That's just bullshit!" She was about to give Smirro a piece of her mind.

Braun put his hand on her arm and shook his head. "I know you're pissed, but I'll do my best to get answers."

Cordy didn't rattle easily. Her gaze followed Smirro as he grabbed the doorknob of the interrogation room. She wondered if he could feel the invisible poison darts she was throwing at the back of his poorly fitted suit.

Braun's lips twitched as he tried to hold back a grin. "I warned you that he was a handful. Take plenty of notes while the old man asks questions. He is renowned for his off-beat interviewing techniques, but he gets results. I'm sure Kildeer will have a few kind words to say about you, too."

Cordy sighed in defeat and then regained her composure. "I want to be inside that room, even if only a casual fly on the wall."

"Oh, darling, you couldn't be casual if your life depended on it," Braun smiled his lopsided grin.

Cordy pulled away. "Don't call me darling!"

"That's what I love about you. You're stubborn and hard-headed, and you don't take advice very well, especially mine."

She stiffened and opened her mouth.

Braun placed his index finger over her lips. "Now, don't be offended. I'm proud you know what you want and will fight to get it." His eyes darkened as he leaned closer and whispered, "Later. Let's see what Kildeer has to say and wrap this up." He took her gently by the elbow and guided her inside the observation room. "His touch left a sweet, tingling sensation that lingered, redirecting her anger to thoughts of future possibilities once they were alone.

Smirro stood outside the interrogation room with a wide, smug grin as if he'd won his first battle with her. "Are you ready? We don't have all day."

Cordy's cheeks burned as her dislike for Agent Smirro grew by the minute. To be honest, at the thought of Braun being allowed in the interrogation, she wasn't all that thrilled with Braun either.

Smirro gave one last dig, "You're lucky I'm letting you watch *my* interview from that observation room. I mean it, you stay put! You handed him over to the FBI, and he's mine now." Smirro turned his back and opened the door to the interrogation room in a flurry.

"Wait." Braun kissed Cordy on the cheek, bolted for the door, and blocked it as Smirro tried to slam it in his face. "I told you, I'm going with you."

Cordy paced, physically shaking to maintain control. I guess I should be happy, *at least Braun will be there.* His sudden kiss had thrown her off balance, so she took extra precautions to ensure she didn't miss any subtle cues, grabbed her cell phone, and hit record. *Now I can replay Kildeer's interview when I'm not so upset.*

Her gaze was fixed on Kildeer through a two-way mirror. The room was sparsely furnished, with only a metal table and four chairs. The windowless walls were cold, gray concrete. The floor was also made of cement, and a camera hung from the ceiling, monitoring every move. Kildeer looked up and smiled as if he knew of Cordy's presence, sending a shiver down her spine.

Thanks to her EMDR training, Cordy could interpret Kildeer's body language during their conversation. She understood that his eyes could convey a lot of information. If he looked up and to the right, he might be lying, and if he looked to the left, he could be thinking or remembering something. Since Cordy's laptop was infected, Cordy made sure to have a pen and notebook ready to take notes on any additional questions and to keep track of the answers.

FBI Agent Smirro introduced himself to Roland Kildeer and his fresh, out-of-law school, court-appointed lawyer. The kid still had blemishes on his face, but his attire, a navy blue pin-striped suit, white shirt, and a maroon necktie, befitted a lawyer.

Dressed in a gray jumpsuit, Kildeer sat behind the table—his wrists and ankles in cuffs. His eyes traveled around the room, but as soon as he saw Braun, he caved in on himself—shoulders drooped, head down, and hands clenched.

The four men gathered around the table: Kildeer and his lawyer on one side, Smirro and Braun on the other. Smirro sat across from Kildeer. After brief introductions, Braun informed the suspect the interview would be recorded.

Smirro took the lead and asked, "Is Roland Kildeer your real name?" Kildeer nodded. Smirro leaned forward. "Is that a yes?"

Kildeer nodded again, but he didn't look at Smirro. Instead, he stared at the two-way window.

Cordy knew the name given to him at birth was Vasily Vladimirovich Petrov. *Will he divulge this information?*

"Speak up! We're recording this," Smirro snapped.

Kildeer's eyes narrowed. "It's the name I go by."

Braun pushed forward, "But it's not the name you were given when you were born." Kildeer's eyes flashed with fire at that comment.

"Nyet."

Smirro glared at Braun, annoyed at his intrusion, then asked, "What name were you given at birth?"

"Vasily."

"Full name and spell it," Smirro said. Kildeer slurred the letters, but Cordy could understand him clearly enough that he admitted his real name.

"Where were you born?" Smirro asked.

"Russia."

Again, Braun interjected, "Where in Russia?"

The small talk continued, but Cordy already knew this information and was impatient for them to get to the meat of the interview. *You're wasting precious moments while a crisis continues to create chaos in New York.* "When were you born? Who were your parents? Spell your mother's maiden name. What was your latest address? Tell me about…" *At this rate, the interview will take hours. Let's get on with it.*

As if Braun knew she was ready to climb the walls, he leaned forward and tried a different tactic. "When did you arrive in the United States?"

Kildeer didn't answer.

His attorney whispered something in Kildeer's ear.

"What does it matter? I'm here now," Kildeer crossed his arms over his chest. The room remained silent. Kildeer glanced once again at the two-way mirror, shifted his weight, and tapped his foot on the floor. "You already know these answers, and if you don't, ask that sexy little receptionist at the Power Station. I think her nametag read Sandy, but I figure she works with you. No doubt, she already has all that information. I'm sure she's out there monitoring my every move."

Not only was Cordy watching, but she had five pages of additional questions that she wanted to ask, and they had been in the room for thirty minutes.

Braun held up the two pen drives retrieved from Kildeer's pocket during his arrest. One was a sleek, silver case no bigger than a thumbnail, and the other was a narrow stick about two inches long covered in black plastic. "Where did you get these thumb drives?"

"We call them pen drives," Kildeer corrected.

Smirro placed his splayed hands on the table and leaned forward, glaring at the suspect. "Don't give me your BS, Kildeer! Just answer the question. Who gave you those drives?"

Kildeer glared back. "I don't remember."

Braun held up the drives and shook his fist. "These contain a virus. Do you deny installing them into the equipment at the Indian Point Power plant in New York City?"

Kildeer shrugged his shoulder. "A virus, you say. How can I tell by just looking at them?"

"These were found in your pocket and activated using the same password used at the Indian Point Power plant."

Smirro moved his right hand in front of Braun to silence him and took over the interview. "Answer the question. Did you activate those pen drives?"

"I didn't activate them," Kildeer denied.

"No?" Smirro asked. "Tell us the truth! Your thumbprint was on the code pad by the back door of the Point Power plant." That was new info for Cordy.

Smirro shook his fist at Kildeer. "You're going down! We can hold you for ten years based on this evidence alone!"

"Ten years in an American prison is a walk in the park compared to my stint in Black Dolphin. Conditions there are inhumane." Kildeer turned to his lawyer. With a quick glance, something was communicated.

Cordy was still trying to figure out the message when Braun asked, "Who provided the 5th Dimension?"

Kildeer swallowed. "What's the 5th Dimension?"

Braun frowned. "You know what I'm talking about."

Cordy saw Kildeer's eyes dilate when Braun mentioned the deadly virus.

"It's on the silver pen drive." Braun held up the stick. "Where did you get it?"

"I got a pen drive from South Africa," Kildeer admitted, "but I don't know what is on it."

"Who wrote the code," Braun asked.

"How the hell would I know?" Kildeer leaned forward in his chair. "But there are people who can target anyone, anything, anywhere. It's going to happen, and you can't stop it. This is only the beginning, or so I've been told."

"That's rather cryptic," Braun snapped. "So, to be perfectly clear, you didn't write the code."

"No. I didn't create the code."

Smirro asked, "Who arranged for delivery of the drive to South Africa?"

Kildeer paused, glanced up to his right, and licked his lips. He shook his head. "I'm not sure."

"Who ordered you to bring the virus to the U.S.?" Braun asked. "You know who your boss is, so tell us."

"I know who I report to, but he's not the boss." Kildeer smiled. "I have no idea who the real master planner is."

Cordy sat outside the mirrored window, ready to fly through the door and ask more specific questions herself. They made her head spin. *Come on. Ask him about Captain Anton and General Urk. Does he know Perry? What about Aqib? Ask why they want to attack the U.S.? Is he working alone? If not, who else is involved? Find out where and why the next hit is planned. We're wasting time.*

"Who do you report to?" Smirro asked.

"I report to Captain Anton Orlov in Moscow, Russia. He sent me to South Africa to get a pen drive."

"Yes," Cordy said under her breath. "I knew it!"

"Which pen drive?" Braun asked.

Kildeer put his elbows on the table, raised shackled wrists, and rested his chin in the palm of his hands. "Ah, it was the one with the black case."

"So not the 5th Dimension?" Braun paused, but when he didn't get an answer, he pushed on, "How did you come by the silver drive? Did you also get it in South Africa?"

Kildeer rubbed his chin. "I've given you enough. Discover the rest on your own." He turned toward his lawyer and gave him that same look as earlier. "I'm not providing any more information."

His lawyer cleared his throat. "We want a deal."

Braun shook his head and said, "No deal! Your client has created a national emergency. Let's move on. Kildeer delivered updated equipment to the William H. Zimmer Power Station in Moscow, Ohio. A bomb was planted in the rear of the 12-wheeler along with the equipment." Braun turned to Kildeer and asked, "You knew there was a bomb, didn't you?"

Kildeer replied, "No comment."

"Not only did you know there was a bomb, but you set the timer to detonate when you were captured. Right?"

"No comment," Kildeer repeated.

Braun continued, "After you set the timer on the bomb, you gave us a warning as the sheriff hauled you to the patrol car, and I quote what you said, 'You have ten minutes.' We called in the bomb squad, who defused the device before it exploded. You know who is behind this cyber attack."

"No deal, no more information," Kildeer repeated.

"Your client is in a great deal of trouble. I suggest you advise him to help in any way possible." Smirro turned from the lawyer to toward the suspect. "Kildeer, you are charged with inciting cyber-warfare, conspiracy to attack public utilities, planting an explosive device, conspiracy to kill U.S. nationals, and that's just the beginning. That alone will give you two or more consecutive life sentences. You'll rot in maximum security. We know you didn't accomplish this on your own."

"He won't give any more information without a deal that protects him from the Russian government," his lawyer said.

"Protection?" Smirro quipped. "That's rich coming from someone responsible for harming hundreds of innocent victims. Ain't going to happen."

"Whistleblowers are considered criminals," his lawyer insisted. "Hired assassins will hunt Kildeer down even in our prison system."

Braun's hands fisted. "We need answers and aren't making any deals today."

But Smirro held up his hand. "Let's not be too hasty here. As you mentioned, we need answers. The FBI might find their way to work out a deal for a lighter sentence if you tell us who created the malware and why."

"What do you mean by a lighter sentence?" his lawyer asked. "Will you offer protection? Promise no death penalty."

Braun turned toward Smirro and frowned. "Lester!"

"What kind of deal would you consider?" the lawyer asked.

"Give me an answer. Why are you in Ohio, and where are you going from here?" Smirro asked.

"That's it?" the lawyer asked. "And then we have a deal?"

"No deals!" Cordy dashed for the interrogation door and threw it open. "I need a word with you, Agent Smirro. I want to hear everything that Kildeer knows about this cyber attack." She turned to Kildeer. "Take it from the top and list everyone involved. When were you brought into the operation, and by whom? Who sent you to the U.S.? Who provided the 5th Dimension and why? Who created the second pen drive, and where did you plant it?"

Smirro's face flushed with anger. He stood up and pounded the table. "This is uncalled for! Get her out of here!"

Braun nearly tipped over the chair as he dashed toward her. He spun Cordy out of the room and closed the door. "This is not protocol."

"Neither is offering to make a deal without more facts!" Cordy shouted. "What the hell is he thinking? You said he has off-beat interviewing techniques, but this is crazy!"

"Maybe, but he's already made the offer," Braun said. "Let's hear what he says before making any hasty decisions."

"What's the matter with you?" Cordy tried to step around him.

"Stay here with me." Instead of returning to the interview, Braun watched through the mirror with Cordy.

As far as Cordy was concerned, Braun stood in her way to prevent her from bolting back into the interrogation room.

Smirro cleared his throat and sat down. "Where were we before that broad interrupted?"

"We were in the middle of making a deal," the lawyer reminded him. His pen was poised to take notes.

Kildeer leaned back in his chair and rocked it on the rear legs. He rubbed his chin, deep in thought. "I don't have all their names, nor do I know where they're located now, but I'm willing to talk to my lawyer."

Smirro raised his voice. "No, you'll talk to me! Give me the names of your bosses and master planners. Tell me what your mission here in the U.S. entailed and what you've done so far. Tell me what else is planned." He turned toward the mirrored window and smiled. "I know just the person who will research everything you give me."

Cordy stopped pushing against Braun. "Did that ogre just admit I might get a chance at those names?"

Braun smiled, "I think he meant me, honey, but we'll run the list together."

"You?" Cordy wanted to slam Braun into the wall. "I'm the one who tracked down Kildeer and figured out the 5th Dimension! Well, that's not really true. You translated the warning. I guess we can work together on this."

Roland Kildeer picked up the pen and paper his lawyer handed him. "Tell me more about this deal!"

"The more you demand, the less I'm going to give you," Smirro said. "You have no idea how much trouble I can make for you."

Kildeer seemed to take his threat seriously and started writing. "Can I get some coffee with two packets of sugar while I compile this list?"

Smirro walked over to the intercom by the door. "Bring in three cups of coffee, one with two sugars." He turned toward the lawyer. "How do you take your brew?"

His lawyer sat up straight. "Just water for me, and I want this deal in writing."

"Two coffees and one water—you catch all that," Smirro asked. "Set up the deal specifics and put them in writing."

"Roger."

"How do I know if the prosecutor will agree to your terms?" the lawyer asked.

"We'll discuss it after I get the list," Smirro said.

"Hang on a minute," Kildeer glared at Smirro. "Are you toying with me? Cuz I don't have to cough up any names. You can scrape up the dregs on your own."

Smirro waved his hand. "The prosecutor and I go way back."

"This is just the beginning," Kildeer bragged. "The mastermind will wipe out any city he chooses. Look at New York. He shut down eight power plants, caused a plane crash, and knocked out all public transportation, including the subway and any car with a computerized engine within five miles. The death toll, I hear, is up to 700 and rising. I certainly didn't cause this destruction. I didn't write one word of code, but you'll never catch him without my help."

"Just give us as much info as possible unless you'd rather rot in a supermax," Smirro said. "I hear they give spies special treatment."

"Give him an hour," Kildeer's lawyer said. "I want protection included in your written deal. If not, you'll never see my client's list."

Kildeer asked, "Are you experienced enough to negotiate this deal?"

The lawyer paled, and his Adam's apple bobbed like a choked swallow. "I'll do my best," he said.

"I'd hate to see what they'd do to you in Russia," Kildeer murmured, then bent his head over the paper and resumed making his list. "Or what someone might do to a young lawyer if he fails?" He smirked. "Not me, of course. I'm innocent, but someone…a friend maybe?"

"What?" Cordy balled her fists. "Kildeer is responsible for a cyber attack that caused the New York power grid to crash and downed a jetliner, leading to the deaths of hundreds of people. It led to traffic jams and deadly riots."

Kildeer continued to compile his list.

Taking a deep breath, Cordy asked, "Braun, since I'm not allowed, are you going back into the room? I want to know who he added to the list."

Braun's eyes narrowed. "I'll go, but only if you promise to stay out here and behave yourself. Smirro won't even speak to me if you make another grand appearance filled with accusations."

"I'll stay here watching, but I don't like it," Cordy huffed. "You know he's making a huge mistake by bargaining in this case. He doesn't even see the bigger picture. It's like a conquest for him. Get the suspect to list a few names, and we're satisfied. Bull shit. Tell that to the hundreds of families who have lost their loved ones!"

Braun paused at the door. "Since this is already in progress, we'll work with Smirro."

"Then be sure Kildeer lists everyone involved in creating the malware on both pen drives. I want to know who sent him to the U.S., why, and who financed his trip. He says this is just the beginning. Find out what else is planned and when—"

"I know your concerns." Braun opened the door and intercepted an officer bringing coffee into the interrogation room. "Thanks. I'll deliver this." He spoke into the intercom, "I have the requested refreshments."

Smirro opened the door and reached for the tray.

"Not so fast. I'm coming in." Braun pushed inside and set down the tray. Handing Kildeer a cup of coffee, Braun glanced at the list. "Only five names? Did you add the financier?"

Kildeer scribbled another name or two. "That's all I'm aware of."

His lawyer shielded the paper. "No looking until I get approval of the deal in writing, and then he will not submit this list unless I approve it."

Braun pushed harder. "I want to know when and where the next attack is scheduled."

Smirro banged his coffee mug on the table. "Braun, I'm warning you."

Braun didn't back down. "We must bargain in good faith. I want specifics."

"The deal is made." Smirro scowled. "They're typing up the details as we speak."

Braun turned toward Kildeer. "When will you have the list for my review?"

Kildeer's lawyer frowned. "We'll see. I must approve it first."

While Cordy waited, she reviewed the suspect's profile and the details of the existing investigation again, including the evidence obtained so far: the pen drives and his fingerprints found outside the Indian Tree Power Plant in New York. There was also the delivery of new equipment in Ohio and the planted bomb, which had been defused moments before detonation. There was no doubt in her mind that Kildeer was guilty. *In fact, he admitted it and even bragged about it, didn't he? I'll go over my recording to be sure.* Her phone rang. Quint's ID popped up.

"Great news, Girlfriend, Chief Jackson freed Sophia and has Floyd in custody. Acting President Harris is back in Washington, D.C. Zac plans to return as president in six weeks, and Perry's code repair for the Big V works like a charm. Having fun tracking down Kildeer's contacts? Things are getting pretty dull around here."

Quint had a way of snapping her out of a funk. "Can you believe it? Schmuck Smirro won't let me anywhere near Kildeer, and he's cutting a deal! I hope to have a few more Russian names for follow-up. You'll hear from me as soon as Kildeer finalizes his list, and we'll wrap this up. Have you heard from Usher? He's tracking Cracker. I understand his flight to Moscow via Frankfurt, Germany, was delayed by several hours, and the FBI agents didn't arrive in Frankfurt in time to intercept Cracker."

"Oh, thanks for sharing. I'll follow up with Usher. Talk to you soon." Quint disconnected the call.

Braun stepped from the interrogation room. "I only saw five names so far, but he added a few more."

"Did you recognize any of the names?" Cordy asked.

"The usual suspects you already know about are Anton Orlov, General Urk, Denys Evanko, Perry, and Alyosha Krackovitz."

"Cracker. I knew it. Quint just called with an update." Cordy texted Quint, "Cracker's on Kildeer's list. Let Usher know." Then she gave Braun a brief review and flipped through her cell phone contact list. "We need to update President Harris. Even though our investigation is incomplete so far, we're making progress, and then I'll have a word with Agent Smirro!"

Braun's eyes sparkled at the thought of his wife talking to Smirro. "I bet you will."

SCAVENGING A SCOUNDREL

Special Agent Usher Hastings feared for the safety of his Russian contact, Vlad. He knew that he would have to travel to Russia at some point. However, when Alyosha Krackovitz, also known as Cracker, cleared customs and headed to Moscow, Usher decided it was the perfect time to follow him.

Usher texted Cordy and Braun, "Heading to Moscow to track down Cracker. I want to know how he escaped from Attica Prison and get the truth about how Cracker murdered FBI Agent Crueger Yates. Thankfully, Cordy's software program identified Cracker's passport photo as he passed through customs, even though Cracker used an alias—C.W. Gresinsky. Talk to you soon."

Braun returned a text, "Beware! People are rioting in Moscow. Let us know when you land, and stay safe."

Rioting? What happened? Usher hunted down a TV while waiting to board his plane, but there was no news report of riots in Moscow—only local news. He shook his head and pulled out his cell to search for the latest details in Russia. "Denys Evanko murdered a top Russian official, General Urk, earlier this morning. Protesters storm Red Square. Death toll rises."

Oh great! Vlad's in the middle of those riots and I won't land until late tonight. I'll have to wait until early morning before making a rescue attempt. I wonder if Reed can stay in Russia to help.

FBI Agents Saul Reed and Zina McLoughlin were assigned to intercept Cracker upon his arrival in Moscow. However, Usher's sudden departure left him with little time to acquaint himself with Reed's dossier before boarding the plane.

CYBER ATTACK AFTERMATH

Cordy tamped down her anger as she spoke briefly with President Harris. Pocketing her cell, she glanced up and spied the source of her ire. Dragging in a deep breath, she exhaled, and the volcano roiling inside finally erupted as she burst into the hallway.

"Agent Smirro, how could you cut a deal without the death penalty? He's responsible for the loss of hundreds, and all he had to do for you was cough up a few names of others involved in this terrorist attack! He gave no leniency for those he killed. I want no mercy for this viper. Kildeer is guilty as hell."

Cordy's opponent, the gray-haired curmudgeon, leaned against the doorframe outside the interrogation room with his arms folded. "So you say."

Cordy clenched her fists. "The 5th Dimension is the most dangerous cyberattack I've ever seen. It shut down New York's power grids, leaving 8.5 million people without electricity, and downed a plane. Personally, it nearly wiped out my laptop."

"It's not my fault that you were stupid enough to download it onto your own computer," Smirro smirked.

Cordy had reached her breaking point. "I've never seen anything this sophisticated. Not in government, our financial data systems, or our highest intelligence agencies. I demand justice!"

"And you had no right bursting into my interview, so I guess we're even!" Smirro had removed his navy polyester suit jacket and rolled up the sleeves of his blue cotton shirt. The shirt was wrinkled with damp armpits. A grin plastered on his face showed his amusement at her defeat. "Go back to your desk, young lady," Smirro said. He straightened and took a step away from the door.

Cordy launched forward, met him toe-to-toe, and poked her finger into his chest. "Without me, Kildeer wouldn't even be here."

"He's mine now, and I'll determine his fate." Smirro's smirk reached his black, beady eyes.

She dropped her voice to a whisper, squared her shoulders, and stabbed a finger into his chest. "I tracked him down." Poke. "I discovered his malware." Another poke. "I quarantined that deadly virus that caused a plane crash." Her finger jabbed into him harder with each word—"That—killed—everyone—on board! Men, women, and children. Innocents."

Smirro, now against the wall, put his hand over his chest for protection, but Cordy had only begun her argument. "Kildeer was in Iran two months ago. I believe he was involved with the missile attack on Air Force One. You weren't there, but I was! That attack could have killed the president and everyone on board."

"There's no evidence Kildeer was involved in that attack," Smirro said. "Besides, that incident has been handled. The FBI captured the pilot and his team in Lebanon."

Cordy wanted to slug Smirro. "Look at the bigger picture. The pilot got his orders from Iran. Do you know what a war with that nation would be like? It could launch us into World War III!"

"I highly doubt it," Smirro said.

"Then you're an idiot! Think what would happen if a network of Middle Eastern terrorists attacked the U.S. Their allies will gladly join in the war—Shiite forces in Iraq, Hamas from Gaza, Hezbollah from Syria, and Houthi forces in Yemen. It would be a massive strike against the U.S., Saudi Arabia, and the UAE. Lebanon would launch a missile attack on Israel—not to mention Iran's loyal fighters in Afghanistan. Iran's Navy could shut down vital oil routes, cutting off one-fifth of the world's energy supply. No, Agent Smirro, you have made a horrific mistake. You negotiated and closed the case. Tell that to the families burying their loved ones. You've set us up for the next war. If you won't deal with this, I will!"

Agent Smirro ran his tongue over his teeth. "I bet you think I'm going to apologize."

Cordy had expected remorse and waited for the words that never came.

"Learn to follow protocol!" Smirro slithered sidewise, slipped on his suit jacket, and walked away.

"The hell with protocol," Cordy shouted at his back. "It'll take weeks for New York to have full power again. There are no backup generators to cool the nuclear cores, and they may still meltdown and nuke the city."

Special Agent Braun Hastings came up behind Cordy, leaned down, and gave her a peck on the cheek. "I'll give you credit. You sure know how to piss off the old man, but I do recall telling my wife earlier today that Agent Lester Smirro was difficult to work with."

Braun's look was so intense it seemed he could read her mind. Cordy huffed, "He made a huge mistake. I could have gotten those names without a deal if he'd only let me—"

"I'm sure you could, but how long would it have taken?" Braun asked. "I hoped this would be faster, and we need those names now."

Cordy's glare made it perfectly clear. She wasn't buying his excuse.

"Wait a minute." Braun held up his hands in surrender. "Don't get angry with the messenger. In all the chaos, I did manage to get a new name from Kildeer's list for you to research. I thought it might make your day." Braun always knew how to defuse her anger or at least deflect it.

"You did?" Her eyes brightened, eager for the name. "Who is it?"

"Not so fast." Braun took her arm and led her toward the front door. "I'll hand it over when we get in the car, and only if you promise to wait until tomorrow for serious searching. Otherwise, you'll be here another four hours, and I have other plans for tonight. You've been working since 3 a.m." His gray eyes twinkled. "I'm very proud of you, and I think we've had a full day. It's time to walk away for a few hours and leave Smirro to his paperwork. I admit it. I'm greedy. We've been married for four days, and I want some of your time and passion for myself."

"Nice try, husband, but I'm not done yet." Cordy shook her head at his laid-on charm. "I still have no reversal for the 5th Dimension. That's the real threat. And whoever is behind that code isn't done writing it yet. My Software Detection Program keeps trapping new additions as the malware worm slithers through the system and disrupts the code. Someone is still out there, and I don't know his plan for the future, but I'm getting reports and reviews of ten to fifteen lines an hour. Then his code again jumps to the program's top, and I can't figure out the next code. It's as if the command lines are jumbled and read out of order. Whatever his strategy, I've got to stop him!"

"I have faith in you," Braun reassured her, setting his plans on hold—for now.

"Enemies already hit the power grid." Cordy paused at the doorway. "What disruption is next—our national defense or financial systems? What about the banking industry?"

Braun opened the front door. "I'll help in any way I can, but tonight is ours."

"Breaking news," announced reporters lurking outside Cincinnati's police station, cameras, and microphones at the ready. "The FBI has completed its initial interrogation of Russian terrorist Roland Kildeer, the cyberhacker who allegedly crashed New York's power grids and downed an airplane, killing all aboard. Stand by for the latest updates."

Still fuming after the chaotic interrogation, Cordy was surrounded by the media the moment she stepped out of the police building. TV news crews, radio journalists, newspaper reporters, and press photographers all clamored for her attention, bombarding her with questions. "What happened in there?" "How did you capture Roland Kildeer?" "Did he admit his guilt?"

Barely able to catch her breath, Cordy's heart rate doubled and then tripled within seconds. She managed to say, "No comment," raised her arms over her face, and turned sideways, trying to push her way through the crowd.

"This is Lisa Pagetti with the latest update." A woman in a red jacket stepped in front of Cordy, shoved a mic in Cordy's face, and blocked any escape. "Tell me about the terrorist you apprehended at the Zimmer Power Plant."

A camera flash nearly blinded Cordy. "Get away from me!"

"I hear you and your husband captured Kildeer."

Cordy repeated, "No comment!" Her nerves were on fire.

Braun bolted from the station and tried to intervene. "She told you, 'No comment.'" He wrapped an arm around Cordy to steer her away from the mob.

The woman refused to get out of her way and plowed on with more questions: "Is Kildeer responsible for the death of hundreds of New Yorkers? Were we next on his hit list?" Another camera flash went off. "Was he going to knock out our power grid like he did in New York?"

Braun grabbed Cordy's elbow. "The lady told you, 'No comment.'"

Other reporters crowded around them. Lisa led the fray as if Braun's "no comment" permitted her to open the floodgates and push even harder. "I hear he's a Russian terrorist. Do you deny it?"

Cordy knew this was no longer her case. Smirro had clarified that, but the question left her in a dilemma. *If I say nothing, the public will assume the reporter is right and panic, knowing that a terrorist is in their city. If I say, 'No,' it will be a lie. Lisa will push even further to find out who the suspect was and why they had arrested him.* Cordy summoned her most confident voice and delivered an answer. "I'm not at liberty to give you any information, but be careful before labeling a suspect as a terrorist without any proof."

The reporter shouted, "You just gave us all the proof we need!"

As Agent Smirro stepped from the building, more questions flew her way, "Ask him. It's his case now." Cordy pointed to Smirro. *It serves him right after how he acted during the interview. He backed down and cut a deal! A deal with a terrorist! It shouldn't have happened, and I wasn't allowed to say a word.*

The crowd shifted toward the new prospect clamoring for answers.

"Run! Hurry—now's our chance to exit this madhouse!" Cordy grabbed Braun's hand as they darted to the parking lot across the street, leaving Agent Smirro to deal with the reporters. "With any luck, I'll never have to deal with Schmuck Smirro again."

Braun clicked his key fob to open the car doors. "Get in. I'm not slowing for anyone."

Cordy dove into the passenger seat and barely had time to buckle her seatbelt when the engine roared to life.

Braun left the lot as a flock of reporters headed their way. Agent Smirro was no longer in sight. Braun sped away from the station and turned right, heading for I-71.

Cordy was still furious, "Smirro completely ridiculed the FBI by negotiating a deal with a Russian terrorist. The schmuck offered a list of all those involved in the cyber plot in exchange for filing lesser charges. However, the list is quite meager and only has the names of a few cyber hackers. I mean, what was he thinking?"

"You did your best, and I'm proud of you." Braun took the Interstate-71 exit. "Let Smirro deal with the outcome. Kildeer is merely a pawn in the massive scheme to cripple U.S. democracy. You have more important things to focus on." Braun smiled.

"Okay, we're in the car now." Excited, Cordy grabbed her laptop. "Agent Smirro can deal with this terrorist, but we're going after the mastermind. Now, what's the name?"

"I'll give you the name, but you promised to wait until tomorrow before launching your next escapade, Cordy." Braun squeezed her hand. "Tonight, we're on our honeymoon. Agreed?"

Cordy crossed her fingers. "Agreed."

Braun smiled at Cordy as if unable to believe her. "You're sure you can wait until tomorrow? It's time for our honeymoon."

It was true. Cordy was always ready for a challenge, but the past month had been both exhilarating and grueling due to the recent events of the Virus X pandemic, which had taken millions of lives worldwide. The virus had even incapacitated the U.S. president, adding to the chaos. Cordy's team had been working tirelessly to find a cure, while Braun Hastings, her fiancé, had embarked on a mission to hunt down General Rutoon, who was responsible for launching the virus.

While delivering vaccines overseas, Cordy met Braun in Tel Aviv. He had recently rescued the new Acting President Thomas Harris from a failed peace conference in Syria. As a gesture of appreciation, Harris invited Cordy and Braun to fly back to the U.S. on Air Force One. To Cordy's surprise, Braun had secretly arranged a wedding ceremony during the flight. Despite not having a wedding gown, cake, or even a ring for Braun, they were happily married.

Their honeymoon was cut short when they diverted a mid-air missile attack on Air Force One. Homeland Security redirected Acting President Harris and everyone aboard to a bunker on Offutt AFB in Omaha, Nebraska. Hours later, a cyber-attack wiped out the power grids in New York City.

Faced with the new disaster, Cordy and her cybersecurity team investigated several documents, emails, and city records. They discovered that many power plants had undergone recent upgrades, and the new software contained malicious components. After delving deeper, Cordy found the Big V, a destructive worm, and an invisible 5th Dimension Trojan hidden within the updated code. She sought Braun's help to track down Roland Kildeer, who had planted the malware. They arrested Kildeer in Ohio, where he was planning his next attack.

Cordy was eager for the name on Kildeer's list. "I know that I promised to wait until tomorrow, but I crossed my fingers. This could be the ringleader." Seeing Braun's smile dip, she added, "Okay, I'll just pass the name to Quint. He can get a head start on the research and fill me in tomorrow." She leaned on Braun's shoulder and pleaded, "Please?"

Braun chuckled. "Risingsickle."

Cordy opened her laptop and pushed the power button. "Risingsickle or risingstar? I already know risingstar is Denys Evanko."

"Who?" Braun asked.

"Denys is head of the Ukraine mafia. He has created malware like the Stuxnet virus that caused the Iranian nuclear program to malfunction. Sections of Iran had no electricity for months." She punched the laptop's power button again.

"Risingsickle is what Kildeer had on the list," Braun clarified.

"That's not a name. It's a code." Her computer still wouldn't power up. "Come on. What's wrong with this thing?"

Braun reminded her, "You removed the battery when Kildeer's pen drive attacked your Darknet account. You better wait until the morning when you can connect it to your desktop."

"Dang it, that's right. I wonder how much damage that virus created." She took nothing for granted and had to know what made things tick. As a child, she took apart every toy and put it back together again, usually making modifications to improve the toy's performance. Not much had changed over the years.

Cordy's cell pinged. "Now what? The message is marked 'Urgent.' I'd better take it."

Braun sighed. "Who sent it?"

Cordy opened the message. "It's from the governor of New York City, Mo Hendrum."

"You might as well read it to me." Braun chuckled, "I'm not going to get much time alone with you, am I?"

"We'll see." Cordy scrolled to the top of the text. "Thanks for helping Chief Jackson free my wife."

Braun nodded. "That is good news. At least they found Floyd Wecholtz after his jailbreak, but his cellmate, Cracker, is still at large."

"We both know Cracker boarded a plane. My passport alert was triggered, but again, Agent Smirro missed his mark, and now it's up to your brother to find him. Governor Hendrum says, 'New York City is facing a growing crisis. We urgently need more help. An electromagnetic pulse brought all traffic to a standstill within a 40-mile radius and downed a jet, resulting in the loss of all lives on board. In the aftermath, all New York airports were closed to prevent another disaster, leaving passengers stranded, delaying deliveries of food and goods, and disrupting corporate activities. Nuclear power plants are without power. There's a brief list of immediate tasks, and it ends with 'Running late. I'll follow up after my press conference.'"

"Let's hear what Mo has to say." Cordy turned on the radio to get an update and hit the scan button. "Deadly Cyberattack Takes Out Power Grid,"… "Software Virus Crashes Plane,"… "Millions Without Power,"… "Chaos Continues."

Braun interrupted, "We already know all that. Why is Hendrum calling us in now?"

The news grew darker with "…New York City tests show their water supply is contaminated…" and "Nuclear meltdown may nuke the city." "There are no transportation systems, hundreds dead—not enough morgues, even more injured, fires burning out of control, and all information systems ground to a halt. Even the well-planned EMS system can't keep up."

"Now I see why he texted me." Cordy immediately contacted Quint, her team coordinator, and explained the situation. "We must reverse hacked codes and get the power grids up and running. After his press conference, Governor Hendrum says we should expect more to address the crisis. I'm tied up tonight, so contact the governor for more details. Give it a top priority to help resolve the situation. Call in Solar Winds and Crowd Strike to help."

"I'm on it, Girlfriend." Quint signed off before Braun could complain about using an intimate name for Cordy.

"How do you put up with him?" Braun asked.

"He's just Quint." Cordy's stomach growled. *Breakfast was hours ago.* "Can we stop for a bite to eat?"

"Sure." Braun searched CarPlay. "Do you want Mexican, Indian, or a plain old burger joint?"

"Somewhere there is Wi-Fi. I forgot to tell Quint I need him to check out the darknet account using a keystroke logger and Gnatcatch Cybersecurity." She sent another text.

"I thought Gnatcatch only worked while the hacker was still online," Braun said.

"If that's what I was using it for, but I have another idea," Cordy paused at Braun's inquisitive expression. "Each hacker has a unique coding and navigation technique to exploit data. What would Kildeer have stolen if he hadn't written the code and only accessed it? We know he had administrative control of the computers at New York's Indian Tree Power Plant. I want to know what files he tampered with, who he sent the information to, and how that differs from the equipment he delivered to the Ohio Power Plant just before we nabbed him."

"Not tonight," Braun said.

"No. I need my desktop for that. It may take days to repair my laptop, but the darknet account can be replicated and isolated. I'll text Quint. He knows all my secrets."

"I hope not all of them." Braun's left eyebrow lifted.

"Not all of them," Cordy said with a sly smile. "I wonder how long before Smirro releases the complete list of names and locations he gathered from Roland."

Braun heaved a sigh and shook his head. "You're all about work tonight, aren't you? You already know most of the people Roland listed."

"I know about Captain Anton and General Urk in Russia." Cordy closed her useless laptop and put it on the floor. "They were on Aqib's computer that you confiscated in Syria. Cracker escaped to Moscow, and Usher is tracking him down. I trust your brother will keep us informed of his progress. Ivanhoe is leaving Moscow and is on his way to Cincinnati. We'll pick him up at the airport when he arrives tomorrow. His partner, Perry, leaves Singapore and will be in Ohio soon, but Risingsickle still baffles me." She sent Quint a message.

Quint texted back, "I'll do my best, but I've been up for nearly 40 hours. A man must sleep to perform at his peak."

Cordy repeated Quint's message and laughed.

Braun chuckled. "It all depends on what is on the man's mind, but with this traffic, Google Maps says our hotel is an hour away. Do you want to eat now or wait until we're closer to the hotel?"

Cordy smiled. "I want to have a relaxing dinner, so let's find a restaurant closer to our hotel, but I don't think sleep is what you have on your mind."

"You may be right," Braun licked his lips, "but fine dining sounds like a plan for an early night of adventure, and maybe we can relax with a nice stroll along the waterfront."

A GOVERNOR IN CRISIS

Sept. 15 – 11:30 a.m. EDT, New York City, New York

Earlier this morning, lawyer Sophia Hendrum faced difficulties navigating downtown New York City due to the many stalled and parked cars blocking the streets. Finding parking was even more challenging because all the garages were full of vehicles rendered inoperable after the 5th Dimension attack. People were paying excessive amounts for parking but couldn't use their cars. On top of that, subway services had been intermittent for the past few days.

Sophia had to park on a side street and walk to her destinations. Her feet ached as she pushed through the crowds, waited at intersections, and finally clattered across the street to OYZ Foundation's old parking garage. At this location seven years ago, her client, Floyd Wecholtz, ran down his boss, CEO Andrew Madeim Edwardo Flinsh Kedderton, known as AK. She met with the supervisor to review the events of that infamous day. "Do you have any records dating back to that time?"

The supervisor shook his head. "I'm sorry, the company has closed, and our policy is to only keep data for five years. Anything older is destroyed."

"Did you work here at the time?" Sophia asked. "Do you remember anything about the incident?"

"I was still in school when the accident happened. I remember hearing about it on the news. Additionally, the maintenance contract for this garage has changed hands twice since then. As I mentioned earlier, we only keep records for a maximum of five years."

Sophia sighed. "Who had the contract back then?"

"One moment, I'll see if I can get that information." The supervisor called his boss and shook his head. "Hard to say—maybe you could check with the city government?"

"Thanks for your time," she flung back over her shoulder. Frustrated at the lack of answers, Sophia gave in to the hopelessness of continuing this line of questioning and headed back outside, plodding the six blocks back to her car.

She arrived on time for Mo's press conference and understood the difficult responsibilities her husband faced as the governor of New York during a disaster. She noticed his troubled expression as he stood behind a podium, bombarded by camera crews aggressively shoving microphones before him, hurling questions with increasing intensity.

"Who is responsible for these attacks?" "What are you doing to address the lack of clean water?" "How long until the power grid is restored?" "Why haven't you put an end to this madness?"

Her husband dutifully answered the rapid-fire inquisition. "I've called in the National Guard. We're trucking in clean water, and I've called in the FBI's cyber team. We're on an emergency backup plan..." The interview seemed like it would take forever but was less than ten minutes when the governor ended with, "No comment. I must return to work."

Waiting in the wings, Sophia managed to bypass the media and weave through a steady stream of government officials to enter the governor's office. Unfortunately, her timing was poor as she walked into the middle of a meeting with a New York State National Guard representative who had already caught her husband before she could reach his office. She asked, "Mo, may I have a moment?"

Her husband peered over at her, his face bleak. "Sorry, Sophia, I can't talk right now."

A frown creased his forehead, and fatigue screamed from every pore of his body. His head slumped forward, elbows on the desk with his chin propped in his hands, and he seemed to have aged ten years overnight. Sophia had never seen him appear so forlorn.

"It'll only take a moment." Sophia turned to the Army officer. "Sorry to interrupt."

"No problem, Ma'am." The officer had the courtesy to back away from the desk to give them privacy.

"What is it, Sophia? I truly haven't any time." His warm brown eyes lingered on her, like a prisoner peering at the sun after days in lockup.

"Have you eaten anything since lunch yesterday?" Sophia brushed a stray chestnut brown curl behind her ear. "You look like death warmed over. You have to take care of yourself."

"Is that what you wanted to tell me?" Mo asked.

"No, but seeing you like this worries me," Sophia said.

The officer cleared his throat. Sophia was reminded that she had interrupted a meeting. *Why didn't I just text him my plans for the day? No, I want to see for myself how he's coping with this stress. And he isn't doing well.* "You told me to inform you of my whereabouts over the next few weeks. Remember, you made me close my office when I started getting death threats. Working from home is better than out of my car, but there's no privacy when our cook hovers over me, so I've rented a safe place."

Mo turned to the officer. "This will only take a moment, but I must talk to my wife privately."

"Yes, sir." The officer headed for the door. "I'll be right outside."

Mo waited until the door clicked. "Where is this safe space?"

"Chief Jackson found a temporary office." Sophia noticed his eyes darken with a hint of gold and knew anger bubbled close to the surface. She rushed on, "I know you're worried about my safety, and the office is secure, but that's not where I'm heading. I'll be at the Southern Judicial District courthouse. Should I try to make it back for a late lunch?"

Mo sighed and checked his day timer. "I have a meeting with a group from FEMA—maybe coffee around 3 p.m.?"

"FEMA again?" Sophia asked.

"Their cyber team is in full force reviewing numerous claims for emergency funding, above and beyond business insurance reimbursements. Oh, wait, I meet with HUD at 3:15 p.m. They finally got authorization for additional funds, and I want to be sure they spend it wisely. We better postpone coffee until 4:15 p.m."

Mo seemed to have his hands in everything. He shook his head. "No, that won't work either. The security board meets at 4:30 p.m. I'll barely have time to review the latest proposal to modify our anti-terrorism plan. Members from the Transportation Committee, water sanitation board, and emergency crisis systems will be attending."

"Okay, dinner at 7 p.m.?" Sophia asked. "I should be able to review Floyd Wecholtz's previous court cases by then."

Mo's face turned red. "I don't want you to touch Wecholtz's case. Ever! Especially after he kidnapped you!"

Sophia was fiercely independent when it came to justice. However, proving Floyd Wecholtz's innocence was more challenging than she had anticipated, and the hearing was scheduled for the following afternoon. She needed more information to strengthen her case.

"Mo, I'm reopening the case," Sophia said firmly but gently. "I have newly discovered evidence that proves Floyd's innocence. I filed a post-conviction petition in district court to reverse Floyd's guilty verdict. Judge Grant has agreed to hear the case."

"How did you get anyone to agree to hear this case when the limitation period for post-conviction proceedings has already run?" Mo snapped. "The period for filing an appeal has already expired."

"I know," Sophia said. "My only option was to file a motion under Rule 440 of the Rules of Criminal Procedure, which I did while I was still Floyd's hostage. I even pushed for a rapid appeal. I had hoped it would get Floyd to release me, and Judge Grant kindly obliged."

Mo wasn't pleased, "So, you're vacating his conviction and sentence?"

"Yes, and I know you're upset, but AK's secretary says she has proof of a newly discovered bank account in Alexa Klinedorf's name," Sophia said. "That's new evidence since Floyd's trial. If you had that info, you wouldn't have sent Floyd to a supermax prison."

"Are you sure that evidence will change the results if a new trial is granted?" Mo asked.

"I've researched other court cases." Sophia handed him a report. "See People v. Latella, 112 A.D.2d 321, 322, 491 N.Y.S.2d 771, 772–73 (2d Dept. 1985), which sets standards for newly discovered evidence. I made the motion as soon as I found this."

"Do you have enough information to make it stick?" Mo asked.

Sophia cleared her throat. "It's a long shot, but I believe the new evidence proves Floyd didn't steal any of the investor's funds. And, I'm sorry to say this, but I suspect his lawyer, Ashton Wellshire, was ineffective or may even have been on someone's payroll to throw the case."

When Mo opened his mouth to protest, Sophia added, "Or maybe it was a flawed prosecutor. I'll have to dig further, but Maude said she tried to reach Ashton and got no answer."

Mo leaned back in his chair. "This whole appeal is a long shot, Sophia. You must be prepared to admit that Floyd Wecholtz is guilty as convicted. And I'm not saying that because I was the judge who sentenced him to life in maximum security. A jury of his peers found him guilty of murdering his partner."

"This is all political," Sophia said. "As governor, you don't want to take the flak for making a major mistake when you were the judge who presided over his case. If freed, you'd worry that a potential killer was back on the streets. I know you."

"You forget the strong possibility that the DA will pull this case from you," Mo said. "After all, you were his victim. Need I mention Wecholtz kidnapped and hid you away for four days before Chief Jackson came to your rescue? It'll be a conflict of interest to represent the man. Not to mention that you're my wife."

"Okay, I may have to twist a few arms," Sophia admitted, "but Floyd knew all this before he even kidnapped me. He's agreed to let me represent him. I'll even get it in writing. If he doesn't assert a conflict of interest, who will? You, Mo? Better not."

"The problem that I see," Mo gritted his teeth as he continued seething at her words, "he will be charged with kidnapping and assaulting his victim. That victim is you!"

"I'll get him off because I'm not going to press any charges," Sophia said.

Mo cleared his throat. "Charging decisions are left up to the prosecutor, not the victim. You know that."

"Yes, but I very much doubt the DA will file charges after I explain that Floyd has a strong necessity defense to the original abduction and that I stayed of my own free will to get his story. Once the DA knows my side of things, I'm betting that the prosecutor will back off, and he'll drop the charges."

"Wecholtz took you against your will," Mo said. "That is defined as kidnapping. You were tied up, injured, and given a drug against your wishes. That constitutes assault."

"Floyd released me unharmed," Sophia said. "I wasn't seriously injured or sexually assaulted, so that would be second-degree kidnapping, but as I said, there is a strong necessity defense. Floyd had to get me to listen to him. I would not have gone to the prison to hear him out, and if he had shown up in my office, I would have called the cops on him immediately. The only option he had to get me to listen to his evidence of innocence was for him to abduct me."

"He didn't let you go!" Mo snapped. "Chief Jackson spent four days searching for you. The police and even the FBI were involved. In the end, the chief used a special forces team to track you down and rescue you. The prosecutor may file charges anyway, no matter what you say."

Mo's brow furrowed. "When the reporters get word of your involvement, there will be a media frenzy."

"Good point," Sophia said. "I'll need to head them off before it comes to that. I'll hold a press conference with Floyd's written consent in hand. If I beat them to the punch, the reporters will have nothing new to report. I'll also address the kidnapping so the whole fiasco will be over before the hearing. But I have to do that by the end of the day."

"There are always leaks," Mo warned. "You better be prepared."

"Trust me," Sophia said. "I have a few ideas on how to circumvent them. I've been a lawyer for twenty years." Precisely what those ideas were haven't bubbled to the surface yet. "First, I need to see that parking garage tape. The NBC tape may clarify a lot."

"Are you going to postpone the hearing until after you get the tape?" Mo asked.

"Judge Grant sent a subpoena. That tape should be here later today." Sophia jotted a note. "I'll need to get my paralegal on board, and I filed a subpoena for Alexa Klinedorf's bank records. Chief Jackson has Cordy helping to check on Alexa's IRS records. She says to send the NBC tape to Professor Seamore Hyde at MIT. I want to know if anyone tampered with the recording. It could be the one piece of evidence that will cinch this case. I'll call my paralegal as soon as the tape arrives and have her forward it to MIT."

Mo's secretary discreetly knocked on the door, reminding her again that the officer was still waiting outside.

"Why?" Mo asked. "Wecholtz is guilty of murdering his partner—ran him down in cold blood. It was an open-and-shut case. I know. I was the judge. That parking garage video captured the whole thing. Are you questioning my decision?"

"You might have missed a few facts, and speaking of that videotape, do you have a copy for review?"

"I doubt it." Mo ran a hand through his hair. "It's a waste of time and—"

"Hardly." Sophia brushed lint from Mo's suit jacket. "The initial trial was a hung jury, so there was some reasonable doubt. Anyway, I gave the man my word."

"Your stubborn mind is already made up, isn't it?" Mo picked up a pile of papers from an open file folder and tapped them hard against the top of his desk. "You don't owe him anything!"

Mo's secretary knocked once again—this time a little louder.

"Come in," he snapped and then turned to Sophia. "Just be sure to take Chief Jackson with you. I can't have you go missing again. It was nearly the death of me. My city is falling apart all around me, and I was worried sick about you. I nearly quit…" He clenched his fists. "No point in arguing. Please, stay safe."

The Army officer opened the door.

Mo slammed the file on his desk and turned toward the officer. "Sorry for the delay."

Sophia knew she had been dismissed, so she returned to the hallway and was glad to see the man she was told to take with her. "Good to see you, Chief."

Jackson's smile blossomed beneath a trimmed mustache. Silver streaked the temples of his ebony hair. His eyes, the color of fine whiskey, flashed concern, and his smile dipped. "He doesn't want you to reopen Floyd Wecholtz's case, does he? I can see it written all over your face."

"Mo's so busy. He doesn't have time to think, let alone make wise decisions. I'm concerned. The stress is getting to him. He hardly sleeps and barely has time to eat, and the city is still in crisis mode. Let's go. I need to check on Floyd's trial records."

"What do you need me to do?" Jackson pulled a notebook from his shirt pocket. "Let's make a list."

Sophia found a corner table in the waiting room and opened her laptop. "We have several interviews. Can you talk to the police who first arrived at the scene and track down all of Floyd's lawyers, starting with Ashton Wellshire?"

Jackson frowned. "That will be a challenge. He's been retired for nearly seven years."

"Do you know him?" Sophia asked. "Maybe you could look him up and set a time for us to meet."

"I haven't seen my old buddy since his retirement party," Jackson said. "The man loves to fish. We used to spend one weekend a month on the lake and compete to see who would bring in the largest catch of the day. I'm sure I can track him down. Who else is on your list?"

"Alexa, if she's willing to talk," Sophia typed on her keyboard, "I already spoke to the parking garage attendant, and I plan to meet AK's secretary, Maude Ingram. They know all their boss's gory details. Can you get a copy of the 911 tape while I go to the courthouse? Then, if you meet with Ash, I'll call Maude. Hopefully, she can meet me for coffee this afternoon since Mo's tied up. Maybe she knows how to reach Alexa."

"If Alexa doesn't talk, you might try the DA," Jackson said. "AK's dead, and you might be able to get the lawyer to talk to you. AK no longer has any privacy rights to protect. Are there any other family members or close friends?"

"I think Alexa is AK's only sibling," Sophia said. "There are others involved—a group of Chinese investors claimed AK's corporation cheated them out of $25 million in the last week of operations. What happened to the money remains a mystery. Floyd denies having any knowledge of the transaction and never could reconcile the books."

"I asked Cordy's team to search the financials. I know she's busy, but she can get someone on her team to help." Chief Jackson made a note. "According to my research, Ashton nearly got him off the fraud charges. I wonder how that transpired since there's no evidence of an overseas account."

"None found to date," Sophia corrected.

"Okay, I'll contact Floyd's lawyer, Ashton Wellshire, and get his old records on file. Maybe you can join me?"

"Call me when you arrange the meeting, and I'll see if I'm available, but I want to be home in time for dinner. Mo needs to relax, and I want to spend more time with him."

They parted ways, contrary to Mo's orders, but Sophia could accomplish more in the short time allotted if they shared the load.

TRACKING DOWN FACTS

Sept. 15 – 12:40 p.m. EDT, Southern Judicial District Courthouse, New York City, New York

Sophia Hendrum called Mo's secretary, Maude Ingram, and they agreed to meet for coffee precisely at 3 p.m.—a little more than two hours from now. Sophia already knew her day would be hectic, trying to cram way too much into it, but that didn't stop her. The trip to the Southern Judicial District Courthouse was delayed due to the New York subway system being out of order and many streets being under repair. *It's not a good day to travel, but I can't stop now.*

Upon arriving, Sophia found the clerk busy on the phone and typing on a computer keyboard. The clerk instructed her to take a number and wait for assistance. As usual, Sophia had to speak to a different clerk to research files, which took some time to complete the paperwork and repeat her request to review court documents. However, finding old records was a hassle as some pre-digital documents were filed on yellowing paper with fading ink. Additionally, other files were stored on an antiquated microfiche format packed in dusty boxes stacked in the courthouse's basement. Today's search for past records was no different.

It took ten minutes before the clerk finally gave Sophia her full attention. "I need Floyd Wecholtz's trial files. I filled out the required request. The date and case numbers are on this form." She pointed to the paper. "I called ahead to have the records pulled."

"How long ago was the first trial?" the clerk asked.

"Seven years ago." Sophia checked her file. "The jury reached a verdict on December 22nd."

"All those records would be in the basement archives."

"Yes, I'm here to review them," Sophia said.

The clerk snatched the form and took it to her computer terminal. After some typing, she heaved a sigh and ran her hand through her graying hair, trapping a few stray strands that had escaped the French roll at the back of her head. "I don't think anyone has pulled them yet. Follow me." She put up a sign, "Temporarily closed – will be right back," over her desk, picked up a ring of keys, and came around the front counter. "We'll have to take the stairs. The elevator doesn't work." Her heels clicked as the clerk walked across the black and white checkered tiles and down two flights of stairs.

Fifteen minutes and ten boxes later, the clerk turned to Sophia. "I can't find even one file."

Sophia was livid. "What do you mean you can't find any of Floyd Wecholtz's trial files? As his lawyer, I must have access to his previous records."

"Wait a minute." The clerk leafed through a thick logbook. "Here it is. They were taken off-site for reproduction three months ago. Let me see if they have been returned. The process takes a long time. We'll have to go back upstairs, where I can access my computer."

Sophia followed the woman up two flights.

The clerk rounded the counter and typed on her keyboard, then paled. "It says here that the files were damaged during the reproduction process. Perhaps you can contact his previous lawyer, Ashton Wellshire. He might still have copies of what was submitted."

"Are you telling me that you have nothing on the case?" Sophia asked. "Not even one file?"

"Sorry," the clerk said. "Maybe the defendant's lawyer can help. It's been nearly seven years. Or you might try the off-site company that replicates the files."

"What's the company's name?" Sophia asked.

The clerk made a few more keystrokes on her computer, "Klinedorf's Archive & Retrieval Center."

"Klinedorf?" The name hit a nerve. Large butterflies with needle-like wings batted against her gut. Something was amiss. Sophia grabbed her cell phone and thumbed through her notes. "Who's the owner?"

The clerk shrugged. "Probably, Mr. Klinedorf?" She typed the company name into Google.

Sophia was doing the same on her cell phone. "Victor Klinedorf. I'll find him and pay him a visit."

"Glad I could help," the clerk said.

"You were a big help," Sophia muttered as she stormed across the floor and slammed the door on her way out. She hoped Mo had kept a shadow file on the case. He had boxes of notes on cases he'd presided over stacked in a storeroom in the basement of the governor's mansion. Maybe she'd get lucky. It was time to track down the chief. *Perhaps he can swing by Klinedorf's while I'm having coffee with Maude.*

Sophia met Jackson in a back room of EMS Dispatch headquarters a block from the courthouse.

"I'm glad you made it." Jackson pulled out a chair for her.

Sophia set her briefcase on the floor and sat down. "I discovered today that Klinedorf's Archive & Retrieval Center damaged Floyd's trial records during reproduction. The owner's name is Victor Klinedorf. That name makes my gut twist. Klinedorf, the same as Alexa's last name, and they have access to Floyd's case Records! How could that happen?"

"Do you think the company deliberately corrupted the evidence?" Jackson asked.

Sophia shuttered. "I'd bet on it."

"I'll check it out," Jackson said. "If Floyd's is the only record damaged during the process, I would be suspicious. And with as many forms, DNA evidence, and lab reports, I can't believe they destroyed everything."

"Fortunately, Judge Grant has already ordered the lab to produce duplicate reports and a copy of the parking garage security tape, which should be sent later today," Sophia said. "It's a crucial piece, and I want to track down the original security recording at the parking garage to be sure there was no evidence of tampering. If they no longer have it, we may be able to get a duplicate copy from one of the lawyers sooner so we can review it in detail. You were a private investigator. Have you had any luck finding the 911 call?"

"It took nearly an hour, but they tracked down the info from seven years ago. The call was made on June 5th at 3:47 p.m. I've listened to the recording once already. It's a confusing message, but 911 calls are like that during a crisis situation." Jackson hit the play button.

"...help! My brother's..." the caller sobbed bitterly, and her words were garbled, but Sophia thought she heard, "My brother's been... hit. The driver didn't even stop!"

The caller continued to speak while the 911 operator said, "Try to remain calm. Where are you calling from?"

"I'm here!" the caller said. "AK! Can you hear me? Wake up, AK! You can't do this to me. Where's the k—"

"We're tracing your call," the operator said. "Help will be there soon."

"There's blood. Oh God, I think he's dead. AK, AK, talk to me. What about the e... ac...? Where does it hurt? You can't die. Not today. Not now. What am I supposed to do? Where do I go? Where's the...No, you can't have that..." There was rustling in the background. "What will happen to me? Our future..."

"Ma'am, we've tracked your location," the operator said. "We have an ambulance on the way. Please stay on the line..."

"I found it! Hurry!" The call disconnected.

"Who made the call?" Sophia asked.

Jackson read the label. "AK's sister, Alexa. I wonder what she found."

"She found her dead brother," Sophia said.

"Yes, that and something else," Jackson said. "Listen carefully to the end of the tape."

"Let's play this again, and we'll record it to review repeatedly at a slower speed. Maybe we can pick up what she says behind the 911 operator."

After hearing the recording a second time, Sophia jotted a few notes. "There are several concerns here. Alexa seems more worried about herself than her injured brother. Why is she talking about their future? And you're right. She did say, 'I found it, and maybe something that he wasn't supposed to have,' like a gun, maybe? Or was there someone else that she was talking to? It makes seeing that parking garage videotape even more important. And I'm unsure if we'll ever get to review it. All the records of Floyd's trial are missing from the courthouse."

"AK's business is also defunct," Jackson said. "I doubt anyone kept old videotapes from the parking garage except maybe the lawyers."

"I better run. I don't want to be late for my meeting with Maude." Sophia gathered her notes. "You can help me check Mo's boxes in storage later this afternoon. I hope he still has Floyd's notes."

"Sounds like a plan to me," Jackson said, picking up his cell phone with the 911 call recording. "I'll forward a copy to you when I get in the car on my way to Klinedorf's. Then I'll plan to meet with Floyd's lawyer."

SOPHIA GETS A BREAK

Sept. 15 – 2:50 p.m. EDT, New York City, New York

Sophia inhaled the rich aroma as she entered an overcrowded New York City coffee shop, anxious to learn more about Floyd. She had no idea what AK's secretary looked like, but Maude Ingram assured her she'd know her instantly.

"I'll be there promptly at 3 p.m.," Maude said. "Not a moment before, nor a moment after. AK demanded punctuality, and I never gave up the habit even after I lost my job."

Sophia found the only vacant table in a far back corner of the cafe cluttered with empty cups, plates, and a tray. Apparently, "bus your table" meant nothing to this college crowd. She set down her briefcase, stacked the dishes and paper cups onto the tray, and headed for a trashcan.

Promptly, at 3 p.m., a tiny, middle-aged woman shuffled through the front door, dragging a wheeled duffle bag behind her with difficulty. The determined look on the woman's face increased as the closing door bumped the duffle, causing her to trip. She was waif-like next to the large duffle, but, in one move, she yanked the door open, wedged it with her narrow foot clad in a black low-heeled pump, and heaved the duffle inside with a slight grunt.

Sophia sprang forward. "You must be Maude. Let me help you with that bag."

"I can manage. I'll follow you." Maude jostled through the crowd, straightened her navy suit jacket, and dropped into a chair across from Sophia. "I've walked five blocks lugging that bag behind me. I never realized how clumsy it would be," She heaved a sigh. "Oh, how rude of me," Maude leaned forward and held out her hand. "I was AK's secretary for nearly five years. I know everyone who worked for the man, including Floyd Wecholtz."

"Thank you for taking the time out of your busy day to meet with me." Sophia shook Maude's hand and was impressed by her firm, confident composure. "I hoped you could tell me more about the man."

"Floyd was very dedicated," Maude continued as if she were an old friend catching up on the latest news. "I can't believe he was charged with murder. Floyd had a rational and scientific mind, excellent math skills, and was honest—a perfect partner who worked overtime without any complaints. He used to drop by here and bring me coffee nearly every morning. The office was just across the street, but another company leased the building."

"It must have been difficult losing your job without notice," Sophia said.

"I bounced back quickly. Good secretaries are hard to find, and I landed a job in a few days, but thanks for your concern."

"Floyd speaks very highly of you," Sophia said. "I hope you can fill me in on some details Floyd couldn't answer. The trial records aren't available yet, so I have many questions."

Maude pulled the duffle closer. "Yes, I figured you would, so I brought everything of interest. I tried to shove it all into my purse, then I tried a paper sack, but the more files I gathered, the more I ran across."

Tiny sparks of excitement bounced through Sophia. "You amaze me. How did you get all this information?"

"I keep a copy of everything and usually bring it home in case the boss calls after hours," Maude said. "You'd be surprised how many times it saved me an extra trip to the office. It's much easier nowadays—I get my copies by email, but we only had paper back then. Let's order coffee, and I'll show you what I have."

"What would you like to drink?" Sophia asked.

"Just plain coffee. Those fancy, frilly drinks are ridiculously expensive and way too sweet for me. A few mocha chocolate frappes later, I'd be a sparkplug."

Sophia shoved her chair back and stood. "I'll get the drinks. Do you want anything to eat?"

"No, just coffee, and I'll organize these papers while you get it." Maude opened the duffle and pulled out several color-coded files.

It took Sophia five minutes to order an extra shot latte with no foam and a large black coffee. When she returned, there was barely room for their paper cups on the table. "What do the colored files mean?" Sophia asked.

"This is my filing system. Red contains failed projects, blue is for potential clients, green is for financial records, yellow is for bylaws and organizational papers, and orange is for my little secrets."

Sophia was intrigued. "What kind of secrets?"

"You'll see, but let's start with potential clients," Maude opened a blue folder. "Floyd was rarely kept in the loop even though he was CFO. I always wondered why he faced such harassment, but I'm just the secretary. I kept my eyes open and mouth shut, but I've seen things since leaving. AK's dead, and I like Floyd. Maybe a bit of a bumpkin, but I always thought he was honest."

"Do you have any information on the Chinese investors who claimed AK's company stole their funds and leveled charges against Floyd for company fraud?"

"That's another incident. So unfair!" Maude snapped. "I know Floyd's innocent on that front. You know, there are some people who you trust. It was like that with Floyd." She blushed and whispered, "Floyd's kind of special. I just like the man."

Sophia wasn't sure what to say, so she picked up the blue files. "The investors would be potential clients, right."

"Yes, they would have been. Unfortunately, I don't have anything about the Chinese group in there, but I have my suspicions." Maude's hazel eyes twinkled. "AK's sister, Alexa, started hanging around the office about a month before the investors supposedly bought shares in the company. That's where my orange files come in. I have the names of three of the five investors and their phone numbers, and I even researched several joint bank accounts."

"Tell me about Alexa," Sophia said.

"She's not the brightest bulb, but she's industrious." Maude sipped her coffee. "It took a lot of patience, but after a couple of weeks, I believe she hit the jackpot—the code to AK's safe. Inside was a list of passwords to our computers. I discovered a list on AK's desk one morning when I arrived early. Alexa would come to the office at night and peruse those password-protected files using my computer and probably AK's."

"How do we get proof of that?" Sophia asked.

"I still have my old computer at home. I can get you a copy of the hard drive."

"That would be helpful," Sophia said.

"I remember one morning, Alexa was on the phone, talking to someone, and she mentioned, 'AK's snoopy secretary, Maude, discovered...'"

"That's when I turned on my cell recorder. I should have recorded the earlier conversation, but I didn't like being called a snoopy secretary."

Maude played back the recording of Alexa, saying, "...One problem is that AK started diversifying, making tracking harder. I created several accounts in Geneva, and the bankers set up real-time information so I could easily trade and conduct business with others in the industry. The funds are secure. Even my brother can't get access. I plan simply to cash in and disappear."

"Do you have a date on that recording," Sophia asked.

Maude nodded and leaned closer as if telling a secret: "Early a.m. on July 5th, the day AK died. One account was opened that same day after AK's death for over $10 million, and I found that account closed ten days later. However, by the time the court case rolled around, the lawyer claimed there was no evidence of any such accounts at the bank. Not true. I have bank records showing otherwise. One of the signers on the account was Alexa Klinedorf."

Sophia's stomach did another flip. "Not Alexa Flinsh, AK's half-sister?"

"Check the signature on my file. It sure looks identical to her signatures, but I couldn't prove it in time for Floyd's trial. His lawyer refused to listen to me. It was as if he already had his mind set against his own client. Of course, it was the last case he handled before retirement."

Sophia's cell vibrated. "One moment, I have a message." She slipped the phone from her purse.

Chief Jackson's text read, "I'm meeting with Ashton Wellshire. Care to join me?"

Sophia typed, "Might be late. Go on ahead. I'll call you when I'm available." She picked up the pile of green files from the table. "These are the financial records, right?"

"Yes, but wait," Maude said, holding up an orange file. "I have more to share with you."

FISHING

Sept. 16 – 2:58 p.m. EDT, New York City, New York

While Sophia headed for her meeting with AK's secretary, Chief Jackson stopped by Klinedorf's Archive & Retrieval Center, but Victor wasn't in. The clerk was a new employee and had no info regarding Floyd Wecholtz's court files, so Jackson left a message that he would call later. Then he tracked down Floyd's retired lawyer.

As expected, Ashton wasn't home when he called, but his wife, Bess was as welcoming over the phone as he always remembered her. "You know how he loves to fish." Her sing-song mid-western accent amused him. "He'll be back home around three, so swing on by before he takes off again. I'll put on the coffee."

Jackson jotted notes in his notebook. "I had hoped that Sophia Hendrum could join us, but she's meeting with Floyd's secretary. I'll be there in time for coffee, but are you sure he'll be back home by then?"

"Ash wouldn't miss a food break. He eats all day long. It's a wonder he can even climb into his boat." Bess gave a hearty laugh. "Best if you come at mealtime, then I know he'll be home for sure. He's always on the go, you know. He's one slippery devil. Guess I caught him during a weak moment, and we've been together ever since." She belted out another chortle. "I'll leave him a voice mail. No cell service on the lake."

"Three it is then," Jackson said.

"I'm running a few errands, but I'll be back in time." Bess added, "Beware of our dog. Pilly sheds like a mountain goat but is a tame little beast. She'll lick you to death before taking a nip."

"Thanks for warning me. See you soon." Jackson disconnected the call and sent a text message to Sophia.

At three sharp, Jackson pulled into the cracked driveway of the Wellshire home and parked alongside a beige station wagon. He got out and walked around his car to meet the retired lawyer, who had just pulled into the garage.

Ashton's flushed face poked through the open driver's window. He wiped a red bandana over his brow. "Chief, you haven't changed."

"Bess said you'd be home at three, so here I am."

"She knows me pretty well." Ashton's gruff voice wheezed a bit as he leaned over the outside door handle and lifted the latch with his pudgy fingers, "Gonna get that fixed one day." He shoved the door open and forced the car seat back as far as it would go. His belly still touched the steering wheel, but he managed to swing his legs around and over the door ledge. His booted feet landed on the pavement with a thud. He rocked his body a few times, then grabbed hold of an edge of the car top carrier and grunted as he pulled his body from the car.

"Catch any fish?" Jackson asked.

"Yup." Ashton hobbled to the back of the car, "Caught my quota for the day." The rear door was stuck shut, so he pounded his beefy fist over the right side, and it swung open, "Gonna get that fixed one day, too." He shoved his waders to the side, removed a cooler, and lifted the lid to show off a string of fish. "Wanna help me fillet them?"

"Think I'll pass," Jackson said. "I'm here on business."

"Bess mentioned you wanna go over Wecholtz's case. I reckon I have his file stashed in my office." Ashton nudged the rear door closed with his hip, then shuffled toward the front of the garage. He set his cooler on a small wooden table. "Guess they'll keep fresh for a few more hours."

Bess opened a screen door between the garage and the house. "Ash, bring the chief inside. It's hotter than hell out here, and I have coffee and sandwiches waiting."

"The boss has spoken," Ashton waved Jackson toward the door. "Enjoy a cup while I wash up and find my files. It'll take a while, so eat up. It's never good to talk on an empty stomach."

"Not that you'd know what that's like," Bess laughed.

"What's that?" Ashton asked, but he smiled and slid his navy suspenders over his shoulders, although his huge gray pants were tight enough to stay up without them.

"Nothing, Dear." Bess backed out of the doorway to let the men inside. A tiny black puffball barked and wagged its tail, then launched toward the door.

"Pilly, stop all that yapping." Ashton swept up the dog in one handful, then nuzzled it nose-to-nose before setting it free to jump up on Jackson. The teacup Pomeranian didn't even reach Jackson's kneecaps when standing fully on her hind legs.

Bess grabbed Pilly and shut her away in the kitchen.

The yeasty aroma of homemade bread greeted the chief as he settled into a dining room chair.

Bess handed him a flowered china cup with a gold rim, then swiped it away. "Bet you'd prefer a mug." She gave him a tall, red cup filled with coffee. "Do you take cream or sugar?"

"Just black, thank you," Jackson said.

"I remember the Wecholtz case," Bess said, "so sad. Both AK and Floyd went to our church, you know. Floyd taught Sunday School, and AK was our largest donor. They volunteered for Habitat for Humanity, and we used to serve Thanksgiving dinners for the needy. AK always donated the turkeys and dressing."

"I heard AK was a philanthropist," Jackson said.

"Not only did he help the poor in this country, but also overseas." Bess handed Jackson a plate of thick roast beef and ham sandwiches on warm wheat bread. "Eat up."

"Do you also know AK's sister, Alexa?" Jackson asked.

Bess shook her head. "She didn't attend our church, but what I don't understand is why she didn't even come to AK's funeral."

That was new information for Jackson. "I heard the 911 call, and Alexa was upset."

"Guess she couldn't take the grief of losing her brother," Bess said. "You know a funeral makes everything so final. Some people don't want to believe the facts. But people from South Africa, Uganda, Sudan, India, and other countries attended."

"Even from China?" Jackson asked.

"Yes," Bess agreed. "I heard several Chinese investors claimed Floyd ran off with their money," Bess said, "but I find that hard to believe. Floyd helped set up the church's financial system. He headed up the endowment fund and did the annual audit free of charge. The children also loved him. He coached the little league team and always cheered the kids on even when they struck out."

Ashton padded his way into the dining room in bare feet, beige shorts, and a faded red and blue plaid shirt. He had an armful of manila files that he piled on the table and poured himself a cup of coffee. "Bessie bending your ear? She has a soft spot for Floyd, but facts are facts."

A timer dinged in the kitchen, and Bess hopped up from the table. "That'll be my angel food cake. I thought we'd have strawberry shortcake for dessert. I'll leave you, boys, to your business." She turned toward her husband. "Ash, try not to eat the plates."

His belly jiggled when he laughed. "Yes, Dear. When you bring the shortcake, I'll have a double helping of whipped cream topped off with vanilla and strawberry ice cream." He reached for the top file and handed it to Jackson. "Let's get started."

Jackson leafed through the yellowed newspaper clippings, court documents, and Ash's notes. AK's photo covered half of the front page news under the heading, "World's Most Generous Philanthropist Murdered. America's business magnate, investor, and most generous philanthropist, who went by the name AK, was allegedly run down this afternoon in cold blood by his CFO, Floyd Wecholtz…"

AK's piercing ice-blue eyes gazed from the photo. His square jaw was set in heroic determination. Thick flaxen hair combed to one side, with matching colored short sideburns, gave an image of prosperity.

Ash pulled the paper closer. "Don't let that photo fool you. It shows manicured nails that defied his calloused palms. He really did use his hands to help others. AK worked with Habitat for Humanity. Floyd didn't have a chance. He was proclaimed guilty from the time that paper hit the newsstand. It was international news by the next day."

Jackson's heart hammered at the thought of being run down and left to die. He hoped Sophia knew what she was doing. The yellowed photo of AK stared at him, forever smiling and forever dead. He spent an hour going over all the information. "Most of this evidence is hearsay. Alexa claims Floyd squirreled away $25 million, but there's no proof of any overseas accounts. Floyd denies ever seeing any funds, let alone opening an account. Who's to say it wasn't Alexa that stole the funds and whisked it overseas?"

"I tried that angle, but Alexa's lawyer always had a plausible answer." Ashton took a third helping of shortcake. "The real clincher was that tape showing Floyd running down AK."

"Do you have a copy of the tape?" Jackson asked. "The court files were damaged during reproduction. We haven't seen the evidence."

Ashton licked his fork after scooping up the last piece of whipped cream. "That's one piece of evidence I don't have. I accidentally slammed it in my file drawer and cracked the CD. I doubt the parking company has kept a copy."

"But you're sure that no one tampered with the tape?" Jackson asked. "Floyd recalls AK standing in front of the car while holding a pistol on him. He panicked and ran AK down, but Floyd swears AK was shouting after being rundown. According to these notes, there's no gun, and AK was left unconscious."

"I know there were discrepancies between the two sides, but the parking video proves there was no gun, and AK was unconscious when Alexa found him. At least, that's what she claims, and the 911 call confirms her side of the story."

"Do you remember that call?" Jackson asked. "I have it along, and I'd like to replay it to refresh your memory. Then I want your opinion about a few things." He replayed the 911 call over his cell phone and paused it after, 'You can't do this to me. Where's the...' "Listen to this again. Alexa mentioned something as the operator said help will be there soon. What do you hear?"

Ashton frowned. "I've heard this tape several times, and it sounds like, 'Where's the key?' But that doesn't make any sense."

"That's what I heard, too." Jackson replayed the tape and went a little farther: "AK, AK, talk to me. What about the...e... ac...?" "I think she said the key again."

Bessie sat down to listen. "This is the first time I've heard the 911 call, but I saw the security camera video. It was played on NBC News. This sounded more like a key account. Finish playing the tape."

Jackson rewound the tape and played it all the way through. "Listen carefully to the end," he warned. "...You can't die. Not today. Not now. What am I supposed to do? Where do I go? Where's the... No, you can't have that..." There was rustling in the background. "What will happen to me? Our future..."

"Ma'am, we've tracked your location," the operator said. "We have an ambulance on the way. Please stay on the line..."

Alexa exclaimed, "I found it! Hurry!" The call disconnected.

Jackson asked, "Why is she worried about herself and their future? And what did she find?"

Ashton shrugged his shoulders.

Bessie narrowed her eyes. "Did she find a gun? According to the security tape, there wasn't any, but if I recall, Alexa was kneeling over her brother's body, and when she said, I found it! She grabbed her purse and then said, 'Hurry!' She made a grand gesture of shutting off her phone on that tape, but I always wondered if she put something into her purse with her other hand. And why did she disconnect the phone call when the 911 operator told her to stay on the line? I heard a siren faintly in the background. Maybe she had to hide the gun before the police arrived—"

"Bessie!" Ashton snapped. "You're letting your mind run away with an overactive imagination. The tape never showed a gun—"

"But she did say, 'I found it!' And we don't know what it meant." Bess sat up straighter and glared at her husband. "She was leaning over AK's body and then fumbled to find her purse. I do remember seeing that on the camera's tape. You refused to believe me, but I know what I saw!" Bess turned toward Jackson. "You have to find that camera feed. I bet her lawyer has a copy of the NBC tape. What was the lawyer's name again, Ash?"

"She had a team of lawyers with Yiddish, Rowan, and Wade. Try Earl Yiddish first. I think he took the lead."

"Thanks for the information. Lunch was delicious," Jackson said. "Sophia will be sorry she missed the strawberry shortcake. She may want to talk with you, too. She truly believes Floyd is innocent."

Ash raised a skeptical brow. "You have your work cut out for you."

"Call ahead, and I'll have the coffee ready," Bess said.

Pilly was barking in the kitchen, so Ashton fetched her as they walked to the front door. "Guess she's saying 'good-bye' in her own way."

Jackson ran his hand over the furball and walked out to his car. His cell phone vibrated. Sophia had left a message. "Sorry I'm late, but something came up. I'm at Klinedorf's. The warehouse is in flames. Can you meet me at my place? I have a lot to share, and I want to hear what Floyd's lawyer had to say."

Chief Jackson returned a text, "I'm on my way."

SOPHIA MAKES PLANS

Sept. 15 – 4:59 p.m. EDT, New York City, New York

Sophia was in hot pursuit of Alexa, AK's sister, and her husband, Victor, after a massive fire destroyed Klinedorf's Archive & Retrieval Center Warehouse, along with Floyd Wecholtz's trial files. It was nearly 5 p.m. when Sophia and Chief Jackson finally sat at the New York Governor's mansion dining room table to discuss Floyd's case. Sophia topped off their cups of coffee. "I know you're dying to ask me why I decided to defend the man who kidnapped me and held me hostage for four days."

"The thought has crossed my mind once or twice," Jackson admitted.

"At first, I only agreed to represent Floyd, hoping he would set me free, but after hearing his story, I was intrigued." Sophia poured cream into her coffee and stirred it. "The first verdict was a hung jury. AK had gunpowder residue on his hands, and a .38 shell casing was found on the floor 200 ft. from the victim. I hate being in the dark when it comes to evidence of a murder, so I asked myself, how did he get exposed to gunpowder? He must have been near a firearm not long before he was struck down."

Jackson agreed. "He would have to be within three to five feet of the gun when discharged."

"Residue was also on the cuff of his right arm," Sophia said. "Floyd vows that AK stood in front of his car, pointed a gun at his windshield, and aimed it directly at his head. The gun went off, and Floyd panicked. He stepped on the gas and ran AK down. He also said that AK sat up and was shouting as Floyd drove away, so he wasn't dead upon impact."

"If you can believe Floyd," Jackson said.

"After hearing that 911 recording, I suspect Alexa isn't a frail little lady sobbing over her brother's body as she would have one believe."

"You think she took the gun?" Jackson asked. "Don't you think the police would have suspected that and checked it out?"

"She may have taken the gun and hidden it. When the ambulance took AK to the hospital, Alexa was free to accompany her brother. Police didn't test her hands for any residue, nor did they search her or her car at the time for any weapons."

Jackson sipped coffee. "Perhaps she found a gun, but we don't have any proof."

"Not yet, we don't, but I'm going to do everything in my power to get to the truth." Sophia said, "I still have many more questions to ask Floyd."

"Is he back in Attica Prison?" Jackson asked.

"No. Sarge still has him locked up while investigating my kidnapping, and I'm hoping I can keep him from ever going back to that hellhole." Sophia pulled out three file folders: orange, blue, and red. "Maude handed me these files. She said she would also make copies for you and will duplicate the hard drive from her old computer that she used at AK's corporation. I'll pick them up first thing tomorrow morning."

"Why the colored folders?" Jackson asked.

"That's her filing system," Sophia pointed to each. "The red folder contains failed projects, the blue is for potential clients, and the orange is for Maude's little secrets. I found the orange one most intriguing. A Chinese investment group accused Floyd of embezzlement of $25 million, but I don't think Floyd took those funds."

Jackson opened the folder and whistled. "Where would Alexa get $10.3 million to invest in this overseas account?"

"Exactly." Sophia sipped her coffee. "One thing is for sure: Alexa knew more about those investment funds than she shared at

Floyd's original trial. Alexa, not the Chinese, made the strongest case that Floyd had extorted those funds, but he claimed he knew nothing about the money. Once accused, Floyd tried to research the corporation's accounts to track them down."

"Did he continue his research after he was in prison?" Jackson asked.

"Yes, but he had limited internet access and couldn't open corporate records from his jail cell."

Jackson shuffled through the pages in the orange file. "How did Maude get this information?"

Sophia chuckled. "Maude has her ways and is also looking into the remaining $15 million. My main concern is that this account is in the name of Alexa Klinedorf, but she didn't marry Victor until four months after AK's death, so was Victor involved in this scam as well?"

"And, if so, how did he find out about the money?" Jackson added.

"Maude mentioned that Victor hadn't met Alexa until the day of the accident," Sophia said.

"I think the first task is to track down that parking garage videotape," Jackson jotted another note. "Ash's CD cracked when it caught in his file drawer."

"It seems unlikely that Alexa would tie Victor's last name to her own after just meeting the man the same day she opened that account." Sophia wrapped her fingers around the warm mug. "I had hoped the video would be here by now."

"That is odd." Jackson studied the data before him. "And you're right. She opened this account on the day of her brother's death. I wonder if she sent the funds before or after his death. Perhaps this is the key account Bessie alluded to when she heard Alexa's 911 call."

Jackson called Cordy to follow up on research on the overseas account. They were still discussing all the information they had collected over the day when a rumbling sound told Sophia the garage door was opening. "That must be Mo." She checked the clock, "Oh, my! It's already 7:30. The cook's off today. I planned on having a relaxing dinner for him, and I haven't even taken the meat from the icebox."

"How about pizza?" Jackson asked. "My treat, but I'm not going to join you. Mo hasn't had a moment alone with you since your rescue."

Mo came through the kitchen door. "Honey, I'm home." He appeared around the corner of the dining nook, leaned over Sophia, and hugged her. "Hi, Chief. Are you still working? Give the lady a break."

"I was just leaving," Jackson said, flipping his notebook closed and pocketing it. "How about that pizza?" he asked Sophia.

"That sounds delicious," Mo said, "but there is no delivery service these days. We still have a curfew. How about we take a rain check?"

"I'll whip up some leftovers." Sophia got up from the table and walked Jackson to the door.

Chief pulled the collar up on his coat. "Thanks. Sleep well tonight. I'll meet you early tomorrow. We're going to be busy."

"That reminds me. I'll pick up a second copy of Maude's hard drive on my way to the coffee shop in the morning." Sophia hugged Jackson, kissing both cheeks as he left. "See you then," Jackson closed the door behind him.

"Hey, how about a hug for your old man?" Mo chuckled and came up behind her. "We could turn in early. What do you say?"

Sophia winked. "Did you say, 'old man'?"

"Hardly. Wait until tonight, and I'll show you."

Sophia turned toward Mo. "How was your day?"

"Don't get me started." Mo slipped out of his suit jacket, tossed it over the top of a chair, and toed off his shoes. "Any luck at the courthouse?"

Sophia picked up his jacket and hung it in the hall closet. "You won't believe it! Floyd's files are missing. I hope you have your notes and some documents in your files downstairs."

"Probably," Mo said, "but don't ask me where."

"You have a lousy filing system," Sophia said. "I searched briefly this afternoon. At least twenty boxes marked legal documents were piled in the storeroom."

"Yes, and I also have two fire-proof file cabinets chocked full of records," Mo said. "At one time, I tried to scan them and make e-files, but that turned out to be a daunting task. I finally gave up on the whole idea."

"Where should I start searching for Floyd Wecholtz's file?" Sophia asked. "I don't want to waste my time if you can point me in the right direction."

"I usually keep any murder trial files in the locked file cabinet, probably in the fourth drawer under W," Mo said. "Start there, but not tonight. I'm beat and want to spend some downtime with the woman I love." Mo wrapped his arms around her shoulders and kissed her. "I'll hunt them down for you in the morning. Let's have some wine and cheese and turn in early."

"That sounds terrific," Sophia said.

Mo barely uncorked a bottle of elegant red wine when his satellite phone rang. "Now what? Oh, it's for you."

Sophia's earlier recorded press conference was released as breaking news. Reporters now had additional questions about Floyd's previous trial. "I'm well aware of my husband's involvement, and we are in agreement," Sophia stated. "That's right," she added. "I've already addressed that concern, and you'll learn more during the hearing." She swiftly disconnected, concluding with, "Nothing is going to get between my glass of red wine and the sweet promise of an early night snuggling with Mo."

FINE DINING

Cordy's plan for a relaxing evening stroll along the gorgeous Cincinnati waterfront was disrupted when Braun's car hit a pothole, resulting in a flat tire. Unfortunately, the rental only had a spare doughnut tire, so their drive was slowed down to a mere 30 mph. To make matters worse, the flat tire happened during the afternoon rush hour, and many tire shops were too busy or closed to offer assistance.

In the meantime, Cordy had received several messages from Quint, a call from Chief Jackson asking for help tracking down some overseas accounts, an update from Usher as he headed for Russia to track down Cracker, and two team leaders who found malware on other electrical grids in Pennsylvania.

The rental car company finally sent them to a garage across town to replace the tire. Braun had to drive 30 miles out of his way to find the station, and then they waited for hours.

Cordy had plenty to do but was ravenous when Braun finally pulled into a parking lot and announced, "Here's Nicola's Restaurant. I hope you like Italian."

"Mmm, sounds terrific." Cordy was already texting on her cell. "I can get Wi-Fi out here in the car. Let me check in with Quint before we get seated."

Seconds later, Quint called Cordy.

Braun rolled his eyes but used the time to catch up with President Harris and his security team. Fifteen minutes later, he cleared his throat. "Wrap it up. I'm starving."

Cordy climbed out of the car but continued to talk to Quint.

"Once I open this door, that phone goes into your pocket, never to be seen again until tomorrow morning," Braun warned. "Agreed?"

"Okay." Cordy smiled and crossed her fingers behind her back. "Quint, I'll talk to you tomorrow. Text me if you find anything." She disconnected the call.

"Crossing your fingers again?" Braun asked. "This time, it doesn't count cuz I caught you."

"Busted!" Cordy chuckled. "What do you have planned for tonight?"

"Ah, yes. I have secrets, too. You'll see." Braun warned, "But we agreed to stop working once we entered the restaurant, and I'm opening the door in three, two, one."

She hesitated. "Quint says he can't sleep because he's too busy, and I'm too upset to sleep."

"That's good because I thought we agreed to some fine dining before turning in."

"Caprese with pesto sauce does make my mouth drool, and I'm ready for a relaxing dinner," Cordy said.

"You always amaze me," Braun found a quiet corner table. "One moment, you're worried sick about your laptop, can't stop to eat because you're hunting down the next criminal, and talk non-stop with Quint to plan out your next ploy to rid the world of villains. The next moment, we're on a wild goose chase hunting down a restaurant. I feel lucky that you found time to spend with me, but all you can say is that you crave a relaxing dinner." He leaned over and kissed her, then pulled a chair out for her.

"Oh, honey, that's not all I crave." Cordy removed her jacket, leaned into him, and grinned as she taunted him. "I'm ready to indulge in the delicacy of Pasta Carbonara, rich with creamy cheese sauce and bacon over spaghetti and a glass of champagne."

Braun whispered in her ear, "Sounds nice, but it wasn't quite what I had in mind."

She noticed his smile dip and added, "Followed by a dark night of bright possibilities." Cordy sat down and peered over her menu at her husband, silently chuckling at his antics. She loved his flirtatious behavior.

The waiter took their order, returned with a bottle of chilled champagne, and poured each a glass.

Braun held up his goblet. "Here's to my adorable wife. May we finally, enjoy a relaxing evening."

Cordy touched the rim of her glass to his and drank. The meal would have been relaxing if she could sit still for two minutes to enjoy the delicacy of cheeses and salami on warm, crusty bruschetta with generous portions of grilled garlic and spicy tomatoes. Instead, her mind bounced from one thought to another as she downed the antipasti. "What time does Ivanhoe's plane land?"

"He doesn't arrive until noon tomorrow." Braun moved his bread plate so the waiter could set down the main course.

"How long will it take to get to Cincinnati/Northern Kentucky International Airport?" She took another sip of champagne.

Braun tried the Carbonara. "We'll leave for the airport early a.m. and stop by to pick up a spare tire rather than a doughnut spare. It should give us plenty of time."

Cordy checked her watch. "Have you heard from Agent Smirro yet? I want to start researching those names."

"I doubt we'll hear anything tonight." Braun took her fork, wound it through the spaghetti, and held it to Cordy's lips. "Eat up. This is delicious."

Cordy took the offered pasta and moaned in appreciation as Braun continued to stare at her. "Aren't you going to eat?"

Braun leaned forward. "I'm admiring the view."

Cordy tuned into the peaceful music playing in the background. The lights were turned down low. "It does have a nice ambiance." She took another bite.

"I wasn't talking about the restaurant." One breathtaking dimple appeared, causing Cordy to flush under his gaze.

"And the food is garnished to perfection," she scooped up another forkful.

"Nor was I talking about the food." Braun's gray eyes sparkled. "You don't know how beautiful you are, do you? I admire you."

"I figured that out." Cordy lazily ran a meatball around her plate with her fork. "Let's eat up and turn in early."

"For once, I'm in total agreement." Braun dug into his meal. He dabbed up the last of the cheese sauce with a slice of bread. "More champagne?" Without waiting for an answer, he lifted the bottle from the ice bucket and poured the remains into their glasses. "We haven't had a break since we got married."

His eyes darkened, making her pulse quicken. She was unable to break eye contact. Cordy lifted her flute, clinked it against his, and drained the glass. "I think it's time to leave before I melt away." She managed to remember her jacket as she headed for the door.

Braun chuckled. "I better pay the bill first." He flagged down the waiter and laid $100 on the table. "Keep the change." He caught Cordy's hand as they left the restaurant. He leaned over and kissed her cheek. "I feel like a teenager, but the backseat of a car won't do for my beautiful wife."

His eyes were pools of moonlight. Cordy leaned into him, breathing in his maleness. "Depends. How far away are we from the Marriot?"

Braun opened the car door. "Get in, my little minx. We'll be there in ten minutes."

EXTORTION

Sept. 16 – 4:00 a.m. MSK, Moscow, Russia/
Sept. 15 – 9:00 p.m. EDT, Cincinnati, Ohio

Freezing rain turned the Moscow roads into sheets of ice, making it an excellent morning to sleep in. However, come rain or shine, the old grandfather clock standing outside Svetlana Orlov's bedroom door kept marching along—tick-tock, tick-tock. Four bongs marked the hour.

"Time to get up," Papa called from the hallway. Svetlana's door opened, and the light in her room flicked on. "You need to pack. Today's the day you're heading to the United States. Your flight is in six hours."

"I'm up." Svetlana stretched. "So you decided to send me ASAP?" Her eyes must have focused. "You're already dressed. Busy night?"

"Yes, I got a mysterious message early this morning," her father said.

"From who?" Fifteen-year-old Svetlana threw back the covers and sat on the side of the bed.

"Alyosha Krackovitz," Papa went into more detail when her eyes narrowed. "You've heard of him as Cracker but never met him. He was a key contact I sent to the U.S. ten years ago to hunt down a mutual enemy, the Journalist. Somehow, he ended up in a supermax prison. Now, Cracker's finally coming home. I notified his wife, Rozalina, sent a few emails, and checked on your flight to Cincinnati, Ohio. Remember, you must dress as Ivanhoe today. That's the name on your passport."

"Da, Papa." Svetlana slid off the bed. "Did General Urk finagle a visa to the U.S. for me?"

Papa nodded. "My boss ranks high up in the Russian government. He didn't even have to pay extra fees. Meet you for breakfast." Papa closed her door.

I hope I'll be back home soon. Svetlana studied her room, remembering her mother making the rose-colored curtains, matching bedspread, and pillow shams. That was three years ago before her mother and twin brother, Ivanhoe, had been murdered during a Chechen raid. Her father was out of the country, and Svetlana had been babysitting at Aunt Inga's. It was the only reason her life had been spared.

Girls were not allowed at the school of Papa's choice, so he made her take Ivanhoe's place. As she had done for the past few years, Svetlana wrapped a strip of cloth tightly around her bosom and slipped into Ivanhoe's best white shirt, black trousers, and heavy Russian boots. Fortunately, she was built slim, small bosomed, and narrow in her hips. Her hair was cut short for a girl, although somewhat longer than most young men, and she knew how to walk with a hint of a swagger, radiating a confidence that Ivanhoe had, although Svetlana, when she was herself, did not.

After dressing, she made sure she had packed everything, including her laptop computer, and threw in a small bag of make-up just in case. Glancing in the mirror, she combed her short, curly blonde hair, grabbed her faux fur hat with long ear flaps from a peg by her door, and placed it on her backpack. Satisfied her reflection could pass as a boy, she hurried to the kitchen.

Papa's office was a small desk to the right of the dining room. "What's for breakfast?" He moved to his usual chair at the table.

"I made scrambled eggs, bacon, and toast." Svetlana brought out two heaping plates and placed one in front of Papa. She set hers down and glanced through the kitchen window before sitting to eat. Something red caught her eye.

Their neighbor, Boris, ran up the walkway with a red woolen scarf wrapped around his neck, and his mouth had ice crystals crusted near his chin—white puffs of steam formed in the cold air with every breath.

Boris burst through the door. "Captain Anton, have you heard the latest news? I thought everything was settled last night when the police called a curfew, and everyone left the park. Now the police have hauled Marot away."

Her papa hopped up from his chair. His fists clenched. "What for?"

Boris shrugged. "He refused to pay for protection."

"I don't blame him." The jagged scar on Anton's cheek blossomed into a deep red. "They were here yesterday and doubled the fee. It's extortion."

"I'm sure the chief of police trumped up some false claim to arrest him." Boris unwrapped his scarf. "I'm frozen to the bone. Got any vodka to warm me up?"

"You know where I keep it." Anton poured a cup of tea and sat back down. "They'll torture him, you know. Chief Ignacio thinks he's still in the KGB."

"Da. Marot's wife won't see him again except in a pine box," Boris warned, "unless, maybe, you come up with the money. His Mrs. asked me to borrow a few rubles."

Svetlana could barely choke down her breakfast. She folded her hands and whispered, "Please, keep Papa safe while I'm gone." Her beloved Papa had been so upset when the police left yesterday that his hands shook. He would now also have to raise his rates for the additional measures he took to keep his clients' businesses safe. *Who better for the job than one who created deadly malware for a living?* Papa was the man behind the scenes, unobtrusively keeping their computers and internet activity from being hacked or infected. This latest round of "protection" affected all of them badly.

Anton shoveled a forkful of eggs into his mouth and walked across the kitchen to his office. His fingers automatically dialed the combination to open the safe. "Is three hundred thousand rubles enough?"

"No, she asked for five hundred," Boris said.

"Five hundred thousand? Are you sure, or does that cover part of your fee, too?" Anton's eyes narrowed as he held out the money. "I had a lengthy talk with General Urk. He promised to stand up to those greedy government officials. No more extortion."

"Good, because the police are brutal," Boris said, "especially the chief. I heard he heads up the Chechen mafia."

"For your sake, you better not spread your opinion to others." Anton set the cash on the table. "Take this to Marot's wife. Hopefully, she's not a widow yet."

"Thanks." Boris helped himself to the vodka, gulped it down, and grabbed the money. He turned to the lad he knew as Ivanhoe. "You're leaving today, right? Going to University in America?"

Svetlana knew it was a lie and peered over at her father, who nodded. The grandfather clock bonged six times. "We head to the airport in fifty minutes."

"Safe travels." Boris shook out his scarf and wound it around his face and neck. "Chess tonight?" His voice sounded muffled.

Anton rubbed his chin. "Not tonight—maybe Saturday."

Boris nodded. "Until then, my friend. Better deliver this." He rushed out the door.

Anton tsked, "I'm afraid Russia's on the brink of war. General Urk better do some fast-talking to turn this country around."

Svetlana swallowed the last of her bacon. "Who in government will listen? They were strong enough to kick out the Chechens a year ago, but a lot has happened since then, and the government is reorganizing its power. They'll do anything to get extra money, and General Urk went missing yesterday. I hope he hasn't walked into a trap?"

"I don't trust the government either, but Urk can care for himself." Papa waved his hand. "Now hurry, Ivanhoe. You must not dally."

Svetlana gathered the teapot and dishes, took them to the sink, washed, and set them into the drainer.

"You have your ticket, passport, and laptop?" he asked.

"Yes, Papa," Svetlana dried her hands, put on a jacket, and slipped on her backpack. "I'm ready, but I'll miss you terribly." She choked back the tears, threatening to spill. "Promise me you'll stay safe."

"I promise, but you must find Roland Kildeer. You know your mission?"

"Yes, Papa. Find Kildeer and modify the code for each power plant. I will not fail you."

CRACKER THE HACKER

Sept. 16 – 4:10 a.m. MSK, Moscow, Russia/
Sept. 15 – 9:10 p.m. EDT, Cincinnati, Ohio

The early autumn morning was typical for Moscow, with blustery rain blowing against the windowpanes. Thirty-two-year-old Rozalina closed her bedroom window and checked her watch—4:10 a.m. The wooden floorboards creaked like they always did as she stepped down the hall to peer in the narrow doorway. An orange glow from a night light bathed the small bedroom where Cracker's nine-and-a-half-year-old twins slept. Rozalina knew she'd have to make other sleeping arrangements soon, but money was tight. She felt blessed when her mother begged her to move in after her father died five years ago. As she tidied the room, her heart raced with a mix of anticipation and anxiety, unsure of what her husband's return would bring.

Rozalina and Cracker's wedding photo sat on a bedside stand so the children could memorize their father's face. She had taught them the ritual of saying good night to their daddy, whom they had never met, and they had more questions about their father every night. "Where is he? When will he be coming home? Why is he on a secret mission in the U.S.? Doesn't he miss us?" Their innocent queries, filled with a mix of hope and longing, echoed in Rozalina's mind, intensifying her own anticipation and anxiety about her husband's return.

Furniture crowded the small space. A four-drawer dresser sat between the twin beds. Across the room was a light brown bookcase

Cracker had built with his own hands. The shelves sagged beneath the weight of so many books, but they lined up in an orderly fashion. It was the way Rozalina kept her house—neat and tidy. All the books were written in Russian. Cracker had underlined several passages he had used as a code when working with 'The Team.' A ladder-backed rocker sat in the corner. The slats reminded her of the prison cell bars that Cracker had been behind for too many years. Rozalina frequently sat in the rocker, rereading those books during the last ten years since her husband left the country on his secret mission to the U.S. It went awry, although Rozalina didn't know the exact details. The mystery of his past and the secrets hidden in those books added to the intrigue of his imminent return.

Satisfied that her children were safe, she returned to her room and opened her laptop. It was time to log in to the underground network like she had every day for the past ten years. She loved figuring out complex issues and could do this within minutes on most occasions. To her surprise, Captain Anton had left her a cryptic message. Her hand flew to her mouth. Tears filled her eyes. She darted to the kitchen and whispered, "Mama, Cracker's on his way home!" She turned the radio on to cover their voices.

"What will you tell him when you see him?" Mama asked. "He doesn't even know he's a father."

"Ah, but there's no denying it. One look at his son, and he'll see his reflection in those deep, dark eyes quietly taking everything in. Regina, on the other hand, is more like me. She has a temper and a mind of her own."

"A brilliant mind," her mother beamed with pride. "She's a force to deal with, but she'll be an influential leader when she grows up. Like you, she'll make her place in the world."

"I didn't even complete my internship," Rozalina sighed. "My medical education was cut short when the twins came along."

"That hasn't stopped you from treating those who can't afford care," Mama cleared off the kitchen table and poured a cup of tea. "When your husband returns, you can go back to the University.

Make that vaccine you've been working on. I know you haven't given up on it. I see you on that computer long after the children have gone to bed."

Rozalina silently cringed. She had lied about her work for so long that it almost seemed like a reality. She even lied to her mother. *If anyone knew what I was really doing, they would have arrested me. I can't let that happen. I love my children and will do anything to keep them safe except stop working on this project. But with Cracker coming home, I must tell Mama the truth.* The weight of this decision and the fear of the consequences filled her with a deep sense of uncertainty and emotional turmoil.

Mama studied Rozalina's face. "What are you thinking? I can see that little crease across your forehead. It only appears when you're deep in thought. You can share your concerns with me. You know, it won't go anywhere."

Rozalina sat next to her mother and brewed a cup of mint tea. "Remember when I was a child? Boris Yeltsin launched us into capitalism. We thought everyone in Russia was going to get rich."

"You might have thought that, but I knew better," Mama chuckled. "Only the oligarchs became rich. Your Papa was only a professor at the University."

"I never felt like I knew Papa." Rozalina stirred the brew and removed the tea bag. "He was never home."

Mama reminded her, "That's because he had to work as a taxi driver every night. My brother was a surgeon, and he used his skills as a butcher to make enough money to put food on the table."

Rozalina admitted, "I know it wasn't easy, and I appreciate all you've done to get me through medical school."

"You wouldn't have gone if Papa and his brother hadn't sold the old farm," Mama reminded her. "But they did, and we are so proud of you. Cracker is a lawyer. He'll come home, and we'll be wealthy."

"Cracker is a brilliant man." Rozalina lowered her voice, "Come, I have something to tell you in private." She stood and motioned for her mother to follow her into her bedroom. "I checked for listening devices. My room's safe, but to be sure," she picked up one of her children's slates and a stick of chalk. "I should have told you this before."

Mama's brow furrowed. "Tell me what?"

Rozalina wrote on the slate. "During college, Cracker worked part-time for SVR foreign intelligence. A few corrupt Russian officials made us pay bribes for protection."

Mama's blue eyes were like ice as she nodded. "Nothing new."

Rozalina erased the board and added, "One day, a tax collector demanded 3.5 million rubles. Cracker refused to pay, and we went into hiding."

"That was years ago," Mama whispered. "Why are you telling me now?"

Rozalina nodded. "The tax man hasn't forgotten. He made up fake charges and threatened to put Cracker in jail. Afraid, Cracker agreed to go to the U.S."

Mama whispered, "So that's why he fled in such a hurry. I couldn't believe he left you all alone, pregnant, and unable to afford even a place to live."

"It wasn't his fault, and I appreciate you taking us in," Rozalina whispered. "The children adore you."

"So, be honest with me," Mama whispered, then remembered to write secretly. "What was he to do in the U.S.?"

"I can't tell you everything," Rozalina said under her breath.

Mama scowled and crossed her arms.

"Don't give me that look." Rozalina put her hands on her hips and sighed. "I know you're trustworthy, but this is for your own protection."

"I can handle interrogations," Mama hissed. "Remember when they came for your father?"

Rozalina nodded again. "You did well, and they freed Papa. Okay, but this is not for anyone else to hear." She wrote, "I don't want you arrested. If anything happens to me, take the children and run."

Mama dropped into a chair. Her hands folded together so tightly that her knuckles turned white.

Rozalina wrote, "Cracker went to the U.S. to track down the Journalist."

Mama gasped, and her hand flew over her mouth. "I know who you mean!"

"Shh," Rozalina put a finger over her lips.

Mama glanced around the room and jotted a note, "Do you really think our home is bugged?"

Rozalina shrugged. "Anton found a couple in the kitchen two months ago."

"Why was Cracker following the Journalist?"

Rozalina wrote, "Smuggled uranium or maybe it was plutonium and sold it to ISIS."

Mama's eyes grew huge in astonishment.

"It's top secret," Rozalina said. "That's why I'm still nervous about telling you. Russia's highest officials will deny everything. Why else would Cracker risk his life to go after this man? Cracker was working with the FBI."

"Why was Cracker put in prison for life?" Mama scribbled, erased the board, and added, "Was he really working with the FBI?"

"I've asked myself that question a hundred times," Rozalina whispered. "That's why I joined The Team.'"

Mama gave her another questioning look.

Rozalina inhaled deeply and wrote, "We call ourselves the team. Captain Anton whisked Cracker away before the Russian police could arrest him. Sending him to the U.S. probably came as direct orders from General Urk. He's our team's leader." She quickly erased the board.

"What do you do for this team?" Mama scribbled.

"Special projects," Rozalina replied.

"Does this team go as high as the Russian president?" Mama gasped.

"Maybe," Rozalina whispered, "but I've never met him."

"Why was Cracker in a U.S. prison?" Mama asked.

"Convicted of murdering the FBI agent he was assigned to," Rozalina wrote, and then whispered, "but I don't believe that for one moment. He was framed. I'm sure, but getting any information from any government official is like falling into a black hole."

Mama nodded. "KGB paranoia, that's why we're talking here in secret."

"Every letter I've sent him was returned unopened," Rozalina wrote. "Anton once told me, 'Cracker is better off in America than here. When an assignment goes bad in Russia, it means death. At least, he may survive and have a chance to return home one day.' And that could be soon."

"It's been nearly ten years since he left Russia," Mama said, clasping Rozalina's hand. "I never thought I'd ever see him again."

"Do you think he'll even recognize me?" Rozalina asked.

Mama laughed. "You've lost some weight since then, but he'll know you instantly. Are you meeting him at the airport?"

"Da. I'll need to make some arrangements," Rozalina said. "I'm happy and scared at the same time. Do you think he's changed after all these years in prison?"

"Of course, he's changed," her mother assured her. "Remember what we've heard about American prisons. He may have been tortured. But, Russian wives are always loyal to their husbands. You'll work it out. I'll stay here and watch over the children."

"Will he be safe?" Rozalina asked. "He broke out of Attica. I heard that it was a horrible place. What if someone is waiting for him at the airport when I arrive?"

"You can't go to the airport," her mother warned. "Find another way. If enemies are waiting, your children will be orphans in an instant! Does Anton have anyone to go instead of you?"

"No, but you're right," Rozalina agreed. "I need to find another way to get him off that plane. Pack and call Uncle Albert to take you and the children to the country. I have a lot of work to do." She took the slate to the bathroom and washed it clean. Her active mind went through several scenarios before settling on a perfect plan. *I am a doctor, after all.*

TIME TO RUN

Sept. 16 – 6:03 a.m. MSK, Moscow, Russia/
Sept. 15 – 11:03 p.m. EDT, Cincinnati, Ohio

Svetlana quickly zipped up her jacket and headed for the door, anxious to catch her flight to the United States. She felt a cold shiver as General Urk's top aide rapped on her father's office window.

"Quick! You have to get out of here!" Leo's voice sounded excited and frantic as he burst through the door. "General Urk is dead. Denys Evanko's men tortured and hung our leader in Red Square. Captain Anton, you were second in command. Now you're in command. Denys and his men will come here next. Your troops are gathering at the Assembly Hall."

Svetlana's heart pounded as she froze at the sound of a hissing screech like a giant blowtorch blasted outside. Rolling thunder ricocheted off the gates surrounding their building. Picture frames rattled from their walls and shattered into pieces as they hit the floor. "What was that?"

Leo craned his neck to watch something streak through the sky. "A military jet—flying too close to the ground. I've never seen anything like it in the city before."

"Take cover." Anton dashed to the back room, threw open his weapon's cabinet, and motioned for Svetlana to join him. "Leo, are you sure about Urk? Did you see the general's body with your own eyes?"

"No. An old man with a thick, scraggly beard was in the park," Leo said. "I thought he was trying to find the entrance to Perry's old lab and was afraid he was after his cousin Vlad."

"I heard Vlad died while in prison," Anton said.

"No, he's in hiding." Svetlana reached into the cabinet and grabbed a pistol, ammo, and an assault rifle. "Where do you want me?"

"You know how to use that gun?" Leo asked.

Working quickly, she inserted the clip into the butt of the gun. It snapped in place. "That answer your question?"

"This changes everything. You can't stay here," Anton said. "You must catch that flight to the U.S. as we've already arranged. It's more important now than ever." He tossed a Kevlar vest at her. "Ivanhoe put this on."

It reminded her that she was dressed as her brother. Her father ensured Leo didn't find out she was a girl.

"Leo, drive him to Vnukovo International Airport. No taxis will be running through the inner city during a riot, and I don't trust the Metro line or Aeroexpress. I'll make sure you're well compensated."

Svetlana dropped her backpack and slipped on the vest. Then she snagged the bag, placed a strap over one shoulder, and sprinted toward the basement. On her way, Svetlana locked the front door. Her fingers shook as she reset the alarm. "What about our rebel forces?"

"From what I saw at the park, they are gathering by the dozens, and police are everywhere," Leo said, "even Chief Ignacio. More men are fighting than last night before the curfew."

"How long before Denys' men reach our gate?" Anton asked.

"They could break through the wall with their battering rams in less than five minutes," Leo said, "but they're rioting in the park and meeting a lot of resistance."

"Take Leo to the tunnels. I'll be right behind you and go as far as the hall to meet my men." Anton loaded his pockets with ammo and grabbed two rifles, grenades, and his vest. "Better get one for yourself, too."

Leo grabbed the last vest and put it on, along with a shoulder holster, then took more guns and ammo. "I'll leave these in the tunnel." He holstered a pistol on his way to the basement.

"Do you trust this man in the park who told you about the general?" Anton asked.

"Yes. I've seen him before." Leo continued down the steps. "He's a known snitch, but rumors were flying from everywhere after I left him. I knew he was telling the truth, so I came to warn you. Denys has a contract out for your life."

"That's nothing new." Anton's face contorted in rage—teeth clenched tight. A furrow twisted over his brow. Fury reddened his scarred left cheek, and his breath came out like short, hard grunts as he fisted his hands. "I have one on him, too, but you're sure the general's dead."

"Yes," Leo said. "You'll be his next hit."

"Go, go, go." Anton pushed Leo forward. They moved through an opening in the wall under the stairway. "Ivanhoe, I must change your mission." Anton lifted a metal plate and placed his face to the glass. A beam scanned across his eyes. There was a click, and he put his thumb to the plate. The door swung open.

"Change my mission?" Svetlana asked.

"Find Roland Kildeer. He hacked into New York City's power plants. You must do everything possible to get the electric grids back up and working. Kildeer's following General Urk's orders. Now, he must follow mine."

"I don't understand." Svetlana hated feeling confused.

"I don't have time to explain," Anton said. "Just do it. General Urk had it all wrong. We need the U.S. to back us."

Svetlana nodded but felt hope fill her chest. "So, you finally agree with me? Peace is the only way."

"Da, but I may be too late," Anton said.

Leo stepped between the two. "We need to go."

"Each of you, place your thumb on the plate to register your prints, or the door on the other end of the tunnel won't release," Anton ordered.

Filled with apprehension, Svetlana opened and closed her fists to relieve the tension, then placed her left thumb on the scanner. "Are you right or left-handed?"

Leo raised his right hand. She showed him how to place his thumbprint onto the scanner and enter a code. "You can use this entrance anytime from here on out." Svetlana's mind raced, knowing she would leave everyone she loved, and she gasped, "Papa, what about Aunt Inga? She'll be here soon."

"Not today," Anton said. "I told her I'd be leaving early this morning. Hurry."

Svetlana blew out a deep breath. "That's a relief." She slammed the door behind them and entered another code. "Security's on."

When the front door alarm screeched, she raced down more steps and hadn't gone thirty feet. "Someone's trying to enter the house."

"No time to waste," Anton dashed forward. They passed a few doorways leading in different directions.

"How do you know which path to take?" Leo asked.

"Right tunnels lead first to the river, second to the Assembly Hall, and the third to Red Square," Svetlana said. "We go left to the park or further to the main highway. Which way to your car?"

"The park. I stopped to check on Vlad and left it in the underground garage." Leo took long strides, and she had to dash to keep up with him.

"Is he going to be okay?" Svetlana asked.

"Yes, we spoke to Perry this morning, and he told us what to do if someone tries to break into the lab. He sure is worried about you. Does Perry know when you're leaving the country?"

Svetlana hoped she could get a message to Perry soon. "Not exactly all the details, but we agreed to talk at ten tonight."

"Stop your chattering," Anton cautioned. "We are nearing the Assembly. I have to leave you now." Anton came to the second doorway to the right. He hugged Svetlana. "Text as soon as you land. This could determine Russia's future."

She didn't want to let him go. "Da, Papa. I know the importance of my mission, and I won't fail you."

Anton turned to Leo. "Make sure Ivanhoe gets on that plane and stay safe."

Leo set down his extra ammo and rifles. "Yes, sir."

"Papa, be careful," Her voice was almost an inaudible whisper.

His eyes locked on hers. "Always. Talk to you soon. We'll make better plans then." Anton went through the scanning process, placed his thumb on the plate, and hurried through the open door. It closed with a slight click, and she knew he'd reengaged security.

Leo raced ahead down the tunnel. "Careful. Stay close to me when we get to the park. You know what the mob was like yesterday. It's far worse, and we need to go across sixty feet of near-open space. The crowd is growing. The police are everywhere searching for the general's killers. Many people are armed."

Adrenaline kicked up her heart rate, sending a surge of blood through her veins. Svetlana's mind whirred. "Maybe we should go to the highway and double back. We can sneak through the alleyways. I used to take them to Perry's lab from school."

Leo hesitated. "That'll take us to the back of Red Square. It might be worse. General Urk's body was—"

"That was over an hour ago," Svetlana said. "The soldiers will gather in the park and march near the Assembly Hall. I'm sure that's where the police are heading. I hope Papa will be okay."

Leo scanned the area. "We're near the park. Let's stop and see what we're up against. If it's too risky, we'll go your way. When do you have to be at the airport? It's still a good thirty-minute drive and maybe longer if we encounter any roadblocks."

Svetlana checked her watch. "I'm okay, four hours before departure." Svetlana stepped to the door and placed her thumb on the scanner. The door clicked, but before she opened it, Leo pushed past her. "Let me check. If it's safe, I'll come back and get you. It'll only be a few minutes."

Terror filled her chest. Almost nothing was visible through the entrance except dust and a thick haze, but the smell hit her hard. There was so much smoke that she feared the whole town was on fire. "I'm going with you. I'm afraid that you'll never make it back through this crowd."

Leo grabbed her hand. "The smoke will cover us as we dash in the opposite direction."

The crowd merged toward them as Leo pushed his way forward. An officer spun around and shoved hard against Svetlana. "Out of my way!"

She lost hold of Leo's grasp. "Sorry." She backed into a middle-aged man who pulled a knife. He swung the blade toward her face, but Leo came out of nowhere. The butt of his pistol caught the man's temple. He dropped the knife and collapsed. People kept shoving and walking over the downed man.

Leo swiped the knife from the ground before a teenager could reach it.

"I saw it first." The grubby boy pushed Leo with all his strength.

Svetlana felt a bone-shaking thump as Leo crashed into her shoulder. "Let's get out of here!"

The teen kept coming. Something shiny caught Svetlana's attention, and she side-stepped before his brass knuckles hit her across the head. She grabbed the teen's arm and spun him toward Leo, who clocked him with his fist. They dashed for an opening at the edge of the field and kept running.

Lightning lit up the sky, followed by a burst of thunder. Rain turned to hail, and the crowd began dispersing. Leo pulled Svetlana into a small grove of trees at the park's edge. "My car's this way, but there are flashing lights ahead. It could be dangerous."

"Do you think they've closed the airport?" Svetlana had to raise her voice as shouts came from near the Assembly Hall. "Papa!" She turned to run toward the hall.

"No, you must catch your flight," Leo reminded her. "I promised."

Torn between staying and leaving, Svetlana heard a rumbling sound as two rusty, dented military police jeeps bounced across the field. They shuddered to a halt. Uniformed police hopped from the vehicles, moved to the rear, and pulled back a tarp. Armed military personnel unloaded. Their booted feet splashed up mud as they charged the remaining crowd.

"Take cover!" Leo yanked her to the ground as the officers opened fire.

Svetlana clasped her mouth to stifle a scream. "They're shooting at Papa!"

The armed troops focused on the crowd near the Assembly Hall northeast of the park.

"Now's our chance. Let's go!" Leo stayed low, ready to sprint.

Frozen in fear, Svetlana couldn't budge. Leo pulled her up by the hand and shoved her toward the tunnel door to Perry's lab. "We'll go out the other way, and you can check on Vlad."

"What about those flashing lights?" Her legs were like noodles, refusing to bear her weight.

"One step at a time." Leo yanked her behind a tree trunk as something whizzed past him, showering them with leaves. "We've been spotted. No time to delay." They took off running, zigzagging to dodge bullets.

"The tunnel's this way," Svetlana pulled Leo toward the entrance's bushes.

"It's too risky. They'll find Vlad and kill him." Leo pointed. "To the garage!" Leo's eyes widened as he flew backward. "Chert!"

Svetlana grabbed his collar and yanked him into the bushes. "Where are you hit?"

Barely able to catch his breath, he gasped, "Chest. Leave me." He held out his keys. "Go, navy sedan."

"No." She quickly entered the code for the tunnel entrance and pushed Leo through the chute. Svetlana's backpack caught as she slid through the door. It took a moment to push the strap off her shoulder and drop it over the opening, and then she grabbed the rope to lower herself. She spied a soldier dashing up to the bush as the door snapped shut.

"Over here!" a soldier shouted. "I saw them here a moment ago. They couldn't have gone far."

Svetlana joined Leo.

His face was pale, but he'd finally caught his breath. "I'm glad Anton made me wear this vest. Even so, it hurts like the devil rammed me with his pitchfork." He checked his watch. "I doubt you'll catch that plane today."

"I must get to the airport," Svetlana insisted. "Papa's counting on me."

Leo rolled to his side and slowly got up. "Vlad, you, all right?"

Svetlana dashed forward and abruptly halted.

Vlad sat glassy-eyed in a dark corner with a pistol pointing at her. "Identify yourself." His eyes, still swollen and purple, squinted.

"It's me," Leo called out, "and you know Ivanhoe."

Vlad lowered the gun. "I'm a nervous wreck and can barely see."

"But you're alive," Leo said. "We're just passing through."

Svetlana moved closer for a better look at Vlad. "You need more rest. You still look awful."

"Thanks. That's how I feel." Vlad pulled himself upright using a small table. "I'll cover you as you exit the other end of the tunnel."

Svetlana bolted for the lab door. "Did Perry leave anything else behind? We used the drones last night. We could relaunch them and see what's happening. I have my laptop."

"Not enough time," Leo warned, but it didn't sway Svetlana.

As she scanned Perry's old laboratory for any additional equipment that Vlad could use, she found another laptop, virtual reality goggles, and a spare cell phone. She also grabbed a satellite phone still on its charger and handed it to Vlad, "Take this. You might need it."

Vlad stood in the doorway. "I wish I'd known about this. I could have reached my American contact using that satphone instead of Perry's old computer."

"What do you mean American contact?" Svetlana panicked. She took a deep breath and felt like she was drowning. *Everything's happening too fast. General Urk is dead, and Papa's in danger. I didn't even get a chance to talk to him about his new plan once I get to the U.S. How will I find Roland Kildeer, and if I do meet him, what will he expect of me? Does he know Perry wrote that code to remove the power grids? Should I even meet with him?*

"Who's your American contact?" Leo asked. "How high up in command?"

"Will he help us?" Svetlana felt her gut twist with concern. "Or should I be afraid even to enter the country?"

"I'm sure he can help," Vlad said. "He's a special agent working for the U.S. president."

"No wonder you were in prison!" Svetlana exclaimed. "I thought the Minister of Finance was after your cousin, Perry."

"He was," Vlad insisted. "They kept asking me for Perry's location. I couldn't tell them anything since I didn't know where he was. No one mentioned my American contact, and you and Perry are the only ones who know even today, so keep it secret. His name is Usher Hastings."

"Are you sure he will help us?" Svetlana had doubts. "Perry's life depends on it. He's dead if he returns to Russia. He no longer has a job in South Africa and will be blamed for the deadly virus that hit New York City if he goes to the U.S." Svetlana thought a moment longer. "Maybe Perry can reverse the damage. Do you think he will be safe in the U.S. if he creates a solution for the damage to the electric grids?"

"Perry talked to Usher and two others yesterday," Vlad said. "He's sending a reversal for the Big V virus, and they know you're heading to Cincinnati, too."

Svetlana closed her eyes and made up her mind. "What? If that's true, why didn't Perry tell me?"

Vlad gulped. "He plans to when he talks to you today."

Svetlana bucked up her courage. "If I'm in danger, I must talk to the U.S. president."

Leo nudged her. "We have to leave for the airport."

"There are two drones, a computer, and a monitor. I will set up the equipment and send up both drones before I leave for the airport. You know how to use these, Vlad, and Papa may want to borrow them." Svetlana turned on the equipment and checked their energy charge.

Vlad nodded. "Are they loaded with weapons?"

Svetlana checked. "One is, but not the other. I guess we used up most of the ammunition last night."

Vlad scooted forward. "Okay, I know what to do. Go! I'll cover you."

"Thanks." Leo darted for the rear entrance.

Svetlana inserted new batteries. "Let me get these ready for launch first. Vlad, I'll leave the weaponized drone for you to activate, but only if Papa's in danger."

"Da," Vlad grabbed the keyboard and initiated the program.

Svetlana called from the end of the tunnel, "Okay. I'll set everything to be activated by you. We'll launch the drones as soon as we get outside, and you control them from here."

"Hurry!" Vlad went through the opening routine, and the tunnel door released. "You're going to be late for your flight."

AIRPORT OR BUST

Sept. 16 – 7:30 a.m. MSK, Moscow, Russia/12:30 a.m. EDT, Cincinnati, Ohio

Svetlana exited from the back tunnel of Perry's old apartment, clutching a weaponized drone, closely followed by Leo with another. As they arrived at the park, she activated her drone and turned to face Vlad, who stood at the door. "Take care. I'll be back soon," she said, her voice tinged with a mix of determination and concern.

"You, too," Vlad replied.

"I'll let Leo know when I land." Svetlana coordinated the drones to Vlad's computer and linked them to her cell phone so she could monitor them, at least while she was still in Moscow. "Release them in opposite directions. Send the weaponized one toward Papa to keep him safe from the attack of Denys' men."

Vlad sent the drones into the air and waved. "Have a safe flight, Ivanhoe."

Leo interrupted her return wave. "We must be in the open for at least a block before getting to the garage. Let's move it."

Svetlana watched the cell phone's blurry image of the drones and noticed more flashing lights blocking the road ahead. "There's no way we'll make it to the garage undetected. Now what?"

"I'll call in a favor from one of my buddies. He has a motorbike with a sidecar."

Svetlana checked the aerial view from the drone. "The main route, along the Borovskoye Shosse, is also blocked by police cars.

We can cut through the maze of alleyways to the E101 and take the M3, but it'll take longer."

Leo speed-dialed a number, his voice filled with determination. "If I get his IMZ-Ural, we'll have you there in no time, guaranteed. It never failed us during the last war," Leo assured, his words dripping with suspense. "All I ask is that you hang on and don't say a word." He was already on the phone with his friend, giving explicit directions, "Meet me behind St. Basil's Cathedral outside Red Square. See you in five."

Three minutes later, Leo donned his friend's lightweight black waterproof jacket, leggings, and helmet. He popped the motorcycle's kickstand, climbed astride the 28 hp, three-wheeled bike, and revved the motor. Svetlana grabbed the spare helmet and climbed into the sidecar.

"Be careful with my bike," his friend warned. "You'll be spotted as soon as you leave the square."

"Who says we'll go through the square?" Leo's grin was mischievous as he gunned the throttle. The bike spun gravel and gripped the grass beneath its wheels, rainwater splashing in its wake. Leo's friend disappeared from view as they rounded the corner, the motorbike leaning perilously on its side. The front wheel found an unseen tree stump, causing the bike to jolt sideways. Svetlana's body jerked toward the driver, but she held on—her fingers in a death grip, her heart pounding in her chest.

"Sorry," Leo's voice muffled in the wind.

Svetlana choked back a gasp as the motorcycle tore across the uneven pavement, slid through trash heaps, and threatened to skid off the path.

Leo drove around barriers and shrubbery. The ground dropped out from under them as they joined E-101, his favorite route out of town. The motorbike hovered over a pool of water filled with slime and weeds before finding solid ground.

Svetlana squeezed her eyes shut as they landed and gasped as water splashed across her face. Her arm flew up to shield herself, but not for long before the bike jerked again. Her body twisted wildly from side to side.

The little ravine had caught Leo off guard, too. He hopped to a standing position to avoid the impact, hitting the seat hard when it flew upward. Leo fought the whirling updraft as they landed on the blacktop and skidded across two lanes of traffic, barely glancing at his passenger to see if she was still in the sidecar.

A driver sounded his horn as a car sped past them. Leo slammed on the brakes and cranked the wheel with all his might to return to his lane. The sidecar rose as the bike rode on the remaining left-side wheels.

Svetlana slumped over the edge of the sidecar, trying to stay upright, then flopped backward as the bike's wheels hit the ground, "Ooof!" It knocked the air from her lungs. "Leo, please, slow down!"

"Da! Da! I'm trying." Leo rounded the bend and joined the straight road that became the M3. He deftly wove around cars, trucks, and vans at breakneck speeds up to 170 kph. Horns honked, and some people yelled out their windows, but he never lightened up on the throttle. The wind whipped through Svetlana's hair, the sound of the engine roared in her ears, and the rush of adrenaline surged through her veins.

All Svetlana could do was hang on, making sure she didn't lose her backpack or get thrown from the sidecar. They were making good time, but Svetlana was butting up against the three-hour window before her departure deadline.

Twenty minutes later, she was at terminal A of Vnukovo International Airport. Svetlana felt like a pretzel. Her fingers were numb from gripping the front bar. She shook her hands out to get some circulation in her fingers. "That was some ride, but thanks for getting me here in time."

Leo nodded. "Call when you land or if you need anything before then."

Svetlana removed her Kevlar vest, left it with Leo, and waved as he drove away from the curve. Then, she went to the Turkish

Airlines ticket counter to get a boarding pass for Ivanhoe. By the time she reached the gate, the plane was already boarding. Relief flooded through her once she placed her bag in the overhead bin and took her seat.

The first tingle of excitement raced up her spine, or maybe it was fear. If all went well, it would take nearly fifteen hours to reach Cincinnati/Northern Kentucky Airport, plus the seven-hour time change. Nervous yet thrilled, she felt like laughing and crying at the same time. Neither would be appropriate for Ivanhoe. It was her first trip outside of Russia. *What will it be like to land in a foreign country? Will I fit in?* Then, the most devastating idea hit her. *What if I fail? That can't happen. If activated, Roland could replicate that virus and plant it anywhere. I must stop him. Papa is counting on me.*

FOLLOW THE LEADER

Sept. 16 – 7:40 a.m. MSK, Moscow, Russia/
12:40 a.m. EDT, Cincinnati, Ohio

After General Urk's death, Anton had to step up as the leader of the most prestigious Moscow unit and inspire confidence in his followers by showing wisdom and natural leadership skills instead of fear. However, Anton was still determining the direction he should lead his team. His sole priority was to ensure Svetlana's safety, but she was going to an unknown location, leaving Anton behind. He followed Urk's orders only because he had to and not because he agreed. Now that he was in charge, Anton was resolute in his determination to protect his team. The Russian government had exceeded its limits, and he believed the country needed the U.S.'s approval and support to remain free.

The men may follow my new direction. Who can I trust? Boris? Da. Yogi? Da. He rescued me on two other occasions. They're strong, and our men will listen to them. Can we trust the police? His gut twisted. *Sometimes, but not if they are under higher orders, and definitely not if left up to Chief Ignacio. Look what they did to Vlad.* Anton heaved a sigh. *I swear the chief of police is behind everything evil, but we must obey or be cut down. I must show no fear, but the doubt lingers.*

Standing tall, he met his team at the Assembly Hall and immediately took charge by dividing his men into three groups. "Lieutenant Yogi, take your troop to Red Square. If General Urk's body is still there, cut him down. Bring him back here so we can give him a respectful burial." Anton's words were filled with trust and respect for his team, making them feel valued and integral to the mission.

"Yes, Captain," Yogi said.

"Don't fire on the police," Anton warned. "Denys' boys are stirring up a riot, and we don't want them mistaking one of us as part of the Ukraine mafia."

"Da, I know what to do." Yogi swung his fist in the air and motioned for his men to follow. "To Red Square—we'll use the tunnel." Yogi's troops followed at a rapid pace.

"Lieutenant Boris, you know the police chief," Anton noted how foreign it felt to call his friend by rank. "Speak to him, and let him know we are on his side. Ask him where he wants you to set up a base, and then take team three with you."

"Where will I find Chief Ignacio?" Boris asked.

"Yogi saw him in the park talking to Sergeant Kraus. The military has unloaded two armored vehicles. Tensions are running high, so watch yourself. We don't want to get caught in the crossfire. Let the chief believe he's in command."

"Da, Ser. I'll take two men with me." Boris pointed to two younger lads.

Anton nodded. "Call me or send word as soon as you find out the police chief's plan."

"Da." Boris left the hall with his team.

Anton motioned to three other men. "Gather the grenades, guns, and ammo in the main tunnel and return them here. The rest of you take positions to protect the Assembly Hall. Wolf, come with me."

A burly, red-faced man with a peach fuzz mustache and auburn hair down to his shoulders stepped up. A Makarov pistol jutted from the holster on the large man's hip. "My name's Hrolf." The man straightened and must have grown another four inches since Anton had seen him last, now towering over his head.

Anton's eyes gazed up at the man. "That's what I said. Wolf, you're Marot's boy, right?"

"Da, they took Papa away."

"I heard," Anton said. "We'll do everything to set him free."

A man with ropey muscles like twisted steel darted in front of Wolf. Dark shadows lined his brown face. A hooked nose twitched. Beady dark green eyes with a hint of gold glared at Anton. "The man said his name is Hrolf." He coughed into his large hand. "Idiot! sir."

Anton smirked and turned to Hrolf. "Who's your buddy?"

"Orel, but you'll probably call him Eagle," Hrolf smirked. "Most people do. Friends, that is, and I'm not sure you're any friend of his."

The hair on the nape of Anton's neck stood on end. He didn't believe in omens, but this was a good sign. "Wolf and Eagle," Anton's voice came out rough as if he'd been smoking a pack of cigarettes a day, which he hadn't done since his teens. "It brings raw energy to my soul. You are my number one team, and you will answer to Wolf and Eagle. Understood? This is not just a mission, it's a bond we share, a trust we build together."

The smile on Eagle's face disappeared. "Da. Let's get that evil bastard! Denys killed my brother two years ago, and I will get my revenge."

The phone rang. "Captain Anton, we are to guard the river's edge to the East," Boris said. "Police are taking the South. Yogi will oversee Red Square and the West. Sergeant Kraus' men have nearly cleared the park and will head north. Send my men out to the ravine. The military has barricaded the roads."

"All roads?" Anton asked. "Can Ivanhoe get to the airport?"

"He should already be there," Boris assured him. "Planes are still flying."

"Good." Anton felt relieved, but in the back of his mind, he was afraid Ivanhoe would miss his flight. "Anyone here from team three? Boris is waiting for you at the ravine."

Boris' men gathered their equipment and moved out of the hall.

"Anton," Boris added, "two drones are hovering above the park. Are they ours?"

"Nyet," Anton was fairly certain of that, "but tell me more."

"They have not tried to interfere," Boris admitted, "but they're hovering fairly low."

"Shoot them down," Anton said.

Wolf grabbed his arm. "Shoot what down?"

"Two drones overhead," Anton explained.

"Leave them," Wolf said, taking out a small oval device. "I want to track them and find their source. Perhaps we can take control. We could use a drone."

Boris clarified, "What do you say, Anton?"

Anton reconsidered. "Be leery, but don't fire on the drones yet. Let me know if they activate any weapons."

"Da." Boris disconnected the call.

HELICOPTER'S MISSING

Sept. 16 – 8:10 a.m. MSK, Moscow, Russia/
1:10 a.m. EDT, Cincinnati, Ohio

Meanwhile, Cracker's wife, Rozalina, was frantically preparing for her own emergency. Every precious second counted as she had to act swiftly as soon as Cracker's plane touched down. It was crucial that her actions seemed genuine, legitimate, and life-threatening. The challenge was that Cracker was oblivious to his critical diagnosis, and so was everyone else on the plane. The plan she had in mind could potentially endanger her husband's life, a risk she was forced to take.

Despite having no direct means of communication with her "soon-to-be" patient, Rozalina was a remarkably resourceful woman who would find a way to rescue him. Her future hinged on this mission, and she was determined to succeed.

It was a freezing day for September—minus 10° C (14° F), eight degrees lower than usual. She blamed the weather change on global warming and dug out her winter sweater. A fine layer of ice covered the streets like slick glass. After 7 a.m., the hospital would be humming with activity—perfect for her plan.

Rozalina couldn't sit still. Pacing, her fingers trembled as she tapped in a phone number she never thought she'd ever dial again. He picked up the call on the second ring.

"Dr. Manaheim. How may I help you?"

"Manny, your helicopter is missing!" Rozalina's voice nearly squeaked. "Time is critical, and I'm joining you for an S and R."

"What time and where?" Manny's reply was calm and steady.

Rozalina nearly choked on the words, "Medical center, 11:03 today—destination Vnukovo International Airport. Contact pilot of Airbus...medical alert. Passenger unknown."

"Roger, 'til then." Manny disconnected the call.

Her mother stood in the doorway. "Rozalina, what was that all about?"

"I called in a favor," Rozalina whispered. "We must remove Cracker from the plane and whisk him away before anyone knows he's landed."

Her mother stepped closer to hear her. "Why did you say a helicopter is missing?"

"This isn't our first mission, Mama," Rozalina felt sweat blossom along her neck. "It's a secret code we use at the medical center. No one must know."

"What does S and R mean?" Mama asked.

"Search and rescue. I must get ready. Take the children to your brother's house in the country. That's where we'll hide out. You must leave in the next twenty minutes." Rozalina didn't wait for a reply, gathered her medical bag, put on her navy overcoat with the medical emblem embroidered on the left lapel, and gathered supplies. The secrecy and danger of her mission hung in the air, adding to the suspense and intrigue of the story.

At 9:40 a.m., Rozalina hugged her children and mother as Uncle Albert loaded them into his car. She locked all the doors and dashed down the street, where an ambulance waited. This was the usual meeting place for such missions, a nondescript corner where they could blend in with the city's hustle and bustle. Igor, her regular driver, held open her door. "Where to?"

Rozalina slid into the passenger seat and gave directions, "University Medical Center, at the usual drop off."

"Yes," Igor hurried around the car to the driver's seat.

Russian police, armed with machine guns, watched over the University campus—frequently stopping to frisk anyone. Two guards stood on the curb when the ambulance approached the hospital. Rozalina bit her lip. "I'm leaving my water bottle in the glove compartment. I'll get it later."

Igor nodded. "What time should I pick you up?"

"I'll call when I need a ride," Rozalina said, opening the ambulance door. "It might be late. Are you sure you'll be able to pick me up at a moment's notice?"

"Absolutely!" Igor reassured her.

She hesitated but stepped from the ambulance, and he drove away.

Rozalina knew that to get results, she needed money. It wasn't easy, as she could barely make ends meet. Although a doctor, she cared for poor people who bartered in return, sometimes paying with goulash, chickens, or running special errands. University Hospital was for the rich, who often purchased medical care with criminal money. She couldn't pay in chickens or soup. It cost her $1,000 in U.S. funds to use the helicopter, but it was worth it, and hopefully, Cracker would help repay her small savings.

Today, she was on a mission and didn't want a delay, so she walked with purpose and spied Dr. Manaheim.

He opened the hospital's front door. "You're late. Hurry!"

She knew this was his way of letting the police know she was no threat, "Coming, Manny." Rozalina waved and rushed to the entrance.

They headed to the roof, where a helicopter waited, fully loaded with medical supplies, including a defibrillator, oxygen tanks, and a variety of medications. She knew the pilot. "Good morning, Rolo. Did Manny fill you in on the flight plan?"

"Da." Pilot Rolo handed her headphones. "We're heading to the airport tarmac before reaching the international gates. A passenger on Airbus needs emergency medical attention."

"That's right." Manny climbed into the chopper. "I contacted my brother at air control. He'll have Airbus stay on the tarmac for our arrival and departure. He radioed ahead to the plane's pilot, who would deliver Rozalina's message verbatim to the passenger in 1-A.

There was no one aboard by the name of Cracker, but this passenger does fit the description and is flying under a Russian passport as C. W. Gresinsky."

As the helicopter took off, Rozalina opened her laptop, logged on to a government database, and hacked into airport records. She altered the passenger list, removing any mention of Gresinsky and a few other files, which would trigger only if necessary after the Airbus landed. She would remove any proof of Gresinsky's flight if need be. A hard copy would still have his name on the list, but Manny's brother would track that and replace it with the revision. There would be eyewitnesses among the passengers, but any Russians aboard would keep their mouths shut. Most had no stomach for spilling information to foreign government officials—especially the FBI. She would implement this plan only as a last resort.

IF DEAD MEN COULD TALK

Sept. 16 – 9:00 a.m. MSK, Moscow, Russia/
2:00 a.m. EDT, Cincinnati, Ohio

Captain Anton's Team 1 hustled to Red Square as ordered. A volley of gunfire erupted from the park, leaving a pungent odor of smoke in the air. An icy chill raced down Yogi's spine when he recognized General Urk's body lying in a heap in the middle of the plaza. The general's Army green uniform, saturated in dark blood, still had his numerous medals honoring his gallant service. Someone had cut the body down but left him on the ground, probably in a hurry before gunfire cut them down, too.

The square appeared deserted except for one policeman, who stood guard over the body. A single streetlamp flickered at one corner. Yogi knew the officer and strolled over for a chat, "Tis a sad day for the general's family and our comrades."

The policeman nodded. "Da. We will get his killer, but oh, the suffering he must have gone through. Look at his swollen tongue. He nearly bit it off—probably during a seizure."

Yogi grimaced. "My men will take his body to wherever you wish, but it is disrespectful to leave him here on the ground in the rain."

The officer tapped his billy club into his gloved hand. "Da, tis true, but I have no orders to move him."

"Surely, we could take him to the mortuary," Yogi offered. "I see no harm in that. It is only out of respect that we would move him."

The officer seemed to think about that. "Perhaps you're right. I could do more good heading to the park and breaking up that riot."

Yogi agreed. "Come, men, let's move General Urk to the mortuary." Yogi didn't wait for the policeman's consent. The men swooped in and whisked the general away, but not to the mortuary. Instead, they brought him to the tunnel.

"I'll get Anton," Yogi said. "He will want to pay his respects before we deliver our commander to his final resting place."

The men laid the general on a table in a back room of the Assembly Hall, and Yogi went in search of Anton.

"I'd like to spend a few moments alone with the general." Anton wondered if the general had left him a clue. Both men had agreed that if possible, in a deadly situation, they would do their best to leave a message.

Yogi left the room and turned, "The officer told me he had a seizure and nearly bit off his tongue. A head injury, or do you think they used nerve gas?"

"Either is possible." Anton bit his lower lip and closed the door. "What do you have to tell me?"

Appalled at the general's condition, he gagged back bile as he searched the body and checked his pockets, cuffs, and even his mouth. The general's tongue was so swollen he appeared to have choked on it. Froth still formed around his lips. He had broken ribs, kneecaps, and fingers. Bruises lined his body, and slash marks covered his back and buttocks. Apparently, whoever did this had undressed the general, tortured him, and then redressed him in a half-assed fashion. Nerve gas would cause respiratory failure, and Anton suspected the deadly Novichok, but he didn't see any clues other than torture.

Anton heaved a sigh and saluted the general. That's when his eyes noticed something unusual. *A double-headed eagle, the Order of Merit to the Fatherland, was pinned upside down on the general's uniform—a traitor in the ranks, but who and how high up?*

Anton removed the medal to return it to its rightful position. On the underside read the letters A. O. etched and sealed with blood. *No, it can't be. That's my initials. Surely, the general couldn't believe I had betrayed him because I didn't.* He rubbed away the blood and saw a faint mark above the etching. *Maybe an upside-down U? That doesn't make any sense.* He couldn't see it clearly, so he took a photo with his cell phone to enlarge it later. Feeling sick and dejected, Anton properly reattached the medal to the general's uniform. *Why this medal, General? Two-headed? Does that mean something? And why my initials? What were you trying to tell me? Did the general know that I would flip sides when faced with facts? It isn't like that. I'm fighting for our country the best way I know how.*

A knock on the door brought Anton back from his scrutiny. He automatically pulled his gun, disengaged the safety, and whipped it behind his back, then padded over to the door. It was second nature to him, an extension of his hand during times of battle.

Yogi didn't open the door. "Captain Anton, we have Denys in our sights, and he's not in Moscow. He's pulling strings from Kyiv." Anton holstered his gun before letting Yogi inside.

"Is it safe to move him?" Yogi nodded toward General Urk's body.

"Da, call the men in to pay their respects, then you can take him to the mortuary. Order an autopsy to determine if he was drugged. We'll have a more formal memorial service when this is over."

FINAL SALUTE

Sept. 16 – 10:00 a.m. MSK, Moscow, Russia/
3:00 a.m. EDT, Cincinnati, Ohio

By 10 a.m., the Russian military and police had subdued the rioters in Moscow. Captain Anton spoke to Chief Ignacio, "This is off the record. I know you are not responsible for your officer's behavior, but the police are jailing several of our neighbors on false charges. Did General Urk come by yesterday to talk to you about the high cost of these protection fees the police are collecting? They have to stop charging so much money!"

"Da, the general stopped by, and we chatted over a drink," Chief Ignacio admitted. "I told him we are doing everything we can to get to the bottom of this extortion."

"I want to know who is behind the high fee." Anton watched Ignacio for any clues. "The government?"

The police chief placed his hand over his mouth and rubbed his chin. "You didn't hear it from me cuz I will deny everything."

"You know I'd never betray you," Anton lied.

"The Investigative Department of the Russian Ministry of Interior has strict orders," the chief whispered as if he were afraid his words would fall on prying ears. "There has been too much embezzlement of funds. We must go to every house to check for anyone defrauding the bank."

Anton leaned closer and whispered, "Under whose orders?"

"Okueva is my bet," Ignacio also spoke softly, "but I've been unable to track him down. You paid what was due, so we let you go, but others refused to pay."

"I didn't admit to any fraud!" Anton hissed. "I paid to stay out of jail."

The chief shrugged his shoulders. "Same thing."

Anton was ready to wring the chief's neck. He clenched and unclenched his fist as he seethed inside. "Was General Urk alone when he talked with you?" Anton asked. "You didn't hand him over to Denys, did you?"

"I'll pretend I didn't hear that last accusation, but you must watch what you say," Chief Ignacio warned. "Some officers are not as generous. To answer your first question, his bodyguards were outside our office and escorted him back to his jeep. I assure you, he was still alive and well when he left our station."

"And you have no idea where he went or what happened after his visit?" Anton asked.

"Nyet and two of his five guards are also dead, two are missing, and one is in a coma in the hospital. We won't know anything unless he wakes up and can tell us. No one claims to have seen anything."

Anton thought hard. "Who's missing?"

"Augi Orion for sure," the chief said, "and he was the toughest of them all. We think he got away. Gabe was the youngest guard and new to the job. We've heard rumors that he was captured, but we're unsure if he's still alive."

Augi Orion, Initials AO. Is he Missing, or is he a traitor? I knew General Urk wouldn't believe that I betrayed him. I bet we'll meet up with Augi again.

"If that's all, I'm a busy man. I sent a man to check on Augi's wife, but I doubt she knows her husband's whereabouts." The police chief dismissed Anton with a flick of his wrist.

Anton wasn't ready to leave. His thoughts went to Gabe, who was the same age as Ivanhoe. "What are you doing to find the lad?" *What would I do if my child were missing?*

"We've been busy, Anton. People are rioting in the streets."

Realizing he would get no more answers, Anton gave a slight bow. "Spasibo, ser." Anton left the chief's side as a messenger brushed past him, anxious to share his news. "Chief, I spoke to Augi's Mrs. Her daughter is missing."

Anton barely took notice and rushed to the Assembly Hall to gather his men.

"Before we move our beloved general, I'd like to give a brief eulogy on his behalf. Many of you knew him as your commander, but I knew him as a friend. If you have anything to add, please feel free to do so. General Urk was a brilliant man, only eighteen when he graduated from law school. He went into the military about the same time as you, Boris."

"Yes, he was just a twenty-year-old lad, and within five years, he became a hero and made general," Boris piped up. "He also worked closely with Galina."

Several of the older men sighed in awe.

A recruit asked, "Who was he?"

Anton's eyes turned to the young man. "Not he. Galina was President Boris Yeltsin's closest advisor, also a lawyer, and one of the most respected females in our country. Galina worked to put the USSR Communist Party on trial, and General Urk worked with her behind the scenes to ban the former party and secret police members from holding office. Then, in 1992, many of the die-hard KGB directly violated Yeltsin's rule and formed an internal party organization. A gunman murdered Galina, but General Urk continued fighting for our people."

Boris nodded. "That wasn't the only time he fought for our countrymen. In 2014, he led a Special Forces unit into Crimea for President Putin, and most of us fought by his side during that war."

The lad who asked about Galina asked, "Why did we fight that battle?"

"I know some of you younger men question the wisdom of that war," Anton said, "but Russians make up more than half of Crimea, and they were under our rule for most of the past 1,000 years."

"That isn't the only reason we fought," Boris added. "Ukraine's economy was awful, and it's still poor. President Putin worried Ukraine would take over Russia's naval base at Sevastopol, our only warm-water port. You know what that would do to our country."

"We had to fight, and General Urk received honors more than once for his bravery," Anton said. "I'm sure Denys is still fuming over that war. He lost his oldest son, and it's probably one of the reasons he is getting even."

Boris reminded the men, "Protection fees have doubled recently, and many of our neighbors are being jailed, like our friend Marot."

"General Urk went before the chief of police asking for help to lower those fees," Anton said. "Not long after his chat, Denys captured our general, tortured and murdered him. With one last salute, I give my deepest respect and gratitude to General Urk and his family."

The men also gave a final salute to their general.

Anton took over as commander. "Yogi, get a team together to deliver the general's body to the morgue. Wolf, Eagle, and Boris meet me in the foyer. I just got word that Denys has gone underground. Boris, line up the artillery, gas masks, drones, and flash grenades. We're going after Denys and beware of Augi Orion. He went missing last night and could be a traitor."

Boris clenched his hands. "I warned General Urk about that goon. He's a raging bull when angered. I suppose that's why the general kept him on as his bodyguard."

"If we find him to be a traitor, he'll be dealt with accordingly," Anton vowed. "We leave for Kyiv before sundown."

"I'll notify my men," Boris headed for the door.

"Wait, we're not taking the whole unit. Just the four of us," Anton said.

"Is that wise?" Boris asked.

"I'm sure Denys has Gabe," Anton said. "His life is in danger, and if a whole team comes after Denys, the lad dies, no questions asked. If we ambush Denys and his men, maybe we can rescue Gabe."

Eagle's eyes darted between the two men as they argued. Wolf tapped Eagle's shoulder. "Let the two of them go. I didn't sign on to be murdered."

Anton snapped, "Who covered your father's debt?"

Wolf straightened. "You did, Ser."

"Damn, right!" Anton glared at the boy. "Marot never neglected his duties. Your father pulled up the morale of our unit, finished his combat tour, and was a hero before he retired. I'm sure this assignment will pay well. Are you with me? I want only the best."

Whether it was the money, his father's honor, or a feeling of pride, Wolf agreed to the assignment.

Eagle didn't hesitate. "This is for my brother. Denys slit his throat during a bar fight last year. I'll gladly return the favor."

AT RISK

Sept. 16 – 11:00 a.m. MSK, Moscow, Russia/
4:00 a.m. EDT, Cincinnati, Ohio

Rozalina's mind spun, filled with rapid thoughts and images as her plan to rescue her husband went into action. After stocking supplies, loading emergency gear, and coordinating with the healthcare team, a medical helicopter circled Vnukovo Airport in Moscow, Russia. "Any sign of the plane?"

The team leader, Manny, leaned forward and stared at the gray sky. "Too far away to tell." He turned to Rolo. "What does the tower say?"

Rozalina gazed down at the runway as Rolo, the pilot, turned left. The rotor blades stirred the morning's frigid air. Rolo landed the chopper in a tree-lined area near the airport tower. A raw wind snatched her breath away when she opened the chopper door. In the distance came a faint roar. "Is that his plane?"

Rolo radioed Manny's brother, Trey, who had taken over operations at the airport tower for this occasion. He used a non-recorded radio frequency. "What's the ETA of our flight?"

Trey said, "The flight's delayed and not due for another thirty minutes, but we are concerned. Two suspicious agents are demanding access to the same plane. What aren't you telling me?"

Rozalina's gut twisted at the response. *The FBI's already here. What should I say?* A blast of air blistered her cheeks, but she had to endure the cold. *My husband's life depends on this mission.* "This is a medical emergency. We'll remove the patient, and then the plane can taxi to the terminal."

"I can't go against airport authorities," Trey warned. "They won't tell anyone who these agents are, but these two strangers were allowed beyond the gate and aren't passengers. That's unheard of, and I suspect government agents. One's a Brit. The other, I'd guess, is American. I'm sure they're waiting to collect a passenger upon arrival. What should I do?"

"Weather conditions are getting worse," Rolo cut in. "If it continues to deteriorate, I won't be able to lift off."

"Change incoming flight to RF 110," Manny said.

"Roger," Trey turned his dial to RF 110, and then there was static. Rolo tracked the new radio frequency.

Manny asked Trey, "Have you reported your suspicion to the plane's pilot?"

"Not yet," Trey said. "You told me this was an emergency."

"It is." Her nerves tingled with apprehension. "Did the passenger aboard the plane get my message?"

"Da, but we haven't heard any request for medical—"

"Vnukovo Tower" sounded in the background. "Co-pilot Hershal here. We have an emergency aboard and request an immediate medical evacuation. A passenger has chest pain and difficulty breathing. We started oxygen."

"Roger," Trey implemented the plan. "Medical services will be on the ground, but the helicopter can't taxi to the terminal. Land, and we'll send flight doctors to your door. Once the patient is evacuated, you can taxi to the terminal."

"That was fast," the plane's co-pilot said. "Will an exit ramp be supplied?"

There was a pause. Trey mumbled something and returned to the radio, "Da, if you take runway A."

There was a slight delay. "There is no runway A," the co-pilot snapped. "I've flown this route for years and never heard of runway A."

"Military access!" Trey said with enough force to convince a general. "You know the drill."

The co-pilot's voice rose in pitch. "Military? I can't! I don't have permission."

"Tower just gave you permission." Trey continued using his most authoritative voice, "Do it!"

"There's no runway there," the co-pilot Hershal repeated. A heated discussion pursued between the co-pilot and the pilot, and then a different voice spoke, "Roger. ETA: fifteen minutes. Ground transport…"

Sept. 16 – 12:16 p.m. MSK, Moscow, Russia/
5:16 a.m. EDT, Cincinnati, Ohio

Boredom set in as FBI agents Saul Reed and Zina McLaughlin waited inside the terminal building at the arrival gate, gazing out the window through binoculars. They had been there for the past six hours and had already encountered four planes, but they had yet to intercept Cracker. Reed lowered his field glasses and strolled over to the gate's agent. "What's taking so long?"

"Poor weather conditions," the agent said. "All our flights have been delayed. We're lucky they haven't closed the airport."

Reed already knew of the delays and hated being stuck in Russia. *It's bitter cold and too much like a military base with no luxuries. Post-USSR days are miserable. Every building is a dingy-gray high-rise made of crumbling cement.* He pulled up his left sleeve and checked the time on his wristwatch—nearly eleven. He sighed. *Only ten minutes have gone by. It 's dark and dreary in this forsaken country. The storm makes it so dark that I'll have to dig out my infrared goggles soon.*

Zina stayed at the window, watching for any movement. "Did someone call in a medical emergency?"

The agent shook her head. "Nyet."

A frown crossed Zina's face. "Why the medical helicopter?"

Reed dashed back to the window and scanned outside through his binoculars. "Where?"

Zina pointed. "Across the field."

Reed squinted and peered through his binoculars once more. "I don't see a helicopter."

Zina pointed once more. "It went behind those trees."

The airline agent called out, "Not to worry. There's no runway over there, and I have no calls for medical transportation. Certainly, I would know if a helicopter was needed."

Reed paced. The terminal was chilly, and he hadn't prepared for such cold weather. "How much longer?"

The agent radioed for an update and reported, "ETA thirty minutes."

Reed's phone rang. "FBI Agent Reed—"

"This is Special Ops Agent Usher Hastings. Cracker didn't land in Heathrow, Rome, Paris, or Nairobi. If he landed in Frankfurt, Germany, no one would be there to meet him, and he must be on his way to Russia. Has the plane landed yet?"

"All flights are delayed. ETA is," Reed rechecked his watch, "twenty-seven minutes. I'll call you as soon as we nab him." He disconnected the call and turned back to Zina. "Let's get a cup of coffee while we wait."

"My gut says something's fishy." Zina stood her ground. "I'll stay and check on that chopper, but you could bring me a cup of hot tea with cream, not too hot, and two sugars. We Brits can't understand your disgusting need for that bitter java."

"Touché!" Reed wandered off.

Sept. 16 – 1:05 p.m. MSK, Moscow, Russia/
6:05 a.m. EDT, Cincinnati, Ohio

Massive clouds rolled in, thick as mushroom soup. Rozalina had a brief conversation with Rolo, who was worried, "Sorry, but there is no way I can lift off the ground in this weather. I'm not even sure your patient's plane can land."

Rozalina cocked her head and listened. "I hear a jet in the distance. Check in with Trey and see what Co-pilot Hershal says."

Trey made contact with the Co-pilot.

"We're landing using instruments only," Hershal said. "We can't see the ground, and a fiery exhaust burns like a blue haze, making our vision even dimmer. We're banking to the right, but ice crystals are bombarding the windshield and getting worse the lower we go."

Rozalina had closed the helicopter door because of the storm, which didn't prevent the cold air from seeping inside the chopper. Her fingers still felt numb.

"You okay, Rozalina?" Manny was concerned. "You're breathing too fast. Relax, we'll be in the air soon with your patient."

Rozalina realized that she had been hyperventilating. She took a deep breath and held it briefly before slowly letting it out. "Thanks, Manny. I'm just nervous." She flinched when Hershal's voice came across the radio. "Where's runway A? I can't see a thing."

Trey said from the tower, "I've locked onto your plane." He gave the coordinates: "You're at 2,000 feet. Stay on course. You'll hit a row of trees if you miss the coordinates by even a tenth of a kilometer."

"Good to know," Hershal said.

The sound of the jet was louder, but Rozalina still couldn't see the plane. Finally, dim lights cut through the mist. Dark round orbs gradually descended until the tires hit the ground, and the aircraft safely rolled to a stop. "They've landed. Now it's up to us." She threw open the helicopter door and hopped to the ground.

Manny shoved a cot loaded with medical equipment beside the rear door and jumped down. They pulled the cot from the chopper and dashed for the plane. In the meantime, Trey had electronically maneuvered a mechanical stairway to the jet's front door. As Rozalina reached the top step, the plane's door opened.

"Where's the patient?" Manny asked, but Rozalina had already spied her husband. His lips were blue even though he had oxygen flowing through a nasal cannula. Sweat beaded his forehead, and his eyes were closed. How did he manage these side effects? Then she remembered his military days and the mock drills he supervised.

A flight attendant grabbed her sleeve. "Hurry! I'm afraid he's dying."

Rozalina followed the flight attendant down the aisle to seat 1 A. "Sir, can you hear me?" Rozalina's voice shook as she tried to contain her panic. Did he really have a heart attack? It sure looks authentic. She grabbed his wrist.

Cracker's eyes flew open, and he said in Russian, "Help me."

"Don't worry, we'll have you at the hospital soon." Manny helped Cracker onto the cot. Rozalina started an IV and injected medication into the IV port while Manny connected a cardiac monitor to Cracker's chest and exchanged oxygen tanks. The attendant took away the old tank.

Rozalina's heart beat nearly as fast as Cracker's. She didn't dare look him in the eye for fear he'd say something or that she might crumble. "Do you have any luggage?"

The flight attendant returned and opened the overhead bin. "This is all he carried on the plane." She handed Rozalina a backpack.

"Thanks for all of your help," Rozalina managed to say without breaking into tears. Relief washed through her as they headed for the open door.

Co-pilot Hershal stepped from the cabin. "Wait! We just got word from security. Two FBI agents are heading this way. You're not allowed to leave."

Cracker's body jerked as if he was having a seizure. Rozalina nearly dropped the cot as they lowered it to the ground.

"This man's life depends on him getting immediate medical attention," Manny ordered.

Rozalina tore open her medical bag and withdrew a syringe filled with another medicine. She injected it into Cracker's IV, noted the time as 1:02 p.m., and nodded to Manny to pick up his end of the cot. "Excuse me," she said, pushing forward. "Let's move!"

The Co-pilot didn't move. "We wait."

I only have an hour to get that antidote. Rozalina panicked. "We can't wait. This man's fate depends on—"

"Let me talk to security," Manny demanded. "This man is dying." Suddenly, the cardiac monitor's alarm screamed in the quiet suspense. "He's in cardiac arrest."

Rozalina nearly sobbed, but she pushed Hershal against the door. "We're heading for the hospital ASAP. You can send the FBI agents there if this is indeed the man they are looking for, but I doubt it. It could be any one of the other passengers on board." They headed down the stairs just as a jeep pulled up.

A woman shouted, "FBI Agent Zina," as she ran from the vehicle. "Where are you taking this man?"

"Medical emergency," Manny said with authority as they laid the cot down on the ground at the bottom of the steps. Rozalina thumped Cracker's chest. He grunted, and the heart monitor rhythm returned to sinus tachycardia.

"Let's go," Rozalina grabbed one end of the cot. "His heart's beating, but I don't know for how long."

The co-pilot stepped from the plane and stood at the door. "I tried to make them wait, but this man must be evacuated ASAP. You're welcome to board now."

"I'm Agent Saul Reed." The man with an American accent dashed past Zina and bounded up the stairs, but Zina stayed behind, pulled out her cell phone, and took a photo of Cracker and the medical team. "Where are you taking him?"

Manny yelled over his shoulder, "University Hospital." He nodded to Rozalina. "Hurry before it's too late." They loaded Cracker into the chopper and climbed aboard. "Rolo, take off."

The chopper blades whirred to life. "I'm not sure it can lift..." The bird vibrated, rose slightly, and then seemed to hang in the air. "Come on," Rolo muttered under his breath. Gradually, the chopper rose and flew away from the airport.

Cracker's monitor beeped again—a few blips on the EKG, then a straight line.

Rozalina thumped Cracker's chest again, but no rhythm returned. As much as she wanted to continue CPR, she knew it would be of no use without the antidote. "There's been a change of plans," she said. "Take us to Sokolniki Park and have an ambulance meet us."

"What if the FBI agents come to the hospital?" Manny asked.

"Fill out a death certificate for C. W. Gresinsky. He died of a massive myocardial infarction." Rozalina squeezed Cracker's hand. "I'll have the ambulance take him to the mortuary."

Manny nodded. "Yes, that would be best. Sorry, we lost your patient."

Rozalina peered down at her husband of twelve years. She hoped with all her might that she was doing the right thing. The FBI agents wouldn't want a corpse. She only had one hour to reverse the meds on board, or his faked death would be permanent. Glancing at her watch, *make that fifty-three minutes.* "I'll call for an ambulance. How long before we reach the park?"

"In this weather, thirty to forty minutes," Rolo said. "Maybe longer."

"That long?" Panic gripped her soul. It would be cutting it close. Too close! The antidote to the drug she had injected into Cracker's bloodstream was in the ambulance. She'd hidden it in the glove compartment inside her water bottle filled with ice. It was a stupid move, but she was afraid the police would stop and search her.

TWIST OF FATE

Sept. 16 – 4:55 a.m. EDT, Cincinnati, Ohio

Sated from a wild night of lovemaking, Braun couldn't get Cordy out of his mind. She remained an enigma to him. *She is definitely passionate about everything she does in life. Stubborn, strong-willed, daring, seductive, reckless, and much too clever, sometimes to the point of infuriating me, but no one can stir lust so easily as my wife. Even after spending a lifetime with this woman, I still will be captivated by her charm.*

Cordy bounced from the bed. "Beat you to the showers."

Braun moved like lightning and blocked the bathroom door. "I'll wash your back if you—"

"If I kiss you?" Cordy laughed and threw her arms around his neck.

Braun lifted her off her feet, spun her around, and walked into the bathroom. He set her back on the floor and then turned on the shower. "You shouldn't tempt me like that. We might easily find ourselves back in bed." But he knew Cordy wasn't one to be summoned or coerced into anything. Everything had to appear as if it was on her own whim. And he loved that about her, too.

"Come on," Cordy grabbed his arm. "Let's shower together, or we'll be late picking up Ivanhoe at the airport, and we still need to buy another tire. It's nearly 5 a.m."

"Back on task so soon?" Braun pulled back the shower curtain. "After you." She stepped into the steaming water. He nuzzled her neck as his hands lathered a bar of soap. Braun watched her as he set the soap bar aside, then gently rubbed the suds over her neck, shoulders, and breasts.

Cordy gave a small moan of pleasure. "I thought you were going to wash my back."

"Front, back, what's the difference? I can manage to wash all of you."

"Two can play this game." Cordy grabbed the shampoo and poured it over his head. She vigorously massaged his scalp and moved the bubbles down his shoulders, back, chest, abs, and lower body. "Put your hands up," she instructed. "You're at my mercy."

He chuckled and backed against the tile wall. "I surrender, but remember, whatever you inflict on me, you get twofold."

Cordy put her index finger over her lips. "Shh." She moved to within a hair's breadth from his mouth. "Inflict? Never. This is a gift from your loving wife." Then she kissed him, teasing his lips open with her tongue. Hot water poured down her back as she leaned into him.

A strong magnetic force pulled them together, poles apart, one positive, and one negative—inseparable upon impact. Consumed with the delight of love's special treasures, they gave their all and then leisurely bathed each other.

After a light breakfast, they headed for the rental car and barely closed the doors before a hailstorm hit. "We can't be late," Cordy said. "This is Ivanhoe's first trip away from home."

Braun headed for the airport as the wind picked up. The hail grew to pea-sized, making it impossible for the windshield wipers to keep up with the slush. Unable to see clearly, Braun pulled onto the road's shoulder. "This will probably delay Ivanhoe's flight."

Cordy checked the flight schedule. "Cincinnati/Northern Kentucky is on a divert status. Who knows what time the plane will land?"

"Or where his plane maybe diverted to, but you promised Perry we'd give Ivanhoe protection."

Cordy shook her head. "No, I didn't promise any such thing, but President Harris agreed to Usher's terms, so I'll do my best to work with Perry and Ivanhoe. We'll see how things unfold."

"This boy is still in high school," Braun reminded her. "It must be scary to fly from Russia to the U.S., not knowing what or who will meet him when he lands. Put yourself in his shoes."

"Maybe you're right, but you heard Kildeer brag that this crisis is just the beginning," Cordy strained to see the road through the fogged windshield and adjusted the defrost button. "There's a mastermind out there who can wipe out any city he chooses. Ivanhoe may not be up to the task."

"Give the lad a chance," Braun said.

"I'll be watching him like a hawk." Cordy pocketed her cell phone.

The hail let up, so Braun pulled back into traffic. "At least we're lucky that Perry agreed to help us."

"Although he wrote the Virus X malware, it's child's play compared to the 5th Dimension," but Cordy agreed Perry had been helpful. "He sent a reversal of his code, and Quint says so far, it works perfectly, and he helped us track down Roland Kildeer."

Braun's phone pinged. "It's Usher. Can you take the call?"

Cordy hit speaker. "Hi, Usher. Braun's driving through fog as thick as pea soup. Where are you?"

"I'm still flying to Russia to track down Cracker." Usher sounded stressed. "There's unrest in Moscow. Have you heard anything more? I can't reach anyone to verify Cracker is in the country, and Vlad doesn't answer."

"One moment, I'll check BBC and CNN News." Cordy did a quick search. "You're landing in Russia at a terrible time. I found two disturbing YouTube videos. Someone murdered General Urk and hung his body in Red Square. People are rioting in the streets."

"Yes, I already know that," Usher said, "but are they still rioting? How bad is it?"

"The police have called in recruits, and many rioters have died," Cordy said. "Please be careful. I'm sending you a link. I may have a few more Russians to track down as soon as we get Kildeer's list, too."

"Great," Usher sounded anything but great. "I'll keep you posted. I may also need your help once I arrive."

Braun warned, "Are you traveling alone?"

"Not intentionally, and I can't reach Homeland Security," Usher said. "Can you notify Guy? I plan to meet up with Agent Saul Reed to help track down Cracker. I want to make sure his paperwork is for a lengthy stay if needed, and I hope Vlad is safe."

"Will do," Braun said. "Stay safe."

"You, too." Usher disconnected the call.

"Pull over," Cordy said. "I'll update Guy from Homeland if you contact your boss, Loran Sloan," Cordy speed-dialed the numbers as Braun pulled under an underpass to keep out of the pouring rain.

"If this weather keeps up, we will have to hunt down where Ivanhoe's plane was diverted to land," Braun mentioned and then called Sloan.

Cordy didn't need more on her to-do list, but Usher's life could be in the balance. *And I still need to track down Risingsickle.*

TEAM TESTING

Sept. 16 – 1:12 p.m. MSK, Moscow, Russia/
6:12 a.m. EDT, Cincinnati, Ohio

Though the weather was bitterly cold in Moscow, Anton ran his team of four through a series of live combat exercises. He already knew he could count on Lieutenant Boris, but Wolf and Eagle were unknowns. They entered the familiar forest outside of town, where frequent fights broke out. It was a perfect place for testing the men on concealment and approach tactics.

"Let's see how close you can come toward me before I spot you." Anton lifted his rifle. "I'll use machine gun bursts over your head when I see you, so keep your heads down. I wouldn't want to shoot you by mistake."

Wolf proved to have expert skills in hand-to-hand combat. On the first round, he crept up to Boris and sliced a finger over his neck in a flash. "If that had been a knife, you'd be a goner!" He always carried two blades on him: one in his boot and another concealed behind his back.

On the first two rounds, Anton spotted Eagle before he got anywhere within killing distance, but by the third round, Eagle had mastered slinking quietly without disturbing a blade of grass. Knives weren't his weapon of choice, but his expertise with firearms was phenomenal. Out of nowhere, Eagle fired a shot. Anton yanked Boris down to the ground as dirt flew up in his face.

"What's the idea?" Anton rolled to his feet madder than a bear shaken out of hibernation. He ranted and raved until Eagle pointed to the ground next to him. The body of a deadly black mamba snake lay coiled near his foot—the head shot clean off the body.

"I guess I should have let it take a nip at you, but there'd be one less person hunting down Denys," Eagle said. "Enough games. We're fit to go."

TACKLING TROJAN MALWARE

Sept. 16 – 1:40 p.m. BST, en flight Moscow to Cincinnati over London/6:40 a.m. EDT, Cincinnati, Ohio

Svetlana spent most of the flight from Moscow to Cincinnati, Ohio, trying to figure out a plan to repair the devastating damage to New York's electrical grid. Reviewing Perry's computer code took hours. She loved simplifying complex problems and coming up with solutions, and she considered computer hacking a game of "cat and mouse."

Perry had assured her his code was reversible if she selected the correct string. She recalled entering a time limit on one aspect of the code, but Perry said he'd "fixed" that alteration. Even after reviewing Perry's virus code several times, she only determined three solutions, but she was sure Perry would have an answer. None of her code modifications would repair the damage already created by the 5th Dimension. She had never heard of that malware and wondered where Kildeer had accessed the program.

Toward morning, her laptop popped up a message, "Runhard973," on her screen. *Finally, it's Perry!*

Perry's message read, "Vlad reached his American contact, Usher Hastings. He's talking to Acting President Harris and working on a deal to grant us safety in the United States. I agreed to help them repair my code and get their electric grid and emergency systems back up and running, but I'll need your help."

Svetlana connected her laptop to the plane's Wi-Fi and, after a few attempts, could contact Perry in person. "I hope this connection is safe."

"One moment." Perry must have entered some code, as there was a ping. "Okay, go ahead."

Svetlana was leery of the FBI. "Are you sure you can trust Vlad's contact?"

"I hope so," Perry said. "An Agent Cordelia-Hastings will meet you at the airport. She prefers the name Cordy and is a computer guru working with the FBI or some top-ranking agency. She also has direct contact with the president. Cordy's anxious to meet you."

"I'm not sure, Perry," Svetlana hesitated. "What if I'm arrested?"

"Please, work with her and give her any information you have about our software virus. It will ensure our safety. The Russian government will think twice before extricating us."

"What if Cordy refuses to let me meet with Roland Kildeer?" she asked. "Papa gave me strict orders to stop his plan to extend the virus."

"I don't trust Kildeer, especially after that incident in South Africa, where they killed my roommate, but Cordy knows all about Kildeer. She'll be meeting him in Ohio, probably before your plane lands, so you won't have to meet up with him. So please, stay away from Kildeer. He's dangerous. Let Cordy deal with the man."

Svetlana sighed. "Okay, if I must."

"Cordy is upset about the virus," Perry said. "It's to be expected, but be as helpful as possible. Our lives depend on it."

Svetlana would have to decide for herself.

"By the way, thanks for launching the drones. Vlad said your Papa tracked them to him, and their team was glad to get access to an aerial view. I'll head to Ohio later today, but not as Perry. I'm flying with a passport from Great Britain under the name Rof Runyard. I already informed Cordy about my darknet account. See you this Wednesday. I have a few ideas, and we can devise a solution together. Have a safe trip, and I look forward to seeing you soon. Spasibo."

Svetlana's heart raced at the thought of meeting these strangers. Everything she had heard about the agency had been negative, and she feared the FBI would implicate her in this computer scandal. She searched the Internet, darknet, and several programs for information on Agent Cordelia-Hastings. Svetlana couldn't find anything. Cordy must be a security master, but she could be a double agent, a darknet hacker, or even an assassin. Why would Perry agree to meet her? At least he was flying under an assumed name.

She wanted to talk it over with someone she trusted, but it was too soon to contact her father. He would be busy hunting down General Urk's killer, and he didn't expect a call until after the plane landed, still several hours from now. Svetlana tried Vlad's account, but he didn't answer. He is probably watching those drones. Svetlana left a message, "How's Papa? Any word on the riots?"

Then, an idea flashed through her mind. Instead of meeting Cordy as Ivanhoe, she would change into Svetlana. The FBI agents wouldn't expect a female; she could observe from afar to see if a set-up existed. If she trusted this agent, she might reappear as Ivanhoe. If not, she'd just walk out the airport's front door and wait for Perry.

As Svetlana thought more about her idea, she found it more appealing. However, she realized she hadn't packed any female clothes. This meant that she would have to be resourceful once the plane landed. Back home, Svetlana usually wore dresses or a skirt and blouse and rarely wore slacks. However, she liked colorful clothing.

Svetlana stifled a yawn as she headed to the small toilet on board. On her way back to her seat, she noticed that most passengers were sleeping, so she quietly studied what they were wearing. To her surprise, many women were wearing slacks or jeans. This gave her an idea. Maybe she could still wear her pants and a T-shirt, but she would remove her bindings. She could fluff her hair and let it flow onto her shoulders instead of hiding it under Ivanhoe's cap. That would make a big difference. Perhaps she could pick up a suit jacket or sweater at the airport.

Glancing down at her feet, she thought about getting new shoes instead of these heavy winter boots. Even her stockings seemed too thick and bulky compared to some passengers who wore short anklets barely showing above their sneakers. When she returned to her seat, she sipped bottled water.

Enough worry about what might happen when I land. It's time to figure out a solution to this malware problem. Svetlana returned to reviewing the code and found a way to trap the worm. Perhaps she could retrace the initial code she entered to limit the Trojan activity before Perry removed it in his final review or quarantined the code. Still, if the 5th Dimension fried the electronic equipment, she doubted anything could repair that. Stifling her third yawn, she decided to sleep on it. Maybe something would jog her mind, like a 5 a.m. epiphany.

LIFE OR DEATH

*Sept. 16 – 1:50 p.m. MSK, Moscow, Russia/
6:50 a.m. EDT, Cincinnati, Ohio*

Rozalina's heart raced as the medical helicopter flew over Moscow through the clouds, hitting pockets of cold air. Her cell phone nearly bounced from her hand as she spoke to the ambulance driver. "Igor, meet me at Sokolniki Park ASAP. Our patient didn't make it, and we must deliver the body to the morgue." Her fingertips tingled once again, even though she tried to calm her breathing. Lightheaded, she barely heard the ambulance driver's voice through her cell phone.

"I'm en route to an emergency," Igor reported. "You'll need to find an alternative ride. Maybe a hearse would be more appropriate."

Rozalina glanced at her watch. Only seventeen minutes left to give her husband the antidote. "No! I must have your ambulance. I left my water bottle in the glove compartment. Please. It is a matter of life or death."

Manny stared at her. "Rozalina, all this over a water bottle?"

"Sorry, I have to sign off," Igor disconnected without another word.

"The patient is already dead." Manny placed a gentle hand on Rozalina's shoulder. "Wouldn't a hearse make more sense?"

Rozalina let the question hang in the air for a moment, then without warning, she thumped Cracker's chest once more, hoping there would be another heartbeat. Maybe she could keep him alive long enough for the antidote, but not if the ambulance didn't arrive on time, and it wouldn't make sense to Manny to start CPR after waiting this long. He'd think she had lost all of her medical abilities. She began chest compressions anyway.

"Rozalina, what are you doing?" Manny moved to stop her. "If you wanted to do CPR, we should have started it immediately. It's too late now."

Rozalina pushed his hand away and continued her resuscitation efforts. The oxygen was still in place.

"Talk to me," Manny demanded. "You're pale as a sheet."

Can I trust Manny? I'll endanger his life if anyone finds out the truth. No, I can't run the risk. This was her husband's life. He was free at last, and she'd just injected him with a potent drug to drop his breathing and heart rate to appear that he'd died. She knew he had a faint pulse but not enough to register on the screen. That was the beauty of the drug, but it would only support life for sixty minutes after the dose was delivered, and that was forty-five minutes ago.

"Rozalina! Stop!" Manny reached across Cracker's body to still her actions. "He'll be nothing but a vegetable."

"I know! It's just not fair." Her hands flew to her mouth to cover the sobs. "Oh, Manny. I lost him. I've lost him forever!" Her head ached from the pressure changes as the chopper fought to stay in the air. She wrapped her hands on both sides of her temples and squeezed, trying to get some relief and to help her think.

Manny laid a hand on her shoulder. "Out with it. What's bothering you?"

"I must get to that ambulance!" Her voice choked.

"Okay, Okay. I'll find out where the emergency is located, and we'll see if we can touch down near the area." Manny radioed the ambulance driver once again. "Igor, this is Dr. Manaheim. Where are you headed? We're going to land the helicopter nearby. Then I'll take your emergency victim to the hospital by chopper while you take Rozalina and her patient to the morgue."

Igor gave Manny the directions, and Rolo changed course. "ETA, ten minutes," Rolo said.

Rozalina gave a silent prayer of thanks and then checked her watch. It would only give her three minutes to spare. *Please, let it be long enough.*

The next ten minutes was the longest time of her life. "As soon as we land, I'm heading for the ambulance." She tapped Rolo's shoulder to get his attention. "Can you help Manny get the patient into the ambulance?"

"Da. I'll help move him," Rolo shouted over the chopper noise.

"Good," Rozalina said.

Rolo nodded but didn't say anything else. The noise was too much.

Rozalina spoke to Manny over the headset. "We'll leave as soon as you get him loaded. I want to be as far away from the hospital as possible in case the FBI comes searching."

Manny frowned. "I get that we are to keep this hushed up, but the patient is dead. Why are you worried about the FBI finding the body?"

"The key word in this rescue attempt is Uranium One." Rozalina stared directly into Manny's eyes. She knew he wouldn't take that topic any further. It would tie her patient's activities clear to top Russian officials, and no one in their right mind would question that relationship. It stretched the truth, but Cracker had gone to the U.S. to follow the man called the Journalist involved in the 2010 Uranium One deal. Cracker found proof that the Journalist had ties to Russian nuclear industry officials, and they were engaged in nefarious dealings, which included extortion, bribery, and kickbacks.

"That high up?" Manny rubbed his chin. "I understand. We'll do everything we can to get the death certificate in the right hands. Are you having the remains cremated?"

"Yes, of course, and as soon as possible." Rozalina hoped she could find a way to make it happen and still save her husband.

Rolo landed not far from the ambulance.

Rozalina checked her watch. There were two minutes to spare as she climbed from the chopper. "Hurry." She ran to the ambulance, threw open the door, and grabbed her water bottle from the glove compartment. Most of the ice had melted, but the antidote was intact. She darted to the ambulance's rear as Manny and Rolo lifted Cracker into the van. "Thanks for all of your help. I know Igor is with another patient, but when you see him, please tell him that I'd like to leave."

Manny nodded. "We agreed to load his patient into the chopper, so it'll be a few minutes before he's available."

"Da, I understand." Rozalina didn't look up as they slammed the ambulance's back door closed. She drew the antidote into a syringe and injected it into the IV port. Then, she started chest compressions to circulate the drug. After three minutes, there was still no heartbeat on the monitor. "Come on! Cracker, can you hear me?" Continuing to pound on his chest created no response. She leaned down to give mouth-to-mouth and noted his lips were warm. It made her work harder at the CPR routine.

Four minutes went by to no avail. "No!" She ripped open a syringe of epinephrine and injected it directly into his heart. A blip leapt across the screen as the helicopter outside roared to life, covering the beeping sound on the monitor.

Igor threw open the back ambulance door. "We're ready to leave."

"I'll ride in the back," Rozalina said.

Igor nodded, closed the back doors, went up front, and started the engine.

Rozalina slammed her fist against Cracker's chest as soon as the door closed and continued CPR as the ambulance swayed and bounced along the unpaved road. Cracker's heart rate was up to thirty beats per minute two minutes later.

Still too slow to sustain life for long, "He needs atropine," Rozalina whispered as she dug through her medical supplies, found the drug, and pushed it into the IV port.

Sept. 16 – 2:08 p.m. MSK, Moscow, Russia/
7:08 a.m. EDT, Cincinnati, Ohio

Cracker opened his eyes. "Stop banging on my chest."

Rozalina said, "Shh. No one must know that you're alive."

"Where are we?" Cracker asked.

"On our way to the morgue," Rozalina said. "You have to play dead."

Cracker's eyes widened. "Rozalina? Is that you?" He gazed into her eyes. "You're amazing. I can't believe you're a doctor now." He glanced around the ambulance, then reached up and kissed her lips. "I've missed you terribly."

Startled by the feel of his soft lips on hers, Rozalina froze as something inside her awakened. To her surprise, she found herself responding. It had indeed been a long time since she had been held, much less kissed, by a man—*my husband*. She had to keep these feelings at bay. "You must play dead!"

"Da. I'm so proud of you!" Cracker said. "I never would have come up with such a dangerous ruse."

Her heart raced. Since last seeing Cracker, he had lost close to twenty pounds. Silver hair streaked his temples, and a small scar ran from his chin to his neck. How did that happen? "There will be time for us later," she whispered. "We still have some convincing to do before we can leave the country."

"Leave the country?" Cracker gasped. "I just got back."

"Things are not safe here," Rozalina said. "I'm worried about General Urk and Captain Anton, and we have to think about our children."

Cracker's jaw dropped. "What do you mean, our children? We don't have any!" He glared at her. "That child had better be nine years old, Rozalina, since I haven't been here. Where did you get children?"

"I was pregnant when you went away," Rozalina said. "You have nine-and-a-half-year-old twins. A boy and a girl, and they can't wait to meet you. I tried writing, but my letters were all returned unopened."

Fifty minutes later, sirens sounded in the background, and traffic picked up until they reached the last two blocks of their journey.

Rozalina quickly ripped off the monitor leads so there was a straight line on the scope. She removed the IV and oxygen.

The vehicle pulled to a stop. The driver's ambulance door banged shut.

"Quick, play dead." Rozalina pushed him back onto the cot.

"We have children?" he gulped another breath.

"Not now!" she whispered. "I have to think of a way to get you out of here—alive!"

Cracker's eyes closed obediently. A crease crept along his forehead as if his mind was dazed, trying to comprehend her words. "I'm a daddy?"

When Igor opened the ambulance's back doors, Rozalina noticed they had driven down a narrow road to a two-story, mud-splattered, white-washed building. A black van had just pulled away, probably delivering another body before their arrival.

"It's a busy night at the mortuary." Igor grabbed the foot of the gurney. "Come on, let's move this body! I have another call waiting. There are riots, and we can't keep up!" He sighed. "It's going to be a long night!"

"Da," Rozalina said. "You can drop us off and then leave. Thanks for everything." She slipped out the back and caught the head end of the gurney as Igor pulled it out of the vehicle.

Igor stopped by the rear of the morgue and pressed the buzzer, waiting for someone to let them inside.

An attendant peeked through a dingy square glass in the mortuary back door, "One moment." The doors slowly swung open with a loud whine. The phone was ringing from somewhere in the building. The attendant's grungy, blood-splattered lab coat appeared two sizes too large. He snapped off his used latex gloves. "Sorry, it's after 3 p.m., and the receptionist already left for the day. We're swamped, and the medical examiner is in the middle of an autopsy. Just leave the body, fill out the necessary information in the logbook, and we'll call you later if there are any additional questions." He rushed off before Rozalina could ask anything of him.

The phone finally stopped for a moment, then rang again. "Do you come here often?" she asked Igor.

"I detest this place, so if possible, I avoid it," Igor replied. "You'll find the logbook on the front desk. The tech is probably busy with phone calls, so you'll have to fend for yourself."

Gravel crunched outside as a hearse pulled up alongside Igor's ambulance. Whoever was at the mortuary door was impatient as a high-pitched buzzer echoed throughout the building.

"Can someone get the door?" sounded over an intercom. "I'm not letting my attendant leave again." The buzzer rang once more, "Anyone out there? Answer that blasted door."

Igor slammed his wrist against the automatic opener and let the hearse driver inside. The driver pushed an occupied trolley ahead of him. Igor's cell phone chirped. "Two more emergencies are waiting for me. I need my gurney, so let's unload our corpse onto a morgue cart." Igor searched for another cart while Rozalina called her Uncle Albert to pick her up at the plaza four blocks from the mortuary.

Igor rolled in a stretcher with a sheet-covered cadaver. "I couldn't find a vacant one, so we'll shove this body off onto another occupied one and load our corpse."

Rozalina grunted as she moved the sheeted mass on top of another body.

Igor grabbed Cracker's shoulders. "Take his legs, and we'll just slide him over from my gurney to the stretcher."

In her haste, she fumbled Cracker's leg, which nearly hit the metal portion of the gurney before she caught it.

The hearse driver grabbed the logbook before Rozalina could get to it, filled out his information, and handed it to her as he left the building.

Igor followed the hearse driver to the door, then turned and called over his shoulder, "I'll come back for you if you need me, but it'll be a hectic night, and I have no idea when I'll be free to get you."

"My uncle has a car. I'll catch a ride from here," Rozalina said. "Take care on the streets tonight."

Igor nodded, wheeled the gurney back to the ambulance, and drove away.

Rozalina kept a watchful eye out for the attendant as she pushed Cracker's cart into the cooler. The phone kept ringing intermittently, so someone must be answering, but no one was in sight. The walls were lined with carts of nude bodies, most covered with stained sheets. Some had two to a cart. "Now's our chance," she said to Cracker. "Get up and help me move one of these male bodies on it instead."

Cracker stumbled as he got off the gurney. "My head's spinning. What did you give me?"

"Sorry," Rozalina said. "Take a few deep breaths and try to remain upright." She dug through her medical bag and found her bottled water. "Take a few sips. You need to flush the drug from your system."

Cracker drank up and moved in slow motion. "What are you going to do with the body?"

"It must be cremated," Rozalina said.

"No," Cracker said. "The Russian Orthodox religion forbids it. The body is God's creation and can't be burned."

"I know," Rozalina said, "but none of these bodies are from Russian Orthodox families, or they would already be crowded in a living room on display for forty days before the burial. We have to choose a body wisely and insist on immediate cremation."

"How do you plan to pay for the ashes?" Cracker asked. "It costs a fortune."

"Wait, I found a body that is scheduled for cremation today." Rozalina pointed to the list. "The log entry says, paid in full."

"I still don't feel right about this," Cracker said. "What if the body doesn't reach everlasting life?"

"We will write a prayer for him and give him a private service at home," Rozalina promised. "Hurry, I need help moving this body." She took the weight of the massive man, leaving Cracker to keep the legs from falling off the table.

Cracker heaved a deep breath as if he'd just run a marathon. "Let's get out of here." He stood shivering at the end of the cart.

"You need warmer clothes." Rozalina handed him a wool vest and a winter coat sitting on the edge of a cart. She shuffled him to the restroom. "Change into these while I place a tag for C. W. Gresinsky on the body's toe. I also need to modify the logbook to match. I'll put the instructions for immediate cremation on his forehead. That's what we used to do at the University, and I see two more bodies in the corner that also have that notation, but they are female."

Cracker sniffed the clothes. "They're musty."

"But warm," Rozalina said. "Put them on."

Cracker grumbled but closed the bathroom door.

After filling out the paperwork, Rozalina walked from the front desk and caught sight of the attendant.

The attendant checked on the "new" body. "Is this the guy you just brought in?"

Rozalina wedged her foot against the bathroom door as Cracker nudged it and then raised her voice as she spoke to the attendant. "That body is scheduled to be cremated. His brother paid in full."

The attendant checked the log. "Wasn't he already here?" the attendant asked. "The entry is halfway up the page from when you came in."

Rozalina had to think fast to come up with a logical answer. "He isn't the body we brought in." She pointed to the cart where the mortician had put their latest arrival. "He is." She pointed to the corpse. "Check the logbook. See the time?"

"Oh, and no autopsy, right?" the attendant asked.

Rozalina shook her head. "No autopsy."

"Good because my day is long enough." With that, he grabbed the body with Gresinsky's toe tag. "I'll drop him off at the crematorium on my way back to the lab. The medical examiner wants to start the next autopsy."

Rozalina shuddered at the thought. She'd seen enough postmortem exams to fill a lifetime.

She moved away from the door, and Cracker stepped from the bathroom. "I'd feel safer if I was out of this place."

"Me, too," Rozalina said. "My uncle will meet us at the plaza. Traffic is awful, so he might be late. You go first."

"Not without you," he warned.

"You remember my uncle, right?" she asked. "He'll meet you at 4:30. Watch your back and go straight to the plaza. His backup team surrounds him, but you will never see them."

Cracker nodded. "Why can't we both leave?"

"I'll stay for a few minutes so we're not seen together."

Cracker's slight hesitation at the back door told her a lot. He was worried. His eyes searched her face. Leaning forward, he stopped short of kissing her and squeezed her hand.

Rozalina's heart broke as she pushed him away. "Go!"

Reluctantly, he turned. "Be careful, honey. I've missed you so much."

A fading "I love you," came from beyond the closing door.

Rozalina stepped away, her mind reeling at all the laws she had broken over the past two hours. She paused and made a mental checklist. *Cracker's on his way, paperwork completed, body on the gurney with Gresinsky's toe tag in place and heading for the crematorium, no evidence left behind, what else?* She placed a jittery hand on the door to exit.

"Wait, you can't leave!" The attendant dashed straight for her. Winded from the sudden burst of energy to block her departure, he blurted, "The medical examiner must speak to you. It's urgent!"

Rozalina's breath hitched in the back of her throat, and she froze in place. Did the FBI contact the mortuary? Are they on their way? I hope Cracker got away. I should have run when I had the chance.

HEELS ON FIRE

Sophia parked on the city's outskirts and walked along the side streets. Her feet ached as she reached Maude's apartment to pick up more information. Rolling thunder echoed in the distance, adding to the dreary day. Fat raindrops landed on Sophia's head, shoulders, and arms as she dashed from the car to Maude's front door, and she seemed to step in every puddle along the way.

"Hello, Sophia. You caught me doing my morning exercises." Maude, dressed in light blue sweats, was in an upbeat mood. "Please come inside and have a cup of tea."

"I wish I could." Sophia, a dedicated lawyer, stood on one foot, trying to ease the pain. "I'd love to get off my feet for a minute, but I'm meeting Chief Jackson at that little coffee shop across the street from your old office. As you suggested yesterday, I stopped by to pick up a copy of your computer's hard drive, which could potentially hold crucial evidence for Floyd's defense."

"Sit! It will only take a minute." Maude motioned Sophia inside and stared at her shoes. "I can see why you look so miserable. My feet would be screaming at me if I wore such high heels. Don't you have any loafers, honey?"

Sophia laughed. "I do. They're in the trunk."

"If I were you, I'd change into them as soon as I got back to the car." Maude puttered in the kitchen and pulled out a chair. "Take a seat! I heated water already." She set down a cup of hot water and opened a wooden box. Inside was a vast selection of teas. "Help yourself while I get that drive. It's in my office."

No one said "No" to this woman, so Sophia gladly sat down, picked out a chamomile tea bag, and brewed a cup.

"I don't know if there's anything useful on this old drive, but I kept it for a reason," Maude called from her office. Her voice grew louder as she walked into the kitchen. "Floyd kept the financial data on his computer, but I have copies of the quarterly reports for the past five years to share. Maybe they will help, and I found a hidden file. Alexa must have used my terminal when she researched some magnesium company."

Sophia spilled tea on her blouse. "Oh, my, I'm sorry." She set down the half-drunk drink and wiped her blouse with a paper towel that Maude handed her. "Thanks for the tea and all your help, but I really must go. I'll keep in touch."

"Will I be called as a witness?" Maude asked.

Sophia got up from the table. "For the hearing, all I'll need is an affidavit from you stating the truth of what you found. Chief Jackson can pick that up from you after you've prepared it. But, yes, I will call you to the stand if we go to retrial. Does that upset you? Remember, a retrial could potentially change everything, Maude. It could be our last chance to prove Floyd's innocence."

"No, I'd love to help Floyd any way I can." Maude placed the hard drive and a few more folders into a paper bag and walked Sophia to the door. "Change your shoes now, you hear?" They shared a sense of trust, camaraderie, and determination to free Floyd.

"I will," Sophia turned and was wrapped in a bear hug.

"I know we can free Floyd. He doesn't deserve to be locked up." Maude opened the door. "If you need anything else, call me."

In a hurry, Sophia waved and climbed into the car. She was about to pull away from the curb when Maude called out from her opened doorway, "You forgot to change your shoes!"

Sophia climbed out of the car, opened the trunk, and held up her loafers so Maude could see them. "Thanks for the reminder."

Maude nodded and closed the front door as Sophia kicked off her heels.

The loafers did make her feel better. New York's traffic bottlenecked downtown, and it was another five miles before she met Chief Jackson at the same coffee shop where she had met Maude the day before.

Jackson sat at a table and waved at her as she entered. He had already ordered lattes. Sophia set down her package and joined him. "What's in the bag?"

Sophia pulled out three file folders: orange, blue, and red. "Maude sat right there and handed me these files yesterday. She made copies for you and duplicated the hard drive from her old computer that she used at AK's corporation."

"I've been thinking, was AK really dead when she found him in the parking garage?" Sophia asked. "Perhaps his condition deteriorated at Alexa's hands."

"Did you get the NBC tape?" Jackson asked. "It should be provided under a Freedom of Information Act request."

Sophia nodded. "It was delivered late last night while we were eating. My paralegal delivered it to Professor Seamore Hyde at MIT, as Cordy suggested. He says he can help us determine if there are any alterations to the tape."

"Many questions are riding on that video." Jackson perused the rest of Maude's files. "I wonder why someone didn't bring this before the judge."

Sophia nodded. "Maude said that Floyd's lawyer spoke with her over the phone, but he never followed up."

Jackson frowned and rubbed his jaw. "I need to talk to Ashton about that."

Sophia stirred her latte. "Maude didn't find out about Alexa opening the account until two weeks later when she picked up the mail at the post office. No one had bothered to look after the little details once the office closed. When she found this letter, she made a copy, forwarded it to Alexa, and called the lawyer."

"Didn't she think to question the amount?" he asked.

Sophia shrugged. "She was busy cleaning out the office and moving on to another position. I don't think she thought much about it until my phone call."

"How will she track down the other $15 million after all these years?" Jackson asked.

"Maude believes Alexa used her computer to research data, perhaps dealing with the investment funds."

"I'd like to have a look," Jackson said.

"I have a copy of the hard drive, so both of us can research the data." Sophia glanced at her watch. "I better go. Do you want the first crack at the hard drive?"

Chief Jackson nodded. "And I want to forward a copy to Cordy. She has tricks that I've never dreamed of. If there's a hidden file, she'll find it."

"Great." Sophia stood and cleared the table. "I want to talk to Alexa, and I hope she's at home since the business burned down. I have tons of questions to ask. Can you join me?"

"I'm free to go now if that works."

"Let's take your car," Sophia said, "it's closer, and even though I changed to loafers, my feet are killing me."

ODOR OF TERROR

Sept. 16 – 2:12 p.m. EET, Kyiv, Ukraine/
7:12 a.m. EDT, Cincinnati, Ohio

The morning had been tough for General Urk's youngest guard, Gabe, and his captain, Augi Orion. They were confined in a locked cell carved out of rock outside Kyiv, Ukraine. Gabe sat at the end of the cot, with his wrists and ankles chained to the wall. He jolted as booted footsteps echoed through the cave's tunnel.

Anger quickened Augi's pulse, spiking a rush of blood through his veins. "Gabe, the thugs are back. Act dazed, or you'll end up dead like General Urk."

Gabe's eyes widened with panic. His face crumpled into agony, lips trembled, and cheeks paled, making his bruised and swollen eyes more noticeable.

The formidable enemy, Denys Evanko, halted outside and stooped to peer into the cell through the bars. He lifted his wrist as if covering his nose to block the dank odor mixed with the coppery aroma of fresh blood that permeated the air. "Unlock this door."

His guard behind him pulled a key from his pocket and held it up for Denys to take. "It's all yours. I can't breathe down here."

Denys stared down his nose at the man.

Augi lunged toward the prison door from inside the cell. "How dare you talk to your boss like that?" Augi Orion had dealt with thugs before. They needed to be in control of every situation. When the guard didn't move, Augi's arms swung from side to side as he moved closer to the door. Great slabs of solid muscle bulged from

Augi's neck and rippled across his chest. His biceps, like knotted ropes, covered in thick, black hair, went all the way down to the back of his hands. "Hand me the key. I'll open it for you, Boss."

Augi detested Denys, but the scumbag had kidnapped Augi's daughter. He would do anything to save Belle, even torture his comrade, Gabe. Augi reached between the cell door bars and snatched the key from the guard's hand. Unaware of his strength, he nearly snapped the key off in the lock. The door swung open.

"Back up!" Denys shouted at Augi, who retreated.

"What have you learned from the boy?" Denys moved to the edge of the doorway but didn't go inside. The cell was barely large enough for his prisoner to reach one end of his cot to a chamber pot in the corner. Manacles and chains were around Gabe's bruised ankles. Most of the blood had been General Urk's, but Denys wasn't aware of that fact.

A slight tilt to the cement floor sloped to an open drain, allowing for easier cleaning after his guests vacated the cell. If lucky, their bones were placed in a pine box, or they joined the many others in a pit outside. Dark stains etched the walls. A single dim light hung at an angle overhead.

"He's just a kid. He doesn't know nothin'," Augi pointed to Gabe. "Look at him."

Denys peered around Augi's shoulder to stare at the boy, who cowered at the foot of the cot. "You do know, don't you?"

"No-know what?" Gabe stammered.

"General Urk hid him so I couldn't get my hands on his son, right?" Denys seethed. "Urk killed my boy, and I plan to do the same to his."

Augi spoke up. "The general gave his own life to save his boy."

"Stupid on his part," Denys sneered. "Two lives aren't enough to repay me. His boy dies!"

A tear trickled down Gabe's cheek. "I've told Augi everything. I don't know anything about the general's son. Please, you must believe me."

Seeing Denys' anger brimming over, he had to diffuse the situation. Augi turned toward Gabe. "I've been easy on you, but if you know anything, you'd better tell me, or you'll end up like the general."

Gabe whimpered. "I know nothing!"

Augi turned to Denys, allowing him to be the decision-maker. "So, what should we do?"

Denys exploded obscenities, clenched the boy's cheeks, and stared into his eyes.

Gabe trembled in his hands.

Augi saw a faint smile cross Denys' face. *He loves the power he exudes over others.*

* * *

Denys let go of Gabe's face, smiling at the whimpering boy, and snatched Gabe's trembling hand, holding it out for Augi to take. "I don't see any broken bones. Get him out of these chains and start with his fingers as you did with General Urk. He's a weakling. Unlike his general, if he knows anything, he'll squeal. Let me know what you find out. The sooner we take care of this, the sooner you'll see your daughter."

The guard outside had already retreated.

A cruel grin curled his lips as Denys walked from the cell, slammed the door behind him, and darted for fresh air.

"Denys has your daughter?" Gabe gasped. "Is that why you killed the general?"

"No. I only roughed him up a bit. Bruno took over, and Denys made the final blows."

Gabe cringed. "What are you going to do to me?"

"Sorry, lad, but you heard the man." Augi's shout was loud enough for Denys to hear.

Screams echoed from the cave. Satisfied, Denys lit a cigar and strolled to his office. *It won't be long now. I'll get my revenge.*

EMERGENCY LANDING

Sept. 16 – 8:16 a.m. ADT, over Atlantic/
7:16 a.m. EDT, Cincinnati, Ohio

It was September 16th, and the A-330's flight 8760 from Moscow was now flying over the Atlantic. Thunderclouds had been threatening to turn into a massive storm most of the way. Pilot Rand called the purser. "Check that all passengers are wearing their seatbelts."

Inside the cockpit, Rand had gained 1,000 feet of altitude, to climb above the storm they had been fighting nearly the whole way, only to be beaten back and losing ground as heavy rains and hail drummed against the hull. "There are days I make the most boring trips and then a night of utter terror. I'm afraid we're heading into the latter."

His co-pilot remained silent but kept turning his head to check on the dials before him and watching the pilot's every move. It was Craig's third trip across the ocean.

Pilot Rand remained alert. No sane man would have such an inexperienced co-pilot take over controls during such a storm.

Craig crossed his fingers. "We might get a lucky break over the Atlantic."

"Maybe for a few hours," the pilot noted, "but the Weather Bureau issued a severe weather warning in Cincinnati, Ohio. The report says it's been raining most of the night and expects half-inch hail, making for extreme conditions and surface winds with gusts up to sixty mph."

*Sept. 16 – 8:55 a.m. ADT, over Atlantic/
7:55 a.m. EDT, Cincinnati, Ohio*

The flight attendant flipped on the overhead lights in the economy class cabin and began serving breakfast. They were three and a half hours outside of Cincinnati.

Svetlana held up her cup for hot tea when the plane hit an air pocket. The tea splashed, and she scooted sideways before it landed in her lap, hitting the seat handle instead. She braced against the seat in front of her as the plane shook and bounced for several long seconds. Glancing around the plane, other passengers clutched their armrests, hung on to their cups, and tried to look braver than she felt, but fear shone in their eyes.

A ping lit up the signs overhead, followed by, "This is Pilot Rand. We're entering a strong turbulence zone. Please remain seated with your seatbelts fastened until I turn off the overhead sign. Cabin crew, halt breakfast service, lock down the carts, and take your seats. There may be a delay in landing. Cincinnati is on divert and has closed its runways to all arrivals and departures. We will keep you posted."

Svetlana lost all interest in her breakfast. *Would a storm close down a whole airport?* This was her first trip by air, and she had yet to learn airline protocol. *What will happen if Kildeer already set off the virus in Ohio?* Acid formed in the back of her throat and blazed a trail to the pit of her stomach. Her gut clenched. *Maybe I'm already too late. If he launched Perry's virus, will this plane be able to land? Will the plane crash?* She stared out of the window but couldn't see anything but dark clouds around the plane.

Sept. 16 – 11:50 a.m. EDT, Cincinnati, Ohio

Pilot Rand had continued to fight the weather, and they were hours behind schedule. When he peered out the cockpit window, he saw lightning bolts crackling across the sky. "Did you get anything on the radio, Craig?"

"Nothing but static," his co-pilot said.

"We're climbing 6,000 feet to see if we can reach clearer skies," Rand announced over the plane's intercom and turned back to his co-pilot. "This doesn't look good. We're fully loaded and have been flying 29,000 feet most of the way. Still no radio response?"

"Nothing but static," Craig repeated into the radio, "This is TK 8652. Request..."

"We're now at 35,000—the plane's bucking and tossing us around like a boat in a whirlpool." Rand gripped the controls until his knuckles turned white.

"Since I can't raise air control, what should I do?" Craig sounded panicked.

"Stay focused." Rand kept his eyes on the controls. "Change frequency and try again."

"Cincinnati ATC. TK 8652. Altitude 30,000. Request change frequency 121.5 International Air Distress." After ten seconds, "Still only static."

"Keep trying," Rand ordered as hail pelted the windshield.

"Shouldn't we climb higher and get out of the hail?" Craig asked.

"We've climbed 6,000 feet. The storm is no better, and it may get worse," Rand warned. "According to my calculations, we can't rise above this storm—it's too dangerous. I'm heading back down."

The plane did a nosedive. The co-pilot let out a gasp. "Lift! Hurry!"

"Can't," Rand's voice came out strained. "We're icing up." He hit the engine anti-ice control. "Get ATC on that radio! Now! We're dropping altitude to 26,000. I don't know what air traffic is in the area."

A strange blue light glowed from the dashboard and traveled between Rand's hands and the controls. At first, he was afraid there'd be a shock or static electricity when he touched the altitude lever, but there was none. He checked the fuel-balancing and fuel gauge. "We've burned through twice as much fuel in the last hour than scheduled."

Craig's eyes widened. "Do we have enough to land?"

"Yes, if we don't make circles while waiting on Cincinnati's tower to grant permission to land." Rand wiped the sweat from his brow with his sleeve. His eyes were glued to the controls.

A voice cut in but disappeared as rapidly. Craig repeated. "Cincinnati ATC. TK 8652. We have severe weather. Request immediate landing."

The engine continued to ice over, pulling the nose down. Rand fought the controls to even out the plane, worried it would crash. "Altitude 23,000." His knuckles were white as his fists bunched on the lever. "Come on, up, level out."

Cincinnati Tower replied, "TK 8652. Approach denied. No flights are landing or departing Cincinnati CVG."

The co-pilot shouted, "We must land. Fuel low, instruments questionable. Engine icing over. Dropping altitude 19,000. Advise information, Descent."

The Cincinnati ATC agent blew out a breath. "Okay, TK 8652. Give us a moment. We'll clear a runway. I'll get..."

A few seconds later, Cincinnati ATC returned, "Reduce speed 250. Maintain 6,000."

Craig confirmed the tower's orders.

The tower agent said, "TK 8652 you are cleared to land, runway 4, left transition, next to land. Maintain 6,000. Proceed..."

While Co-pilot Craig continued communicating with the Tower, Rand wrestled the controls. The instrument panel started blinking. The anti-ice mechanism wasn't staying ahead of the storm, even after the plane descended in altitude. He yanked the nose up again and again to maintain balance.

"Pilot Rand, passengers are becoming ill," a flight attendant warned.

"Deal with it," Rand snapped. "I have too much going on here."

"Yes, sir," the attendant announced, "Aisle clean-up needed at C-23—"

Rand didn't hear the rest as he fought to keep the nose from diving too fast, and the altimeter dial fluctuated, leaving him unsure of the plane's air pressure level.

Cincinnati Tower replied, "TK 8652, taxi to runway 4 via Alpha, hold...Approach now." After a brief pause, they returned with, "We thought you were looking good for a transition and descent. Something Wrong?"

The co-pilot gasped, "We're unable—having problems here."

"Can you do an RNAV arrival?" came from the tower.

Craig stared at Pilot Rand, "What's going on?"

The Cincinnati tower agent said, "You've already crossed our emergency landing zone. Can you still program your computer to..."

Rand grabbed the radio. "Negative. Can't steady nose. Engine icing over. Manual only. Going to 5,000 trying to maintain. Reducing speed 190."

Cincinnati ATC: "Affirmative. Turn right."

Rand grabbed the controls and turned, but the plane wobbled, refusing his commands. The aircraft was now at 4,000 and continuing to dive.

"I said, turn right," came from the tower.

Rand said through gritted teeth, "Can't level. We just lost instruments."

Craig's hands shook as he relayed the message to Cincinnati Tower. "What should we do?" Craig shouted into the radio. "Are we going to crash?"

"Don't panic. We'll get you down," a much deeper and calmer voice came from the tower. "Lunken is a little better site. Wind 150 at 8, visibility 10,500..." he continued, ending with orders to change radio frequency.

"So, we're heading to Lunken?" Rand asked.

"There's traffic on your left. To your left, came from Lunken Tower, 8 o'clock, 5 miles northbound. It's a twin Cessna. Watch your left, LEFT!"

Rand compensated in time and glanced at Craig, whose eyes were squeezed shut as he muttered a prayer. "Craig, I need you with me, boy. Get dispatch. We need a plan B!"

Craig's eyes flew open. "Sorry, sir. Of course."

"Just do it!" Rand snapped as he managed to steady the plane at 2,000. Wind gusts threatened to blow him off course. "We only have thirty minutes of fuel."

Sept. 16 – 12:10 p.m. EDT, Cincinnati, Ohio

Back in the economy class, Svetlana stared out the window, fighting to keep down the few bites of egg she had eaten. The plane reeked of puke. A gray-haired gentleman in a navy blue suit sat beside her, fighting dry heaves. He'd already lost his breakfast twice. Mostly coffee, but he'd used both his and her barf bags.

The crew refused to let passengers get up to use the bathroom, and she desperately needed to go. Crossing her legs helped for a while, but she was afraid her control was losing the battle over time.

The plane took another dive, and Svetlana thought no more about her bladder. She worried for her life. Luggage fell out of an overhead compartment and landed on passengers' heads. A child who stood next to her father fell into the aisle. The plane bounced again, and Svetlana's shoulder slammed against the window.

The gentleman next to her reached for her arm. "Oh my God, we're going to crash. I've never been on such a bumpy ride, and I've flown three times a week for the past ten years."

"This is my first flight," Svetlana admitted. "I'm scared, too."

Although the flight crew was supposed to strap themselves into their own seats, passenger safety demanded action. The attendants clung to seat backs as they moved up the aisle, tried to assist others, shoved bags back into the storage areas, and closed the bins. Children across the aisle buried their heads into their mothers' shoulders or cried out in fear. Some people chanted prayers.

"Ladies and gentlemen, we have permission to land," came over the intercom. "We'll arrive at Cincinnati Lunken International Airport in five minutes."

A sigh of relief seemed to fall across the cabin. Svetlana needed clarification. Lunken? She checked her ticket, which read Cincinnati/Northern Kentucky International Airport. Had the flight attendant made a mistake?

No one around her seemed upset, so Svetlana asked the gentleman beside her. "Did she say Lunken Airport?"

"Yes," the man said. "There are three airports in Cincinnati. I guess someone diverted us, but don't worry. The airlines will make sure we get to the proper destination. Perhaps they'll have buses to transport us. I, for one, will be happy to be safely on the ground no matter where we land."

"How will my contact know where to find me?" Svetlana asked.

"The airport will have that information, so don't worry."

Svetlana was feeling anxious. She wasn't sure if she wanted to meet Agent Cordelia, even though Perry trusted her. Perhaps Cordy was everything Perry had described, but she would never meet her. This made things worse because then she wouldn't get the chance to speak to the president. Svetlana was frustrated with the confusion and pressure her father and Perry put on her. She didn't know where to go or if anyone would be waiting to meet her.

A few people screamed as another plane came into view. The plane lurched to the left as they barely missed a collision. Svetlana held her breath, her eyes gaping wide. She could even see passengers through the windows of the other plane. Many had their hands in front of their faces. "If we live through this, I will never fly again."

Her head ached, and at times, her ears popped as the plane's altitude fluctuated.

Sept. 16 – 12:21 p.m. EDT, Cincinnati, Ohio

In the cockpit, pilot Rand gasped, "We've lost pressurization. We can't go any higher. How far are we from Lunken?"

Craig got back on the radio. "Twelve point three miles, sir."

"Tell Lunken to keep an eye on us. We need to go lower. Speed 180."

"Runway 4L cleared for approach. Number 1 to land," came from Lunken Tower. Craig communicated the information. "We have permission for an emergency landing."

Rand contacted the flight attendant, "Just lost cabin pressure. Did oxygen masks deploy?"

"No," the flight attendant said.

"Activate manually and make sure everyone has a mask. Assume emergency positions and prepare for landing."

Sept. 16 – 12:27 p.m. EDT, Cincinnati, Ohio

The crew went into immediate action amidst panic within the cabin. A fistfight broke out toward the back of the plane. A teen in a red sweatshirt screamed, "That's my mask! This one is deflated." He punched the woman next to him, giving her a bloody nose.

"All are deflated," the woman called out and slammed the teen in the gut with her elbow. It knocked the breath from the lad who held his ribcage. "I can't breathe."

A flight attendant raced down the aisle, tripped, and hit her head against the leg of a seat next to Svetlana. More crew members ran toward the back to break up the quarrel, nearly trampling the fallen flight attendant. "Take your seats! Now. We are landing, and everyone needs to buckle up, put your arms over your heads, and brace yourself against the seat in front of you. The oxygen masks do not inflate, but oxygen is indeed flowing," came across the intercom. The purser finally got the two in the back to take their seats.

Fear left Svetlana as she climbed over the gentleman beside her and helped the downed flight attendant. She dabbed blood from a cut above the attendant's left eye with a napkin. "Hold this tightly over the wound," Svetlana instructed.

"Thank you." The attendant struggled to walk back up the aisle. Svetlana helped her to the front. And then, using the moment of confusion, she darted into the restroom—relief at last.

Svetlana slipped from the restroom and rushed to take her seat. "Emergency vehicles on the tarmac," Craig said over the intercom. "Does anyone need assistance?"

A crew member explained they had three passengers and an attendant needing medical care. The plane bounced a couple of times as it landed. "Welcome to Cincinnati. Please remain seated until medical personnel board and assist those needing treatment. Then, proceed in an orderly fashion inside the airport. Once you've cleared customs, identify your luggage. We'll have a bus to transport you and your bags to your scheduled airport. We apologize for any delays or inconvenience. The local time is 12:27 p.m."

"Three hours late." Svetlana's mind whirred with disjointed thoughts. Her heart raced like a ticking time bomb, ready to explode, and her nervous fingers shook as she reset her watch to the local time. *I made it this far, but now what?* Everyone spoke in rapid English—most too fast for her to translate. She stayed close to the man sitting beside her on the plane. At least he spoke Russian, had traveled to the U.S. frequently, and offered to guide her through the dreaded customs routine. *I can't fail—Papa's counting on me.*

HOLY ROLLER

It was a cloudy day in New York City. Sophia and Chief Jackson had been watching the Klinedorf residence for 20 minutes when Victor finally pulled his silver BMW into the driveway. Sophia stepped onto the street and met him as he opened his car door. "Good afternoon, Mr. Klinedorf. I heard about the terrible fire at your plant. I hope you and Alexa stayed safe."

The sallow-complexioned man bounced the keys in his hand. His nails had been bitten to the quick. Victor's brow furrowed, and he stepped away from the car. "I was in the back of the warehouse when the fire started. I nearly choked to death. Thank God Alexa was safe, but in a matter of minutes, my whole life went up in smoke." His eyes were still red and puffy.

Sophia moved aside as Victor shoved past. "Do you know what caused the fire?"

Deep red flushed his cheeks, and his voice went up a notch. "The police are still investigating."

Sophia already knew this, but she wanted to hear Victor's version. "I hope your insurance will cover the damages."

"Fortunately, I have good insurance, but getting everything back in order will take weeks. Who are you? Some reporter?"

"No," Sophia answered. "Sorry, I should have introduced myself. I'm Sophia. I just stopped by to see Alexa. It must be hard running a business. What did you do before starting this company?"

He paused. "That's really none of your business. Look, I'm rather busy right now."

"Of course. Is Alexa here?" Sophia asked.

Victor tensed. "Does she know you?"

"Yes, well, actually, she knows my friend. She frequently plays the ponies, so they got to know each other. Alexa's last tip paid off quite well."

"That's good to hear," Victor heaved a sigh and seemed more at ease. "Alexa isn't here right now. She's at some meeting at her church. It's a big day for her."

"A big day?" Sophia asked. Fortunately, she had looked up Alexa's church when Maude had mentioned that Alexa hadn't attended AK's funeral.

Victor continued walking up to the front door. "I told her not to go, but she wouldn't listen, so I guess this means a lot to her." His right eye gave a nervous tic. "That's all I'm going to say on the matter. You'll need to talk to her directly."

"Oh, that meeting," Sophia didn't know what meeting was held at the church but wanted Victor to feel comfortable answering her. "It's at Christ Church on Park Avenue. My friend goes there, too. When will Alexa be home?"

"I don't know her plans," Victor said. "Stop by tomorrow. What's your name again? I'll let her know you will be by."

"I'll do that." She headed back to the car and then turned. "Name's Sophia."

Victor was already unlocking the front door. He briefly turned and watched Sophia enter her car before entering the house.

Chief Jackson was on the phone talking with Floyd's previous lawyer. "Thanks, Ashton. I'll be by later this afternoon to pick up your notes on Victor. Say hi to Bess for me." He disconnected the call and buckled his seatbelt as Sophia started the car. "What did Victor say?"

"Not much, but Alexa is at some meeting at her church," Sophia said. "Victor told her not to go, but she went anyway. Also, he wouldn't tell me where he last worked."

"That's because he used to work as a guard for a parking garage," Jackson said. "Bet you can guess which one. Ashton mentioned that he represented Victor in a DUI case two months before Floyd's court hearing. He got Victor off on a technicality. He was single then, and as far as Ashton knew, Victor didn't know Alexa before Floyd's trial."

"I wonder if Victor met Alexa one fateful day when her brother was run down in the parking garage." Sophia made a U-turn. "Let's visit Christ Church." She headed for Park Avenue and pulled into the parking lot outside the Romanesque church made of marble.

Jackson climbed out of the car and met her on the sidewalk. "What a beautiful church."

Sophia pointed up. "That stain-glass window was made by one of Tiffany's employees. And wait until you see inside. This building is so large it may take a while to find Alexa's meeting."

"Perhaps we should go separately in case she recognizes you," Jackson said. "I'm an out-of-towner."

"I like your idea," Sophia said. "I'll go in first, and you come in a few minutes later. You can follow me, but we won't talk openly to one another."

To their surprise, Sophia and Chief Jackson discovered Alexa was attending Gamblers Anonymous. It was a modified closed meeting allowing only those who admitted they were gamblers to attend. Sophia opted not to go into the meeting, but Jackson professed a gambling problem and joined the seven other members.

Sept. 16 – 10:00 a.m. EDT, New York City, New York

Chief Jackson entered the dimly lit room and discretely took an empty chair in a circle across from Alexa, who stood by her chair to tell her story. Jackson straightened his jacket and fumbled to turn on his recording tie tack in the shape of a gold leaf with a small shiny stone. At least, it appeared to be a stone, but it was a camera eye—a gift from Cordy.

Alexa was in the middle of her life history and didn't even pause to look in his direction. Her thick, curly brown hair draped over her shoulders and bobbed as she spoke with such animation and sincerity.

Alexa's amber eyes glittered with tears. "…felt lonely and isolated. I was still single in my thirties and bored with my job. My only excitement came from betting on the horses. Family members hounded me to stop throwing my money away, but then I'd hit it big, and they'd shut up for a while until I'd lost it all and started begging for another loan, which I rarely paid back."

Chief Jackson listened intently to her story.

"My one hope was my brother. I remember AK's words as if he had spoken them just yesterday. 'A major storm will hit the U.S. someday soon. I'm not talking about the weather—a financial crisis. It will hit like a tsunami. I'm unsure when or where, but you must become financially secure.' I asked him, 'How have you prepared? After all, you're always in the limelight as the world's leading philanthropist. You're wealthy, well-respected, generous, and concerned for human welfare.' At least, that was what he portrayed on the outside. But I knew him as family.

"'Come help me at the office,' AK said. Maybe you'll learn a few tips of your own and, believe me, I need someone to work with that I can trust.'"

Chief Jackson leaned forward, making sure his pin could catch every word.

"…I never lacked male company, but finding a man to build my future with never came to fruition until seven years ago. It was the worst day of my life. I visited my always-perfect brother in his office. He was Papa's pride and joy; he never made an investment error in his life. At least, that was my father's opinion, but I know better. He was in the middle of a scam up to his eyeballs in money laundering. Millions of dollars invested in gold, diamonds, and magnesium." Her hands flew into the air. "Yes, that's what I said. Magnesium!"

Jackson wondered why magnesium. There was no formal open market for the metal.

"You know the Chinese have an 80% market share. So why would this make such an impact on my life?"

She appeared to be rambling, but Jackson listened carefully for any cues.

"My brother was killed in a hit-and-run accident—run down by his own CFO. The worst day of my life became an opportunity of a lifetime. I'm not going into the details here, but that's when I met the man of my dreams. He wasn't some highfalutin bigwig who could tell me what to do—nothing like my family. No, he was a talented mechanic who was down on his luck. He took a job as a security guard at that same parking garage where my brother was rundown. He saw everything happen on the monitor and came down to lend me a hand."

Her lips curled upward in a faint smile. A blush tinted her cheeks. She made eye contact with Jackson and held it for longer than usual as if to test Jackson's response. Watching him watch her, a bit of intrigue lit up her face as if to check that he saw her in the right light. He briefly lowered his eyes. Satisfied, she, too, looked away.

Jackson clicked a remote in his pocket that took a series of photos of Alexa's expressions. *So that's when she met Klinedorf. And AK was money laundering? I wonder if he was involved with any Russian activities. I better check with Cordy.*

Alexa refrained from glancing his way again. "We married four months later, and I've never worried about money again. Victor's a smart investor. He knows electronics like the back of his hand and deals with powerful people in the right places. Now, I admit that I'm a gambler. But he was the best bet I ever made. He wants me to stop gambling. I thought it was a simple request, but it hasn't been easy, and he's threatening to leave me if I don't quit. That's why I'm here today, asking for your support to help me stop gambling." Alexa wiped a sleeve over her eyes and sat down.

Jackson thought it was an impressive performance, but why did she mention the Chinese magnesium? *That's something more to investigate.*

TOO LONG TO WAIT

Sept. 16 – 4:36 p.m. MSK, Moscow, Russia/
9:36 a.m. EDT, Cincinnati, Ohio

Cracker didn't want to leave Rozalina in the icy and putrid-smelling mortuary. However, she pushed him out the door and whispered, "Hurry! I'll be right behind you after one last check." Cracker's mind was still hazy as he ran down the alley until he reached the street. He paused, shook his head to clear the cobwebs, and tried to figure out where he was and what had happened. His last clear memory was boarding a New York plane heading to Russia.

The flight was going well, and then the flight attendant delivered a message, "Don't panic. You'll be home soon." She gave him a glass of vodka.

"Panic," he hadn't heard that since he'd left home. Rozalina had hypnotized him using that word, but he didn't believe in such nonsense, which happened more than ten years ago. Within minutes, Cracker began to sweat. A dull ache ran through his left arm and into his jaw. His heart skipped several beats. Soon, it felt like an elephant was sitting on his chest, and he couldn't breathe—gasping for air. His fingers trembled over the button to call for the flight attendant.

"How may I help you?" echoed through a dull roar. Gray dots floated before Cracker's eyes. He couldn't remember why he summoned her. "I can't…breathe!"

The flight attendant hooked him up to an oxygen tank, and the remaining flight became a blur. He woke up in the back of an ambulance. Rozalina was at his side. She admitted that she'd injected him with something, and whatever drug, it was still in his system. *Think. What did Rozalina say? Uncle Albert. Right, I'm supposed to meet Uncle Albert, but where?*

Cracker closed his eyes and heard a car approaching. Instinct told him to run. He hid amongst nearby shrubs. Rozalina will be here shortly. He waited for ten minutes, but there was no sign of his wife. Where is she? I don't want to leave without her. Not after all they had been through to reunite after nearly ten years. One look at his lovely wife told him that he didn't want to continue living alone. He'd been without her for too long, and he yearned for his marriage and his family. She said they had twins. *I don't want to live alone ever again.*

As twilight turned into darkness, Cracker was still waiting. No matter how hard he tried, he couldn't remember where to meet Uncle Albert, and it was time to return to the morgue to collect what was his. *After all, Rozalina risked everything to save me. What if she is in danger now? I should have insisted on both of us leaving together.* Guilt seized his soul.

Cracker studied the dirt road to his left. It was all clear. He checked the path he had taken from the mortuary. A few people with lit candles had gathered under a tree not far from the back door to the morgue. They were chanting or singing—he couldn't tell which. Surely, they were no threat, so he stepped out from the shrubs.

A car pulled around the corner, and headlights nearly blinded him. "Get in!" a graveled voice sounded from the vehicle. "I've been searching for you for nearly an hour."

Cracker stiffened. "Are you talking to me?" He hated being caught off guard and took a fighter's stance.

The driver wore a black Ushanka. The fur cap's earflaps were attached to the crown. A squat spark plug of a man layered in bulges of muscle climbed from the car and removed his cap, exposing a shiny bald head. "You are Cracker. Right? I'm Uncle Albert. Rozalina said to meet you at the park, but I was afraid something went wrong when you didn't show."

"Have you heard from her?" Cracker asked. "She shoved me out the back door and said she would soon follow. I've been waiting, but there's no sign of her. I was about to return to the morgue to check on her."

"You stay here," Albert said. "I'll search inside the morgue." He returned to the car and drove down the dirt road past the candlelight ceremony.

Cracker grew tired of hiding and followed behind on foot. Staying in the shadows, he watched the car pull up to the morgue's back door. Albert got out and rang the bell. The back door opened, and Albert went inside. Cracker inched his way closer.

Sept. 16 – 4:40 p.m. MSK, Moscow, Russia/
9:40 a.m. EDT, Cincinnati, Ohio

Rozalina had barely closed the mortuary's rear door after pushing Cracker outside, when the attendant blocked her departure and blurted, "The medical examiner must speak to you. It's urgent!" It's the FBI. They must have called ahead, raced through her mind.

The attendant continued talking, "…his office immediately."

Rozalina's instinct was to run after Cracker, but all her efforts to save him would have been futile.

The attendant tapped his foot with impatience. "Are you coming?"

"What? Coming where?" she stammered.

"Did you hear anything I said?" The attendant's voice had gone up a notch. "The medical examiner wants you in his office now!"

"Why?" Rozalina's fingers were going numb again. She had to force herself to breathe normally, or she'd pass out. "I followed protocol."

"I never said you didn't," the attendant snapped. "Please, follow me."

A man dressed in soiled green scrubs leaned over the railing and called down, "Thank you for taking the time to meet with me. It's important."

"I was just leaving for another appointment." Nauseated by the potent enzyme disinfectant and decade-old formaldehyde, Rozalina didn't want to waste another minute in the morgue.

"I understand you're a doctor," the medical examiner said.

That shocked her. "Do I know you?"

"I'm Dr. Manaheim's older brother, Feliks. He was tied up when I called him and asked for his professional opinion about my situation. He informed me that his doctor friend would be dropping off a body, but I was not to ask any questions. I'm not asking who you dropped off or why, but I'm extremely overworked and have puzzling information on one of my clients. I wondered if you could lend a hand."

Rozalina clenched her fists. "Manny wouldn't have told you any such thing." She saw him lower his eyes and bite his lip. *I'm right. Manny didn't blow my cover.*

"You're right. Someone from the FBI called asking about a body dropped off at the morgue," Feliks admitted, "but I did call Manny for help, and he said he was on a mission. I know what that means. Then you appeared at the morgue. I'm not a stupid man."

"So you're blackmailing me?" Rozalina spat out.

Feliks shrugged his shoulders. "No, I need your help. Manny trusts you, so I will, too. I'm falling behind schedule, especially with the current riots."

"How do I know you're telling the truth?" Rozalina asked.

"Call Manny and ask him," Feliks added, "but I need your help and can't pay for professional advice."

Rozalina stood her ground. "That's good because I am a professional and won't work for you!"

"Please, I only need a second opinion," Feliks insisted. "I don't care who you are or who you brought to the morgue. If you help me, I'll forget that I ever saw you, and as far as the FBI is concerned, someone dropped off the body and returned to their business as usual."

Rozalina paused. Something else was going on behind this request, but what? "I must leave. I'll let you know my decision in the morning."

"I need your help now." Feliks added, "I just finished an autopsy on General Urk's body. It's a nasty piece of work, and his burial is scheduled for tomorrow at 1 p.m."

Rozalina gasped, "General Urk's dead?" With Urk gone, what will happen to the team?

"Tell you what," Feliks said. "I'll make you a deal. I need to show you something in the chromatography/mass spectrometry unit. Please, it'll only take a few minutes, and then you can leave." He didn't wait for an answer. "This way."

Rozalina was intrigued. What does he have to show me? It has something to do with General Urk. Curious, she followed.

Icy air blasted toward her when Feliks opened the steel gray lab door. Flecks of paint had chipped away over the years. "The spectrometer is in here." He stepped over the threshold. "You don't want to get your clothes soiled. Hang your coat on that peg and replace it with a lab coat so you don't freeze."

Rozalina gladly slipped into the lab coat despite its dark, reddish-brown colored spots. She told herself it wasn't blood but knew better. A gasp escaped her lips when the door clicked shut behind her. A shiver crept through her despite the coat. The walls appeared a muddy blue-gray in the dim light. One corner of the room was crowded with dead bodies. Metal tables, scales, and overhead trays also cluttered the space. There was a faint drip, drip, dripping sound from a pipe above the stainless-steel sink. The formaldehyde odor grew stronger the farther she entered the room. She covered her nose and mouth with her hand and tried not to gag.

"You get used to the smell," Feliks said. "We'll go to the makeshift lab where the air is more tolerable." He turned left past the restroom. At the end of the hall was another office. "This is the toxicology lab." He moved behind a desk, pulled a file, and handed her a computer printout.

She studied it. "Is this from General Urk?"

"Yes."

"Was he a diabetic?" she asked. "Ketoacidosis maybe? What was his blood sugar?"

"He did not have diabetes," Feliks said. "His glucose level was 92, and no evidence of ketones."

"Then why is the report positive for ethylene?" she asked.

"I knew it!" Feliks sounded elated. "You agree with my analysis. It's the third positive case I've had in two days, and I've rechecked the results. This is not a lab error or a false positive. I know it's real."

Rozalina's interest was piqued. "It's definitely ethylene glycol. I can think of only one other cause, but how did antifreeze get into his system? And who were the other cases?"

"Now, the question is, do I trust you?" Feliks said.

"Manny does," Rozalina reminded him.

"Oh, I don't need to know anything else," Feliks said. "Actually, you'll want this information in your line of business. It may protect you or your loved ones." He gave her a knowing look. "You're part of the team, aren't you? I'm the missing link you don't know about."

"If that's true, who are the other members?"

"General Urk was our leader. I'm sure that Captain Anton will take his place. Then there's your husband, but he went to the U.S., and that's when you joined the team. Need I say more?"

Rozalina thought a moment. "Why have you remained as an anonymous member?"

"I get my assignments directly from the top."

"Even higher than General Urk?" she asked.

He nodded. "But, I'm not going to say who."

"Not from Pres—"

"Not that high, but I'm not at liberty to say," Feliks whispered.

"So, who are the three cases in which you have had positive results so far?" Rozalina asked.

"The first was a high-ranking official, but we can't release his name yet," Feliks said. "The police are still searching for his family. The second case is a woman who worked for the police chief."

The attendant rapped on the door. "Excuse me. A man downstairs says he's here to give the lady a ride home."

Rozalina blew out a deep breath. "I must go now. Tell the man I'll be right down."

The medical examiner handed her his business card. "The information I shared with you is top secret."

"Why are you confiding in me?" Rozalina asked.

"I'm warning you to beware," Feliks whispered. "Things are not as they seem. All three victims saw Chief Ignacio within three hours before their deaths. Two of them had a drink with the man, and the woman who worked for him may have, too."

"What are you saying?" Rozalina asked.

"If you run into the police chief, I'd decline anything he offers to eat or drink. Why is the FBI...? Never mind, I promised no questions, but stay away from Manny. I don't want him involved in any of this."

"Rozalina," Uncle Albert's graveled voice sounded muffled. "Let's get out of here. I can't stand the odor."

"I must go now." Rozalina yanked off the lab coat and dashed from the toxicology lab. She grabbed her jacket from the peg, hung up the lab coat, and tugged on the door. It opened with a whoosh of air. She nearly collided with her uncle as she fled down the stairs.

Feliks called over the banister, "Thanks for your help, and remember, it's dangerous out there! Be careful."

SUBTERFUGE

Sept. 16 – 6:35 p.m. EET, Kyiv, Ukraine/
11:35 a.m. EDT, Cincinnati, Ohio

Augi stood over Gabe and unlocked the shackles. "Denys forgot something." Augi smiled, held up the brass skeleton key, and placed his finger over his lips. "Shh. I'm not going to hurt you, but you have to scream and moan as if I'm pounding the life out of you. Your pathetic howls will keep Denys away. He hates being around anyone while being tortured. I was shocked to see him come to witness General Urk's beating. I thought I'd rough the general up a bit, maybe give him a black eye, but I guess Denys wanted revenge for his son. He had Bruno take over, and then, at the last minute, Denys delivered the final blow. I was locked outside of the cell and couldn't intervene."

Gabe glanced toward the cell door. "Bruno will be close by. I've seen his shadowy figure make regular rounds, and he's even bigger than you. What will you do if he comes?"

"Denys let Bruno go to town. I guess as a celebration."

"Denys has your daughter," Gabe said.

"Yes, and I need you to help me locate her." Augi felt his anger rise. "Tonight, after dark, we'll strike back."

"Where did Denys take her?" Gabe asked.

"I'm not sure, but he'll want her to join him for dinner."

"What about his other guards?" Gabe asked. "Someone will be keeping an eye on us."

"Yes, but there are only a few guards at the moment. Denys sent most of his men with the general's body to cause riots in Moscow."

"When are they due back?" Gabe asked.

Augi shrugged. "I don't know yet. I need to win over one of the guards to get more information. Okay, keep screaming and begging for me to stop."

Gabe played his part, yelling until he was so hoarse that his voice was barely a whisper.

The squeak of the top gate warned Augi that someone was on their way down to check on them. "Go over to that downspout and roll in a pool of the general's blood. It hasn't completely dried yet. You need to look like you've been beaten and bleeding."

Gabe did as he was told while Augi rubbed his hand over the charcoaled wall and rubbed black over the back of his knuckles. Then he smeared soot over Gabe's eyes and cheeks to appear more bruised and added a trickle of blood over Gabe's face. "Act like you passed out."

A light flashed along the cave walls, and a slurred voice yelled, "Denys told me to check on the boy. You get anything out of him yet?"

Augi glanced at the boy. "He's unconscious, but you can come to take a look." He lumbered to the cell door while rubbing his bruised knuckles. The guard reeked of booze. A bright light flickered through the bars, and a beam shone on the boy's face as blood continued to ooze down one side. Splotches of red soaked his shirt and pant legs.

"You've been a little too enthusiastic, Augi," the guard said. "What did he tell you?"

"General Urk sent his son away to Prague," Augi lied. "We were working on where in Prague when he passed out."

"Wake him up," the guard ordered.

Augi suggested, "Fetch a pail of cold water from the stream. That should revive him."

"Nyet." He backed away from the door. "I'm not your stooge. Keep the screaming down. Denys is dining in. He has mighty fine company tonight, and we're not to bother him."

"My daughter, no doubt," Augi sneered. "He better treat her well."

"What can you do about it if he doesn't?" The guard gave a hearty laugh. "You're locked up in this cell. At least she'll have an excellent last meal. Cook's been preparing a feast all day. I'm sure he plans to entertain all night."

Augi moved toward the boy, grabbed a handful of hair, and lifted his head, making sure the guard saw how bloody he looked. "You want to watch him while I fetch the water?" Augi stepped to the cell door.

"I'm not that stupid," the guard said. "He's out cold, and I'm not waiting for him to wake up. I have a cute little chambermaid to keep me bed warm tonight." The guard stumbled a bit.

Augi asked, "Have the men returned from Moscow?"

"Nyet!" the guard yelled over his shoulder as he retreated. "Get back to work!"

Augi waited until it was quiet, then unlocked the cell door, stepped into the hall, and relocked it. "Be right back. Don't move."

The guard left the top gate unlocked as he headed for the rear entrance to the main mansion. Augi didn't meet anyone as he fetched a pail of water from the stream. Something buzzed above him. "Damn, bats." The area was renowned for them.

Augi glanced toward the veranda as he hauled the water back to the cave. Gas lights lit up the place. Denys stepped outside with a couple of filled wine glasses. Sitting at a small table, his daughter had a blue shawl wrapped around her slender shoulders. It took every ounce of stamina to prevent Augi from attacking the man, but a guard stood outside the door with a machine gun over his shoulder, ever observant. *Not yet. He'll shoot Belle and me. Wait until dark.*

Augi hurried into the cave, unlocked the cell, and offered Gabe fresh water. "Sorry about pulling your hair while the guard was here. I was afraid he might want to have a go at you."

"You even asked him to watch over me." Gabe shivered at the thought. "I nearly puked."

"I figured if I offered, he would decline. Men like that hate being told what to do."

"Did you see your daughter?" Gabe asked.

"Yes, she's on the veranda, but it's too risky with Denys and the guard nearby. It's nearly 7 p.m. Move up close along the wall. If another guard comes by, drop to the floor. I'll pick you up and take you to the trash heap out back, claiming you didn't live through the ordeal. You can get away when they're not looking. If caught, I'll say I'm looking for Denys to give him additional news."

"What news?" Gabe asked.

"That General Urk's son is at a monastery outside Prague. You had no idea which monastery."

"I hope he believes you." Gabe's eyes darted around the cave as he headed from the cell. "It's dark down here. I can't see anything."

"Feel your way along the walls," Augi said. "There's a steep step leading outside. When you reach the step, don't move until I check the area first."

A loud noise shattered the night, causing the ground to shift under their feet. "Wait here!" Augi warned and crept forward.

TYING UP LOOSE ENDS

While Chief Jackson attended the Gambler's Anonymous meeting, Sophia waited inside the church lobby and called Maude, AK's secretary, to ask a few more questions. "How well do you know Victor Klinedorf? He worked at the parking garage and was on duty the day your boss was run down."

"I've known him since he started working at the garage," Maude said. "A gentle soul when sober, he would help unload heavy boxes of files, suitcases, and other items from my car and get someone to carry them to the office, but he was an ogre when drunk. AK nearly fired him a few months before that fatal accident."

"What happened?" Sophia asked.

"Victor came to work drunk and got into a brawl with an investor who drove into the lot against a one-way arrow. Victor was strict on rules and wouldn't let anyone, especially a foreigner, question his authority. He gave the man a shiner. When AK heard of the incident, he called the police, but Victor fled before they arrived."

"Why didn't AK fire him for leaving his post?" Sophia asked.

"Victor was involved in a fender bender and ticketed for his third DUI, which landed him in jail. There was a trial, and a judge ordered Victor to attend one year of AA meetings involuntarily plus thirty days of probation as an alternative to jail. AK agreed to give him another chance. I don't have access to the parking garage's personnel records, but you might talk to his lawyer. Now that I think of it, he had the same lawyer as Floyd Wecholtz."

"Thank you, Maude," Sophia said. "I'll do that." As she disconnected the phone, she spied Chief Jackson, leaving the gamblers' anonymous meeting.

He smiled at her and made an about-face, so she followed at a distance. When he reached the exit, Jackson held the door open for her to leave. "Nice day. Care for a cup of coffee?"

Sophia nodded, and they headed for the car.

Once inside, Jackson said, "Ashton is pulling his files on Victor, and Bess makes the best cookies, cupcakes, and coffee I've ever tasted. I promised I'd give him half an hour before heading over. We've given him that amount of time and more. Jackson punched the address into Sophia's GPS device. I have to warn you: Ashton is a retired old duffer. He'll talk your ear off if you let him."

Sophia asked, "Did you find out anything new about Alexa?"

"Yes, she mentioned that AK was laundering money and something about the Chinese and magnesium. I want to do some more research on that."

Sophia and Jackson arrived at Wellshire's home and found Ashton scaling and filleting a fish on a wooden table outside his garage. He chucked the fillets into a bucket of water, wiped his slimy hands on a newspaper, and headed toward the car. "I wondered if you had forgotten about our meeting."

Sophia climbed from the passenger's seat and was met with a large hand still glistening with bits of fish guts. She stuck her hands in her pocket and turned sideways. "It's nice to meet you."

"Ash!" A plump woman darted from the house. "Where are your manners? Go inside and wash up while I do the greeting. Men!" She smiled at Sophia. "I'm Bess, and you must be Sophia. I've heard nothing but the best about you from the chief." She wrapped Sophia in a gentle hug. Then she opened her arms to Jackson and gave him a bear hug. "It's wonderful to see you again. Come along; coffee's getting cold. I made fresh peanut butter cookies. I know how much you like them."

When Bess opened the door, a black furball darted through. She caught the yapping Pomeranian mid-stride as it launched for Jackson. "This adorable pup is Pilly. She won't bite but loves to bark and lick you when you're not looking. Ash, we'll meet you in the dining room. Better hurry, or all the cookies will be gone," she chuckled. "That'll get him here in a heartbeat."

Ash padded into the dining room barefoot. He held an oversized folder in one hand and a pair of torn sneakers in the other.

"That's a thick file," Jackson said. "You must have slaved to get all that data."

Ash dropped his shoes onto the floor with a thud and fell into his chair. "I lived through one trial after another, working my ass off."

Bess quipped. "It shows."

Ash's eyes twinkled even though he frowned. "Let's just say I've lived that high-profile life, getting sleaze balls off for stupid stuff, and I'm glad to be done with it. These cases never go to a jury. Lawyers defend the hell out of the case, wrack up obscene fees, and then advise their client to settle. It's an ugly game out there. I didn't want any more of that, so I retired."

Jackson studied Ash. "Is that what you did with Floyd?"

"Naw, his case was different. I really tried to get him off, but Alexa's lawyers were always one step ahead of me. It was like they had inside information on the case. I had no stomach for it anymore, and Bessie, I don't need another wisecrack."

Bess kissed the top of Ash's bald head. "I wasn't going to say a thing."

Ash squeezed her hand. "It was time to retire and spend time with my sweet cakes. Sit," Ash instructed and handed the file to Jackson.

No one had to ask Chief Jackson twice to sit at Bess's table, loaded with delicious cookies. Of course, that wasn't all there was to eat. Bess was a Midwestern woman, and entertaining meant no one was allowed to leave hungry. Bess passed a plate of sliced ham and roast beef, another with homemade bread hot out of the oven, followed by slices of Colby and Cheddar cheese. "Key lime pie for dessert."

Sophia passed on the meat but spread melting butter over the bread and added a slice of Colby. "Fill me in on the Klinedorf case."

"Victor is a piece of work." Ashton sliced a wedge of ham piled on mustard, followed by Cheddar, Colby cheese, and a dill pickle. "According to court records, Victor is a recovering alcoholic who often relapses. When he's drunk, he becomes violent and has attacked family members, his ex-wife, and people close to him. When he met Alexa, he already had two restraining orders against him. The forty-three-year-old, who worked part-time as a mechanic, has been convicted of two criminal charges for assault, and driving under the influence."

Jackson chewed on his second cookie. "According to Alexa, Victor's the best thing to happen to her. Guess she hasn't spoken to his ex."

"His former wife said he trolls for emotionally fragile women then weasels himself into their lives." Ashton took a plate of key lime pie from Bess. "Alexa was quite broken up over her brother's death."

"Maybe this time is different," Sophia said. "He seems to care for Alexa."

Jackson set down his coffee mug. "That's because she has access to lots of money, as I hear it. No one has found the millions AK received from his Chinese investors, although I have my suspicions."

Jackson's fork was poised for another bite. "But no proof?"

"No proof," Ashton agreed. "I interviewed his ex-wife, father, and AK at the time."

"What was his childhood like?" Sophia asked.

Ashton drank half his cup of coffee in one gulp and then dug into his pie. "According to his father, school didn't come easily, and he had trouble fitting in socially. Victor beat up the little kids in the neighborhood. At some point, he was diagnosed with a learning disability, and his parents enrolled him in a private mechanics school.

He later joined the Army, and when he got out, he had a good job, got married, and had one child."

"Does he see his child very often," Sophia asked.

Ashton shook his head. "She'd be in her teens now, but when his ex-wife divorced Victor, he refused to pay child support. His ex was fine with that, as long as he vowed to stay away from them for the rest of their lives."

Jackson flipped a few pages in the file. "Says here that booze takes over his brain and turns him into a monster. He was convicted of assault and battery and spent three years in prison after beating up his ex's boyfriend. I wonder if he stays in touch with any of the inmates. Alexa mentioned that he makes wise investments and knows some powerful people in the right places."

"That I don't know," Ashton said around another mouthful, then swallowed. "I wonder, with his history, how his company got the State contract to copy court files."

Sophia nodded. "I'll check into that. Do you have any other information on Victor?"

"Not at the moment," Ashton said. "Take the file and review it at your leisure. Better yet, Chief Jackson can return it, and maybe we'll find time for another fishing trip."

ALL SYSTEMS GO

Sept. 16 – 7:09 p.m. EET, Kyiv, Ukraine/
12:09 p.m. EDT, Cincinnati, Ohio

Captain Anton and his tightly knit team flew from Moscow, Russia, to Kyiv, Ukraine, in under two hours. However, securing a military plane proved time-consuming, pushing their arrival past 7 p.m. The small team finally landed in a field two miles from Denys' location. Anton skillfully taxied the plane under a stand of tall pine trees. The leaves lay decaying in the damp woodland, giving off a ripe, earthy stench as fungi digested the ground's debris. The temperature dipped to 28°F, well below the usual 40. The team, having meticulously prepared for the mission, was undeterred by the challenging conditions.

Anton, a seasoned professional, enlisted the team to set up a bat drone, a testament to their thorough preparation. The drone, equipped with two cameras for day and night surveillance mounted on a wingspan that could open up to three feet, was launched to locate Denys' hideaway. A signal sent to each of their phones, complete with GPS coordinates, let them know where to search, which further highlighted their readiness for the mission.

Anton watched his screen for a few moments and then pointed to an image of an area covered in brush—small outcrops of cement buildings sprinkled across the land. The infrared camera brought up heated figures, so Boris moved to the regular lens view.

"Look, I think that's Augi down by the river filling a bucket of water. I knew we couldn't trust him." Boris enlarged the image and moved it as the drone flew over the veranda to the main mansion. "There's Denys, and who's that young lady?"

Anton put on his reading glasses. "I've seen her before, but I can't quite place where." Seeing Augi jarred his memory. "Wait, I have something I want to show you. General Urk and I had an agreement. If anyone ambushed us, we would try to leave a message for the other." He flipped to the camera on his phone and found the photo he had taken of the back of General Urk's badge. "What do you see?"

Boris stared at the photo. "A crooked letter, maybe an A and a circle. Or AO." A frown crossed his face. "Anton Orlov?"

"I thought that at first, too, but there's more that I don't understand." Anton passed the photo to the rest of his team.

Wolf traced the letters. "I see an AO, but something obscures the clarity. Is there a circle around the letters?" He moved the phone for a closer look. "No, it's more of a curve like an upside-down U. I don't know what it is?"

Eagle took the phone and held up his torch. "That looks like a bell. See the etched line under the letters?"

Anton gasped. "Not a bell, but Belle. That girl on Denys' veranda was Belle. AO could mean Augi Orion, and I bet the Belle refers to Augi's daughter. I overheard someone report to the police chief that she was missing. Do you think that's what the general was trying to tell me?" Anton's left cheek puckered around his scar as he pondered the new information. "I found the badge pinned upside down on General Urk's uniform. You know what that means?"

Boris nodded. "Traitor, but maybe there's a reason. What would you do if someone had kidnapped Ivanhoe?"

Anton nodded. "I'm glad I didn't have to choose between the general and my child. I want to find Augi before we do anything foolish. If Denys kidnapped Belle, Augi would fight beside us."

"Remember, Gabe could be down there somewhere," Boris said. "Maybe Augi knows where they're hiding him."

The drone continued to hover over Denys' fortress, a large two-story country house surrounded by fifty acres of pine trees. It was challenging to maneuver the drone through the forest. Still, when it got closer to the ground, the team discovered two smaller cottages on the land: one located outside a large brick-walled gated enclosure and the other about 100 yards inside. No doubt, these housed Denys' guards, officers, and other members of his staff.

Razor-barbed wire covered the top of the six-foot barrier surrounding the mansion. Motion detectors and spotlights were also located every 100 feet around the wall. A large building inside the barricade was used as an aircraft hangar, a few jeeps, and a Hummer. An assortment of other vehicles, two SUVs, trucks, and cars, were in a wide curved driveway in front of the house. Two guard dogs roamed freely.

A single road led through the gate. Other than the dogs, very little activity appeared in the area. Infrared showed two sentries at a steel-reinforced gate, one inside and the other outside the barrier. Boris zoomed in the camera lens, showing each sentry toted an AK-47. Nine people were inside the mansion, two on the veranda, which they had already identified as Denys and Belle.

Anton pegged the figure as Augi. He had entered a grove, or perhaps a cave with a bucket of water, and his infrared blob dimmed. When Boris flipped to the regular lens screen, Augi had disappeared, but now there were two infrared blobs in that area.

"I think that's an underground cave," Eagle said. "Perhaps we'll find Gabe inside."

"How do you want to approach the property?" Boris asked.

"Send the secret weapon through the front gate," Anton ordered. "Eagle and I will wait for the chaos to set in and make our way inside."

Boris muttered, "They have surveillance cameras around the perimeter. I'll send the drone closer to check the wall. Maybe there's a chink in their armor."

"That's a good idea," Anton said. "Block any signals. We'll need to knock out those motion detectors, and then we'll move closer. It'll be twilight in half an hour. Plan to attack after dark."

The men returned to the plane, got their equipment, and headed for the mansion. Boris removed the most significant piece of equipment, another unmanned aerial drone, and activated it for live ammo. The drone was large enough to launch a missile through the gate, or at least they hoped so. It was still in beta testing, but this would be a good target.

Anton peered at the faces of each of his team members. "We tried to prepare for every contingency, but a lot can go wrong. Rely on your training, experience, and gut reaction. If we don't screw up, we may see each other again." He pulled Boris aside. "If I don't make it, take care of Ivanhoe."

"Da," Boris said. "We'll be home before you know it."

Like shadows in the night, they dashed through the forest. The beta drone hovered a few feet from the ground as Boris set its path. The drone's missile device could launch a bomb, followed up with three grenades. If the drone didn't send the missile far enough ahead, it would self-destruct. That was the key problem that Anton hoped had been resolved.

"Boris, switch to thermal sensors and fly that drone over the encampment." Anton paused to check the feed to his cell phone from the bat drone previously launched to locate the guards on duty. "They're completely unaware and chatting with one another through the gate."

Boris made the adjustments on the drone. "Someone must have fed the dogs. They're unusually quiet."

The bat drone circled the outer wall, but no hidden cracks were evident. Anton replayed every scenario in his mind before making the decision. Denys was responsible for murdering hundreds of innocent people. He strapped explosives to women and children who blew themselves up at marketplaces, mosques, and schools, killing children, families, and soldiers. He brought his fighters to Russia, kidnapped the general, tortured, and murdered him. And Denys would continue devastating raids if left unchecked. Anton was convinced this was the right maneuver and set everything in motion.

"Okay, we go in the front gate," Anton said. "Load the missile and cover Boris." All three men, armed to their eyeballs with automatic assault rifles and sidearms, covered Boris as he set up the missile with explosives, adjusted the timers, and attached them to the drone.

"I locked the device targeting the front gate," Boris whispered. "The first grenade hits within three seconds, knocking out any guards in the area. Ten seconds later, a second grenade is set to take out the inner guard building, and thirty seconds later, the third will destroy the aircraft hangar."

Anton nodded. "Wait for the third grenade before we enter the grounds. Wolf hits the veranda and rescues Belle. Eagle, head for the cave. If Augi's down there, send him to me and rescue Gabe. Boris, after the drone launches, grab your ammo, and head for the mansion's rear."

All eyes locked on the drone, firing the missile. A flash exploded, and the front gate blew off its hinges. The outside guard flew through the air, dead on impact.

Eagle lay on the gravel, crawling, making slow and measured progress, and halted one hundred yards from the gate. Guard dogs ran forward. The guard inside reached up to sound an alarm, not that he had to. There was enough noise to wake the dead. The first grenade cleared the area. The second and third hit seconds later. Eagle rounded the gate with his weapon raised, and he dashed for the cave.

Anton followed and then covered his men with a salvo of gunfire.

Wolf was right behind him. He dropped to the ground. A few men darted from the inner building, but Wolf's gunfire cut them down.

Augi nearly ran into Eagle as he rushed from the cave. He raised his hands. "Don't shoot. I'm unarmed."

"It's me, Eagle. I'm on your side. Get Gabe, and let's get out of here."

"Give me a gun," Augi said. "Denys has my daughter."

Gabe raised his hands and came into view. "Da, I want a pistol, too, if you have one. I'll go with Augi."

Eagle didn't hesitate. He handed each a pistol and two grenades to Augi. "Anyone else down here?"

"Nyet," Gabe said as Anton entered the cave. "Augi, I hoped I'd find you."

Augi raced forward. "We're going to the mansion to get my daughter. Denys was there earlier, and he has a drunken guard with him. The cook and a few workers are probably inside the house, too, so proceed with caution."

* * *

No one was on the veranda when Wolf appeared. He darted around to the back of the building, found the kitchen door, and climbed three narrow stone steps. The lights were off. As Wolf reached for the knob, a guard pushed the door open. Wolf leapt aside in time.

The man pulled up his suspenders and muttered, "What's going on? Can't a man have a moment's pleasure?"

Wolf slammed his rifle butt across the back of the man's head, knocking him out. He stepped over the drunk and darted through the doorway. Someone flipped on the kitchen light. Denys sat on a chair with a gun pointed at Wolf's chest. "Drop the rifle!"

Wolf let go of his AK-47.

"Care to tell me what's going on?" The muscular man with a reddish mustache stood. Denys' movements were smooth and graceful for such a large man. "You wouldn't happen to be searching for this beautiful lady, would you?"

Belle appeared in the kitchen at gunpoint. "Please, let me go." The man behind her nudged her in the back with his pistol.

"I want you to see what happens to this man who's risked his life to save you." Denys' finger pulled back on the trigger as Boris burst through the door, knocking Wolf to the ground and shooting Denys in the chest. Denys also fired as he flew backward. His bullet went astray and hit the stove, which ricocheted, barely missing Wolf.

Belle let out a blood-curdling scream, and her knees wobbled.

Wolf grabbed a knife from his boot and tossed it over Belle's head, hitting the man behind her in the eye with a sickening crunch of bone. The man fell back with a gurgle, landing on Belle, who had fainted onto the floor, crumpled like a damp tissue.

Augi and Gabe came through the kitchen door with their guns raised. "Belle!" Augi shouted, his face paled when he saw her in a pool of blood on the floor next to a collapsed man. Augi ran to her side and cradled her head in his lap. "My baby." His eyes filled with tears as he stared down at the daughter he had almost lost.

"Belle's safe." Boris hovered over her. "She just fainted."

"Spasibo! For a moment, I thought she was dead." Augi brushed a damp curl from her face. Tears flowed down his cheeks. "She looks so much like her mother."

Eagle came from the back door. "I found keys in the Hummer. Let's take it back to our plane."

Boris peered around Eagle. "Has anyone seen Anton?"

IVANHOE OR SVETLANA

Landing at Cincinnati Municipal Lunken Airport was a lucky break for Svetlana, who deplaned, dressed as Ivanhoe, and headed to Passport Control. Her eyes widened as she followed the other passengers down a hallway. *The airport is huge! Where are the guards? I thought everyone in the U.S. had guns, but there aren't even any soldiers in the hallway.*

Passengers from her plane merged with others and filtered into rows heading toward glassed-in booths where customs officers sat stamping passports, one at a time. Confused, she tapped the shoulder of the man sitting next to her on the plane. "Which line for Russians?"

He smiled. "Follow me. You mentioned this is your first time in this country."

"Yes." Svetlana took out her phone. "I can't wait to show Papa a photo—"

The man grabbed her phone. "Nyet, no photos allowed!"

She gasped, "Will I go to jail?" Turning, she searched for the police. Relief washed over her when she didn't see anyone dashing toward her.

The man laughed. "Sorry, I overreacted. You are not allowed to take photos until you pass through customs and baggage claim. Then you can take all the pictures you want."

"Oh, I didn't know." Svetlana stuffed her cell into the pocket of her pants. "Thanks for telling me, my friend. There are so many rules, and everything is so modern. I feel like someone transported me in a time machine. Look. TVs are everywhere. The walls are colorful, not dirty, beige and cement, like at home. The people are organized in rows instead of shoving ahead to get to the front of the line. I think I'm going to like it here."

Her friend waved her ahead of him in line. "You can go first. I've been through here many times."

"What should I do?" she asked.

"Just hand the agent your passport and smile. He may ask for your fingerprints and will take your photo. Answer any questions without hesitation and thank him before you leave."

"Next," the immigration officer said.

Svetlana's heart thumped loudly as she stepped to the window and smiled. To her surprise, the immigration officer smiled back. Before she knew it, he stamped her passport and returned it to her.

"Enjoy your stay." The officer turned and motioned. "Next."

Svetlana moved aside and waited for her new friend. The officer stamped his passport, and he walked toward her. "Where do I go now?" she asked.

"Do you have any luggage?" he asked.

"No, just my backpack," she was careful not to say Nyet.

"Then you can leave. Hand the declaration form you filled out on the plane to the customs officer as you exit the baggage claim area. I have to wait for my bag. Do you have any other questions?"

"Where is the bank? I need to exchange rubles for dollars."

"There's an exchange booth beyond security before you exit the building."

"Thank you for all your help," Svetlana said. "Safe travels."

"Same to you." He waved and walked to the baggage claim.

Svetlana handed the form to the officer and exited security. She found the airport currency exchange booth and took out her wallet. "How many rubles is $1,000?"

The clerk shook her head. "The maximum amount allowed is $500."

"Then I need $500." Svetlana pulled out a wad of rubles.

The clerk entered numbers on a calculator. "That will be 43,904 rubles." Svetlana counted out the bills and received the money. Rumors had spread that everything in the U.S. cost a lot of money. She hoped it would get her across town and maybe pay for a hotel room. She'd buy her own groceries. The thought of eating in a restaurant was tempting but too expensive.

Instead of heading to the Embassy Suites, where she had planned to stay, she decided it might not be safe, as the FBI might be waiting for her. She watched several hotel vans pass by. They didn't seem to stop, so she thought they must only deliver passengers.

Svetlana recognized the name of a hotel printed on the side of a van. It must be an international hotel chain. A long line of cars was under a taxi sign, so she found the first available driver. "How much does a ride to the Hyatt Regency cost?" She made sure to use proper pronunciation.

"The Hyatt has a van that runs for free every thirty minutes, but if you're in a hurry, it's $38.50."

"That's a lot of money." Svetlana backed away. "I'll wait for the van."

"Here's my card if you need a ride later." The driver smiled and pointed her in the right direction to catch the van.

"Spa, ah, Thank you." She walked further along the sidewalk until she reached the "hotel shuttles" sign and waited until the Hyatt Regency van stopped beside the curb. When the automatic door opened, she climbed into the back seat. Two men boarded the van behind her, causing an initial alarm, but she breathed a sigh of relief when they didn't pay any attention to her.

"Do you have a reservation?" the driver asked.

Both men said, "Yes," so Svetlana, still dressed as Ivanhoe, pretended she was with the other passengers.

The driver slid into the front seat and pulled into traffic. "We'll reach the hotel in about twenty minutes. Sit back and enjoy the ride."

Svetlana scooted toward the window, her forehead pressed against the glass, watching in awe as they passed by trees growing along the highway, flourishing in autumn colors of red, orange, and gold. *Americans drive on the right side of the road, too,* she noticed. *Lines marked the smoothly paved roads to tell people what side to move on, and everyone actually stayed in their own lanes except to pass. The cars on the road were all new and shiny—no rusted-out bumpers, missing headlights, and probably no holes in the floorboards like back home. No horses were pulling carriages or dogs running wild along the streets.*

They drove past one-family houses. *There were no crumbling concrete high-rises, all grey and sooty. These were brick houses with white or pastel-colored shutters and wooden doors, most probably with welcome mats. Everyone must be wealthy.*

She checked her phone for a cell signal and then made a hotel reservation before arriving. Traffic backed up as they reached the inner city, but she didn't mind watching people darting from their cars and ducking beneath overhead awnings to get out of the rain. Oddly, few people use umbrellas, and only some wear trench coats or rain cloaks. How do they stay dry?

The shuttle pulled up to a stylish several-story building with a black awning with Hyatt Regency Cleveland at the Arcade printed on the flap. A whole mall was inside. Svetlana looked forward to doing some shopping for female clothes.

The hotel lobby welcomed her with its vivid red, yellow, and blue Oriental carpet spread as if waiting for royalty. People sat on elegant chairs and sofas in a lounge section of the main lobby. Svetlana eyed each person, wondering if one was Cordy, and felt relieved when no one glanced her way. She saw young children playing on iPads and cell phones, and some even had computers. *They must be rich.* She stepped up to the curved desk to check-in.

"Good afternoon," the receptionist greeted her. "Do you have a reservation?"

"Yes. Ivanhoe Orlov." She handed over the passport.

The receptionist typed on a keyboard, rechecked how to spell the last name, opened the passport, and examined it. "What language is this?"

"Russian."

"One moment." The clerk took the passport to a back room.

Svetlana's gut clenched. *Is the FBI already looking for me?* She backed away from the desk, ready to run, but needed her passport. *What should I do? This was a bad idea.*

The receptionist returned to the counter before Svetlana could make up her mind. "You're in Room 425. Enjoy your stay." She handed over a plastic key card. "Unfortunately, we are backed up. After we finish processing all the paperwork, you'll have to come down and get your passport later this evening. We'll call you when we're through with your passport. I'm sorry for any inconvenience. Don't hesitate to call the front desk if you need anything."

Svetlana wanted to protest, but when she saw the line behind her and heard the same story given to the couple beside her, she thanked the clerk and headed for her room. She was looking forward to taking a shower and going shopping.

WHERE'S ANTON?

Sept. 16 – 7:54 p.m. EET, Kyiv, Ukraine/ 12:54 p.m. EDT, Cincinnati, Ohio

Gunfire erupted from the rear of Denys' hideaway in a forested encampment south of Kyiv, Ukraine. A gust of wind blew snowflakes across Anton's face as he dashed from the cave. Squinting in the darkness, he saw headlights rapidly approaching as a heavy vehicle bounced over remnants of the cement wall and demolished gate. He raced through the darkness and ducked back into the cave so the driver couldn't see him. *Surely, the rioters haven't returned from Moscow already.*

The engine whined, brakes squealed, and the massive vehicle stopped outside the main house. Anton glanced at Bruno, who was climbing out of the truck and slamming the door.

The muscular mass darted toward the cave, his bald head covered with a black Ushanka cap, its fur flaps hanging loosely over his ears. As he reached the cave's entrance, an automatic rifle was poised in his hands.

Anton retreated further into the darkness, staying in the shadows.

After a brief pause, Bruno listened intently, then turned and headed toward the back of the house.

Worried about his men inside, Anton stepped out of the cave only to be spotted.

The brute moved with incredible speed, lunged forward, and was upon Anton in a flash. Bruno's right hand whipped from behind his back, and a wicked eight-inch knife blade whizzed past Anton's ear.

Anton became a blur and leapt aside in time, but Bruno was undeterred. He launched forward with a well-practiced street fighter's move, slicing a mighty upward swing meant to cut through flesh and bone—*a killer's blow against anyone else.*

Anton caught the brute's wrist with both hands and twisted his forearm. The bone snapped and tore through flesh in an arterial spray.

Bruno shrieked in pain.

Anton retreated, believing Bruno would bleed out shortly. He moved toward the house's back door to check on his men. He caught movement and a glint out of the corner of his eye.

Bruno grunted as he propped his left arm onto his stomach and aimed his Tokarev pistol.

Anton cursed at being such a fool and dove for the ground. A bullet ripped through Anton's arm before the sound blasted. Anton rolled. Another round hit his leg as he struggled to get away, and he couldn't stand. Maybe a third bullet entered his body, but he didn't know for sure. He ached all over. Adrenaline pumped through him. Dots floated before his eyes. Anton's hands trembled so much that he lost grip of his gun and couldn't sit up. The smell of gunpowder burned his nose. Warm blood oozed down his arm. He swallowed and tasted bile.

A round of gunfire erupted from behind Anton, and Bruno's body bounced as the bullets pelted him. *Surely, he's dead.*

"Anton, are you hit?" echoed from a distance. *That's Boris,* but Anton couldn't form any words to reply. Feeling a cold breeze let him know that he was still alive, but for how long? The sky opened into fluffy white flakes. He felt lighter than air.

Lieutenant Boris repeated, "Anton, can you hear me?"

The voice faded away. *I'm sorry, Svetlana.* His wife, Maria, floated above, reached down, and took his hand. His pain disappeared. Her touch let him know that no one could ever hurt him again.

WHERE TO HUNT?

Sept. 16 – 8:38 p.m. MSK, Moscow, Russia/
1:38 p.m. EDT, Cincinnati, Ohio

Special Agent Usher Hastings pulled his cell phone from his pocket as the plane landed at Vnukovo International Airport in Moscow. Braun had sent three text messages with updates on Cracker, and Cordy also wanted Usher to track down Risingsickle. *Whoever that was.* He barely had a scrap of intelligence to guide his investigation. Still, Cordy narrowed down his search based on a phone call from Quint and a few emails sent to Aqib's computer. Risingsickle had sent a message to Aqib from a Starbucks in Moscow three weeks ago. He also sent five earlier messages from the same location, so Usher hoped Risingsickle hadn't left the area.

A new text message from Agent Saul Reed popped up. "Sorry, Usher, I left Moscow earlier today. Good luck."

"Great!" That only left FBI Agent Zina McLaughlin to help him rescue Vlad and locate Risingsickle, and Usher had no clue about her background. Usher sent an urgent text message to Zina's cell, "There's been a change of plans. Don't board the plane to London. I must talk to you in person. I just found out that Agent Saul Reed is already on his way to Chicago, so I must speak to you. Fortunately, your Russian VISA allows you to stay in the country until the end of the week."

People packed the plane's aisles, and Usher was in the middle of the aircraft, making it difficult to rush into the airport for a meeting.

His cell phone gave three chirps as he grabbed his bag from the overhead bin.

Zina texted, "No time to meet. BTW, I go by Zina and am heading to my parents in Dublin, Ireland. I'm boarding a plane in 5 minutes. Call me in the morning."

"No!" Usher gasped.

A man in front of him turned around and muttered, "Go? I can't move any faster. Everyone's always in a hurry."

"Sorry, I wasn't talking to you." Usher dialed Zina's phone number. It rang twice before an irate agent answered, "I can't talk now! I'm already in the boarding line."

"Cancel your flight!" Usher ordered. "I want an update on what happened to your assigned fugitive, Alyosha Krackovitz, better known as Cracker. How did you and Reed let him slip through your fingers? If he required medical assistance, why didn't you follow him?"

"A medical team whisked him away by helicopter, and we didn't have any say in the matter," Agent Zina said. "And we did follow up, but he never arrived at the hospital. He died en route, and they diverted his body to the morgue as is their custom."

Usher raised his shoulder to hold the phone to his ear as other passengers nudged him along. "Did you check at the mortuary?" He forged forward when he noticed an opening and squeezed to the front of the line. "What gate is the flight to Dublin?" he asked a clerk.

"You have to go through customs first, sir," he said.

"Yes, and where do I go if I'm going to Dublin?" Usher got directions when he deplaned. He was upset at himself for not reviewing Zina's agent record, but he was sure he'd be working with Agent Reed, so he didn't take the time.

He nearly dropped his cell when Zina replied, "I don't know who you're talking to, but answering your question, we didn't go to the mortuary. What was the point?" She sounded annoyed. "In my defense, I did speak to the medical examiner. Cracker was already cremated by the time we discovered where the emergency team had taken his body. I've written up our report, sent off the file, and completed my assignment. Now, I'm going home."

"No, that doesn't make any sense," Usher said. "Cracker was Russian Orthodox. He'd never be cremated. It's against his religion. Plus, I need your help to find someone who goes by the name Risingsickle. I'll be there in five minutes."

"I can't help you." Zina sounded miffed. "I'm late for my sister's birthday party. Find someone else for the job."

"Flights come here only once per day. It'll take another twenty-four hours before another agent can fly here." Usher used his in-charge voice. "You're already in Russia. I need your help, so step out of that line, and I'll meet you at gate 2." When she hesitated, he added, "I don't want to pull rank, but I will if you make me."

"Fine!" Zina disconnected before he could say another word.

Yeah, fine. What a great way to start a working partnership! Usher hastened his already long gait and entered the airport, barely noticing the pouring rain. Water flew off his hair as he shook his head like a dog and ran a damp sleeve across his face. Standing in the customs line, Usher wondered if he could even work with the insolent woman. His colleagues never challenged him when he gave orders. It was unthinkable. *Agent Zina sure had her nerve. He'd let her know who was in charge.*

After all, he wouldn't have asked for help if he didn't need it. The level-headed older brother of the Hastings boys knew where his responsibility lay, and today was not the day to challenge it. Not after rescuing the president, tracking down the pilot and his accomplices who nearly shot Air Force One out of the air, and then dealing with a cyberattack in New York City, causing major security issues threatening his country. He'd had too little sleep over the past four days, and flying all day didn't help. He never could sleep on an airplane, and this trip hadn't been any different.

The uniformed customs agent motion, "Следующий!"

Usher wasn't as fluent in Russian as his brother, Braun, but he decided it meant "Next," so he stepped up to the window.

"American passport." The agent glanced up, "Visa?"

Usher set down his suitcase, turned to a back page in his passport, and pointed to his VISA sticker. It hadn't been an easy document to obtain on short notice.

The officer thumbed through the passport for a blank page. "Here for pleasure or business?"

"I hope for both." Usher shifted his weight from one foot to the other, wanting to get moving again. He wasn't sure if Zina would wait or board the plane.

"How long are you in the country?" the agent asked.

"A few days, maybe longer."

"You have a departing flight," the agent said. "It's required, so how long?"

"Seventy-two hours." Usher decided to cooperate and smiled. "You have a beautiful country. I've been here before."

"Da." The agent stamped the passport and then handed it back to Usher. "Have a nice stay."

Usher nodded, grabbed his bag, and dodged around several people as he headed to gate 2, expecting to find a severe, irate, middle-aged woman asserting her displeasure at being grounded instead of going home. Gate 2 was in sight when he abruptly stopped.

Only one woman stood in the area with shoulder-length raven hair pulled back with a gold-colored barrette at each temple. She wore black slacks and a maroon cotton shirt with rolled sleeves, revealing tanned, well-toned arms. Long, graceful hands tapped impatiently on her narrow hips. Dark brown eyes with a hint of gold snapped back at him in irritation. "Satisfied? My plane left without me."

Usher opened and shut his mouth like a fish gasping for air before finally stuttering, "Yeah, well, okay, sorry about that." He couldn't stop smiling, a slow, lazy curl of his lips—one side higher than the other. *This could be fun!*

"Wipe that boyish grin from your face," Zina snapped. "I'm here now. What's our plan?"

"Um, we don't have much intelligence to guide us," he admitted.

"I can see that," Zina huffed.

Usher let the sarcasm roll off him. "How about we stop at a restaurant and discuss it? I'm famished."

Zina shook her head. "That will be a problem. You couldn't have picked a worse time to come to Moscow. The president called in the militia to squelch riots in the streets. Nearly a hundred people have been killed, even more, arrested."

"I know. My Russian contact is hiding out in the middle of the most violent section of town. We'll rescue him after dark."

"What's this 'we' shit?" Zina's voice went up a notch. "I thought you were here alone and required my help to find someone, Risingsickle. Now, you tell me you have another contact? Why do you need my help?"

Usher cleared his throat. He wanted to chuckle. "Okay, we'll find a restaurant at the airport, but I'm still hungry. Let's go."

Zina nudged a suitcase with her foot. "You only have one bag. You can take this one as well." She picked up the smaller of her two suitcases and walked past him. "Are you coming? I thought you were famished."

Usher quietly picked up her luggage and followed. He couldn't help but grin as he watched the rhythmic sway of her hips. *Oh, yes, I might enjoy this assignment after all.*

NOWHERE TO RUN

Sept. 16 – 2:29 p.m. EDT, New York City, New York

Svetlana had made it from the Cincinnati Airport, taken a van to the Regency Hyatt Hotel, and checked into Room 425 as Ivanhoe Orlov without any FBI agents detaining her. Her frayed nerves were beginning to calm as she quickly unpacked. She removed the binding around her chest and found a shirt with ample room to cover her bosom.

She stood before the mirror and fluffed her blonde hair into some semblance of a shaggy hairdo. Nodding with approval, she could pass as a girl, then grabbed her key card and left the room to go shopping at the mall next door. The hallway was empty, so she darted to the elevator and patiently waited for it to reach the fourth floor. A slender strawberry-blonde woman dressed in a royal blue sweater and jeans was talking to a tall man with a powerful frame as the elevator door opened. Her hands waved as she spoke, then she smiled at Svetlana. "Good afternoon."

Svetlana nodded, stepped to the side, and lowered her head as the couple got off the elevator, and she slipped inside.

The man wore a long-sleeved gray shirt, unbuttoned at the collar, accenting his gray eyes. As she passed, she noticed a bulge at his back and wondered if he was carrying a weapon.

The woman studied a sign on the wall. "Room 425 is that way," she pointed down the hallway as the elevator door closed.

Svetlana knew in that instant that the woman was FBI Agent Cordelia. *They've tracked me down. There's no place to hide or time to make a better plan.* Cordy seemed pleasant enough, but Svetlana wanted to know more about the couple before meeting them in person. Instead of pressing the button to the lobby, she went down only one floor, got off on level three, and headed for the stairwell. Taking the stairs to the fourth-floor landing, she stopped, peered through a small window, and opened the door. Unfortunately, she was at the wrong end of the hallway to see her room, but she could hear a woman call out, "FBI, open the door."

A moment later, the man said, "Clear! There's no one here. What do you want to do?"

"We'll wait," Cordy said.

"I'll go downstairs and check the lobby," the man said.

Svetlana's heart hammered against her ribcage. She couldn't move. Her feet were like blocks of wood as the fear washed over her. She took a deep breath, trying to calm down. How long will they wait? I need to contact Perry. However, her computer was in her room. She managed to get back onto the landing.

As she held the door ajar, the man in the gray shirt rounded the corner and headed her way. She gasped and was sure he'd head downstairs, so she crept up to the sixth floor as quietly as possible. Holding her breath, she heard his footsteps descending. *Should I return to my room now that Cordy is alone? I'll have to meet her sooner or later. Maybe I could walk down the hallway and peek into the room. After all, the FBI agents are looking for a boy, not a girl. It might work. Why did I tell Perry that I'd meet her?*

Convinced that she must meet with Cordy, Svetlana walked down the sixth-floor hallway and nearly bumped into a maid's cart. Plan B popped into her head. Two doors down, the noise of a vacuum cleaner masked the sound of moving the cart to the elevator. Svetlana pressed the down button.

As she waited, Svetlana slipped into a black sweater she found strewn across the top shelf. Then, she saw an apron on the lower shelf and pulled it over her head. When the door opened, she moved the cart into the elevator, pressed number four, and down they went.

While riding the elevator, she rummaged through the cart, found a rubber band, and pulled her hair into a stubby ponytail. Before returning to the hallway, she pinched her cheeks to bring some color into them.

Svetlana was surprised to find the door to Room 425 open. Cordy stood at the end of the bed, peering around the room, and then she moved toward the table by the window where Svetlana had placed her backpack. Not wanting Cordy to invade her privacy further, Svetlana rapped on the door, "Maid service."

Cordy jumped and accidentally knocked a glass off the table. "Sorry, I didn't mean—"

"Don't worry. These things happen." Svetlana forced herself to remain calm. Then, remembering that she was playing a maid, she got a small broom and dustpan from the cart and started to clean up. "Is this your first visit to Cincinnati?"

Cordy moved closer to the door. "No. Have you been working here for long?"

Svetlana didn't look up. "I started this week. Are you traveling alone?"

Cordy shook her head. "Braun went downstairs to talk to the manager. Maybe you can help me." She reached into her pocket, pulled out a photo, and handed it to Svetlana. "I was wondering if you have seen this man earlier today."

Svetlana didn't take the photo but glanced at it briefly. *Ivanhoe.* She dumped the swept-up glass fragments into a wastebasket as she thought about what to say. Her mouth went dry, and she licked her lips before answering, "No. Who is he?" She had to be sure to speak clearly with an American accent. Cordy didn't notice any flaw in her speech pattern, but her partner might bring the hotel manager here soon. He would know that she wasn't the actual maid.

"One moment, I can still see glass splinters on the carpet," Svetlana said. "I'll be right back." Rummaging through the cart, she ran across a roll of thick packing tape on the bottom shelf. She tore off a strip and wrapped it around her hand, then went back into the room. She noticed that Cordy had moved the backpack from the table to the bed, but she still hadn't opened the bag. The tape she patted over the carpet picked up most of the splinters. She tore off another piece of tape and wrapped the roll over her wrist. "I'll need a vacuum cleaner to get anything I've missed."

The elevator pinged. That must be her partner. Svetlana moved with her back against the door and turned toward Cordy. Her hand slid a strip of tape across the lock as she spoke, "I'll move the cart down the hall out of the way and will be back later to finish cleaning your room." Svetlana pulled the cart four doors down and scooted behind it to listen.

Fortunately, Braun was alone. Cordy rushed to the door, glanced up and down the hall, and pulled Braun inside.

Braun shut the door behind him, but the tape prevented it from closing completely. "No sign of Ivanhoe?"

"Not yet," Cordy said. "The maid stopped by a few moments ago but hasn't seen Ivanhoe."

Svetlana inched her way closer to hear more clearly. She wasn't sure what to think about the FBI agents. They'd entered her room, but no one had opened her backpack so far. *Perry had promised that Cordy would protect them, but would they really?*

Cordy's cell phone rang. "It's Quint."

Braun said, "Put him on speaker. I want to know what he's—"

Before he could finish, Quint blurted, "Hi, Girlfriend. Do you know those two pen drives Braun took from Kildeer and you downloaded to your darknet account? They contain deadly Trojan malware. You say Perry created this code?"

Svetlana's heart leapt at the sound of Perry's name. She wondered how Cordy would react.

"Yes," Cody replied, "and he sent a sample code to repair the virus so you can test it to ensure it knocks out the original worm. What else did you find?"

To Svetlana's surprise, Braun sounded like he was speaking through clenched teeth as he interrupted, "Never call my wife Girlfriend again! This childish banter has to stop."

Cordy shushed him. "This could be our breakthrough. Leave him alone!"

Quint piped up, "Okay, I get it. This is a male thing. I'm just giving Braun a hard time, but you know, your woman has layers—many layers—so be proud, old man, that she picked you. Anyway, back to this Big V Virus—*that's what Perry calls it.* I've tested the code and Perry's solution on three machines. All three reversed themselves after being infected."

At that moment, Svetlana felt proud to know Perry, but her pride was dashed when Quint added, "However, the 5th Dimension is another story. I loaded it onto a burner computer, placed it in a protective casing, and it blew up the code in nearly every program."

Svetlana nearly barged into the room to defend Perry, but Cordy jumped in to defend her friend first. "Perry has no clue about that virus and wants to see the code."

"I've studied the code from one end to the other and have never seen anything like it," Quint said.

Svetlana's concern about the 5th Dimension Malware grew during the phone conversation. She had heard the virus had killed hundreds of people. Something she wanted no part of, but if they could save even one life.

"There's a third problem," Quint said. "Someone has written an entry code, and when accessed, it allows the person to see everything on the entire network."

"Perry never mentioned that code," Cordy said. "Is he keeping that little surprise to himself?"

Svetlana blinked back rage at that comment. *Perry wasn't hiding anything. He had even agreed to fly to Ohio to help these FBI agents. Maybe he is walking into a trap.* She had to know the truth. It was her job to protect Perry. *Well, perhaps not her job, but she wouldn't let anyone hurt him. That was a given.* Her fists clenched and unclenched.

Then she stepped to the door. Relief washed over her as she heard the rest of the conversation.

"No, it's not Perry's code," Quint said. "I can tell a change in coding techniques. This is a third person entirely."

"Perhaps it was Cracker," Cordy said.

"Have you spoken to Ivanhoe?" Quint asked.

"We've tracked him to the Hyatt Regency, but he isn't in his room, and we haven't found him yet," Cordy admitted. "You don't think Ivanhoe wrote that code, do you?"

"No," Quint continued. "And you might ask me why I think it's not Ivanhoe's code. I found a few interesting modifications to Perry's code that were written very similar to Perry's technique. It limited the malware to 72 hours, and everything would be reversed. That's what I believe is Ivanhoe's code. Then Perry reversed the modification at a later date."

"Interesting," A frown crossed Cordy's face.

"Perry's new code repairs the Big V," Quint said. "I believe he is being honest when he asks for protection, and he's agreed to help reverse malware damage. Using the new code proves his integrity, and we need to get New York City's electricity back on the grid ASAP."

Cordy agreed. "Nothing we accomplished today would have been possible without Perry's help. I was skeptical about allowing him into the country, but if he and Ivanhoe have a solution, we must work with them."

Braun piped up, "And to protect them."

"Yes," Cordy nodded. "I have changed my mind about protecting Perry and Ivanhoe. We can't do this promptly on our own, but I plan to be with them every step of the way. We will work together as a team. I know that I don't always play by the rules, but my gut says we must welcome their help."

"I agree completely," Braun said. "Sometimes, we find ourselves in sticky situations, and it wouldn't hurt to expand our resources."

Quint sighed. "My time has been stretched so thin it'll tear, and I'll need to darn it soon." He chuckled, but Cordy cleared her throat.

Svetlana mulled the conversation over once more before making any decisions. She liked Cordy, and maybe she would make a good mentor, but only time would tell.

"Okay, Gir...Cordy. See, I remembered. Back to the grindstone—the easy entry code is already on the new software loaded into William H. Zimmer Power Station's new hardware. Kildeer also placed the Big V and the 5th Dimension on the equipment, but he hasn't launched any more malware to date. What do you want to do next?"

"Before connecting the new equipment to the power plant, I want to enter Perry's fix and see what happens," Cordy said.

"Done," Quint said. "This equipment better not blow up in our face."

Svetlana leaned closer to the door. Did she hear that Quint was going to boot up a program that still had the 5th Dimension? It sounded like it.

"I'll let you know what happens," Quint was saying.

Svetlana burst through the door to Room 425. "Wait! Quarantine the 5th Dimension before booting up the equipment!"

Cordy gasped and fumbled the phone. "What?"

Braun stepped between the two women. "Who are you?"

"Quint, are you still there? Quarantine the 5th Dimension ASAP!" Svetlana blew out a deep breath. "I've been reviewing the code all night, and I have no fix for that specific malware. It will blow up in your face."

"Who am I talking to?" Quint asked.

"I'm Ivanhoe or rather Svetlana." She flushed and backed up toward the door, ready to flee. Her heart pounded in an unsteady rhythm.

Quint interrupted, "I guess you found Ivanhoe. Is there anything else for me? I need to contact Chief Jackson with the latest information he requested."

"Go ahead with the 5th Dimension quarantine," Cordy ordered. "I'll talk to you soon."

"Then later, Girlfriend," Quint chuckled before disconnecting.

Braun smiled at Cordy. "Geeky little imp!"

Svetlana saw Braun's eyes sparkle as he grinned at Cordy. They seemed honest, but...She backed further into the hallway.

"Whoa," Cordy said. "Come back here. You're safe. We won't hurt you, but we do need to talk."

Braun stepped closer and held out his hand. "Glad to meet you, Svetlana."

She stared at his hand, but he didn't pull away, and she made no effort to take it. "Am I free to go?"

Cordy picked up her backpack and walked with it to the door. "I believe this is yours." She held it out to Svetlana. "But before you go, can we talk?"

Svetlana reached out and grabbed the backpack, then glanced up and down the hallway. Cordy and Braun didn't follow her. Svetlana turned back. "You promise to protect Perry?"

Cordy nodded. "Yes, even if you decide to leave, we'll protect Perry as we promised."

"How can I be sure?" Svetlana kept her eyes glued on Cordy.

"I guess that will have to be your decision, but we'll respect it," Cordy said, "no matter what you choose to do."

"Because you can hold Perry as a hostage until I return?" Svetlana pulled the apron over her head, removed the sweater, and shoved them onto the cart.

"No," Cordy said. "Because we need your help, and I made a promise. That's something I don't take lightly."

Svetlana stayed next to the cart, eyeing the hallway as if she debated running.

"I can see that you're unsure of talking with us." Braun offered, "Would you like to go downstairs, where more people are around, and have something to eat as we talk?"

"No," Svetlana said rather quickly. She turned back to Cordy. "I don't know if I should trust you, but Perry's in great danger. Russian agents will kill him. They murdered his roommate and nearly killed his cousin, Vlad."

Cordy said, "Yes, we spoke with Vlad. He's the one who introduced us to Perry. Did you know that Vlad is also working with the FBI?"

Svetlana nodded. "Are they going to protect Vlad, too?"

Cordy hesitated. "That's not up to me. His contact is Braun's brother, Special Ops Agent Usher Hastings, and he's talking with the president of the U.S. to determine the next steps, but our job is to protect you and Perry and to get the electric grids back up and running. We had a near miss here in Ohio, and fortunately, we caught Kildeer before he could shut down another power plant."

"You caught Roland Kildeer?" Svetlana asked. "That's good. I think. I need to check with Papa, but I was to stop him if possible. Now you already have him."

Braun interrupted, "Are there others in jeopardy?"

"Not that I'm aware of. But, I have to reach Perry."

"Maybe you could clear up one question that has been going through my mind since I met you," Cordy asked. "We've been searching for Ivanhoe. What happened to him?"

"It's a long story." Svetlana bit her lower lip. "I'm both Ivanhoe and Svetlana. My twin brother died a few years back, and I took his place. Perry was his best friend."

"Does Perry know that you're a girl?" Cordy asked.

Svetlana pursed her lips and nodded. "Is it okay if we call Perry? I should let him know I've made it to Ohio and met you as promised. The call must be private. That's why I can't go to the lobby."

"Do you want to make the call in your room, or is there somewhere else that is safe?" Cordy asked.

Svetlana studied Cordy, then Braun. "I prefer to call from my room, but I don't want either of you to speak to him after I make the call unless I say so."

Braun said, "Fine by me, but we're not leaving."

Svetlana backed against the wall as Braun went to sit in a chair near the table.

"Do you want to use your phone or mine?" Cordy walked over to the table and pulled out a chair next to Braun.

Svetlana cautiously moved through the door, pulling the tape away from the lock as she entered the room. She flipped the lock and checked the door before placing her backpack on the bed and pulling out her laptop. "I only use the darknet to reach him. Are you familiar with that term?"

Cordy nodded with a knowing grin. "Are you comfortable talking with us?"

"I'm still testing the water," Svetlana admitted. "Look, I want to help, and I know you haven't a clue who I am, but you can ask me any questions. I'll tell you as much as I know, and I have a few questions of my own. Hopefully, they will be off the record. Is that how you say it?"

"While you girls chat, I'm going to book us a three-bedroom suite for the next few nights," Braun phoned reception. "I'll order up some dinner, too."

Twenty minutes later, they moved upstairs. Svetlana ran to her bedroom window and gasped, "Look at the view! I've never had a room like this. Are you sure you can afford this?"

Braun laughed. "If you're helping us catch a terrorist, it's the least we can do. Are you hungry?"

"Maybe a little," Svetlana said.

Cordy set up her laptop on the desk in the living area. Her message alert popped up. She had finished running Maude's drive data through her detection software system for the past three hours, and it had just finished a forensic analysis report that found several secret files. She sent a copy to Sophia and Chief Jackson.

Jackson sent her a thank you on her darknet account.

"You're welcome. Call if you have any further questions," Cordy texted Jackson.

"Svetlana, let's eat before your dinner gets cold," Braun said. Cordy joined them for an appetizer of mushroom soup, a Caesar salad, pork roast, and mashed potatoes.

A half-hour later, Svetlana retired for the night.

Cordy would have worked late into the night, but Braun used tender kisses to coax her to bed.

USHER BLINKS

Sept. 16 – 9:32 p.m. MSK, Moscow, Russia/
2:32 p.m. EDT, Cincinnati, Ohio

Special Agent Usher Hastings' first stop was the airport's ATM, which refused to cough up any rubles even after trying his bank card, VISA, and MasterCard.

"Probably out of cash," Zina said. "The money exchange kiosk has closed for the night, too. Hope you can get by on credit."

"I'll stop by the bank in the morning." Usher headed for Sixt to pick up a car. At least the rental agency took his credit card with only a few murmurs of inconvenience. The Lada Vesta was a dark gray compact car with a few dings, but it would be easy to park.

Usher pocketed the key. "Let's get something to eat before heading into the city. How about Grenko Pub? They've taken my credit card in the past. It's not the cheapest place to eat, but we can get real food there."

Zina nodded. "I hear they have good sausages, but their waiters are not so friendly."

"I want food even if I have to cook it myself." Usher headed for the pub.

"So, you can cook?" Zina's footsteps marched three times for every two of his, but she didn't waver and kept close to his side. "That's good to know."

Usher found a seat along the back wall. An old habit, he never sat with his back to any door. Before perusing the menu, Usher's eyes swept over the pub, checking for anything unusual. Spying two older teens playing footsy under the table, a young couple with a toddler, and a guy at the bar already tipsy, Usher was ready to dive in and eat.

"What'll it be, Ma'am?" A waiter asked Zina.

"I'll have a Caesar Salad with extra anchovies and iced tea."

"Coming right up." He took two steps before Usher called, "I'll have the same, but hold the anchovies. Make it hot coffee instead of iced tea, and give me an order of grilled Kolbasa with sauerkraut and onions."

The waiter frowned. "We're out of Kolbasa."

"Okay, then a Polish sausage," Usher said.

The waiter shook his head. "Nyet. Maybe we have stew at this hour. I'll check."

Usher nodded, but the waiter was already heading for the kitchen.

"I know Big Brother is alive and well, so fill me in on our mission." Zina placed a napkin in her lap. "I can't wait to see what I'm getting into."

Usher lowered his voice. "What do you know about a code name Risingsickle? I don't know his given name, but I'm here to track him down."

Zina pursed her lips and thought. "Haven't a clue who you're talking about."

"According to our records found on Aqib's laptop, Risingsickle made several lucrative deals selling uranium to extremist groups in the Middle East. That was until ten years ago when a high-ranking member of the Russian government accused him of embezzlement. After two attempts on his life, he fled the country."

Zina asked, "Where did he flee to?"

"We think he went to Syria, initially, but that's not a proven fact," Usher said. "With no more access to uranium, his money supply dried up quickly, and he simply disappeared."

"Wait, Risingsickle. He's accused of murdering several high-ranking officials in Great Britain." Zina studied Usher's face. "What aren't you telling me? I can see a frown across your brow. The same frown I saw when you met me at the gate. I'm known for reading expressions."

Oh great. Another Cordy. Usher made an effort to hide his feelings. "I have a contact in Russia. I need to meet with him in person. Vlad may have some additional knowledge."

"You mentioned Vlad earlier." Zina's eyes narrowed. "No, there's something else."

"We also must find Cracker," Usher said.

Zina shook her head. "You're still not telling me everything."

Usher rubbed his chin. "Alyosha Krackovitz, you know him as Cracker, was found guilty of killing an FBI agent, Crueger Yates."

"The same Cracker we were to intercept at the airport?" Zina asked.

"Yes, and I'm not convinced that he's dead. We'll track down his wife before we leave Russia."

Zina took a deep breath and blew it out. "So you don't believe me. Interesting."

"No, that's not true," Usher whispered. "I think you may not have all of the facts."

Sept. 16 – 10:08 p.m. MSK, Moscow, Russia/
3:08 p.m. EDT, Cincinnati, Ohio

Zina couldn't understand why Usher upset her so. *I usually back down when confronted by a man, but I've learned my lesson—never again. I'll say what's on my mind, no matter what. After all, I missed my flight home to help this idiot.* "So you don't trust me. Very well. May I have access to the FBI files?"

"Yes," Usher opened his briefcase and handed over two large folders. "Take them all and read through them tonight. You can return everything in the morning."

Zina shoved the folders into her bag and pointed inside his case. "Why the second phone?"

"My agent's phone." Usher paused as the waiter appeared with their coffee, iced tea, and salads. "Stew will take another hour," he said.

Usher was already exhausted. "Fine. Forget the stew." He relocked and set down his briefcase before digging into his salad.

Zina placed a fork in her left hand with tines down and chopped the salad with a knife in her right hand. The palms of her hands hid the handles. Once she cut a bite-sized piece of food, she placed the morsel straight into her mouth with her left hand. She used the blade of the knife to guide the food onto the back of the fork and continued to eat daintily using the European custom, then paused. "What's the plan for tomorrow?"

"Risingsickle sent a few emails from a Starbucks in Moscow," Usher said. "We'll meet there at 7 a.m. and check if anyone has seen him lately. If we're lucky, we may even run into the man."

There's more than one Starbucks," Zina said. "Which one?"

"The one in Afimall City," Usher pulled up a map on his cell phone and pointed the location. "Can you find it? Or should I pick you up in the morning? We can drive together."

"No, thanks," Zina said. "I can manage quite well on my own." She finished her salad and laid down her silverware for the first time during the meal. "Excuse me while I powder my nose." Zina reached for her purse, but it caught under the leg of his chair.

Usher stood, retrieved her bag, and placed the strap over Zina's shoulder. "I'll summon the waiter."

Something about this man infuriated Zina. Inhaling deeply, she forced her gaze away from those clear, smoky-gray eyes. The dim restaurant lights added a shimmering glint, hinting at intrigue and depth. His touch left lingering warmth on her shoulder. She hated to admit it, but Usher Hastings was getting to her. *He was a man of contrast and contradictions. One moment, he was harsh over the phone, demanding she stay in Russia. The next moment, he agreed to carry her suitcase.*

Her cheeks flushed as she moved quickly to the ladies' room. The restaurant seemed oddly quiet—only her footsteps echoed as she walked across a cracked linoleum floor. She didn't need the facilities. It was an excuse to get away. A chill raced down her spine whenever she thought of Usher, and he kept popping into her mind. *Why? This can't be happening. After being stood up at the altar, not once, but twice, I know better. Well, I'm not going to let another man in my life. Love isn't everlasting, and I won't fall for it again. Not ever!*

With that decided, she called a friend to ask a huge favor. "Hello, Pastor Gustav. This is Zina. Does that offer to stay at your fiancé's place still hold? I missed my flight and need a ride from Grenko Pub…Thanks. I appreciate it. How long before you get off work?"

Relief flooded through her when he said, "I'm heading to the car now. Church let out ten minutes ago, and I should be there in twenty minutes."

"I'll wait for you outside the front door." Zina disconnected the call and then refreshed her lipstick. Making her way back to the table, she scanned the room. The waiter was clearing the plates.

"How much do I owe you?" Usher pulled out his credit card.

"No credit," the waiter said. "Cash only."

"You took credit cards the last time I was here," Usher insisted.

The waiter glanced toward the door. "New management. No credit."

"I have U.S. dollars," Usher said. "Either that, or we can wash the dishes."

"Rubles only," the waiter said.

"What's this we business?" Zina smiled at Usher's dilemma but didn't offer to pay. "Are you really planning to do the dishes for your meal?"

"You have any better ideas?" Usher asked.

"I'm not wasting my manicure on dish soap," Zina laughed.

"I don't suppose you're flush on rubles tonight?" Usher asked.

Zina shrugged, "Enough to pay my way, but sadly not yours." She fished out 500 rubles, laid them on the table, and put on her coat. "See you in the morning."

"Where are you spending the night?" Usher asked.

"I have friends. Meet you at Starbucks at 7 a.m. Oh, I'll take my bags now. Gustav is waiting. I hope you find your contact. Bet you're sorry you prevented me from boarding my plane." She plucked up her luggage and left the restaurant, chuckling.

Sept. 16 – 10:33 p.m. MSK, Moscow, Russia/
3:33 p.m. EDT, Cincinnati, Ohio

Usher got up and dashed after her, hoping to borrow some cash from her friend. By the time he reached the street, Zina had climbed into her friend's car. She waved as they drove away. He turned to go back into the restaurant.

The bouncer, a brick wall of a man, stepped in front of him. "You left before paying your bill." A familiar bulge under his jacket told Usher the man carried a gun. He most likely had a concealed knife, as well. It was common in Russia to be well-armed for an unsuspected attack.

"Fine, lead me to the kitchen," Usher said. "I'll wash the rest of your dishes tonight in payment for my meal." The bouncer hesitated. "Come this way. I'll have to ask the manager."

Usher followed the bouncer back into the restaurant, picked up his bag and briefcase, and entered the kitchen.

"Set your bags down in the corner." The bouncer headed for a small alcove off the kitchen, which couldn't have been much larger than a pantry. "I'll be right back." He closed the door.

Usher set down his bags and searched for an apron. Grit stuck to his shoes when he walked to the counter. Greasy plates were stacked high on both sides of the sink. Silverware, cups, and glasses filled the basin, sitting in cool, gray, sudsless water. No one else was in the kitchen. Voices came from beyond the closed door.

Usher opened a cabinet under the sink to find dish soap and a cloth.

The office door opened with a bang. The bouncer appeared. "We've decided you don't need to wash the dishes. We have a better payment system."

A skin-headed man stepped forward and smiled, showing off a gold tooth. "So, you have no rubles? I exchange money for a fee." He turned toward the bouncer. "Leave him to me. I know what to do with freeloaders."

"Don't rough him up too much," the bouncer warned. "He's American. Word on the street says he's a government or special agent."

"Even better," Gold Tooth said. "We have people who'll pay for his hide." The impact was swift. Air rushed from Usher's lungs as he crumbled to his knees. Cursing, he rolled and scrambled to all fours before being hammered again. He should have seen it coming. His sixth sense rarely let him down, but he'd been preoccupied with Zina.

The bouncer launched forward and landed full force on Usher's back. The weight knocked him to his elbows. He squirmed with every fiber.

Gold Tooth grazed a sharp object over Usher's cheek, drawing blood. The two men hauled Usher outside the back door and dropped him on the ground like a sack of cauliflower. An unmistakable sound of ripping duct tape came from behind him. Rage poured from every cell as Gold Tooth moved a swatch of tape toward Usher's arms.

"Get away from me!" Pulling his legs into a fetal position, Usher kicked out and drove his heels into the man, knocking him to the floor.

Gold Tooth's nose cracked. Blood and Russian swear words spewed from his mouth.

"Who is your boss?" Usher asked. He didn't expect an answer, and none came. Instead, two more men came running through the darkness—one swinging a brass-knuckled fist straight for Usher's jaw.

The other pulled a knife and ran full bore, holding the blade like an ice pick, ready to chop and slash.

Usher had spent years perfecting his weaponry skills. He grabbed the brass-knuckled fist, twisted the man's arm, and spun his body into the blade, racing toward Usher's chest. The man's gurgled scream was short-lived. Usher spun the knife-wielder around and knocked him off balance.

A quick wrench of the man's knife hand and the weapon clattered to the ground. Giving a vicious twist to the man's wrist, it snapped. Jagged bone broke through his skin, and arterial blood spurted as he howled in pain. The bouncer scurried back inside the restaurant.

Usher dropped $20 U.S. at Gold Tooth's feet. "Consider this payment in full, and don't bother to follow me."

Gold Tooth spat at the bill but didn't make another attempt to fight.

Usher didn't wait for the bouncer to return with recruits. He dashed to the restaurant to get his bag and briefcase, but the back door was locked. The lights went out, and the restaurant was closed. He went to the front, which was also locked, but Usher knew someone was still inside.

His cheekbone throbbed, and his eyes swelled so much he could barely see. His ears rang as if standing below a bell tower, and any movements made him dizzy. Blood and grit drooled from his mouth and dripped down his chin. He couldn't even muster enough energy to spit.

There was a day when all four thugs like these would lie dead as Usher walked away, ready to fight another day, but not tonight. He wasn't here to kill anyone who got in his way—certainly not for a meal costing 500 rubles. That wasn't his style. Although he had to admit, he'd enjoyed the meal—well, not so much the food, but the company, although Zina left him to face these spies on his own.

"He was familiar with Russian tactics. Someone had identified him not just as an American, which was obvious, but also as a special agent. Espionage was deeply rooted in Russia. Who had identified him? He wasn't going to leave Russia until he found his adversary, but first, he needed to reach his car, figure out a way to recover his briefcase, and locate Vlad."

Close to vomiting, he wasn't in any shape to drive. He managed to get away in the darkness. Finding his car was a gut-wrenching trek, but once he spied it, he fumbled with the key and climbed into the driver's seat. Usher planned to return to the restaurant but passed out before he started the engine.

JUSTICE

Sophia Hendrum had made a 440 motion on behalf of Floyd Wecholtz, and Judge Grant of the New York Criminal Court agreed to expedite the hearing scheduled for September 16th at 3 p.m.—an odd time for the court as they usually started early in the morning. However, the regular schedule was full, and this slot opened when the previously scheduled case settled out of court. Scheduling the hearing later would have taken another three months, so Sophia gladly took the opportunity to present Floyd's case.

At 2:58, two officers escorted Floyd Wecholtz to the hearing. Floyd greeted Sophia and held out his wrists to have the handcuffs removed. Then he sat in the chair next to her. "It's so embarrassing to be here in this orange jumpsuit, but my only suit coat went missing."

"We'll see what we can do if we have a trial," Sophia reassured him.

"Thanks. Who is the DA?"

Attorney Ron Moore-Les entered the room and peered at Sophia through his narrow reading glasses. He removed the specs to improve the glare.

Sophia's breath hitched. The man's expertise and aggressive behavior were legendary among her colleagues. She knew today would be an uphill battle, but fortunately, Judge Grant would preside over the hearing. He was renowned as strict but fair.

Moore-Les took his seat at the council table. Sophia opened her date book and jotted a note. A trickle of sweat dampened her collar.

Floyd reached for her arm. "He seems very confident. Do we even stand a chance?"

"We are well-prepared." Sophia had to remain calm, if not for her sake, at least for Floyd. She licked her dry lips and wondered if there were any holes in her logic that Moore-Les would pounce through. She had taken great care to prepare for this case, but what if she had missed an important factor?

At the stroke of 3 p.m., the side door opened. A man stood at the front of the room. "All rise for Judge Grant."

All eyes turned as Judge Grant entered the room. This wasn't a courtroom but a hearing room, so he sat in front of a wooden table on an overstuffed leather chair facing Sophia.

A court reporter walked behind him, carrying a machine and tripod. The official court clerk entered, too, and arranged himself at a table off to the side. His job would be to mark any exhibits and control the flow of any paperwork used as evidence in the case.

"Good afternoon, counsel, and parties. My name is Judge Milhouse Grant, and I am the presiding hearing officer for New York State vs. Floyd Wecholtz. Sophia Hendrum has brought up this case for our review. The counsel for New York State is Ron Moore-Les. Gentleman and lady, are we ready to proceed?"

"Ready." Sophia placed her palm over Floyd's folded hands.

Moore-Les sat erect and faced the judge. "We're ready."

The hearing officer continued, "The court's ruling is final subject to the party's right to appeal. That appeal would go to the Supreme Court of New York. I am the presiding judge."

Judge Grant spread a small stack of papers in front of him. "Let's begin. The burden of proof rests with Floyd Wecholtz, so as his counsel, we will hear your statements about what you intend to prove and your witnesses first."

Sophia cleared her throat and stood. "We have recently discovered new evidence that throws doubt on the original verdict."

Moore-Les piped up, "How do we know that your client didn't deliberately neglect this evidence so when he was convicted of murder in the first degree, he could challenge that verdict by revealing this evidence after the trial?"

A stickler for rules, Grant raised his hand in his trademark gesture, silencing Moore-Les.

Sophia stood tall and ignored his previous remark. "I propose to nullify the verdict based on new evidence discovered since the previous trial, which resulted in a guilty verdict. The defendant was unaware of this evidence and could not have discovered it, even with due diligence. If this evidence had been presented during the trial, the verdict would have been more favorable to the defendant, and he would have been acquitted."

Judge Grant asked, "What new evidence have you obtained that was unavailable during the previous trial?"

Sophia presented Maude Ingram's documents. "The defendant was found guilty on two counts—embezzlement and first-degree murder by running down his boss, Andrew Madeim Edwardo Flinsh-Kedderton known as AK, with his car, suggesting pre-meditation rather than self-defense."

Grant nodded. "Proceed."

"In the case of embezzlement, my witness, Private Investigator Chief Jackson, obtained the documents I have entered into evidence as exhibits 1a, 1b, and 1c from AK's secretary, Maude Ingram. She found the documents after the initial trial. I now call Chief Jackson to the stand."

Jackson was duly sworn and testified, "The first document is a record of a Geneva bank account opened on the day of AK's death for $10.3 million and is registered in the name of his sister, Alexa Klinedorf, which is odd. That was four months before Alexa married her current husband, Victor Klinedorf. Her name at the time would have been Alexa Flinsh. Based on her original trial testimony, she first met Victor Klinedorf on the day of her brother's death—"

Moore-Les lifted his left arm and waved his hand. "I object. Alexa, whatever her name, is not relevant to this case."

Sophia turned toward Judge Grant, "I assure you, she is relevant if you'll hear Chief Jackson out."

Judge Grant's dark brown eyes darted toward Sophia. "Then proceed."

"Alexa claims that Mr. Wecholtz embezzled $25 million from Chinese investors, which has never been recovered," Jackson said. "Yet, $10.3 million was deposited in an off-shore account on the day of AK's death. AK's secretary discovered someone had opened that Geneva Bank account while using her computer."

"How do you know that Maude didn't open that account?" Moore-Les interrupted.

"It was an encrypted file accessed by user code 10200, which—according to Maude—was assigned to Alexa two weeks before AK's death," Jackson answered in his authoritative voice. "Maude's affidavit confirms everything."

"Let it show that Ms. Ingram's affidavit is entered as exhibit 1d, along with Agent Cordelia-Hasting's forensic analysis of the computer hard drive marked as exhibit 1 e."

Moore-Les again raised his hand. "Objection, Mr. Wecholtz was the company's CFO, so he had access to her user code."

Floyd hopped up from his chair. "That's a lie! I never had access to anyone's code but my own. It was company policy."

Judge Grant banged his gavel. "Be seated, Mr. Wecholtz." He turned to Chief Jackson. "Would you care to explain?"

"Yes, Your Honor. According to Alexa's previous testimony, she has no recollection of the account, and her financial status at the time was a net worth of only $380,000."

"So, how do you explain the deposit of $10.3 million to the Geneva account?" Moore-Les asked.

"My point exactly," Sophia said.

"Perhaps Mr. Wecholtz set up the account in her name to divert the funds and tried to frame AK's sister."

Sophia stiffened. "Floyd did not know of the funds until the amount was brought up during his trial. Further research shows those funds are no longer available, but seven years ago, on July 5th, Geneva Bank sent this notice verifying funds arrived in this account. When we subpoenaed the record, the bank later reported they never had any funds in that account. Evidence marked 1a proves the contrary, and 1b shows a record of $10.9 million cashed out ten days after it opened, on July 15th, also in the name of Alexa Klinedorf. Yet, we cannot trace that amount anywhere on Alexa's tax returns."

"What about the other $15 million the Chinese claim to have invested?" Moore-Les asked.

Sophia nodded for Chief Jackson to answer, "We discovered a hidden file on AK's secretary's hard drive, also entered by code 10200, and has Alexa Klinedorf investing $15 million in a Chinese Magnesium Corporation as already noted in exhibit 1c, and is verified by a national cyberthreat and research analyst expert, Agent Joshtine Cordelia Hastings," Chief Jackson testified. "That investment was also on July 5th, only hours after her brother's death. To my knowledge, Floyd Wecholtz never embezzled the Chinese investors' funds."

Sophia stated, "The defense places the affidavit of Agent Cordelia-Hastings as exhibit 1f."

Grant leafed through his notes. "You stated here that you have strong evidence that Mr. Wecholtz did not murder his boss, AK. Is that true?"

"Yes," Sophia referred to the exhibit marked 1g. "After several attempts, I finally accessed NBC's copy of the parking garage videotape showing my client running down his boss, AK, with his car."

"So, wasn't that proof of your client's guilt?" Grant asked.

"No," Sophia said. "Someone tampered with the videotape."

Moore-Les stood. "I object!"

"On what grounds?" Grant asked.

"Because we've seen this video ad nauseam at his original trial," Moore-Les insisted. "The general public has also seen it in its entirety, and without the original, how can you prove any tampering?"

Sophia turned toward Moore-Les, "I can prove it and will be happy to do so. May I proceed?"

"Yes," Grant said.

"No," Moore-Les shouted. "The original tape was destroyed in a fire."

"Proceed," Grant overruled. "And Mr. Moore-Les, sit down."

"Although a fire destroyed the original tape, I can still prove someone tampered with the evidence," Sophia said. "We sent the NBC copy, a duplicate of the original, to Professor Seamore Hyde at MIT. He ran a digital video analysis and found several areas that had been cut and spliced throughout the tape. The professor's affidavit stating that the video had been tampered with is marked exhibit 1h. I offer the exhibit to the court. I've marked each area and will play it with your permission."

"The exhibit is received. Please, proceed," Judge Grant said.

The court clerk, a slender man in his mid-thirties, placed the videotape into a VHS machine.

Sophia added, "Before starting the video, I want you to listen and watch closely. As the professor noted in his affidavit, there are abrupt changes in background sounds during the cuts. Lighting goes from dark to black, then pops back to the original colors, making the video appear jumpy. There are digital numbers hidden on the tape, which also advances from 15:45:12 to 15:47:38; another skip occurs from 15:48:16 to15:49:07, and there are three more skips with the last one at 15:52:28 to 15:54:42. The tape began again six seconds before the ambulance and police arrived. There is no further evidence of any tampered information." She turned to the county clerk. "Please, start the tape."

Floyd leaned forward and watched with renewed interest. Sophia paused the tape at each jump in the timeframe, made a few comments, and restarted the video. When the clip was over, she noted, "What happens during those missing time frames is of the greatest importance."

"And why is that?" Judge Grant asked.

"My client swears that AK had a gun pointed at him. He panicked and ran his partner down. Then AK shouted at Floyd as he drove away. The tape, on the other hand, shows AK, without a raised gun, standing in front of Floyd's car when he ran AK down. The next scene has AK unconscious and perhaps even dead—that's when his sister, Alexa, finds him. She called 911. Her initial call is not on the tape, but it picks up mid-sentence. We have a copy of the audiotaped 911 phone, exhibit 1i for comparison. When you play both tapes together, pieces are missing from the parking garage video."

"Turn down the lights so we can get a better view and replay the video," Judge Grant ordered, "and then play the 911 audio." The room fell silent.

After hearing the 911 audiotape, Grant said. "Interesting. Play that videotape again and put it in slow motion at the end as Alexa leans over her brother. Something is missing. On the 911 call, Alexa said, 'No, you can't have that,' but it doesn't appear on the video, so match the audiotape with the video for the last three minutes."

The clerk replayed as requested. When Alexa said, "You can't have that' on the 911 call," a rustling sound followed. At the same time on the video, Alexa was leaning over her brother. Something shiny glinted as she slid her hand into her purse, and a shadow fell over her. The purse disappeared from the tape. As the lights returned, Grant asked Sophia, "How did you interpret the last three minutes?"

"I believe Alexa slid a gun into her purse—the same gun that AK used to threaten Floyd Wecholtz and sent him into a panic, causing Wecholtz to run down his boss. Alexa covered her actions by leaning over her brother, but she definitely slipped something into that purse. A purse that disappeared on the tape, and there was no purse found at the scene when the police arrived. AK had gunpowder residue on his right hand and the right cuff of his coat. That evidence was presented in the original trial but ignored by the jury."

"Was any residue found on Alexa's hands?" Grant asked.

"No one thought to check at the time of the incident," Chief Jackson said. "She was quite upset, and the EMTs allowed her to follow the ambulance to the hospital. AK was pronounced dead on arrival, and Alexa was free to make funeral arrangements."

"Do you wish to cross-examine?" Grant asked Moore-Les.

Moore-Les shook his head.

Grant said to Sophia. "Thank you. You may sit down. Mr. Moore-Les, you may proceed."

After the video, Moore-Les opted to make a brief statement, and the hearing went into a recess until the judge had time to decide.

Fifteen minutes later, the hearing resumed. Judge Grant reentered and sat down. "Based on the new evidence presented here today, the court overturns the previous conviction of guilty and grants a new trial." He slammed down his gavel, and the room cleared.

Moore-Les gathered his papers and stuffed them into his briefcase. He left the room without as much as a handshake.

Floyd tapped Sophia's arm. "What just happened?"

"We won, for now." Sophia smiled. "You'll have a new trial. The newly discovered bank records, Maude's hard drive, and the proof of the tampering with the videotape are so strong that the DA won't appeal to the appellate courts." She waited for the officers to return Floyd to jail, and then she met Chief Jackson in the hallway outside the hearing room.

"Congratulations." Jackson hugged her. "Now, the real work begins."

"I'll be up all night." Sophia gathered her files and placed them into her briefcase. "I can't believe the trial starts tomorrow morning. It's a tight turn-around, but the slot came open when a previous case was postponed, and I gladly took the opening."

GETTING TO TOWN

Sept. 17 – 2:00 a.m. MSK, Moscow, Russia/
Sept. 16 – 7:00 p.m. EDT, Cincinnati, Ohio

Vlad was an old man living in a young body. His eyes were ancient, a pale blue the color of a summer sky, yet they had seen war, witnessed the death of innocence, and strained under heavy abuse. The youthful muscles of his twenty-four-year-old body used to propel him to the mountain top with the ease of a simple stroll to the market, but not today. His fair skin suffered bruises from torture from the very people who were there to protect him, the police.

He'd married young and fathered two children. Then war descended on his family's village, flattened by airstrikes. Ground troops followed, killing his wife and daughter. His two-year-old son was yet to be found. Probably kidnapped, swept up, and sold at a profit. At least, Vlad hoped he was still alive. It was incentive enough to join the resistance movement and to become a contact for the U.S. FBI. Now, he waited for Agent Usher Hastings to make a personal appearance.

Fighting in the park had been violent for most of the day and didn't die down until after midnight. It was nearly 2 a.m. when Vlad's satphone rang. Woken from a sound sleep, Vlad was groggy. "Привет." It sounded like privet, meaning hello in Russian.

"Hello," Usher said. "I have a situation here, and I don't know if I can reach your hideaway."

Vlad rubbed his tired eyes and spoke in English. "What type of situation?"

"I had a little run-in at Grenko Pub." Usher's words slurred. "I wasn't able to retrieve my bag, but my briefcase is what I really need ASAP. It's locked, but I'm sure that won't stop anyone who wants to open it. Thank goodness, I gave Zina my paper files, but there's a thumb drive hidden in the lining. Whoever sent those men is probably searching for my hide."

"Don't report it to the police!" Vlad said. "The chief is bad blood. He'll kill you himself if given a chance and make it look like self-defense. Where are you now?"

"Trying to make it into the city, but there are roadblocks everywhere."

"Give me a few minutes," Vlad said. "I'll call my Army buddy, Leo. He knows all the back roads and will bring you here unharmed."

"Where exactly are you?" Usher asked. "I can't locate this call on my GPS."

"I guess you haven't met Perry yet. My cousin is a fanatic when it comes to security. You'll never find this place on your own. Hold, please." Vlad called Leo and then reconnected with Usher. "Are you on M3?"

"Yes, but I had to turn back or be trapped in a roadblock," Usher said.

"Go back to the restaurant," Vlad said. "It will be closed by now, and I bet your bag and briefcase are in the dumpster behind the pub. Unfortunately, they'll have stolen anything of value. You might find a few clothes. Trash will be picked up around 3 a.m., so you don't have much time."

"I'm glad I didn't bring my laptop," Usher said.

"Grab what you can, and Leo will meet you there."

"How will he get here?" Usher wiped his brow.

"Leo will probably take Боровское or another route, and he knows the tunnels to my location," Vlad said. "He'll be riding an IMZ-Ural. There aren't many around, so you can pick him out in a crowd, but no one will be there at this hour."

Sure enough, Vlad was right. The trash was overflowing when Usher pulled up in the back of the pub. His suitcase was torn to shreds, and his clothes were strewn in a heap of goulash and other unidentifiable, slimy rubbish. His suit had also been slashed. Usher picked up a cotton shirt and his shaving kit but left the rest. He'd get new clothes rather than fetch his underwear, socks, and T-shirts from decaying fish guts, congealing beet juice, and rotting cabbage.

His briefcase was another matter. The itinerary lay torn and scattered amongst the rubbish. He found his new throw-away agent phone cracked and stuffed into leftover pelmeni. The pastry dumpling filled with meat sauce would have made an excellent dinner if he'd known they had it—especially if slathered in butter topped off with sour cream. His stomach rumbled.

Usher doubted his cell would function but scooped it up and wiped off the grime as best he could. Fortunately, he hadn't activated the phone yet. He continued to dig through the trash heap. The main compartment of his brown leather briefcase was empty and slashed down to the false bottom, but it was still intact. He found the hidden thumb drive unharmed, tucked along the back outer side under a steel-reinforced fake siding.

His sister-in-law, Cordy, had given Braun an identical briefcase last year for Christmas. Usher, awed by the gift, had one made for himself. She sure knew how to build secret panels. He would get her to order him a replacement. In the meantime, he'd make do with the sliced-up case. He placed his shirt, itinerary remnants, and shaving kit inside. It was all he would retrieve from the heap.

A dark-haired man in his early thirties drove up on a motorcycle with a sidecar. "You must be Agent Usher Hastings. It's good to meet you. Vlad said you'd be in the back of the pub, but I didn't know you'd be pawing through the trash."

"I'd shake your hand, but I'll spare you." Usher wiped grime onto a pair of his trousers from the heap.

"That's a nasty bruise on your jaw," Leo said.

"Caught me off guard," Usher swiped blood from his cheek. "I wasn't expecting an attack. Glad I have a hard head."

Leo parked his motorcycle and walked to the pub's back door. "There's a faucet over here. Sorry, no soap, but at least you can get rid of most of the slime and some of that crusted blood from your face."

"Thanks." Usher headed for the faucet. "How do we avoid the roadblocks getting into town?"

"I know a place where we can hide your car." Leo picked up a stick and sifted through the clothing piled on the rubbish. "Do you want any of these? It gets cold out here. It could be 10° C by morning."

"I'll buy used clothes if I have to." Usher shivered as he stuck his head under the faucet of running water and dabbed away crusted blood from his cheek and chin. "If I ditch the car, getting around the city will be harder."

"Maybe, but it'll be easier to sneak past any traps on this bike. You can ride in the sidecar but need a heavier coat than your suit jacket." Leo pulled Usher's black down-filled jacket from the trash heap and wiped away some slime with the torn trousers. "This one isn't too badly soiled. Follow me."

"Thanks." Usher plucked the jacket off the stick, slipped his arms into the sleeves, and zipped up the grubby flap. "I don't like being without wheels."

"I have a few Army buddies who can loan you a motorcycle," Leo offered. "Have you ridden one before?"

"I grew up on them," Usher said. "It's my preferred mode of travel. Take me to Vlad. I need to clean up and get to Starbucks by 7 a.m." Usher climbed in his car and followed Leo for nearly three miles, then turned off onto a dirt road that continued into a wooded area.

Leo pulled over and stopped, motioning with his arm for Usher to pull his car under the trees. A tractor-trailer was parked halfway in a barn near a farmhouse about two hundred yards ahead. The lights were off.

Usher scanned the area. "Are you sure this is a safe area to leave my car?"

"I can't think of a better place," Leo said. "This is my uncle's farm. He's away for the week, and I come out here frequently. Hurry. Hop into the sidecar. We have another fifty minutes before reaching Vlad's hideaway. The way back jogs between several routes to avoid roadblocks, and one area is quite risky. We'll have to see what we encounter."

DISTURBING

Sept. 17 – 5:00 a.m. MSK, Moscow, Russia/
Sept. 16 – 10:00 p.m. EDT, Cincinnati, Ohio

It took over an hour for Usher and Leo to get from the airport pub to downtown Moscow, but Leo did an excellent job avoiding any roadblocks until they reached the inner city. He pulled the motorcycle behind a group of trees. "This is the tricky part. I think we'll walk from here. The Ural may draw too much attention." Taking his cell from his pocket, Leo called the vehicle's owner. "We're back. Thanks for your help. I parked the IMZ just below your office. It should be safe there. No guarantees, but hopefully, I won't need it again today."

Usher brushed a hand through his wind-blown hair and climbed from the sidecar. "How much farther?"

"Six blocks to the Kremlin and Red Square," Leo said, "and then to a hidden entrance near Park Zaryadye."

As they entered the city, dawn was on the horizon, but the soaring red brick buildings were still in shadow, framed by the familiar round towers topped with ruby stars. The Kremlin was walled off as usual, but the number of guards had increased tenfold.

Usher had strolled through the most famous area in Russia four years ago. The bright domes of St. Basil's Cathedral bloomed like an ornate stone flower planted in the 16th century. All the principal streets of Moscow radiated from Red Square.

Today, the area had changed. The aroma of gunpowder, stale tobacco, and smoke hung in the air. Streetlights were dark. Rioters had shot out the Windows of the famous Gum building, many lamps adjacent to the Cathedral had also been smashed, and glass shards still lay on the ground below. Soldiers patrolled the area. Temporary five-foot metal grids surrounded the square. Usually, merchants would enter at this hour, but all was quiet.

Leo moved like a fox, darting from one building to the next while staying in the shadows. Usher was shocked by the damage to the park. Military tanks had left a trail of cracked cobblestones and deep gouges rooted up the grass. Several trees, stripped of their leaves, and limbs and branches lay broken on the ground. Aspen lined one park area, and evergreens lined another—low-lying scrubby shrubs nestled between the trees.

Leo used his leather gloves to push aside a thick, prickly shrub to reveal a metal manhole-like cover over the entrance. "There's a bullet hole next to the latch. That wasn't here before." He quickly placed something round, like a key fob, in the upper right corner. A grinding sound came from the door, and something shiny appeared in the top right corner. Leo pressed his thumb to the plate. Nothing happened. "It worked yesterday."

Leo tried again, pushing against the latch with all his might, but it still wouldn't budge. "We better go around to the other entrance."

A flash of bright light nearly blinded the two men. Usher leapt back and lost his balance. The manhole flew open. A metal cord shot out of the gaping hole and snaked around Usher's ankles.

"Wait, it's Usher," Leo said.

Too late, Usher was yanked by his ankles through the hole and down a chute. He landed with a thud at the bottom and stared up at Vlad. "Good morning to you, too."

Vlad knelt beside Usher and released the cord. "Sorry about that, but there was an attack last night, and one can't be too sure, so I set the trap."

Leo slid down the chute. "What was that bright light? I still have spots in front of my eyes."

"A flash grenade," Vlad said. "Perry rigged it to explode when anyone breaches the latch."

"It wasn't breached," Leo said. "I entered the code, and my thumbprint like Ivanhoe showed me."

"That bullet probably damaged the latch." Usher rolled to his feet and got his first real look at Vlad. His cheeks still had a sickly greenish hue. Both orbits were dark purple. One puffy eye stared back at him. The other eye socket was still swollen shut. "The police did a number on you. Your lips are puffy and cracked."

Vlad opened one swollen eye and stared at Usher. "Me? What about you? Your lip is swollen, too, and your eyes will soon be as black as mine were a few days ago."

"You should see the other guys," Usher said.

"We'll need to program an access code for you," Leo said, hunting down the computer and repeating the process Svetlana had programmed for him before leaving for the airport. "I'll need your thumb and fingerprints before this will work."

Usher followed Leo's instructions. "Thanks for bringing me here. We have much to discuss, but first, I must clean up. How far is it to Afimall City?"

"That should take about thirty minutes, but how will we get you there?" Vlad asked.

Leo added, "Afimall's Starbucks is probably open, but I'm not sure today is the best day to go there. You haven't slept all night, and the streets around here are heavily guarded."

Usher nodded. "You may be right, but I'm meeting my partner there at 7 a.m." He ran a hand over his chin and flinched. "I'll call her. It's unwise to bring her here. Where's another safe place for us to meet?"

Leo was on his cell phone, trying to procure a motorcycle for Usher. He glanced up, "This is the safest place. I can pick up your partner, but I'd rather wait until after dark."

"How much sleeping room do you have down here?" Usher asked.

"There are two bedrooms plus an alcove off the lab, a kitchen, and this common area," Vlad said. "I think we could arrange for all our needs, but Leo, our pantry, could use more food."

Usher dialed Zina's cell. It rang four times before she answered in a sleepy tone. "Hello. Who's calling at this hour?"

"Good morning. This is Usher Hastings. Are you safe?"

"Yes. Why wouldn't I be?" Zina snapped.

"So, you can talk without being overheard?"

"Yes, I'm at a friend's house. Alone, in my bedroom, sleeping until you called."

"Good," Usher said. "There's been a change in plans. We're not meeting at Starbucks, after all. I'll pick you and your luggage up at 5:30 this afternoon. So sleep in and enjoy the day. I haven't gotten to bed yet."

"And you're hungry again, right?" Zina said. "I'm not sure I'll be able to meet you at 5:30. I have dinner plans with my friends."

"Break the plans," Usher said. "We have work to do."

"Somehow, I knew you were going to say that." She blew out a deep breath. "Guess we'll go out to lunch instead. Where should I meet you at 5:30?"

"That depends," Usher said. "Where are you now?"

"Oh, no! That information is strictly off-limits, and I'm not having you storming over here on a whim. This is my secret hideaway. I'll meet you in front of St. Basil's Cathedral."

"That place is huge," Usher said. "Meet me in front of the Monument of Minin and Pozharsky."

"I know the place," Zina said. "Now, let me sleep."

"Be careful," Usher said. "There are guards all over the square. I'll be watching, and if the square has a curfew or is closed, I'll set up another meeting place. By the way, bring your luggage. We are on the move, and I have another safe hideaway where you can also meet Vlad, and we can make plans—"

Zina disconnected the call before he could add, "to track down Risingsickle."

Usher stifled a yawn. "Does this place have a shower?"

"Yes, and a washing machine," Vlad said. "I think those clothes could put it to good use. Leo will get us some breakfast, and I'll find some clean clothes for you, although you're about eight inches taller than me. How about Perry's robe? After your shower, we can eat, and you can catch a nap."

"Sounds good to me." Usher followed Vlad down the hallway past a small alcove with a washer, dryer, and a bathroom just beyond.

Leo called out, "I'm going out the other door. Be back with coffee and whatever else I can dredge up in fifteen minutes."

Usher called Braun for a brief update. The men discussed what they knew about the Journalist, his deadly attacks on high-profile foreign leaders, and smuggling of uranium to Iran, but they still didn't know his name.

Leo returned with three bags filled with groceries, placed them on the counter, and then left to find a motorcycle for Usher. Ten minutes later, he returned for a breakfast of fried eggs and warm bread, which hit the spot. Usher removed the chip from his agent's phone and tried replicating it but failed. "I'll send this to Cordy and see if she can retrieve anything."

"By the way, I'm going to get you a new phone to replace the cracked one," Vlad said. "I did see a few contacts pop up on the screen. To be safe, you might want to save that information."

"Most of that data is also on my backup drive," Usher said. "Has Perry made any progress on travel plans?"

"I'll check in with him while you sleep," Vlad said.

"Thanks," Usher dabbed the last of his eggs with his remaining toast. "I've been on the go for days. Give me four hours."

An hour later, Usher lay on a foam mattress in a small, windowless alcove by the lab, exhausted, yet his mind refused to quiet. Thoughts of Zina kept floating to the surface. It was absolutely absurd. Acting like a lovesick adolescent, the woman mystified him even though she could barely tolerate his presence. To think he'd been vain enough to believe his charm could disarm any female.

Well, Zina had put that little lie to rest. She left him to fend for himself with a simple wave of her wrist. *Who is this Gustav? A lover, or just a friend, as she claimed.* Usher was unashamedly jealous of the man. Wait, didn't she say that he was a reverend? Still, this was a strange feeling, and it irritated him.

He adjusted an ice pack over his swollen eye. The purple line beneath it promised to blossom into a full-blown shiner by nightfall. He ached all over.

LIMITED FREEDOM

Sept. 17 – 6:30 a.m. MSK, Moscow, Russia/
Sept. 16 – 11:30 p.m. EDT, Cincinnati, Ohio

Alyosha Krackovitz, nicknamed Cracker, counted the days he'd been a free man—sixty-six days, eight hours, and thirty-seven minutes, to be exact, from the time after his KP Duty at Attica Prison ended. That's when he and Floyd Wecholtz officially climbed out of the trash cans mistakenly wheeled to the curb.

The prison went dark during lights out, and the two men never looked back. Floyd Wecholtz went his way, and Cracker flew back home to Moscow to his attractive wife, Rozalina. He loved running his fingers through her silky blonde hair, amazed by her unlined skin and sturdy body, even though she had given him two children that he never knew he had: nine-and-a-half-year-old twins, a boy named Yosha, and a girl named Regina.

Yosha sat on his lap, reading a book. Regina was creating computer code for a Sphero robotic ball, making it roll across the floor on its own. He savored every minute, knowing how precious each one was. *I'm never going back—at least not willingly.*

Rozalina sprang to her feet when her phone rang. She checked the caller ID. "It's Manny." She scooted away from the kitchen table to talk privately, but Cracker followed her into the bedroom. She gasped, "Yes, that patient was my husband. How did the FBI agent find out?"

"This is about me, isn't it?" Cracker said. "Put the call on speaker. I want to know what's going on."

"Cracker is standing next to me." Rozalina hit the speaker button. "I'm including him on this call."

"Welcome home, Cracker," Manny said. "I have some bad news. Some woman, an FBI agent, left here a few minutes ago. Wait, I've got her name right here. She says she knows you aren't dead and buried. She tracked down the mortuary and says she put two and two together when she realized your Russian Orthodox religion forbids cremation."

"I don't understand," Rozalina said. "She was heading back to England when last we spoke."

"She missed her flight but made some connection with another American, Agent Hastings. He refused to let her leave for some reason, but I'm unsure what they are doing. Nosy Americans. She figured it all out, and now I am not safe either. Why didn't you fill me in on your mission, Rozalina? I might have been more prepared."

"I'm sorry, Manny," Rozalina said, "but I tried to keep you safe. I didn't mean for it to backfire on you."

"At least I know that Russia wouldn't extradite me to America, but the FBI could just as easily have me killed along with you and Cracker. Maybe I am on some hit list from here, too. I know it wasn't your fault, Rozalina, but you must get these people off my back."

"So, how did Agent Zina find you?" Rozalina asked.

"It was only by accident that the FBI agent discovered my part in the rescue mission yesterday. Zina's staying with Nancy, who is my nurse. They were having breakfast together today. Nancy mentioned how hectic yesterday had become with all the riot victims and that she was working on her own. When the agent asked, 'Why?' Nancy told her, 'because the doctor she worked with was on an emergency run to the airport.' The agent put two and two together. That's when she came to see me."

"Does the agent know about Rozalina?" Cracker asked.

"I didn't mention her by name, but the agent saw all of us at the airport during the rescue, and she took a photo on her cell phone,"

Manny said. "I'm worried because the agent said Cracker broke out of prison. Is that true? Were you convicted of murder?"

"Yes, I was falsely accused of murder, but I didn't do it. I know who did murder FBI Agent Yates, and I can prove it as soon as I track down the culprit."

"You may not get the chance," Manny said. "I don't know how much longer before they find you."

"I'm never going to run again," Cracker vowed. "I'm in Russia, and I'll be damned if I ever go back to the United States. This is my home, and no one will deport me."

Manny sighed. "These are dangerous times, my friend. The whole country has changed since you left. All hell is breaking loose around us. We don't know who is in charge or who to trust. The police are corrupt. The few that aren't are outliers being shot in the back by their comrades."

"How do I reach this Agent?" Cracker said. "I have the information she wants; maybe I can trade it for our safety."

"No," Rozalina grabbed his arm. "They'll take you away. I'll never see you alive again."

"From what Manny says, I'm better off dealing with the FBI than facing the Journalist on my own. He'll sell me to the old KGB members I've been hunting down for years."

Cracker grabbed the cell phone. "Thanks, Manny, for the warning. Give Agent Zina McLoughlin a message to meet me at midnight at the American Embassy. I'll be alone."

"No, you won't!" Rozalina's voice shook. "You said you'd cut a deal with the FBI the last time before going to the U.S., and look where that got you. I'm coming along."

Cracker glared at his wife, wondering when she got so spunky. She never used to speak to him with such authority. "I'll be alone!" he disconnected the phone call. "Get me everything you have on the Journalist."

"His name is General Surko Okueva." Rozalina dashed to the small office off her bedroom and returned with a thick file folder.

"I've been researching him for years, running into tight-lipped bureaucracy, hitting dead ends, closed security files, and classified documents that disappeared as soon as I chased one down. Then I got a break. Okueva has several hiding places, but I tracked him down once in a resort town near the Czech border. Last year, he moved to a small flat in an unnamed passage off the Khamovniki district here in Moscow. I know it's a front. There's no such address, but I found a recent photo."

She thumbed through the file and then pulled out a glossy print. "Okueva has changed his looks completely. See, without a uniform, he looks just like any other man, and now his blond hair is no longer short, but he has curly black locks down to his shoulders. He must be dying his hair. Even his beard and a droopy mustache are much darker than two years ago. You still can see the scar over his right eye."

"Do you think he's hiding in the same district?" Cracker asked.

Rozalina shrugged. "Hard to say. Let's research this some more. I haven't checked his whereabouts since I heard you were heading home."

"It would be wise to gather all these facts before meeting with Zina." Cracker followed Rozalina into the office. "Wish we had more than one computer. Do you still have my old desktop?"

"It's over ten years old and outdated," Rozalina said. "Use mine. My cell phone can do as much as that old computer. I want to check out the darknet. That's where I get most of my information."

CRACKING CODE

Back in Ohio, Cordy, Braun, and Svetlana went downstairs for a hearty breakfast and then returned to the hotel room. Cordy opened her laptop and downloaded the latest analysis of Kildeer's thumb drives.

Braun sat next to her, reading text messages from the president's team on his cell phone.

Svetlana tapped on her computer keyboard to place an urgent call. The message pinged. "Perry must be midair. The call won't go through."

Cordy glanced at the computer. "Tell him to call back on a secure line."

While they waited for Perry's call, Svetlana tapped Cordy's shoulder. "I don't know much about Kildeer's code. If you can, would you tell me about it?"

Cordy shook her head. "Let's not talk about that code. Let's talk about Perry's. Can you even comprehend the damage his virus has done? New York is still under attack. It brought down power grids, oil and gas companies, and that's only the beginning. The nuclear plants' backup systems have failed, and the energy companies fear a meltdown of the nuclear core. If they explode, it will expose everyone within a five-mile radius to toxic materials. More if there are severe winds. We have contaminated water treatment plants, emergency communication systems are down, security, airport infrastructures, and healthcare systems also have been compromised."

Svetlana's eyes widened as Cordy continued to speak. Svetlana lowered her head. "You're right. I had no idea, but Perry's code couldn't have caused all that damage. It was only to interrupt utility services. And if he'd left my code in place, it would have been for a limited time only. What you're talking about is far worse, and the deadly 5th Dimension virus on top of that. I feel awful about this, and Perry and I will do everything possible to reverse the code. Please, trust me. I believe we can help."

"I'm not sure what to think," Cordy snapped in irritation. "This is a bigger crisis than the both of us. I'm throwing everything I have at it—running a complete forensic analysis on everything on Kildeer's thumb drives. The whole security team is backlogged, and we're also checking for other spies who are stealing and selling U.S. secrets." She hesitated and glared at Svetlana for a response.

Svetlana bit her lip. "Did you download Aqib's computer?"

"Yes, and I was lucky! I barely got it copied before someone wiped the hard drive clean!"

Svetlana flinched at the comment and blushed. She refused to make eye contact.

Cordy pointed at her. "It was you, wasn't it?"

Svetlana hesitated, and her eyes glistened with tears. "I didn't want to tell you because I thought you might arrest me, and I didn't want to get Perry into more trouble. Are you planning on putting us in prison?"

"Not at the moment, but I might consider that option in the future."

"In my defense, I didn't know what was on his computer, but Papa was worried that Aqib's programs would be linked back to him." Svetlana swallowed hard. "That scared me, too."

"Did you just erase the whole computer?" Cordy asked.

Svetlana gasped and placed her left hand across her mouth as if she just remembered something important. "Yes, I did." Then she stared at the floor and admitted, "I examined a few of Aqib's programs before deleting them, and I ran across suspicious code written by two students. I think they were living in Kansas. Did your analysis system track them down?"

Cordy ran through several pages of highlighted source code. "Portions of analyzed data have been quarantined, but nothing regarding students pops out at me. Show me where you found their data."

Svetlana moved closer to Cordy's computer. "I think I can replicate my earlier actions."

"Wait! No typing on any of my accounts. I can't compromise my findings, but explain every step you took."

"I understand you still don't trust me, so I'll do one better," Svetlana said as she grabbed her laptop and opened a blank text editor page. Her fingers tapped away at her keyboard as she talked. "I believe sponsors from Syria, Russia, and elsewhere paid for the students' education. A bank account was attached to the file that also provided students' college grades, but that's not what caught my eye. They hacked your defense system, and I found a few viruses. One was a worm."

"We must find that code immediately." Cordy's fingers raced frantically to initiate a search. "So, a student managed to breach the U.S. national defense systems, and another introduced a worm, right? This is a serious breach that demands our prompt attention."

Svetlana nodded, "but I didn't take the time to check where he planned to plant it."

"It may explain some of the inconsistencies my analysis is showing, and we can prevent further damage." Cordy's message alert flashed on her cell, and she stood to move away from Svetlana for privacy.

Quint left a detailed text. "Wolf Creek Nuclear Plant in Burlington, Kansas, has been tampered with, but your system quarantined Trojan malware in time to prevent an explosion. We don't know where else this may have gone, but I know that Perry, Kildeer, or whoever created the 5th Dimension didn't write this code—totally different programming styles. I'm launching a more extensive search nationwide. We need additional help now. Do you trust Svetlana?"

Torn between trust and fear of betrayal, Cordy paced as she weighed her options.

Braun stepped into her space and nodded. "Give her a chance."

Cordy wondered how much to share. She glanced over at Svetlana.

Tears pooled in the girl's eyes. "I hope you can trust me. I do want to help." She swiped a sleeve over her face and took over pacing around the room.

Cordy tilted her head and studied Svetlana. "There's something else you haven't told us."

Svetlana paused and then sat heavily into a chair. "I'm afraid for Papa. His life is in danger, and he must leave Russia—sooner, the better. Just before I left Moscow, there was rioting in the streets. Papa's boss, General Urk, was murdered, and all our lives are in danger, but Papa is second in command. I don't know what to do or how to rescue him. I beg you to help me, and the only way I can ask you is to prove that you can trust me. I'll do anything!"

Cordy took a deep breath and stared at Quint's message. "Okay, maybe you can help. I believe you may have uncovered something important regarding the students. Does the code name Risingsickle mean anything to you?"

Svetlana gasped and covered her mouth.

Obviously, the kid knows something. Cordy wanted to question the girl as frightened as she looked. *If it's her father, will she tell the truth? Or maybe it's General Urk. Let's see how she responds.* "By your reaction, you know who that is. Tell me what you know!"

Svetlana trembled as shock gripped her. She sat like a statue, unable to answer any more questions.

Cordy stared at Svetlana until Braun interrupted. "What are you trying to hide? If you know Risingsickle—"

Svetlana jolted. "I'm not hiding anything!" Her voice shook. "Risingsickle is General Surko Okueva's code name. Okueva is Papa's nemesis!" She crossed her arms protectively across her chest as if trying to shrink. "He killed Ivanhoe and Mama." A tear splashed when she blinked.

For a moment, Cordy saw Svetlana as a scared kid.

"Papa hates Okueva. He's been hunting that ugly Chechen commander down for three years. Every time Papa gets close, the man disappears."

Cordy turned to Braun. "Have you heard of General Okueva?"

Braun shook his head. "No, only Risingsickle and we have no proof except Svetlana's word. I lean toward believing her, but President Harris needs sound evidence. You don't have much to go on so far, but there must be a trace of him somewhere."

Svetlana clasped her hands around her middle and rocked slightly in the chair. "I may never be able to go home again. How am I going to get Papa out of Russia?" She bit her lip. "I need to call him right away." She stood and turned toward Cordy, and as an afterthought, she added, "If Okueva's team hacked into the U.S. defense system, your whole nation is at risk. He's dangerous, Cordy. Papa wasn't able to stop their cyber attacks on three occasions. It was like their malware code self-destructed after implementation."

That sounds exactly like the 5th Dimension Virus. Cordy felt her blood pressure rise with the fear of one more urgent threat she must deal with immediately. For a moment, she was afraid she couldn't handle it. She typed, frantically researching her programs for General Okueva.

Svetlana's computer chirped. "It's Perry." She waited until Cordy nodded and connected the call to the speaker. "Hello."

"Ivanhoe, where are you?" Perry asked.

"Ohio." She turned to Cordy. "I want to talk to him alone for a moment."

Cordy stopped tapping on her computer and glared at the girl. "No, I'm not leaving this room! I'm responsible for both of you, and if you have to say anything to Perry, you will say it in front of me."

"Perry, hold for a moment." Svetlana took the call off speaker, cutting Perry off mid-sentence.

Svetlana slipped back into Russian and mumbled a few words. "Да, наставник."

Braun smiled. "Too bad Cordy didn't understand that."

Cordy turned her head toward Braun. "What did she say?"

"She thinks you'd be a great mentor," Braun chuckled.

"I don't believe that's what she said for one moment," Cordy huffed.

He glanced at Svetlana, then back to Cordy, and laughed. "Something like that, but I wouldn't worry about it."

Svetlana snapped her head up, and she told Cordy, "Sorry. I didn't mean to offend you. It just slipped out. I said, 'Yes, teacher.' But you would make a good mentor."

Cordy narrowed her eyes, but inside, she was impressed that Svetlana felt comfortable enough to admit her feelings. "Let's make it perfectly clear. From here on out, we have no secrets. You got that? And speaking in Russian so I can't understand won't build bridges to our relationship."

"Right, no secrets. No Russian." Svetlana agreed. "I want to tell Perry about the latest update from Quint," Svetlana hesitated, "if that's okay with you."

"Let me think." Cordy crossed her arms over her chest. "I'm not leaving this room." Annoyed and frightened by the enormity of everything happening, she wanted to scream.

Svetlana took a step back. Her eyes were wide with apprehension.

Cordy was surprised at how snappish she had become and pursed her lips. She wasn't sure if she could trust either Svetlana or Perry. *Perhaps this would be a good test.* "We'll tell Perry together and get his input."

"Fair enough." Svetlana hit the speaker button. "Perry, Cordy, and Braun are here with me."

"I thought I heard voices in the background. I'm glad you found Ivanhoe."

"More like Svetlana," Braun was still chuckling.

"Oh, they know then," Perry said. "That's a relief."

Cordy typed something into her computer, set the record button, and then locked it down while Braun spoke to Perry. Taking a deep breath, Cordy slowly exhaled and joined the conversation. "Did you have any trouble getting out of Singapore?"

"No, everything is going as planned." Perry sounded relieved. "Thank you for your help."

"Perry, I have so much to tell you." Svetlana bubbled over, then paused, and glanced up at Cordy, who again nodded approval. Svetlana went on, "We found more hackers trying to access U.S.'s national security, and I think they are linked to Risingsickle. You know what that means."

"Yes. The Journalist is at it again. Cordy needs our immediate help," Perry warned. "I'm working on an entrapment code as we speak. We must work fast to prevent any further damage."

Braun's cell phone rang. "It's Usher. I need to get this." He answered the phone and headed to the hallway to take the call.

Perry said, "I have some bad news, too. Vlad had a visitor a few hours ago…"

Cordy dashed after Braun and poked her head out the door. "Tell him the Journalist is General Surko Okueva. That's who he needs to track down, and if Usher can find Cracker, he may know more about the general. Also, I need to talk to Homeland Security. If Guy is nearby, let me know when he's on the line, then come and get me."

Braun nodded and moved farther down the hall to continue the call.

When Cordy returned to the room, Svetlana sat on the bed with her legs tucked under her body. She cradled her computer, sobbed, and rocked silently. Tears streamed down her cheeks. "Are you sure it was Papa?"

Perry spoke softly, remorse in his voice. "I hate breaking this news to you. I wanted to be with you when you heard it."

"Who told you about Papa's death?" Svetlana asked.

"Your neighbor, Boris, visited Vlad in his hideaway." Perry's voice shook as he spoke. "Boris just got back from Ukraine after hunting down Denys Evanko. They successfully wiped out Denys and his guards—probably six to ten men."

"Papa led the raid on Denys Evanko, right?" Svetlana asked.

Perry confirmed her suspicion. "Yes. Boris and two other men flew to Ukraine with Anton."

"How did Papa die?"

"Boris mentioned one of Denys' men shot him," Perry's voice cracked.

The death of Svetlana's father loomed large in the room. Cordy's heart went out to the girl. She sat on the side of the bed and tentatively put her hand on Svetlana's shoulder. Shocked at the girl's bony arms, Cordy realized she was only an undeveloped teen carrying adult responsibilities and secrets for a long time. "I'm sorry." She knew what it felt like to lose her father.

Svetlana leaned toward Cordy like a frightened child. "If only I had been there, I could have prevented his death. They didn't need to go after Denys."

Cordy recalled that Svetlana's mother and brother died three years ago. Now, Svetlana was an orphan. Unable to resist, she wrapped her arms around the girl. Svetlana released her computer and returned a brief hug.

Perry cleared his throat. "At least you're not alone, and I'll be there soon. Boris is willing to care for Ivanhoe, but he says he's never been a father and isn't sure if the boy will return to Russia safely. I guess he doesn't know about you, Svetlana. He only mentioned Ivanhoe."

Cordy drew Svetlana closer. "What can I do to help?"

"Just let me stay here another moment as I think this through."

Cordy nodded. "I'm glad you're safe."

"Am I safe here?" Svetlana's voice was barely a whisper. Her hands clasped together so tightly that her knuckles turned white. "Americans don't like Russians."

Cordy gazed into her eyes and said in a firm voice. "That's not true, and yes, you are safe with us. You can trust me to keep you out of harm's way, and we'll figure out the rest as we go."

"If we can get this cyberattack under control, we'll both be more secure in America than in Russia," Perry said. "When you left, Moscow was in the middle of a riot. It only got worse. The Kremlin declared a national emergency. The president sent in the military to squelch the violence. Many protesters were shot on sight—over 100 fatalities so far. Others are being deported back to Ukraine under threat they will be shot if any return to Russia."

"Is Vlad safe?" Svetlana asked Perry.

"Vlad is still in hiding."

Svetlana peered up at Cordy. "Are you and Braun going to send agents to get Vlad out of the country?"

"I'm not sure what we can do for him," Cordy said. "We'll need to talk to Usher and President Harris."

Svetlana hugged Cordy. "Braun's on the phone with Usher. Can you go ask him?"

"I'll see what we can do after our call," Cordy released Svetlana. "Remember, I'm here if you need me, but we still have a lot of work to do to turn around this crisis. Perry, we look forward to seeing you soon."

Perry tried to console Svetlana. "Your father died a hero."

"But what am I supposed to do now?" Svetlana asked. "I can't go back home. There's nothing there for me. I have no money, no home, and no family."

"Your Aunt Inga will take you in," Perry suggested.

"That's another concern," Svetlana said. "My aunt made all her money working for Papa. I won't burden my aunt and don't know how to earn more money. I can't think about this right now. When will you arrive in Ohio?"

"My plane lands in three hours. We'll talk more about this then. I hope to finish the entrapment code by the time I land. I want it to capture hacks throughout any coding system. Remember, I'm flying under the name Rof Runyard."

Svetlana asked Cordy, "May I go along to the airport?"

"Absolutely, we'd love to have you," Cordy said. "Perry, we'll meet you as you leave baggage claim."

"Can't wait. Until then," Perry disconnected the call.

Cordy was sitting next to Svetlana when Braun knocked on the door. He poked his head in the doorway. "Guy from Homeland Security says he'll talk with you as soon as he updates President Harris and his security team."

"I'll go freshen up a bit." Svetlana went into the bathroom and closed the door.

Braun entered the room, a set of earphones connected to his cell phone. He removed one earbud and handed it to Cordy. "You can say hello to Usher while you wait."

She placed it in time to hear Usher say, "Harris spoke to the Russian president a few moments ago. Things are still chaotic in Moscow."

Braun said, "News is that Cracker died. We're closing out the file."

"Wait. Put a hold on closing his case. He's alive," Usher said. "I plan to track down Cracker as soon as I get some rest, and now that I know the Journalist is Okueva, I hope he'll help us capture the general. I want to find out more details on Agent Yates death. That's why I'm in Russia."

Braun asked, "Guy, are you on the line? I have Cordy waiting to talk to you."

"I'm here." Guy seemed out of breath. "What's up, Cordy? You needed to speak with me?"

"Do you or anyone in Homeland Security know General Surko Okueva?"

Guy gasped, "Have you heard from him?"

"Not me directly, but Svetlana says he's Risingsickle, her father's nemesis. She says that Okueva is a murdering tyrant who killed her mother and brother three years ago. It appears he now has his grubby fingers on students here in America, paying them to hack into our security systems. We need to stop this immediately." They discussed the need for expanded security services, research, and forensic analysis.

Guy said, "I know you work closely with the National Security Agency and the U.S. Cyber Command."

"Yes, and our teams at Solar Winds, Symantec, and CrowdStrike," Cordy added. "I need all the help we can get, and Svetlana just heard from Perry that her father was murdered. These teenagers will also need our support."

"Acting President Harris is calling another meeting after speaking to NATO. I'll update the team." Guy paused, "Hold on a moment. Carl needs to talk to you."

Carl from DoD mentioned, "I overheard your conversation with Guy. General Surko Okueva has been on our radar for years. The FBI also calls him the Journalist. Finding out that Risingsickle is his codename was a missing link we've been searching for. Good job. He's extremely dangerous, Cordy. If he's involved with hacking into our security software, we need to prepare the nation for another major attack. Be careful, and keep me informed of everything you discover—"

Usher interrupted, "If he's in Russia, I'll track him down."

"That is exactly what President Harris will expect," Guy admitted. "Cordy, fill Usher in on everything you know about Okueva. I'll tell President Harris of your news, and I'm sure he'll want to talk to both of you directly. Will you be available for a phone conference in the next hour?"

Cordy glanced up at Braun. "What about Perry?"

"You stay here and be on that conference call," Braun reassured her. "Svetlana and I will pick up Perry."

"Yes, I'm available," Cordy said to Guy.

"What about you, Usher?"

"I'll keep you posted by text," Usher said.

"Will do," Guy said. "What do you have to report, Cordy?"

"I'll pull the latest software analysis update to share with the team and return you to Braun. I need to check on Svetlana."

Braun stayed on the line for more details. "Take care, Usher. If I know you, you'll try to do this on your own. Be sure to partner up with Agent Reed."

"Reed flew back to the U.S., so I'm partnering with Officer Zina McLaughlin," Usher said. "I need to sign off now. Vlad's waiting to update me."

Cordy knocked on the bathroom door. "Are you okay?"

Svetlana blew her nose. "I think so."

"You can come out now. I'm off the phone."

Svetlana stepped into the room. She had taken the rubber band from her hair, washed her face, and touched up her mascara, but her eyes were still red and teary. "Thanks for helping bring Perry to the U.S. and not arresting me or sending me back home. I'm afraid I don't have enough money to support myself for long, and if I do go back to Russia, I probably will be arrested. You don't know how much I appreciate all of your help."

Braun disconnected his phone call. "We better head to the airport."

Cordy was already on the hotel's phone, contacting the concierge. "I need a conference room for the rest of today and tomorrow." She paused and added, "Yes, I'll meet you in three minutes."

Braun asked, "Ready, Svetlana?"

"I can't wait to see Perry again." Svetlana ran to the mirror for a quick inspection. She applied lipstick and stepped to the door. "Ready."

"It sounds like we'll be working long hours together," Braun said. "This will give us a chance to know each other better."

They all took the elevator to the ground floor and split ways. Braun and Svetlana went to the parking garage while Cordy headed for the Conference Center. Cordy's mind raced through a list of all the people she must contact and how to get the equipment she needed to work throughout the night.

Cordy took her responsibilities seriously, but having Svetlana and Perry assist her now could cost her career, especially since they had a hand in the destruction. Trust had to be earned. Svetlana seemed sincere, and Perry's life really was in danger back in his home country. Cordy felt like she was sitting on a ticking time bomb, but what if they could be proactive in preventing another crisis elsewhere in the nation? It was better to know where the two Russians were and what they were doing than to put these young ones in jail or, worse yet, return them to Russia, where they might be tortured and killed.

She wasn't sure what to expect on her phone conference with the president's team, but Cordy was sure her country's future depended on what she did over the next twenty-four hours. The thought was overwhelming.

VLAD'S NEWS

Sept. 17 – 3:30 p.m. MSK, Moscow, Russia/
8:30 a.m. EDT, Cincinnati, Ohio

Another rainy day in Moscow, and it was after 3 p.m. when Vlad roused Usher. "Get dressed. We've tracked down Cracker."

"As I thought, he's not dead." Usher pulled the sheet around him and stood at the side of the cot. "He must have had a lot of inside help to get by our folks. How did you find him?"

"I didn't find him." Vlad stared at the floor. "Promise you won't get angry with me. You left your cell phone on the dryer after speaking to Braun. I heard it ringing when I transferred your clothes from the washer. At first, I ignored the phone, but after the third call in fifteen minutes, I thought it might be important, so I answered. It was Agent Zina. She tracked down Cracker."

"Alone? Where is he now?" Usher was impressed with Zina's skills but not at all thrilled with her foolhardy approach to working alone. She should be working with other agents. She should be working with him. He would see to it before she put all their work at risk. "Give me my phone," he grumbled. "How long ago did she call?"

"Two hours ago," Vlad said, "not long after you finally got to sleep."

Usher ducked his head to clear the doorway, stormed out of the bedroom, and down the hall to the dryer. "Why didn't you wake me? She could be in danger."

"No, she's fine," Vlad said. "Leo is on his way to bring her here. And, for your information, I did try to wake you, but you were sound asleep. I thought it was important for you to recover before going out. It would be best to be well-rested before you meet Cracker at the American Embassy tonight at midnight. She has all the details and will be here shortly."

Leo called out from the back entrance, "We're finally here. The streets are still under heavy patrol, and going out after curfew will be dangerous. This will need to be well-planned before we leave tonight. I'll put on some coffee while you show Zina to her room."

"No java for me," Zina said. "I need tea and plenty of it. I must be alert for this almighty case that dragged me thousands of miles away from home. Where's Usher? Is he still sleeping?"

Usher grabbed his clothes from the dryer and darted into the bathroom. A few minutes later, the toilet flushed, and he opened the bathroom door. "I'm awake." He padded into the hallway in bare feet. His shirt was unbuttoned, and his slacks were wrinkled, but he was dressed. For the first time in his life, he worried about his appearance, dressed in freshly laundered apparel, his only remaining clothes, and his presentation to Zina.

She stared at him. "What happened to you?"

"I had a little run-in at the pub after you left," Usher said, pleased that she expressed any interest in him at all. "You should see the other guys."

"Guys?" she asked. "You were attacked by more than one?"

"Four to be exact, but they didn't get away with more than my itinerary, which I've already trashed, so they won't know where to find me. I'm glad I sent the files with you. Let's get down to business. We haven't much time. How did you track down Cracker?"

"Let me show her around before we get into that and then make plans for tonight," Vlad said.

"Fine, I'll check in with Cordy while you do that. She may have more information on Okueva." Usher speed-dialed his sister-in-law. The line was busy, so he left a message.

Zina filled the team in on Cracker's terms for their meeting.

Usher then called President Harris. "We've tracked down Cracker in Moscow, but there's a hitch. Cracker wants a full pardon, or he won't work with us to capture Okueva. He did give us some vital information. Perhaps we can use it as bait."

EMERGENCY TEAM MEETING

Sept. 17 – 11:05 a.m. EDT, Cincinnati,
Ohio, and Washington, D.C.

Cordy sprinted back to her room at the Regency Hotel in Cincinnati, Ohio, to grab a few files and quickly called her cybersecurity contact. Returning to the conference room in time to join Acting President Harris' team on the phone conference, she explained her discovery of General Surko Okueva's backing of International students and using them to hack into vital networks, including the national defense system and the Pentagon.

The head of the FBI, Loran Sloan, gave background data on Okueva. Cordy typed notes as she listened, then she asked, "How did he get the nickname, the Journalist?"

Loran paused. Cordy heard paper shuffling as if he were checking his file. "Okueva wrote articles for an online video channel and declared the Russian Federation a dominant nuclear power during the post-USSR era. The news went viral. Okueva went on to publish his book and became known as the Journalist."

"More like a political activist," Guy cut in. "His name soon became associated with the murders of several high-ranking officials in Europe, China, and the U.S. FBI Agent Crueger Yates, who headed up our investigation of Okueva's Middle Eastern deals, was murdered."

Loran added, "After a lengthy trial, Okueva was found not guilty of murder, and he went underground. We haven't heard much about him until now."

"Do you have a photo of this man?" Cordy asked.

"The file has several New York Times articles about the trial," Loran added. "I'm sure they included several photos. He was in his early forties, clean-shaven with a short military haircut, and stood rigidly as if ready to salute."

"Cordy, since we have you on the phone, give us an update on New York City's status," President Harris said.

Cordy gave a brief rundown of the software forensic analysis but kept it simple, adding, "I called a contact at FEMA. They found the old generator equipment for the R. E. Ginna Nuclear Generating Station and are running Perry's malware repair along with the Cybercrime Detection System before restarting the generator. All systems will go live in twenty-four hours if they pass the inspection. It should provide electricity to 5% of New York's population, which isn't much."

"It's a start, but I'd hoped to reach more people by now," Harris agreed. "What about the Indian Point Energy Center? How extensive is the damage?"

Cordy shook her head. "There's no hope in getting those reactors up anytime soon. We're researching the possibility of restructuring two decommissioned reactors on site as a temporary solution, but it'll be another two weeks before that can go online. In the meantime, the National Guard is installing an expansive fleet of power generators brought over from Connecticut. Solar panels are being erected on each block and are going live as soon as they can be activated. That may cobble together basic lights and power for cooking, but no A/C or heating."

Harris frowned. "Mo wants to cover 80% of the city by the end of the week."

"They're working round the clock," Cordy reassured him. "Water is still being trucked into the city, but the treatment plant discovered the contamination source. They isolated the area and cleaned it up. If all goes well, the plant will go online tomorrow but won't be back to full production for another ten days to two weeks. Even then, residents may need to boil water before consuming it."

Carl from DoD added, "LaGuardia will remain closed until FAA determines safe tower control for take-off and landing. It'll probably be another twenty-four hours."

Cordy leaned closer to her screen and took notes. "Usher is in Russia. His key contact, Vlad, has been compromised during the riots. Is there any way to get him out of the country?"

"I'm leaving that decision up to Usher," President Harris said. "I spoke with him earlier, and I understand he is partnering with Zina McLaughlin. Usher will have a better idea once he can assess the situation, and since he's already in the country, he'll also track down Okueva. Usher left a message for Braun but hasn't heard back from him yet."

"I'll let Braun know when he returns," Cordy said.

"Are there any more questions?" Harris asked.

"Not at the moment. Thanks for the update." Cordy checked her watch. "Braun will be back from the airport shortly with Perry and Svetlana. We'll be in Ohio for another day or two. Keep me informed, and I'll do the same." The call disconnected.

Cordy went back to setting up the conference room. Fortunately, she had a high-powered laptop with a ten-hour battery and two power packs. The hotel furnished a computer with a large-screen TV, and the FBI provided a desktop computer and multi-window screens that allowed her to view several files simultaneously. She set up a password management program using a five-step verification system when accessing government files, which included fingerprints, an iris reading, and three passwords.

Braun's and Svetlana's laptops, and probably Perry's, could also be connected to the screens so everyone could view multiple data, but Cordy made sure she had control of accessibility. Quint and other National Security Agency and Homeland Security members would be available online as needed.

Guy Weimer had permitted the installation of her OptiSnatch detection software on every public service electrical, oil, and gas plant nationwide. Once installed, the program immediately trapped malware from plants throughout the country. That was how Quint discovered the breach at Wolf Creek Nuclear Plant in Burlington, Kansas.

The questionable code had been quarantined, and now it was her team's job to deconstruct the malicious viruses and figure out who was responsible. They would recover and upload working software programs to replace damaged files. Perry's sample code had reversed his original virus, but the 5th Dimension still loomed over them.

Quint called with an update.

"Did you discover more information on Kildeer?" Cordy asked. "I've been working on Okueva."

"Yup," Quint shoved the bridge of his sliding glasses back on his nose. "An MPEG-4 video feed, probably from Kildeer's cell phone, recorded a trip up a mountain to an estate somewhere in Russia—perhaps Okueva's headquarters. Several cars were parked outside, complete with license plate numbers, which I also ran. Several people attended the meeting. General Rutoon and Kildeer were among the attendees. I'll play the highlights."

Cordy's computer turned black, and then a scene fast-forwarded. Inside the house, seven people sat around a table. "That's Kildeer, the second man to the left of Rutoon, who seems to keep his head down, but I still recognize him." She studied each person, memorizing their features. "Is that Okueva at the head of the table? I'm not sure who else is at the meeting."

Quint said, "I ran each of the men's faces through a facial recognition system." A blue screen popped up with "Match ID," and columns of data scrolled across the screen for each man, except one. Kildeer's identity came up, but no further information.

"Denys Evanko," Cordy exclaimed. "That's the man that Svetlana's father tracked down and killed. I've never heard of the other three men." She studied each face again. "Deen P. Fjords' face is always in the shadows, but something about him looks familiar. Wait, that name says Andrew Madeim Edwardo Flinsh-Kedderton. That's AK, the well-known philanthropist that Chief Jackson asked me to research. What is he doing at Okueva's meeting?"

"I'll forward the information to Homeland Security," Quint said.

Cordy moved closer to the screen. "AK's dead, allegedly run down by Floyd Wecholtz, Cracker's cellmate. Let Homeland Security do further research. There may be more to AK's story, but let's go back to Surko Okueva. Usher is trying to track him down, so send me all your data."

"Will do," Quint said. "Okueva left Libya and returned to Moscow, where he still is, according to President Spendorf."

"How can we be sure?" Cordy asked.

"I put out a satellite search," Quint said. "A black SUV that picked up Okueva at the airport two days ago matches one of the cars in the film. A close-up of the license plate confirms the match."

"Thanks, Quint," Cordy said. "I'll send this information on to Usher. Let me know if you find anything else."

"Later, Girlfriend." Quint disconnected the call.

This would be a long night, so she ordered pizza, drinks, and other refreshments. Cordy's cell vibrated. Pulling the phone from her pocket, Braun's ID popped up. "We just arrived, and Rof is checking in," Braun said. "We'll take his luggage to the room. Where are you, or should we meet you in the lobby?"

"I'm in the Bluegrass Room," Cordy said. "It's perfect. The hotel set up two cots in the kitchenette area so we can take turns resting, and refreshments are on the way. I've already met with the president's team, and Usher left you an encrypted message."

"Thanks. We'll be there shortly." Braun disconnected the call.

PERRY ARRIVES

Sept. 17 – 12:40 a.m. EDT, Cincinnati, Ohio

Braun cleared his throat as he entered Cincinnati, Ohio's Hyatt Regency conference room. He carried Perry's backpack over his left shoulder and his computer case on his right.

Svetlana and Perry walked into the room hand-in-hand. They were chatting in Russian but became quiet as soon as Cordy glanced their way.

Svetlana set down her backpack and tugged Perry by the arm. "This is Cordy."

Perry released Svetlana's hand, ran his palm down his pant leg, and stepped forward. "I'm pleased to meet you, Ma'am." His handshake was firm, and his smile genuine. The young man seemed respectful enough.

"Just call me Cordy." Perry didn't look anything like what she had pictured in her mind: a geek with Coke-bottle thick eyeglasses, something like Quint. No, Perry was actually quite handsome. The young man was pale and slender, almost too skinny. His navy blue suit jacket hung loosely over a light blue shirt. The unbuttoned collar revealed a jagged scar from his left ear down his neck. His beige Dockers had been pressed with a crease down each leg. "How was your flight?"

"It went by too fast." Perry's English was impeccable. "I barely had time to compile my research and complete the entrapment program. We finished the code in the car on the way to the hotel. Svetlana was able to help me figure out a few flaws in my logic." He peered over at Svetlana. His broad smile reached his eyes, crinkling the corners.

Cordy noticed Svetlana blush. "We have a lot of work to do. Braun, would you connect Perry and Svetlana's computers to my laptop? Before linking them to the network, I need to scan them on my OptiSnatch program." Cordy did all her research and data analysis on the darknet. It was the most secure platform available, and she had created additional encryption and cyber-trapping programs as filters.

Svetlana dug through her backpack, removed her laptop, and handed it to Braun without hesitation.

Braun set Perry's bags on a table and held out his hand for Perry's computer, which led to a heated conversation. "Of course, you must hand over your laptop. You agreed to help, and we are responsible for your welfare. If anything personal, intimate, or romantic is on your computer, remove it before handing it to Cordy, but she'll find it anyway." Perry glanced over at Svetlana.

Her brow furrowed. "Is there a problem?" Svetlana asked. "I trust Cordy, and you must, too. Our future depends on how much we can help."

"Do they know about your father?" Perry asked.

"Yes," Svetlana said. "And if you're hiding anything, please share it with us."

"Everything?" Perry tensed. His eyes darted between Cordy and Svetlana.

"Papa is dead," Svetlana said. "We will share everything because we have nothing to hide."

"Do they know about The Team?" Perry asked in almost a whisper.

Svetlana flinched. "Papa worked for them, but I don't know exactly what his role entailed."

Perry crossed his arms. "There were seven of us, remember? Oh, that's right. It was Ivanhoe, not you on The Team. I only know six. The seventh member has always remained a secret."

Cordy turned to Braun. "I've never heard of The Team. Have you?"

"No," Braun said. "Who are they?"

Perry bit his upper lip. "General Urk headed up The Team. Svetlana's father, Anton, was second in command. I was only a hacker and peon, Ivanhoe died, and I guess Svetlana was never privy to The Team's business. Our missions were top-secret, and General Urk got orders from the highest government officials. That's where I was ordered to develop the Big V and deliver it to Roland Kildeer."

"You only mentioned four members. Who else was on The Team?" Cordy asked.

"Alyosha Krackovitz, nicknamed Cracker," Perry said.

Cordy's eyes captured Braun's. "The same Cracker you've been tracking? The man who broke out of Attica Prison nearly two months ago? How was he a member of The Team from Attica Prison?"

"Cracker's wife, Rozalina, became the sixth member. She took over after Cracker left Moscow to come to the U.S. in pursuit of the Journalist," Perry said.

Braun was already on his cell phone to Usher when he heard, "Journalist." He spun around and asked, "Cracker was following the Journalist? Was he working for Russia or the U.S. government?"

"No, Cracker was working with an FBI agent, but instead, the Journalist murdered the agent and pinned the crime on Cracker, who was sent to prison for life."

"I'm confused," Cordy said. "Why would Cracker work with the FBI? Did Loran, Guy, or Carl ever mention Cracker?"

Perry dug through his backpack for his computer. "The Journalist is a case officer responsible for handling black operations for Russia. I didn't know the man's real name was Okueva until Svetlana tied him to Risingsickle, but I'm very familiar with the Journalist. I also know of Okueva's reputation, but as I mentioned, I just realized they were the same person. This explains a lot."

"Okueva was buying and selling Plutonium," Braun said. "But you're saying he is also the Journalist. He killed one of our FBI agents and pinned the deed on Cracker. Am I getting this straight?"

Perry nodded. "I believe so."

"I transferred Cracker's case to Usher after Cracker left the country," Braun said.

Perry's eyes narrowed as he watched Braun's reaction, and then he turned to Cordy. "Am I in trouble for mentioning this?"

"No." Cordy asked Braun, "Do you think Cracker is innocent?"

"I don't know," Braun said, "but I will tell Usher what we just learned. He'll want to talk to you, too, Perry."

Braun and Perry moved to the far corner of the room and spoke to Usher while Cordy ran Perry's and Svetlana's computers through her detection system. Usher informed them that Cracker was alive and planned to meet with him around midnight.

While Cordy's program worked in the background, she reviewed Perry's new code. It wasn't as thorough as hers, but it could be customized to analyze source code on single-line edits, looking for consistency within code blocks. This helped to determine individual entry styles. Cordy hoped to narrow the search tight enough to identify individuals.

Perry's second feature was that his software was explicitly written for power plants. Cordy was surprised to learn that he knew so much about the plants. It was evident that he had done a lot of research. She turned toward Perry. "Where did you develop the ideas for your computer program?"

"I studied the Ukraine incident and how they resolved the cyber attack on their power grid," Perry said. "They took the electronic grid totally off the operational network to minimize external hacking. It may seem antiquated, but using old-fashioned analog switches limits anyone from tampering with the device, at least initially, until a more secure system can replace it."

"That's a good idea," Cordy said. "I'll pass the information on to Carl and FEMA. Now, let's track down those student hackers that Svetlana mentioned earlier. I'm sure they created a back door to allow them to enter administrative access as they please, which means Okueva also has access."

"Are these doctoral students?" Perry asked. "That sounds like his MO. He recruits several brilliant young students who want to pursue their education but can't afford the fees. He enrolls them in international universities and pays their enrollment fees, room, and board. In return, the students help him by writing code. They have to write their programs privately on computers with no Internet connectivity. If they don't comply, the student is immediately deported back to their home country."

Svetlana nodded. "The catch is that none of the students know the end product. They are only assigned small tasks to write code. With some fine-tuning, Okueva melds the codes together and creates some of the most deadly computer viruses known so far."

Cordy took a deep breath and added, "So Okueva has access to various companies' operational programs and can insert the viruses whenever or wherever he chooses. The students have no reason for alarm since they have no clue what they've just created."

"That's right," Perry admitted. "I saw this scenario in Russia, Ukraine, and South Africa."

"Do you have any names of students so far?" Perry asked.

"When I wiped Aqib's computer, I found two students in Kansas City," Svetlana said. "The file also included a list of grades for several students and financial records. Cordy has backup data. It's a start."

"In the meantime, I'll search for any data to or from Okueva on Aqib's laptop," Cordy said.

"When I grabbed Aqib's laptop in Syria, I had no idea it held such critical information," Braun said. "It was just a gut reaction."

STRAIGHT A STUDENT

Sept. 17 – 11:52 a.m. CDT, Wichita, Kansas/
12:52 p.m. EDT, Cincinnati, Ohio

Four students in Wichita, Kansas, spent the last nine months at individual computer terminals, each crafting destructive codes capable of disabling any computer program upon system login. Their most recent projects are their deadliest yet, posing a grave threat to our digital world. After almost six months of intense work, they are now gearing up for the testing phase.

The most experienced student was a Russian named Xander, short for Alexander, the same as his father's and grandfather's names. He'd always been a nerd and spent most of his time surfing the net, leading him down the darknet path. Hacking became second nature. The greater the challenge, the more he liked it. Three years earlier, he'd applied for a grant to study IT at an American university and was thrilled to get accepted. He gladly left his small village along the Volga River.

The financier, Mr. Smith, was friendly at first. "We'll cover all your expenses, tuition, room, board, and textbooks. I'll even furnish a new car and a state-of-the-art computer system. You only need ten hours a week to work on a little project. It will be easy with all your expertise."

Xander looked forward to working on the computer. Initially, the projects were no challenge and didn't threaten anyone as far as he could see. Then, Smith increased the workload. Ten hours became twenty. Simple hack jobs became more dangerous. The risk caused deep concern, and Xander finally had enough. "Mr. Smith, I can't maintain straight A's in school and complete your projects, too. I need to cut back my hours."

"No," Smith said. "This project must be finalized in two days. You've been working on it for months, and where will I find someone to pick it up and continue at this point?"

Xander shrugged his shoulders and headed for the door. "Good luck with that."

Smith snapped his fingers.

A heavily armed man with bulging muscles blocked Xander's path. A black, sleeveless T-shirt clung tightly to his chest. Each upper arm displayed a tattoo of a six-sided star with the wheel of eternity inside. The symbol caused Xander to gasp. He recognized the victory sign of an uprising Russian political party. This sun wheel and the swastika share a common origin dating back to 5,000 B.C. The tattoo seemed to pulse as the man's arms flexed. "You'll regret your actions, boy."

"Let him pass," Smith said. "This is just a warning. Go home and study for your final exam, but I expect you here tonight promptly at 10 p.m."

Two hours later, Xander received an urgent message from his father, "A group of four men just hauled away your brother. I don't know who they work for, but they have an odd six-sided star on their arms, and they were all armed. No charges have been made, but we've received death threats, and I'm told it's your fault. What's happening?"

"I'll take care of it, Papa." Xander gathered several papers and notes of the codes he'd written. He stuffed them into a paper sack and hid it under his mattress. Angry, he left the apartment. His hands shook as he locked the door. It was the last time he'd been at his apartment.

HACK ATTACK

Sept. 17 – 2:50 p.m. CDT, Cincinnati, Ohio

From the moment Cordy had first logged into Aqib's computer, even while aboard Air Force One, she knew it held deadly hidden files. Going into his backup made her more aware of the evil that lurked in that data. They were using students to hack into the nation's security systems. Before handing over Aqib's backup files for further review, she reran them through her security analysis, copied the backup, and sent it to three secure sites.

"I'm going to brief my team," Cordy said. "President Harris assigned Braun to another project, so we're on our own. Svetlana, since you're already familiar with Aqib's download, you can use your computer to find the students' files by linking them to this account." She gave her access to one of the backup files she had just created. "Get as many names as possible from the grades and financial data list."

"What should I do?" Perry asked.

"I need you to compile additional data on General Surko Okueva," Cordy said. "He is somehow linked to Aqib. Find any financial data on the man. You can use this computer while my program scans your laptop."

Perry agreed.

Cordy was on the phone to her contact when Svetlana gasped, "Come quick!"

"Not now." Cordy turned and saw the girl's face pale. "Quarantine whatever you're looking at! Sorry, Lucy. Text me when the next generator is up." She disconnected her call.

Perry took over and typed madly on the keyboard. "No, oh, No! I can't trap it!"

Cordy, the lead cybersecurity analyst, nearly collided with Braun as they rushed to Svetlana's laptop. Svetlana was in a state of panic. The screen read: deleted file <filename1>, deleted file <filename2>, deleted file <filename3>, and it continued to roll down the screen, adding the next consecutive number after the filename, deleting file after file on its way into oblivion. "Why didn't my scan catch this?" Cordy exclaimed, her voice trembling with fear.

There was no Break command key on her laptop keyboard. With a few keystrokes, Cordy pressed the Ctrl+Pause keys—nothing. She typed Ctrl+Fn+Pause, then tried Ctrl+Fn+Scroll Lock—again nothing. One of those should have broken the command sequence and stopped deleting files, but Cordy wasn't controlling the computer. Some alien code had taken over, and that backdoor command told the computer to ignore her latest entries. All of the data was being gobbled up by this ravenous computer, byte by byte.

Perry called out, "It's a worm, not a virus."

"Aren't they the same thing?" Svetlana asked. "I thought a worm was a virus."

Cordy was too busy shutting down the computer to answer.

Perry pulled Svetlana aside. "Don't interrupt her," Perry ordered. "This is serious. A virus attaches to a single program, destroying the files within, which is bad enough, but a worm can propagate itself throughout multiple programs. It wiggles and slithers from one program to another and does whatever the command tells it to do, usually deleting the data."

Cordy grabbed her laptop, ran her detection analysis against the backup file Svetlana had been working on, and then went to the code. "Gotcha!" Cordy found the command which read: delete log*.*. Then she read the rest of the hacked code. It appeared clean and well-written, unlike most foreign code with typos or the use of words in the wrong context.

Braun glanced over Cordy's shoulder. "How could this happen?"

"That code was inserted sometime during the last hour after I ran my security scans, but why wasn't it quarantined?" Cordy quickly traced the malware. "It's attached to a rootkit of the New York Stock Exchange! I'm afraid we have an inside hacker trying to take control of the U.S. financial system. It'll be next to impossible to discover how this code got here."

"Fortunately, the Stock Market is still closed," Braun said, "but as soon as the bell rings in the morning, all hell will break loose." He continued to read over Cordy's shoulder. "Oh, check this out." He pointed to the code toward the bottom of the screen. "Amazon, Google, and other key stocks are already primed for selling short. Whoever is set up to buy already knows the market will crash. Who's the primary buyer?"

"My God, it's General Rutoon!" Cordy knew it wasn't possible. "He's been dead for over a month. Could he have set this up that long ago?" Fear jolted through her at the thought.

"Not likely." Braun stepped away to place an urgent call. "Get me, Guy, at Homeland Security ASAP!" Braun lowered his voice and ended the call, "Have him call me at this number. It's urgent."

Cordy took a screenshot of the code and transferred it to another program for a more detailed analysis. "This code was installed two days ago, but something went wrong, and it squeaked by because it wasn't set to launch until only ten minutes ago. Svetlana, you did a great job finding this. It could have wiped out everything! Thank you."

"I didn't do anything," Svetlana said. "It just appeared on the screen."

Cordy had to admit that whoever the hacker was, they knew English quite well. The hacker's code was sophisticated and very similar to her style. So much so that she tapped a few keys. A hidden text popped up behind the code. Her hand flew to her mouth at the sight of the unique code letters she used to sign off every entry she made, *zxjc*. She knew that she hadn't entered that code. There was only one other person who knew her secret—*Quint.* Her gut clenched at the thought. *No, it can't be.* She glanced up at Braun.

"I've seen that look before." Braun smiled. "You think you know who the hacker is, don't you?"

"I sure hope I'm wrong, but in the meantime, we must reverse this immediately." Cordy knew there had to be another explanation. *If not, Quint, someone is trying to frame me. But who? How do they know my secret entry signature? And how is General Rutoon involved in all this? He's dead!*

I'M NOT ALONE

Sept. 17 – 10:00 p.m. MSK, Moscow, Russia/
3:00 p.m. EDT, Cincinnati, Ohio

Cracker studied General Okueva's photos from Rozalina's file. One blurry, black-and-white photo was in the *Moscow Times.* "Rozalina, did you read this article below the general's photo?"

Rozalina stopped typing on her cell phone. "Probably a while ago, what does it say?"

"Police activity has risen seven-fold over the past two months. They routinely change speed signs, set up road-work detours, and make parking restrictions along the riverfront and warehouse districts. I suppose it gives officers an excuse to stop vehicles to search for contraband. Foreigners have gone missing—three girls from Cambodia, two from Ukraine, and an Asian."

"Missing? Or sold into slavery?" Rozalina went back to her search.

"Remember what that mortician said about the police chief?" Cracker asked. "According to the paper, there has been a flurry of raids. Many prisoners vow they're innocent, and they are found dead within days of their arrest. Do you think the police are behind these deaths?"

Rozalina paused and bit her lower lip.

Cracker smiled at the familiar habit. "You don't have to answer that. I was thinking out loud, and it's not our focus for now. I'm going for a stroll. Don't wait up for me."

"But it's already 10 p.m. Where are you going at this hour? You don't meet Agent Zina McLoughlin until midnight."

"I want to check out the area before they arrive, so I have an escape route if needed."

"Let me go with you," Rozalina begged.

"Absolutely not!" Cracker said. "Stay home and take care of our children. I'll be fine. I know what I'm doing."

"Mama can take care of the children," Rozalina said. "They're already asleep, so she won't have to do anything. Surely, you can't go alone."

"I'm not alone," Cracker said. "Your Uncle Albert is taking me."

"Is he staying with you while you meet those agents?" Rozalina asked.

"We'll see."

There was a knock on the door, and Uncle Albert wandered into the room. A bulge over his right hip let her know that he was packing.

"So, you're expecting violence?" Rozalina asked in alarm.

"No, honey." Cracker pulled her into his arms. "Your uncle's a war hero. I'll be safe with him."

She blew out a sigh of frustration. "You better be careful."

"Always." He skimmed a kiss along the line of her jaw, and then crushed her against him. "Wait here for me. I'll be back before sunup, and we'll be together for the rest of our lives." He broke away and bolted for the door. "Coming, Uncle Albert?"

"I'm right behind you."

HAIR-TRIGGER ALERT

Sept. 17 – 11:20 p.m. MSK, Moscow, Russia/
3:20 a.m. EDT, Cincinnati, Ohio

Usher couldn't believe Zina had arranged to meet with Cracker without discussing the operation with him first. *What idiot would allow Cracker to pick the time and place of the meeting? Security might be compromised.* Usher preferred to meet on his terms, assuring tight, fully informed plans to prevent his opponent from gaining unexpected advantages. *Will Zina know what to do? We've never worked together before, and we could be walking into a trap.* "Vlad, how far is it to Russia's American Embassy?"

Vlad pulled up a map and pointed. "It's in Moscow's Presnensky District, about six km from here. It'll take twenty minutes at normal road speed. You'll have to walk beyond Red Square before starting any motorized vehicle. Leo will show you a shortcut."

Leo nodded and sent a message on his phone. "We'll need to backtrack to where we left my friend's IMZ-Ural. That will be the riskiest area, so to minimize our exposure to danger, I'll have my friend bring the motorcycle to our rear entrance to save time. He knows a secret passage. Then we can cut across back alleys to the main highway."

Usher was still worried about Zina. "It would be easier with only two riding the Ural."

Zina stiffened, furrowed her brow, and didn't hesitate. "Okay, then, Leo and I will tell you how tonight went. Stay close to your phone."

Usher scowled. "That isn't what I had in mind. Leo and I make a good team—"

"Not happening!" Zina's finger jabbed his chest every time she said I. "I tracked down Cracker. I made arrangements to meet him and plan to do just that. You and your male chauvinist attitude won't stop me."

Usher opened his mouth to argue, but Zina continued to rant.

"I will bring him in. Do I make myself perfectly clear?" Zina's cheeks flushed in anger. With fists clenched, she began pacing. A pulse beat rapidly in her neck. "I hate it when men think the little woman should stay home and mind the fires, cook, wash, and care for the children."

Usher tried to break the tension. "I didn't know you had any children."

"This is not the time, nor the place to joke around!" Zina got in his face. "You know what I mean, and I won't tolerate it."

Usher still wondered what real experience she had, but he admired her spunk. Zina reminded him of Cordy in so many ways, which made him respect her all the more.

Zina shoved her arms into a black fleece jacket. "We're wasting valuable time. I'm going, and that's final. Come, Leo. Lead the way." Dressed all in black, she pulled up the hood, strode to the rear entrance, and tried to open it. The door didn't budge. "How do you get out of here?"

"One moment," Vlad inserted his code, and the latch clicked as the door unlocked. "Once we have Cracker, where will you take him?"

"First, we'll question him and then confine him until the FBI decides his fate," Usher said before Zina could answer. A rap on the unlocked door startled him.

"That's our cue," Leo lifted his sleeve to check the time. "Synchronize our watches. I have 10:48 p.m."

Usher nodded while Zina reset hers.

Vlad waved. "Set Zina up with a door code and stay safe."

Leo agreed. The door clicked shut behind the team of three, and a slight grating sound followed. Leo entered four digits on the code pad. "Place your thumb over this plate to get back inside."

Zina repeated the drill. The door opened and relocked.

Rough-looking armed men guarded the streets as they headed away from Red Square.

Leo whispered, "I'll walk a few blocks ahead with the Ural. Stay in the shadows, and if approached by the police, tell them you just went out for dinner and are heading to the hotel for the night. They shouldn't bother you."

Before he could move, a rugged man with wavy gray hair briefly paused and glanced their way. Leo shoved Zina back against the brush. "Shh. Stay here and count to fifty. I'll draw his attention away from here and move the Ural over the grass so it won't crunch on the gravel. Usher, you know the way—lead Zina through the back bushes." Leo slipped into the night, cunning as a fox.

Zina counted, "One, two, three, four…Sixteen, seventeen," Zina fumed, turned her back on Usher, and walked a few steps away. "Twenty, twenty-one…"

"Zina, please don't wander. We must work together." Usher grabbed her gently by the arm. "I was here this morning. I know the way, and we don't have time to argue with the police."

"Twenty-six, twenty-seven…" She removed his hand from her arm. "I understand, but don't touch me. Thirty, thirty-one, thirty-two…"

"Roger," Usher snapped to attention. "Don't touch. Got it, but once we get in that Ural, it's going to be crowded, bumpy, and I can't promise—"

"Whatever," she whispered. Leo was nowhere in sight. "Forty-nine, fifty. Okay, where to?"

"Three blocks straight ahead, then turn right. Leo should be waiting at the end of the block." Usher glanced over his shoulder. The coast was clear, so he motioned for her to follow as he sprinted from the back of one building to the next, ensuring he was close to the cement walls. The only light came from the moon. He made his steps carefully so he didn't trip over branches or small shrubs hidden by the darkness, aware that any misstep could be their undoing.

Zina amazed him as she kept up with his long-legged stride. A noise came from off to his right at the corner of the building. Usher paused.

Zina collided with him. "What are we waiting for?"

"Shh." Usher pressed his pointer finger over his lips. "Listen." Muffled voices in the distance grew louder, signaling imminent danger. He had faced enough Russian thugs on this visit. The police were known to strike first and ask questions later. He had to protect Zina at all costs and pulled her to the ground as a shadow appeared in the corner.

A hint of tobacco wafted through the air. A flickering light glowed brighter as the shadow inhaled. Embers fell from the cigarette tip and landed on the ground. The shadow appeared nervous, glancing from one side to the other. He opened a backpack and removed something that caught his eye, a metallic object that glinted in the moonlight. Tucking the object under his arm, he slipped the backpack over one shoulder and limped across the street, followed by a second man. They didn't seem to notice two bodies huddled together behind a shrub.

Usher waited until the men were out of sight, and then stood up for a better view. When nothing happened, he signaled for Zina to move quickly. A wave of relief briefly washed over him, but not for long—the tension ripe with anticipation.

A cloud passed over the moon, plunging the area into total darkness. Usher couldn't see his hand before his face. To his surprise, Zina clung to his arm, her fear distinct in the pitch-black night.

A flash of bright light blinded Usher, followed by a rush of heat and a deafening boom. The earth shook beneath them. Usher threw Zina under him to shield her as dust and cement chunks rained over them.

The bomb's strong odor of stagnant motor oil gagged Zina. Coughing and sputtering, she tried to breathe. "I need air." She moved and then covered her mouth with her hood.

Screams erupted from rooftops while Guards rushed toward the burning buildings across the street. The tall wall had flattened. The view left Usher speechless. Flames spewed skyward and spread quickly from one rooftop to the next. An unquenchable appetite engulfed a proud stand of trees, leaving nothing but smoldering embers.

Usher's eyes burned and blurred with smoke-filled tears. He and Zina were totally visible now, but the guards pushed past them toward the destroyed building. Usher grabbed Zina's trembling hand and pulled her to her wobbly feet. He shielded them with the flap of his jacket. "Let's get out of here!" They retreated as flames licked the night air, growing closer by the second.

Leo appeared out of nowhere. "Quick! Climb aboard."

Usher lifted Zina into the sidecar. Then he hopped in the back of Leo. "Go!"

Leo gunned the engine as police yelled, "Stop!" Bullets flew around them, but Leo zigzagged the Ural between buildings and across the grass, finally reaching the main road. No one spoke until they were two kilometers from the fire.

"That was too close," Zina shouted. "Why'd they blow up the building?"

Leo revved up the Ural "Someone's in deep trouble with the mafia—maybe a warehouse full of drugs or contraband. We should be at the American embassy in five minutes."

Nothing could have been further from the truth.

CRACKER'S BARGAIN

"Can't we go any faster?" Usher shouted over the ruckus created by the explosion outside of Red Square. The Ural tipped to the side, nearly pinning Usher's leg to the gravel.

"Slow down!" Zina yelled from the sidecar, which hovered in the air. "I'm not ready to die!"

"I'm doing the best I can." Leo stood, leaning forward on the handlebars, and pivoted the motorcycle, which landed on all three wheels with a thump.

Mud splattered the vehicle and caught Usher's pant leg. He turned toward Zina. "Did we have to meet at the American Embassy at midnight?"

"Back off, Usher! It's the only time Cracker would meet, and I'm tired of being blamed for everything. At least I tracked the man down while you slept away like a baby. You're lucky I got him to meet with us at all."

Usher muttered under his breath but managed to quell his anger. He was pissed off at himself more than Zina. She could have been killed in that explosion. He'd never forgive himself if she were injured in this fiasco. Silently seething, the trip went well once they were on the open road.

Leo roared into the Embassy lot and parked the Ural. "We made it with two minutes to spare."

Usher hopped off the cycle and offered Zina a hand. She declined and managed to climb out of the sidecar with minimal effort. "Across the street." She motioned for the men to follow and led the way.

When Usher reached the front door, he folded his arms and glared. "Well, Zina. Where is he? Surely, the embassy isn't open at this hour."

Zina peered around and tapped her foot in disgust. "Cracker said to meet outside the building by the front door."

"And that seemed like a logical place to meet?" Usher snapped.

"I agreed because you said 'he was of great interest to your country.' You've come all the way to Russia to bring him back to the States. I thought a meeting would please you no matter where or when. My mistake! You aren't pleased with anything we do. The sooner we finish this meeting, the sooner I can go back home to Dublin."

Usher would have had it out with his partner without hesitation if Zina had been a man. But she was a woman—a supercilious woman who needed to be put in her place. "Agent McLoughlin!" She winced when he used her last name and opened her mouth to speak, but Usher raised his voice and bulldozed forward. "This is not your assignment. You are here to assist me! That means you do as I say in the manner I tell you. And if I tell you not to do something, you will also obey. Do you understand?"

Zina glared and stepped forward. "Oh, yes, I understand perfectly. You are an arrogant fool!"

"That's rich coming from the most arrogant, haughty, overbearing woman I've ever met." Usher backed up. *She must be in shock. Well, what woman wouldn't be after such an explosion?* "Okay, Zina, I'll cut you some slack after that bomb back there."

Zina shook her finger. "Listen, Agent Hastings, don't you dare patronize me—"

Usher eyed her for a few seconds. There was some chip on her shoulder, and he had no clue what caused it. All he needed was for her to work with him for the rest of this assignment. Maybe he'd made the worst mistake of his life by keeping her here against her wishes. Could he even trust her?

"Men!" Zina said under her breath. "We have work to do."

"Guys, maybe you can discuss this another time," Leo warned.

It went unheeded until a short, stocky man dressed in a brown military uniform with numerous military medals covering his left chest walked around the corner of the embassy. "Hello, Leo. It's good to see you again."

Usher assessed the situation. "You know this man?"

Leo saluted. "Yes, we were in the military together. Then, we both joined the Resistance Army."

"Are you two agents working on the same side? It scarcely seems like it." The soldier chuckled and then became serious. "I am Marshal Albert Chernyshevsky, retired from the Russian Federation as one of the highest-ranking commanders in our country, but you can call me Albert. My last name is a mouthful. Which of you is in charge?"

"I am." Usher stepped forward.

"And you are?" Albert asked.

"Agent Usher Hastings of Joint Special Operations Command."

"You're here to see Cracker, right? So that you know, he's under Russian protection and won't be leaving the country."

Zina deliberately stepped in front of Usher. "Cracker talked to me. He promised to meet, and I want to talk to him in person." She glared at Usher. "Alone. I'm here to see that he gets fair treatment from the FBI."

Albert seemed amused. "How can you be such a skeptic when you are both on the same team?"

Usher cleared his throat. "She works for me, and I want to talk to Cracker directly."

"I work *with* him, not *for* him," Zina clarified her position.

Usher flicked his wrist in her direction. "Whatever. Where's Cracker?"

Albert stood ramrod straight as if at attention. "Not going to happen."

"I am here at President Harris' request," Usher asserted. "Now, you and I can play games or work together. Have I made myself clear?"

"Quite clear, but that will be up to Cracker," Albert said, stepping closer to Usher. "He is under my protection. Oh, by the way, you will not meet in person tonight."

Usher moved quickly and was about to strike Albert when Zina stepped in front of him. "Marshal Albert, we wish to treat you with the utmost respect, but there is a limit on how far that respect is maintained."

Usher wasn't going to let Zina have the last word. "I know Cracker is here, and I want to know why he set up this meeting and then refused to meet with us."

Albert stood glaring at Usher.

Usher stepped around Zina. "At some point, you will let us speak to Cracker. The only question is how difficult you want to make this."

Albert pulled up the left sleeve of his coat. Something shiny glinted.

Unsure of Albert's intentions, Usher pushed Zina behind him, but she craned her neck and insisted, "Marshal Albert, I must meet with Cracker."

"No, he will not meet you," Albert insisted, pointing toward the top of the building across the street. "My men surround you, so don't get any ideas."

Usher scanned the area. "They hide well." But he was ready to strike if Albert made one false move.

"Yes, on rooftops." Albert spoke into the object on his wrist, "Dimitri, Larensky, Lukovich, check in."

A flash of light came from the rooftop across the street and on either side of them. Usher reached inside his jacket pocket. "I'm not asking again. I want to talk to Cracker…Now!" Usher placed a hand over his revolver.

"Don't bother with weapons. My men have already moved." Albert spoke once more into his wrist gadget. "Cracker, can you hear me?"

"Yes, Uncle Albert. I'm quite impressed. Even I did not know you had your guards with you."

"That was only my front line," Albert said. "So, these agents are here at your request?"

"Yes, I want to make a deal." Cracker's voice sounded tinny coming from the gadget's speaker, "My freedom for the capture of General Surko Okueva, better known to the FBI as the Journalist."

Usher's stance was poised for action. "How do we know we can trust you?" His eyes narrowed, and he rescanned the area.

"That is a good question." Cracker sounded bitter. "I believed in your organization once and found myself in a supermax prison. My contact Agent Crueger Yates was murdered, but not by me, and I'm not going back to the United States."

"I'm afraid that's not a decision I can make." Usher's inner voice added, *Nor will I make.*

"No, but President Harris can," Cracker said. "I know you have his ear. If you want my help, you must commute my sentence to the time already served. Better yet, I'm innocent. I want a full pardon. The Journalist murdered Yates and framed me. Now, it's time for his punishment."

Usher stepped closer to Albert. "I can't promise—"

"I'm not asking for promises!" Cracker said. "I want my freedom—to live with my wife and family. And I want to hear from President Harris directly—a full pardon or no deal."

"How can I be sure that you're trustworthy?" Usher asked.

"Oh, that's a good one," Cracker cackled. "Trustworthy. Like, I trusted your FBI, and what did it get me? Life in prison. You don't have to trust me, but I must trust you. Is that how you play the game? I've never hurt anyone who didn't deserve it. Never killed anyone who didn't deserve it, and I'm not about to start now."

"How can we be sure?" Zina asked.

"Do you think you can track down Okueva without our help? Think again. What do you really know of this man?"

"He's a military expert," Usher said.

"Yes, one who knows how to use any weapon, including cyberspace," Cracker said. "He sold plutonium to Syria, wiped out New York City's electrical grid, downed planes, nearly blew your president and you out of the sky, and that's just the beginning."

"Cracker is a genius coder," Albert said. "His wife makes a close second. You'll spend years and have nothing to show for your efforts. Okueva's brother is the police chief, so you won't get any help from them. I know this city, Okueva's contacts, and his hiding places. Beware, this isn't about money or politics. He wants the fame and power of knowing that he can do anything, anytime, anywhere, and to anyone."

"You can have the glory of bringing him in, but you need me to find this devil." Cracker said. "He's slippery as an eel and has more disguises than you can imagine. He has moles planted everywhere. I'll hold up my end of the bargain."

Usher pointed out, "You've been out of the country for years—"

"And my wife has been tracking him every minute since I was in prison. I want him more than your FBI. He's destroyed my life. Okueva started this. I'm going to end it!"

"Da, and he'll have my team at his back." Albert beamed with pride. "You can't ask for a stronger lineup. Do we have a deal?"

Usher wasn't sure what to think. "I need to check with President Harris."

"I want this behind me," Cracker said. "How long before you can arrange direct communication?"

Usher hesitated.

"Do you want this guy or not?" Cracker asked. "I plan to move on with my life."

Zina nudged Usher. "You said you have direct access to the president. Do you or don't you? If you're not going to make a move, I'm flying back home on the next flight out of Russia."

"Step out here and meet me face-to-face," Usher said.

"It's not going to happen until I talk to your president," Cracker said. "Many issues are going on behind the scenes that I doubt you're aware of."

"Name one," Usher challenged.

"To begin with, student hacking into your nation's vital systems," Cracker said. "And I have a hunch there is a terrorist cell ready to attack on command."

"Al Qaeda, ISIS, Daesh?" Usher asked. "Where?"

"Probably out of Libya," Cracker said. "I don't know for sure yet, but your country needs my help. Let me talk to your lead security officer. We can work together, or if you don't want to work with me, try to breach Okueva's code on your own."

Usher wouldn't let Cordy get anywhere near this danger, but the more he thought about it, he realized she was already involved. "You better not be making this up to suit your needs."

"Check it out for yourself," Cracker said. "I'd start with General Rutoon."

Usher sneered. "Not likely. He's dead."

"But not fully buried," Cracker warned. "His plans are on the move, and so are Okueva's funds—cashed out a few hours ago. Better make up your mind before it's too late."

"Give me one hour," Usher said. "I'll see what I can do." *But first, I need to have a long chat with Zina. How dare she threaten my authority?*

UNDER THE GUN

Sept. 17 – 4:48 p.m. CDT, Wichita, Kansas/
5:48 p.m. EDT, Cincinnati, Ohio

Back in Wichita, Kansas, Xander's heart raced, sweat dripped from his forehead, and his nerves sizzled at the thought of his brother back home being kidnapped by thugs—*the same gang with the star tattoo as Mr. Bully at Smith's office. It's up to me. If he dies, it's my fault. All because I wanted to keep my straight A average, and I couldn't stop spending my time on these hacked programs.* Xander clenched his fists and burst into Smith's office. "Release my brother. I'll do whatever you ask, but leave my family alone."

There was a ruckus outside of Smith's office door. The burly man with the tattoos marched behind three blindfolded young men. They were in leg chains and shuffled their way into the office. "I've rounded up the students as you requested. Is this the last one?"

It caught Xander off guard, and he didn't dare move as Smith grabbed his wrists and pulled them in front of him.

"Yes." Smith snapped on a zip tie. "Take them away, and don't let them go until the project is finished."

"What do I do with them then?" Tattoo man said.

"That depends on how well they do the job," Smith said. "Kill them if they fail or give each of them $10,000 if they succeed."

Xander felt panic as a blindfold was placed around his head, and a strong arm grabbed his shoulder, pushing him forward. Memories of Russian thugs beating him in a back alley flooded through him, and a flash of anger tore through his fear as he tried to pull away, only to receive a brisk slap across the face. His heart raced, and he felt a throb in his neck with each beat. A salty, metallic taste reached his tongue as blood trickled from his lip. Although it had been rough growing up in Russia, he had never experienced violence in America. His cheek stung, but the terror dulled the pain as he wondered, *What are they doing to my family? What will they do to me?* The alarm made him hyper-alert to every sound.

The powerful arm led Xander down a long passageway and then stopped. He could hear several footsteps behind him that also stopped when he did. A grinding noise, like the opening of a garage door, sounded. A blast of cool air hit him, along with a stench of gasoline and motor oil. He was nudged into a vehicle. Someone strapped a seatbelt over his shoulder and around his waist with a click. Chains rattled and then landed with a thump as they hit the concrete. The other boys must have been freed of their leg chains. He heard five more seat belt clicks. The zip ties on Xander's wrists cut in as he tried to get comfortable.

One boy asked, "Where are you taking us?" There was a slap, and the lad cried out.

"Zev, are you all right?" a panicked voice piped up.

"Hush, Jabril," Zev whispered, "I'm fine."

No one else spoke.

"Take them away," Smith said. "Make sure they finish the job by noon tomorrow," Smith whispered something in Belarusian.

The other students probably didn't understand, but Xander knew enough of the language to make out, "Everything is rigged to blow tomorrow at 12:01 p.m., so clear out as soon as they're finished. I won't be seeing you again. Payment will be in your accounts." Xander could hardly breathe through the dread that gripped him. A cold chill raced up his spine, yet he broke into a sweat.

Smith switched back to English, "Oh, and boys, don't try to escape. We have your families in custody. They'll be dead within minutes of your departure. It doesn't matter who flees. All family members will perish, so keep an eye on each other."

The engine roared to life, and the vehicle's wheels crunched over a gravel road, then turned into a smoother ride. They sped up, and the tires whined over a paved highway. It seemed like forever, but it was probably less than an hour before the ride became bumpy again. Something scraped against the van.

The driver pulled to a stop. "Open the gate."

The van's door opened, and a scent of pine wafted into the vehicle. Xander focused on the sounds. A squirrel chattered its dismay at being disturbed. A screech came from outside. "The damn gate's stuck!"

The driver swore, and then the vehicle swayed as he climbed out. There was grunting and more cursing, and something metallic clanked. The van bounced again as the men climbed inside, slammed their doors, and drove only a short distance before coming to another halt.

"The research laboratory is under those trees," the driver said. "Get the boys inside, and be sure they each boot up their computers before you return to patrol the area. I'll hide this vehicle and will be back shortly."

The side door slid open, and someone released Xander's seatbelt. The blindfold came off, and his eyes stung from the bright light. The tattooed man used a small knife to cut through the zip ties restraining Xander's wrists. He rubbed the areas to get back his circulation.

"This way," Tattoo man pointed his pistol at Xander and the other three students, "Inside that white building." He motioned with his gun to three steps that led up to the door of what looked like half a mobile home.

A boy with a reddened left cheek marked in the shape of an open hand stepped forward. He grabbed another lad's arm. "Let's finish this up so I can go back to Iowa. I have finals next week."

"I don't think you'll ever see Iowa again, Zev. It's too risky, and we need each other for protection."

"Nonsense, Jabril," Zev whispered. "Just do as they tell us. Everything will be okay."

Tattoo man turned toward the two students who were talking, "Shut up and move!"

"Yes, sir." Zev bounded up the steps and opened the door.

A man in a camo-colored turban greeted them. A jagged scar ran across his left cheek, causing a white streak in his otherwise black beard. "It's about time you got here. I'm Termine. You'll do as I say, complete the files you've been working on over the past few months, and adapt them in your folders as I've instructed. I'll be watching everything you code. You can't hide anything from my oversight program. Which one of you is Cadden?"

A tall, lean lad with golden-brown skin stepped forward. "I am, sir. Let me know what you wish, and I will do my best to achieve the goal. I am a man of peace. My family means everything to me."

"Yes." Termine motioned Cadden to a corner computer terminal. "I am also Punjabi. We work hard and want to be treated fairly. You can expect the same from me. This is your assignment." He opened a folder and gave Cadden his login code and password. "If you have any questions, you may talk to me, but not to the others about your project. Is that understood?"

"Yes, sir." Cadden didn't hesitate, sat down, and logged into the computer.

Termine called upon Jabril, and then Zev, who sat next to each other on the opposite side of the room.

Xander wiped the sweat from his upper lip. Banks of monitors surrounded an area on a desk in the front of the room between the four smaller terminals—probably Termine's security system. The room hummed with the high-pitched sound of computer fans, which almost drowned out the annoying buzz of the fluorescent lights overhead. When Xander got an assignment, he asked, "Is there air conditioning?"

After a brief rundown of Xander's project, Termine nodded to Tattoo man standing at the door. "Go out back and turn on the air. It'll be hotter than Narak in here before long."

Tattoo man grunted. A buzzer sounded as the door opened.

The driver walked inside as the man left the building, "Everything under control, Termine? Did you show them the refreshment area and the toilet?"

"Not yet," Termine said, "but they've each been briefed and have logged into the system." He motioned to the back room, where refreshments and the bathroom were located. "No more than two at a time are allowed to leave your stations, and no discussion of your projects. Agreed?"

The students nodded their heads. "Agreed."

Termine handed bottled water to each of the students. "Keep hydrated, my friends. This will be a long night."

Xander sized up Termine. Although he sounded friendly, he had an authoritative attitude and was proud of his heritage. Yet there was a certain twinkle in his eye when he spoke with Cadden—an underlying glance that gave away his concern for the boys. He didn't want to be here any more than they did. *Perhaps we will survive this ordeal after all.*

"Are you spending the night with us," Termine asked the driver.

"On the grounds only, but I'll be back here tomorrow at 11 a.m. We'll load you and the necessary equipment."

Xander wondered if the students were considered necessary or not. *I must communicate with the other students. They were the brightest kids in class. Somehow, we must find a way to call for help.*

Xander's assignment was to break into the New York Stock Exchange. After a brief review of the assignment, Xander realized a flood of cash would be automatically dumped into key accounts as soon as the NYSE opened for business. Within twenty minutes, stocks would hit all-time highs, upwards of 40,000, and then plummet drastically by noon. Anyone selling short would make a fortune.

Sept. 17 – 10:33 p.m. CDT, Wichita, Kansas/
11:33 p.m. EDT, Cincinnati, Ohio

It was nearly midnight CDT when Xander's first opportunity to call for help came to light, but Xander didn't initiate the idea. Wrapped up in his coding, he was startled when someone tapped his shoulder.

Cadden stood beside Xander. He cleared his throat and slipped a note under Xander's mousepad, "Read and destroy." Cadden slinked back to his station and busily typed away as if nothing happened.

Xander glanced around the room and noted that Zev and Jabril were in the back room with Termine. Tattoo man had gone outside for his hourly rounds. No one watched them, but he remembered that everything the students typed was monitored. He checked Cadden's note. "After lights flicker, keep coding and insert your message using one word at a time, underline the word, and locate the position based on prime numbers only. 'Help! Vital *threat*. NYSE in Lahore buildings in danger.' We only have three minutes to complete before we go back online. These underlined coded words will immediately disappear at that time."

Zev returned to his station. Cadden caught his attention and lifted his mousepad. Zev's brow furrowed with confusion.

Cadden dropped the corner of his pad, lifted it again, and pulled out a piece of paper.

Zev did the same and glanced around the room before palming the sticky note. A few moments later, he crumbled the note, cleared his throat, and nodded.

Cadden mouthed, "Tell Jabril." Zev nodded once again and went back to work.

Jabril came into the room talking to Termine, "Why the Pentagon?"

Termine shushed the boy, "Just do it. Okay, Cadden and Xander, time for your break."

Xander got up and followed Termine to the refreshment area, where fresh pizza and Coke awaited.

"Do you have any questions?" Termine asked.

"No, but it will take all night to get the code to perform correctly." Xander took a bite of pizza and washed it down with Coke.

"I've given you special access," Termine said. "Just type in the code."

Cadden stepped into the backroom. "Pizza! Thank you."

Termine turned to the boy. "Best eat up. It might be a while before you eat again."

After taking turns using the restroom, both boys returned to work.

Termine opened his computer system and seemed pleased with the progress. The overhead lights flickered.

"Keep working. Your terminals are on battery power," Termine said. "I'll see what's interrupting our power." He went outside.

Xander heard Termine talking to Tattoo man. "Now?" he asked Cadden.

"Now!" Cadden said. "The first underlined word starts with the prime numbers. Then, the third, fifth, seventh word, etc. There are only three minutes before we go back online. I must send it before the lights go out."

Each of the students rapidly typed their part of the message. Xander typed, "Help! Send For messages vital to the threat. General Rutoon immediately NYSE and in payout at 7:15 a.m. Lahore sharp buildings account number 2367A8923G68Z in to be collected danger." Xander whispered, "I'm done. Where should I send it?"

"Leave it," Cadden said as he entered his last keystroke. "My program will pick up all the underlined text and merge the message in order."

Zev whispered that he was done, but Jabril was having trouble with his message and perhaps hadn't understood Zev's feeble attempt to communicate Cadden's instructions.

Cadden darted to Jabril's station. "Move over. I'll finish it. Oh my, you're breaking into the Pentagon?" His fingers flew across the keyboard, "Done." The lights blinked once more as Cadden returned to his terminal, and he hit the send button. Everything went dark for twenty seconds.

Xander held his breath.

"Get those lights back on," Termine yelled. Then the lights returned.

Xander glanced at his code, and the underlined words had disappeared. He chanced a breath and realized everyone had quit typing. "Get back to work," he whispered. All they could do now was hope their desperate message had been sent and someone would respond.

If no one received it, panic would rip through the U.S. By noon, the financial system would have crumbled, and the nation's security system would have been breached, maybe even starting WW III. Xander's biggest fear was by 12:01 p.m. tomorrow, the students and all of their families would be dead.

BEAR TO BEAR

Sept. 18 – 6:00 a.m. MSK, Moscow, Russia/
Sept. 17 – 11:00 p.m. EDT, Cincinnati, Ohio

Cracker hadn't gotten much sleep. It was rather stupid, believing Agent Hastings had access to President Harris and a pardon would be granted overnight. He'd still hunt down General Surko Okueva, with a pardon or not. They were hot on his trail and narrowing the distance. Today would be the day. Moscow's Kazan Cathedral Church bells rang—6 a.m.

Rozalina set a mug of coffee on the table and sat across from him. "Still no word?"

Cracker sipped the brew while he jotted another item on his list. "I had hoped for a better outcome, but as usual, only lies."

"It was the middle of the night," she reminded him.

"Not in D.C.," Cracker corrected her. "When I left the embassy, it would have been just after 4 p.m. They've had plenty of time to get back to me. I'm afraid we're on our own."

"I'm surprised," Rozalina said. "You sound as if you looked forward to working with the FBI again."

Cracker reached over, placed his callused hand over hers, and gave a gentle squeeze. "I want to be free, and I had hoped this would benefit all of us."

"Did you locate Okueva's cell activity?" Rozalina asked.

"Yes, but his cell was heavily encrypted, and it took all night to crack his code. Here's a map of all the cell towers Okueva's calls have bounced off in the last twenty-four hours. It took a while to run down a list of numbers that also touched those towers at the same time. Albert and I tracked the origin, and your Uncle thinks he's located Okueva's headquarters. He's checking it out."

Rozalina scooted her chair back and leaned over Cracker's shoulder. "Is that the list of supplies you need?"

Cracker nodded. "I think it's complete."

"Good," Rozalina pocketed the list. "While we wait for Uncle Albert's call, I'll drop the children off at school and pick up these supplies."

Cracker nodded. "Thanks. I inventoried what we have on hand here and will pack them."

Rozalina gave him a peck on the cheek. "I'll wake the children."

"Let me," Cracker offered. "You have had that privilege for years, but I appreciate each day of freedom and want to be with our children every minute I can." *Our children.* The words filled his heart. His wife had done well in raising them during his absence.

Rozalina laughed. "Have fun waking Regina. She's a bear, like you, in the morning. Yoshi, on the other hand, will gladly let you tickle him awake."

"If Regina is like me, I know what to do." Cracker chuckled as he headed down the hallway. "Oh, my darling children, rise and shine!" He sat on Yoshi's bed and sang, *Eensy, Weensy, Spider,* as he moved his fingers along his son's neck.

Yoshi giggled. "Where did you learn that song?" He hopped from the bed and tickled Cracker under the chin. "You need a shave."

Cracker ran a hand over his face. "So, I do. Let's gang up on Regina."

"Oh, no," Yoshi tore out of the room. "I get the bathroom first. You wake her." The hallway door slammed shut.

Cracker moved to Regina's bed. His daughter lay wrapped up in the covers like a blintz. Her feet stuck out of one end, and golden curls poked out of the other. He flipped on the lamp.

She turned her head to face the wall. "Shut off the light!"

"My Regina Bear, it's time to get up." Cracker sang in a sing-song voice, "Mama says you wake up as grumpy as me. But I know better, and that can't be. I am the grumpiest bear, you see. Grr..." He tiptoed to the bed and pounced.

Regina laughed and pulled the covers over her head.

"Can you make up a better rhyme?" he asked.

A challenge, something she never could let slip past her. She threw off the covers. "Papa doesn't play fair, and I don't care. Giving me a great dare," she paused and jumped out of bed. "He's my favorite growly bear. That's you, Papa." She flung her arms around him. "I'm so glad you are home."

Cracker kissed the top of her head. "Wash up, get dressed, and let's eat." He'd missed so much of their lives, but never again, not if he could help it.

He worried until 1:30 p.m. when the expected call from Uncle Albert came. Rozalina had just arrived home after taking the children to school and running errands to gather surveillance equipment. Cracker assumed his mother-in-law would pick up the kids from school.

* * *

One year ago, General Surko Okueva met U.S. National Security Advisor General Rutoon at a summit in Tripoli, Libya, along with terrorist leaders from the Palestinian and Egyptian Islamic Jihads, Hezbollah, al-Qaeda, and Hamas. Okueva recalled the events as clearly as if they were yesterday.

"I just got back from the G-7 annual meeting," Rutoon had said. "We have some pressing issues to discuss: crisis management and global security. The leaders seek stiffer sanctions. My brothers will not tolerate this." He waved his hand around the room's periphery, where a dozen young men stood at quiet attention, their Uzis held ready across their chests, which included Aqib, Denys, and Roland Kildeer.

Okueva was already seething at this slight to his fatherland's honor. Russia had not been included again this year—a member of G-8 since 1998, but dropped in 2014, as the now G-7's solution to Russia's annexation of Crimea. Their demands to stop interference with Ukraine went unheeded.

* * *

Rutoon was the product of an American father and a Libyan mother. His older half-brothers had never visited the U.S., and government sanctions made it rough living in Libya. Rutoon had married once, lost his young American wife to cancer, and they had no children. He never remarried, and his work was his life. Initially, he worked hard for his country, fighting one war after another, but nothing ever improved. That's when he began understanding the depth of the U.S. government's corruption and decided to flip sides.

As the president's National Security Advisor, he was in a perfect position to fulfill his goals. Government officials saw him as a diplomat and held him in the highest esteem, allowing him to work behind the scenes in relative secrecy. He did his work in full sight of others, and no one was the wiser. He needed to weaken the country and used his trained mind to find flaws in the system, then exploited existing loopholes that would support a bioterrorist attack. That was already in the works, followed by cyber warfare. Okueva would plan that phase. Then, after the U.S. was reeling in chaos, they'd launch the final phase—a "ghost attack." No one would see it coming until it hit full force.

"We need to get the capitalists' attention and stand together," Rutoon said. "Unemployment rates continue to rise. Sanctions, bans on nuclear weapons, trade embargos, freezing billions of dollars in assets, gold, oil reserves, and other resources, not to mention prohibiting free trade, have all stifled our growth."

"What do you mean—our growth?" Okueva asked. "You're a top official of the U.S. government. You have President Spendorf's ear. What's in this for you?"

"I'm glad you asked," Rutoon stood tall. "I work with top officials in Libya and North Korea. They are my brothers, and I have furnished them with weapons." Rutoon enjoyed the silence that filled the room after he dropped that information and waited. Tension built within the room as unsaid questions grew, yet Rutoon continued to wait, knowing it would come.

* * *

"And you could do the same for us?" Okueva's voice hesitated in disbelief at this stroke of good fortune. Rutoon looked at him directly for the first time. Okueva braced himself and asked, "What kind of weapons?"

"M-4s, laser illuminators, scoped optics, and explosive devices, to name a few," Rutoon had said. "They are the latest models and top of the line."

"What exactly would you want in return?" Okueva felt a flutter of hope. He would never launch an attack on the U.S. unless confident of success. It required thorough planning, loyal, trained resources, and massive financial investments to make it happen.

"That is none of your business, but I want to make changes and end corruption," Rutoon had said. "If I am in charge, I can accomplish much good."

"I thought you were the president's best friend," Okueva said.

Rutoon grinned but said nothing.

A vote went around the room. Only one man hesitated but rapidly agreed when four Uzis appeared, leveling at his chest. Fortunately, it had been a private meeting held in a secure place.

Rutoon had delivered on his promises, but he died prematurely of a lethal virus that he had planted.

Now, it was up to Okucva to lead the attack. Since that first meeting, today's date had been circled in red on Okueva's calendar.

This was it. An attack in London had already been launched. Then, another strike would hit other major cities at two to three-hour intervals, ending with Rome, and then the U.S. Okueva had also considered Canada and Japan, as initially planned, but time was limited. *Let the enemies wonder who is next.*

Funding wasn't a problem, especially when his ingratiated students finished their hack jobs siphoning money from American Express, Wells Fargo, and the NYSE. That, on top of the flood of revenue streams from Iranian and Syrian sources, allowed secret cells to organize terrorism around the world. With plans triggered to launch a financial collapse, violence would bring these democracies to their knees. When the capitalists' world imploded, he'd be there to scoop up the pieces. Everything was going as planned, and with Rutoon out of the picture, his team would gladly take over the U.S.

STUDENTS FOR HIRE

Sept. 17 – 11:40 p.m. EDT, Cincinnati, Ohio

Svetlana had been reviewing her laptop backup of Aqib's files regarding foreign college students being forced to hack into major U.S. corporations as part of repayment for school loans. A shiver raced up her spine, and she slipped into a sweater as the AC in Ohio's Hyatt Regency conference room seemed to drop back below 66° F. The room was either too hot or too cold. Her stomach growled, but she kept typing. She grabbed Perry's hand when his stomach played a duet with hers. "It's time for some pizza, and I need to show you some disturbing files I've been researching."

"Pizza sounds terrific, so let's talk." Perry opened the door to the kitchenette and found two Cokes, while Svetlana heated two slices of pizza.

"Shh, don't wake Braun," Svetlana whispered.

"I'm up," Braun said, "I'll join you."

Svetlana handed Braun a slice. "I'll be right back."

Braun heated the pizza and had his mouth full when Svetlana returned with her laptop. "You don't have to work while you take a break."

"I know, but I have some concerns." She set the laptop on the table and opened a few files. "I tracked down two students, and my gut says there are more. I'm afraid they're hacking skills are…"

A sound came from the main conference room. "That sounds like Cordy." Braun hopped from his chair. "Something's upset her. I'll check." Braun slipped into his shoes. "She'll want to hear about this, too."

RUTOON'S HIDDEN MESSENGER

Sept. 18 – 12:00 midnight CDT, General Rutoon's Office, Washington, D.C.

It was either late at night or early in the morning, depending on how one considered the stroke of midnight. Of all the idiotic things Quint had done in his life, agreeing to his boss's latest request was the stupidest yet. As a key Intelligence Officer, Quint felt obligated to say yes when the ailing President Zac Spendorf called asking for a favor. However, the more he thought about it, the more he wondered if his boss had all his marbles.

"Someone's impersonating Rutoon," Spendorf insisted. "I'm still getting messages from the general and tracked them down. They're coming from his office. I know that's impossible. The man's dead, and I'm sure his office has been cleaned out by now. Please check it out."

Quint couldn't believe he'd agreed to sneak into the Pentagon and search for answers. *What if I get caught? After all, Spendorf is on medical leave. Will I get fired for this?* With a flashlight in hand, he barely breathed as he tiptoed through the building, trying to make as little noise as possible. Eerie shadows flickered over dusty furniture, reflected off dark windowed doors, and he couldn't help but feel haunted by occasional rodents. Finally, he made it safely through the secret passageway, took the stairs to the mezzanine level, and entered Rutoon's office.

Quint scanned the shelves lined with books, knick-knacks, and personal journals. One spiral tablet lay flat on the shelf. A loose page slid from the journal when he picked it up for a better look. It had a drawing of two triangles in the shape of a six-sided star. The star was surrounded by foreign letters and numbers that seemed random.

Inside the star, there was a circle with eight waves intersecting in the middle. Curious, Quint used his cell phone camera to take a picture of it. He then placed the piece of paper back into his notebook and returned it to the shelf.

Next, he went through the filing cabinets—there were two, but one was locked, precisely the one he wanted to get into. He searched the desk drawers, hoping to find a key. No luck, so he became creative with a paperclip. It took several minutes and made more noise than he wanted, but he managed to get in. A clicking sound startled Quint.

He rotated the beam of light around the room but didn't notice anything unusual. Perhaps it was the heater, but Quint was frightened. He worked rapidly in the darkness, shading his flashlight to focus solely on the labeled tabs and selected files that caught his attention. He discovered three large folders stuffed with CDs and two thumb drives in the third drawer. He found a cell phone hidden at the back under multiple folders in the bottom drawer. He opened a directory of essential contacts and discovered Zac Spendorf's name. Near the top of the list was Deen P. Fjords, who had an asterisk in front of the name. Other key individuals also had asterisks beside their names, but for some reason, Fjords was between Okueva and Spendorf, which fell out of the alphabetically ordered list.

Cold sweat beaded Quint's face. The clicking sound stopped, making it too quiet. Quint wiped his forehead with his sleeve, still feeling hot and sticky. If the heater clicked off, he should have been relieved, but the longer he stayed in Rutoon's office, the more fidgety he became. He copied the thumb drives and removed the large folders and cell phone so that he could take more time with the data. Quint checked each drawer. Everything looked untouched, so he relocked the cabinet.

At 12:17 a.m., his phone vibrated briefly, alerting him that his ShadowNavigator program had intercepted data pinged from an NSA Satellite. These messages are often linked to terrorist networks, and his system could track their locations. To his surprise, the message he received was well-encrypted, and he didn't have time to break the code, so he downloaded it to his darknet account and urgently contacted Cordy.

Two minutes after reaching Cordy by phone, a loud crash sounded from somewhere down the hall. Quint's heart leapt at the sound. His body tensed, ready for action, "…sending info to your darknet. Gotta go before I'm caught." He disconnected the call, grabbed Rutoon's cell, and folders, and ducked behind the two file cabinets. He clicked on his video record button. On second thought, he made sure the video feed was recorded onto Cordy's darknet just in case something happened to him. He'd also send her a download of Rutoon's phone data.

Faint voices came from outside the office door. Quint wedged a large trashcan against the wall next to the cabinets and briefly held his breath to listen. Peeking through a small crack between the two cabinets, he held up his phone for a better view. The image shook in his nervous hand, so he propped his cell along the metal edge of the cabinet. He tried to calm himself, but his body wouldn't obey. The suspense was unbearable as wild imaginations kept running through his mind. After swallowing spit that wouldn't form, he took regular breaths and tried to think straight.

A faint ray of light appeared through the small glass in the main door. "I don't see anyone," a low male voice said.

The door swung open with a bang, and someone turned on the overhead office lights. A woman in a green Army uniform walked over to the desk. "Someone was here. Look at the phone cord. It's caught on the arm of the chair. I know it wasn't that way last night." She moved the office chair, stooped, and checked under the desk.

"It was probably the janitor. There's no one here now," the man said as he poked his head into the room.

The stale scent of cigar smoke irritated Quint's nose. Afraid he'd sneeze, he covered his nose with his sleeve. Quint couldn't get a good view of the man but thought he recognized his voice. It drifted through his mind but wouldn't stick long enough for him to recall a name.

"Come on. Let's go before the janitor returns. We've kept Rutoon's accounts open long enough. Wait until tomorrow when the stock market opens. We'll get our funds and close out his account."

The woman peered around the room, narrowed her eyes, and approached the bookcase. She picked up the journal lying on the shelf, tapped the bottom edge against the ledge to straighten the pages, and placed it upright. "I don't like it. Something's not right. This journal contains all of Rutoon's secrets, and we need to make sure it's safe."

"You've been jumping at shadows all week," the man said. "Rutoon's dead. He can't hurt you anymore, Dora. Let's leave."

"Not yet." She didn't turn around. Her eyes searched each shelf meticulously, like a detective on a crucial case. "General Rutoon used to glare at me like I was lower than a worm. He'd bark out orders and treat me like an idiot. Can you believe it? Even after all that, I kept his sorry ass out of trouble more times than I can count. Now I'm ousted out of service like an old used car. It's not fair. Only six months before retirement."

"You served him well for nearly twenty years. He owes you, and it's time to collect your dues."

Quint bit his lip when he realized the woman was Rutoon's secretary. *Of course, she would have access to all of Rutoon's data, probably his usernames and passwords, but who is with her?* The man finally came into full view. Quint didn't recognize him. *Hopefully, Spendorf will know him when he sees the video.*

"I swear, at times, I still see Rutoon's ghost." She gave a visible shiver and grabbed the man's hand. "You're right. Let's get out of here!"

"Perhaps that's what you saw tonight," the man said. "Clearly, there's no one here."

CAUGHT SNOOZING

Sept. 18 – 12:17 a.m. EDT, Cincinnati, Ohio

It was 12:17 a.m., and the conference room at the Hyatt Regency was so quiet that all Cordy could hear was tapping computer keys. She'd gotten a message from Usher saying he was meeting with Cracker, and she hoped they'd track down General Okueva soon.

Perry and Svetlana had each taken a two-hour nap at different intervals, and it was Braun's turn to rest. Cordy was used to long hours of research, but she knew how crucial sleep was to productivity, so she sipped coffee and made sure the others got adequate downtime. It was essential so they could continue their research around the clock.

A buzz of Cordy's cell phone caused her to jump out of her chair. She must have dozed off briefly. The caller ID was unfamiliar, "Agent Cordelia. Who's calling at this hour?"

Quint launched into an exciting dialog. "I found it. A satellite sent odd signals over New York City."

"What?" *Why's he calling me?* "Slow down, Quint. Did you discover signals sent by satellite over New York? Is that what you're telling me? What's so unusual about that?"

"This is different," Quint said. "It lasted only a few seconds."

"What did they send? Do you have the coordinates—" Cordy heard a loud bang over Quint's phone.

"Shh," Quint whispered. "They're encrypted. Unable to decipher, but I've captured the signal. Sending to your account—gotta go before I'm caught."

"Where are you?" Cordy asked, but the line went dead. *What was that all about?*

Sept. 18 – 12:22 a.m. EDT, Cincinnati, Ohio

Braun entered the conference room and found Cordy absently staring at her phone. She jolted when Braun massaged the back of her neck. "Quint in trouble again?"

Cordy rubbed her tired eyes. "I don't have a clue what he's up to."

"Play back the message," Braun said, "I know you automatically record all calls—even mine." The corner of his lips lifted into a boyish, lopsided smile.

"And the GPS coordinates of his location, if I'm lucky. Sorry to cut into your break time."

"I was getting up anyway," Braun said. "Then I was going to make you take a break, but that won't happen. Will it?"

Cordy shook her head and handed him her phone as she booted up her account designated for Quint. "I'm running the message through my encryption program," Cordy said. "I hope to have answers soon."

Braun listened to Quint's phone call. "What do you suppose he's doing now?"

"Million-dollar question," Cordy traced the signal and played it. I can't interpret the cipher, but it only lasted eighteen seconds. Do you think it was sent by accident?" A list of satellites in the area popped up on her screen. "It pinged off the NSA satellite."

Braun pulled up a chair next to her. "Several scenarios are racing through my mind, but none make any sense."

"My thoughts exactly," Cordy said. "These are sophisticated hackers. If they've managed to camouflage their activity so far, why did this one get through?" She sent it to another decrypter, and while she waited, she did more research.

Sept. 18 – 12:37 a.m. EDT, Cincinnati, Ohio

Cordy's decrypter program dinged. The message read, "Help! Four students hacking vital systems under threat of death at gunpoint. White pre-fab lab in Lahore by abandoned buildings, barbwire, wooded area, Wichita, KS., NYSE, banks, and Pentagon in danger. Come quick! zxjc."

Cordy's heart skipped a beat. *There it is again. My darknet signature—and this time, a backdoor does not even hide it—out in the open for anyone to see. Who's doing this? If Quint thinks this is funny.*

Braun read the message over Cordy's shoulder. "I wonder if this is a second attack on the New York Stock Exchange or the same one you just fixed."

Cordy didn't respond, so he tapped her shoulder. "Earth to Cordy," he repeated his comment.

"Don't know."

"How many abandoned buildings are in Wichita?" Braun asked.

Cordy searched on Google Maps, "Too many. We need to narrow our search."

"Where is Lahore?" Braun asked. "Is that a suburb of Wichita?"

Cordy typed again, "No matches found."

Svetlana stepped up to Cordy and handed her and Braun a hot pizza slice on a paper plate. "Did you find the students?"

Cordy hesitated and glanced at Braun, who scarfed down his pizza in four bites.

"I think we can share the information," Braun said around a slab of pepperoni before he swallowed. "After all, they've been researching data on students all evening."

Cordy took a nibble of her pizza, but it was too hot, and she wondered how Braun downed his so fast. She turned her laptop toward Svetlana as Perry joined them. "Any ideas what this means?"

Svetlana squinted at the screen. "It's signed zxjc. That would be Zev, Jabril, and Cadden. They are some of the students we've been investigating. But who's the X?"

Perry had a handful of notes. "I've been researching Cadden Singh. He's from Pakistan, and his native language is Urdu. He's in his final year of medical school and is a front-runner for Valedictorian of his class."

"Oh, makes sense. Lahore is an Urdu word," Braun mentioned in passing as he ran a greasy hand over his gray pant leg, leaving a tomato stain, and then placed a call on his speaker. "Guy, sorry to wake you, but we have an urgent situation."

"Great, it's not even 1 a.m., don't you ever sleep?" Guy from Homeland Security snapped. "This better be important."

"I wouldn't have called you otherwise," Braun said.

"That means I'm up for the day," Guy yawned. "What's so urgent?"

Cordy typed Lahore into the computer once again and searched for an Urdu-to-English translation, "Joyland? Does that mean anything to you, Braun?"

"What are you talking about?" Guy asked.

Cordy updated Guy on the latest message. "We need feet on the ground in Wichita, Kansas."

"Did you just say, Joyland?" Guy asked. "There's an abandoned Joyland Amusement Park in Wichita."

"Is it in a wooded area?" Cordy typed Joyland Park into Google Maps. "Oh, yes, I was there once as a little girl. It looks very different fenced off in barbwire."

"I'll get a hostage negotiation team up there ASAP, and they may need SWAT backup. We'll keep you posted." Guy disconnected the call.

"Good work, Perry," Cordy said. "What about the other students?"

"I found a lot on Zev," Svetlana said. "His formal name is Zev Abadi from Israel. He's also in his last year of school but studying computer engineering at the University of Iowa. I don't know how he ended up with the others, but Jabril Pacaud appears to be Zev's cousin. Perhaps he stopped in for a visit, and both were forced into the group. I have no proof of that, however."

"Did you find any students' names beginning with X?" Cordy swallowed a bite of now-cooled pizza and washed it down with a gulp of cold coffee.

"No," Svetlana said. "There's a Mahir Fazil from Syria and a female named Aria Esfandiari from Iran. Both are attending the University of Texas in Austin. A sixth student, Hala Hariri, returned to Jordan last year and was found dead at home. It was thought he committed suicide."

Perry said. "I'm researching Baogem Wang from China. He's a third-year PhD student in microbiology at Stanford University. So, I'm not sure who X stands for. Maybe someone we haven't run across yet. And I don't know how the other three students are involved so far."

Cordy hoped the initials represented these students, but it was still a huge coincidence, and she didn't believe in such things. "Good work. Take another short break while Braun and I make a few phone calls. It might be a while before you get another break."

"A second slice of pizza sounds good!" Svetlana said. "Should I microwave one for you and Braun, too?"

"No, thank you." Cordy held up her plate with a half-eaten slice on one corner. "We'll join you later."

Svetlana grabbed Perry's arm and led him to the kitchenette.

Cordy opened Quint's message and gasped, "He called from a landline at the Pentagon. That's what it looks like, but why?"

Braun plugged his earphones into his cell, handed a bud to Cordy, and then called Guy once again.

PANIC ATTACK

Sept. 17 – 11:38 p.m. CDT, Wichita, Kansas/
Sept. 18 – 12:38 p.m. EDT, Cincinnati, Ohio

The power outage at the lab hidden away at Wichita's Joyland Amusement Park created temporary chaos. All students were uneasy when the lights came back on, especially when Tattoo man returned to threaten them. "Light out, not good for the family."

Typing ceased. All eyes darted between Tattoo Man and Termine. "We're working as fast as we can," Zev said.

"Please, give us more time," Jabril added. "This is impossible."

"Don't talk to the students," Termine warned Tattoo man. "They need to concentrate."

The brute dashed toward Zev, who was nearest. The boy threw his hands over his head and ducked. "Don't hit me again."

"Back off!" Termine shouted.

Tattoo man launched his body into Termine, knocking his hip into the corner of his desk.

Termine took a step away and held up his hands in surrender when Tattoo man raised his fist for another attack.

The driver called Tattoo Man's radio in a panic. "I need your help out here. I see lights in the distance. Hurry."

Tattoo glared at Termine and pressed the reply button, "Da! Where are these lights?" He mumbled several foreign words under his breath and stormed out of the lab. The door slammed behind him.

Xander flinched at the language as if he had understood, but the rest of the room breathed a heavy sigh of relief.

"Did he hurt you," Cadden asked Termine.

Termine rubbed his injured hip and shook his head. "Get back to work." He wiped sweaty hands down his loose-flowing black shirt made of thin cotton. His baggy dhotis wound around his legs were gathered around his waist in a bunch and tied with a string. He already had pain in the pit of his stomach from the tension and fear that wouldn't go away, day or night, and the bulk further irritated him. He had kicked off his leather hiking boots hours ago, longing for his broken-in sandals. Feet needed to breathe, and he never got used to wearing those heavy shoes.

"Will he be back?" Cadden asked.

"It's not our concern." Termine noticed the boys flinch and softened his tone. "Okay, lads, I know you're all worried about your families, but I assure you, the sooner we accomplish our tasks, the sooner you will see them alive and well." He hoped his wife and family were safely hidden away in the small hut in Amritsar, but he'd called her four times and never got an answer. These men were brutal, and it concerned him.

He needed to listen to his gut. *These boys and I may share the same fate, but how can we free ourselves and save our families, too? Tattoo man plans to eliminate the evidence, and maybe all of us. What can I do?* Termine returned to his large screen, thinking of how he might create a diversion, or blow up the men outside, or... He didn't know what to do.

His large screen was divided into four smaller areas, duplicating each student's terminals. He rapidly assessed each student's code to determine whether they were on task to complete the assignments. It was up to him to make sure their projects were on track.

Jabril typed a line of code and then deleted it. He tried again, but the content was filled with typos, causing Termine to bite back an oath. He walked behind Jabril to give him a tongue-lashing and paused.

The keyboard was slick with sweat. Jabril's fingers trembled, fumbling to hit the correct letters. Termine hoped the boy was close to being finished. They were running out of the one thing they had the least of—time.

Jabril bit his lip and shook his head. "I can't. I can't do this anymore!"

"Yes, you can," Termine said. "All of our lives depend on it."

Jabril glanced up. "You, too?"

Termine nodded. "I have a wife and five boys. We are in this together, so let's keep working. I'll help you."

"How?" Jabril wrapped his arms around his knees to keep from shaking. "Each of us has a different project."

"That's true," Termine said. "Try breaking your project into smaller pieces. Set short time limits to do the first task. Take a break as a reward and move to the next step, but stay focused. During each break, relax, drink water, and eat food. We can do this together. It's the only way we can survive. Let's start with you first. Come."

Jabril followed Termine to the back room. "Tell me about your family."

"My Eema is already frail." Jabril's eyes filled with tears, ready to spill. "This could kill her. The pressure is too much for her."

"They're safe." Termine knew it was a lie. *The boy was to be eliminated. But the work had to be done, or Termine and his family would be executed. How could they get out of this hopeless mess?* He gave a fake smile of reassurance and handed Jabril a bottle of water and a cookie. *It's better not to let the boy know.* "I know this is hard. You have one of the riskiest projects of all—finding a way into the Pentagon. How would you divide this task? Do it for your mother."

Jabril thought for a moment. "We need personal data from the gatekeepers and passwords that keep changing. I've logged in using a back door method, but we can't leave any footprints. Getting in without getting caught takes time. Too much time for Smith to obtain the complex work they're doing."

"Can you get better data more quickly?" Termine asked.

"Maybe…if…" Jabril ran his fingers over his chin while he concentrated. "I can redirect each person to an update page when they first log in. We need to record their keystrokes so that we can duplicate them. Then there is the issue of the iris scanning. The code must capture that to fool the system?" He took out a pen and scribbled on a napkin. "Let's see. I'll need to get names, departments, and new passwords." His eyes brightened. "Yes, I might be able to do it!"

"What systems will you attach the update to?" Termine asked.

"That's something I hadn't thought of." Jabril pondered for a few minutes. "Let's see what the branches of the military are." He jotted his ideas from time to time. "I studied them in class—Department of Defense, the Army, Navy, Air Force, Marines, and the National Security Systems." He lifted his head. "I can also add an invisible camera eye on the screen and a recorder, so anything said in the room will be spoken directly to us, as though they were right here with us."

"That's smart. You're doing well," Termine praised the lad. "How will you prevent anyone from getting suspicious after you get in?"

"The only warning is one flicker of green light," Jabril said. "It is our most vulnerable moment, and it will be quick, but it is still possible to be caught by a sharp-eyed person. However, they won't know what to do because the information will already be trapped once the light blinks. They will be too late."

"I knew you were right for the job," Termine said. "What will happen to the photos and recordings?"

Jabril drummed his fingers on the lunch table and paused. "Whatever faces the monitor will be digitally recorded. Let's see. It will record every document, face, or fingerprint, and feed it back to our master files. They will be encrypted so no one can track it to us."

"And that finishes the project," Termine said, "ready to get back to work?"

"Yes," Jabril said.

"You think you can do this?" Termine asked.

"Yes, but what about Zev? His family lives in Israel, too. How will we be sure they are freed when we're done?"

"I'll send you a message," Termine said. "I'm sure your family will contact you soon, too."

"Thanks. I'll send Zev back here." Jabril hurried from the break room and tapped Zev's shoulder. "You're next. Termine's waiting. He helped clarify my project, and I know he'll help you, too." Jabril went back to his terminal. His fingers now typed with assurance.

Termine went through the same process with Zev, who was assigned to hack into American Express to acquire access to over a hundred million accounts.

"I don't like this project," Zev said. "The more I realize what we're doing, the worse I feel. I want to go back to Iowa and finish school. If this succeeds, I will bring great shame to my family. Papa will not be proud of me. I have made his life miserable."

"You want them to live, don't you?" Termine asked. "We don't have a choice here. This is beyond you and me."

Zev choked on his water.

Termine slapped the boy's back. "Better?"

Zev nodded, but his fists remained clenched.

Termine didn't know if it was from fear or rage. "Will you be able to finish your project?"

"Oh, yes," Zev said. "I'll finish this project. And when this is over, I will hunt down Smith. You can count on that."

Termine felt some of his own powerlessness come over him and wondered again how he could get them all out of this mess when he couldn't even hope to tackle the brute Tattoo man.

Cadden was next. "I have three fund accounts to set up at Wells Fargo."

"Your task is going well," Termine said. "How far into the code are you?"

"I'm about halfway, but I can copy some of my initial code to speed the process," Cadden said. "I'm done with the first one—a mutual fund totaling $14 million, and I'm working on an International account for $30 million."

"The third is a money market fund for another $16 million," Termine added. "Do you need anything from me to finish the job?"

"Not to code the project," Cadden said, "but I want to know what happens to us if anyone gets caught? Are we going to jail? What about our college? Will our families be held responsible for our actions? The government will never forgive us for this, and I am worried that we might get killed anyhow. After all, we know what we've done, but others will soon know, too. They will hunt us down."

Termine privately agreed with the boy, but he had no better option. "Calm down, son. I'm not going to let anyone harm you." Worried about Smith's direct orders, he realized Tattoo man might eliminate him, too. "We have to stick together. No, we *must* stick together. Think of this small group as also your family."

"What if anything happens to you?" Cadden asked.

"We'll figure it out," Termine said. "Now go back to work. Your project goes live at 10 a.m. I still must talk to Xander."

Cadden stopped off at the restroom before returning to work.

Xander flinched when Termine tapped him on the shoulder. "I'm working as fast as I can." His head flexed from side to side to release the tension.

"I know, son," Termine whispered. "It's time for a break."

Xander glanced around and noticed Cadden heading back to his seat. Jabril and Zev were busy at their terminals. Xander's left ankle had gone to sleep, sending a zing up his leg when he stood, causing him to stumble to keep upright.

Termine caught him before he fell. "You okay?"

"Yes," Xander snapped, but he softened his voice. "Sorry, I'm worried about my family."

They walked to the back room. "All of us are anxious for this to be over, but this is the only way they will return our families to safety," Termine said. "You'll see. I'm quite satisfied with the results so far."

Xander washed a bite of cold pizza down with warm Coke while he gave Termine an update on hacking into the New York Stock Exchange.

Termine's message alert vibrated in his pocket. He checked the device. "It's Mr. Smith. I need to get this. Don't take too long a break."

"I'll return shortly," Xander said to Termine's back.

Termine logged into the pre-arranged darknet account.

Smith sent an encrypted message. "Give me results only."

Termine glanced up as Xander returned to the room, barely having time to read the text. "All is going as scheduled."

"Plan A on time?" Smith typed. The message flashed once and automatically disappeared.

"Goes live at 9:30 a.m.," Termine replied by text. "Plans B and C follow at 10."

"And the big D?" Smith texted. "It's most urgent. First SC launches in Paris at noon, and in U.S. at 3 p.m."

SC? Secret cell launches at noon. The U.S. is doomed by this afternoon.

"On task," Termine replied.

"Perfect," Smith texted. "At 12:01 p.m. sharp. All traces are gone."

"Yes," Termine replied. "And the boys?"

"All evidence will be destroyed!" The text disappeared, and Smith logged off.

Termine's heart skipped a beat. *Including the boys? So, I was right.* There was no further communication, and Termine knew precisely what that meant. He broke out in a cold sweat. Glancing up, he noticed his team was busy at work. Overloaded with fear for his family, the boys, and their families, he blew out a shaky breath. *These students have done everything they were ordered to complete. Why has it taken this long to dawn on me? Smith won't leave <u>any</u> evidence. I'm evidence, too. No one has given me any exit plans. I have no driver, no bodyguard, and no money. I am collateral damage. He intends to kill them and then me. I have to find a way out of this.*

SWAT ALERT

Sept. 17 – 11:09 p.m. MDT, Fort Collins, Colorado/
Sept. 18– 1:09 a.m. EDT, Cincinnati, Ohio

Guy Weimer, head of Homeland Security, knew exactly who to call at an ungodly hour of 1:09 a.m. It was before midnight in Fort Collins. He searched contacts on his cell phone and speed-dialed Russ Bracken of the Federal Protective Forces in Colorado. "I just got a call from Agent Cordelia-Hastings. She discovered there's a group of students…"

Cordelia-Hastings? It caught Bracken off guard. *So Cordy finally got hitched.*

Bracken had dated Cordy for nearly six months before she broke it off. She had worked with Bracken's SWAT members in the past. Once, when Braun and Usher became trapped in an underground bunker filled with C-4 explosives and again when Chief Jackson had been kidnapped.

Before working SWAT, Bracken had been a Navy Seal Explosive Breacher. He'd grown up as a Navy brat, pulling up his roots every few years. It only seemed natural to follow his father's career path and move beyond to serve his government. He lived for the unexpected. New adventures, plotting solutions to problems, and successfully combating the odds thrilled him. Those twists and turns kept him alert.

Guy cleared his throat, and the line went quiet.

Bracken realized he'd zoned out briefly. "What's that you said about students?"

"Someone's holding them captive at gunpoint in the abandoned Joyland Amusement Park in Wichita, Kansas. They are literally hacking into our financial and security systems as we speak."

"Did they get beyond the firewalls?" Bracken asked.

"Yes, Cordy says someone penetrated the New York Stock Exchange. Thousands of people will lose their funds as soon as the doors open in the morning. They've also targeted the Pentagon. We have to stop these attacks before they occur. Further investigation found two large banking systems also compromised." Guy continued with what he had learned so far.

"How do you know these students are the hackers into these vital systems?" Bracken asked.

"Cordy tracked them on the darknet," Guy said, "and got a message that they are being held hostage at gunpoint. She is still researching the situation, so check in with her for the latest details. In the meantime, I need you and your team out there ASAP. The Army has a BATT ready for your use. Standard ballistic supplies only, so if you need anything special, transport them with you."

"Yes, sir," Bracken said.

"Who's available?" Guy asked.

"This team is home-grown." Bracken unwrapped a stick of gum and popped it into his mouth—a new habit since he'd quit smoking. "You won't find a better group of men. I was their platoon sergeant in Afghanistan, and since then, we've spent five years working SWAT in Fort Collins. You've met Poncho. He's A-one, top of the line—a quiet man but always observant. No one questions his authority. He is my second in command and will head up team two. Chico is my hero. I wouldn't be here if he hadn't raced me through open gunfire. Chest wound. I owe him my life."

"I've met both men," Guy said.

"There are two other SWAT members, two bomb disposal officers, and a medic," Bracken said. "I'll arrange everything on this end, and we'll be in Wichita in three hours, tops. Have a BATT at the drop site, and I'll plan to meet your negotiator outside Joyland Park around 4 a.m. CDT."

"Terrific." Guy sent GPS coordinates of the location. "Two drones are hovering over the area, taking pics. The hostages are being held in a pre-fab laboratory parked by a few abandoned buildings. The area is wooded and surrounded by barbwire. Negotiators will meet you outside Joyland, but this is a dangerous mission, so be ready to act immediately. I'm sending photos. Any questions?"

"Not yet. I'll contact you when we land." Bracken disconnected the call and then speed-dialed Poncho. "Guy Weimer has an assignment for us in Wichita, Kansas. Contact our bomb squad. Ensure Desmond and Sergeant Foley bring all their supplies, as I don't know what to expect. Snipers may be onsite. Explosives have not been ruled out."

Bracken filled Poncho in on what little details Guy had mentioned. "I'll contact Chico, Officer Kayman, and George, our medic. Then we'll get an update from Cordy when we're in the air. Flight leaves in forty minutes."

"Roger," Poncho said. "You can count on the team."

TRACKING QUINT

Sept. 18 – 1:36 a.m. EDT, Cincinnati,
Ohio, and Washington, D.C.

In her usual way, Cordy was doing three things: tracking down Quint while deciphering encrypted text messages and coordinating a SWAT team's rescue of international students hacking into the vital U.S. financial systems. "Braun, call Guy and see if he can help find Quint. He's in the Pentagon somewhere."

Braun plugged in his Bluetooth earphones and speed-dialed Homeland Security.

It took three rings before Guy answered. "Sorry for the delay. I know it's been a whole 30 minutes, and that's a lifetime for Cordy, but I'm still working on getting a negotiator for the SWAT team to send to Wichita. They should arrive by 4 a.m. In the meantime, the FBI is sending up a drone over Joyland. We'll forward the photos as soon as we get them." Guy cleared his throat. "Did you get another message?"

"No, I'm calling about another matter," Braun said. "Did you or any of the president's team send Quint to the Pentagon?" After another pause, Braun added, "I didn't think so. Yet the geek is on location and seems to be in some danger."

"Where in the Pentagon?" Guy asked. "It's under constant renovation and covers twenty-nine acres. That will be like finding a needle in a haystack."

"Not if you know where to search," Braun said. "Cordy, read off the GPS location."

After hearing the coordinates, Guy said, "Northwest wing of the Pentagon, mezzanine level of ring B. That would be the Army division. Wait, that's General Rutoon's old office. Surely, it's been cleared out by now. Wonder what the lad's up to."

MISSION WICHITA

Sept. 17 – 11:40 p.m. MDT, Fort Collins, Colorado/
Sept. 18 – 1:40 a.m. EDT, Cincinnati, Ohio

Bracken, the first to arrive at the Fort Collins, Colorado, airfield, warmly greeted each team member as they boarded the Blackhawk Helicopter. Their faces were familiar, like those of brothers. It took twenty minutes for the team to fully assemble, each member bringing their unique skills and experiences to the mission.

As the last member arrived, the team erupted in cheers. The medic handed Bracken a red metal emergency box, a symbol of their preparedness, and climbed aboard, each member confident in their role and the mission ahead.

"It's about time." Bracken loaded the box along with the rest of the team's gear. "We're sweating out here, all dressed up in our gear while waiting on you." The team members, though visibly tired and impatient, maintained their composure and focused on the mission ahead.

"Sorry, I'm late." George strapped himself in, grabbed the bulky headphones, adjusted the microphone over his lips, and then plugged the long black cord into a jack in the ceiling. "Let's go. There is no breeze, and the diesel fumes are stronger than usual."

Bracken stepped to the front, folded his long legs so his knees were nearly touching his chest, and strapped himself in, then turned to face the rest of the team—six men dressed in flak vests over the mixed green and tan desert camouflage fatigues. Bracken made the seventh. "We're behind schedule. George, download the drone photos. Chico and Foley, you're with me. As usual, Poncho's head of team two, Kayman and Desmond, are on his team. I'll brief you in the air." He turned back and signaled to Poncho to start the engine.

The Blackhawk lifted off the tarmac and into the cloudless sky. The seats in the helicopter's rear had been removed to allow for tactical equipment, a testament to the team's preparedness. Kevlar vests, goggles, helmets, and thick leather gloves, along with ammo and emergency and trauma equipment, were all in place. It was an awe-inspiring sight, a reminder of the team's formidable capabilities. Bracken settled in for the flight and called for an update.

"This is Agent Cordelia-Hastings. What's up, Bracken?"

"Guy assigned us the Wichita Mission." The sound of her voice made Bracken smile, and for reasons he shouldn't bring to mind. She sounded tired, but that would never stop her from hunting down villains. He wished she'd chosen him to spend the rest of her life with, but it wasn't to be. A touch of envy crept into his soul. *I can't go there. Not now, not ever.* He cleared his throat. "Anything new since you last talked to Guy?"

"Mixed news. The good news is we think we can block the student's attack on the New York Stock Exchange, so perhaps our economy won't crash, but we found disturbing malware on Wells Fargo and American Express corporate systems, and the Pentagon may be compromised. Joyland Amusement Park has been closed since 2006. There's a high fence covered in graffiti, but several areas have been breached. The drones have located two armed guards outside the pre-fab lab. Heat sensors show five people inside. We believe there are four students and perhaps a guard. Bracken, be careful out there."

So, she does have a small space in her heart for at least a bit of concern for my welfare. Bracken became serious. "We'll be fine, but it won't be as easy without you at the BATT controls watching over us. George will be filling in on your behalf. Hopefully, we won't need his medical expertise."

"He's a good backup," Cordy agreed. "I understand an armored transport vehicle will be waiting for you. The fence is topped with barbwire all around the complex. Bramble and brush have collected around the fences, so it's hard to see." Her agile mind raced ahead, plotting out solutions. "Use heat sensors to locate the—"

"That's just like you, Cordy. Telling me how to do my job," he chuckled. "I sure do miss you. Hope Braun's treating you right. If not—"

"Yeah, I miss sparring with you, too, but I'm happy, Bracken," Cordy said. "Did you get the drone pics?"

"George is downloading them to our cell phones."

"The place is surreal, dark, and looks like a haunted jungle." Cordy recalled the area, "Many high areas are great for hiding—especially from the old rollercoaster. I'm not sure how safe it would be, though. The railing is falling away from the tracks. Many of the structures have been demolished. Tall trees are growing up through the Ferris wheel. Machine gears and rotted wood clutter the uneven ground and cracked concrete. I especially remember the Whacky Shack, which is now in shambles. Happy memories from long ago have now turned into a nightmare. Oh, gotta go. Quint's calling." She disconnected.

Bracken glanced at the downloaded pics that George had forwarded. Cordy was right. Joyland was anything but amusing. "It's time for our briefing." Bracken went through the photos, brainstormed with the team, and set a plan. *Hopefully, the negotiators will be successful, but things could quickly get out of hand.*

QUINT'S ON THE PROWL

Sept. 18 – 2:47 a.m. EDT, General Rutoon's Office, Washington, D.C.

Quint digested every email, phone call, fax, and text message he could find in General Rutoon's files. There were messages from the land, sea, and National Security Agencies worldwide. He ran each through a watchlist program laced with hot words such as cyber, attack, explosives, anthrax, polio, etc.

One call stood above the rest. Three days before Rutoon's death, a message came from Syria logged in at 2:53 a.m. Eastern European Summer Time Zone. It took three rings before Rutoon answered the phone.

Start of Transcript: "General, it's me, Gertie. Can…hear me?"

"You're breaking up," Rutoon said. "Where are you calling from?"

"Damascus International," Gertie said. "Risingsickle's on the prowl. What are you waiting for?"

"I don't have orders to move," Rutoon said in a low voice.

"But you're going to move on this, right?" Gertie asked.

Rutoon hushed her. "No one can know my plans. Where is he now?"

"Syria, heading back to Moscow. His seeds are planted in London and other major cities, including the U.S. They will reap harvest soon. You must be ready."

"Where in the U.S.?" Rutoon asked.

"SC planted in Wichita Falls in Texas. They'll attack NYSE, the Pentagon, and…" There was a loud crackle and then a single gunshot blast.

"Son of a bitch!" Rutoon yelled. "Gertie! What just happened?"

A gruff voice with a thick Russian accent broke out in laughter. "Better find a new stooge!"

"Surko Okueva?"

"Guess again."

"No, Ignacio, what have you done?" Rutoon shouted.

"Gertie already told you the SC is in Texas. That's a secret cell command force, right? You set it up with my brother, Surko, but don't worry. He's at the top of my kill list. I'll be taking his place soon. Beware, General Rutoon. Once I off my brother, you're next on my hunt list." The line went dead.

Quint listened again. He sent the message to Cordy's darknet account and the camera photo of the six-sided star surrounded by random letters and numbers. Inside the star was an odd circle filled with wavy lines.

Sept. 18 – 3:12 a.m. EDT, General Rutoon's Office, Washington, D.C.

Cordy answered after two rings. "Hey, Quint. Are you still in Rutoon's office?"

"Yes. I sent you a message, and I found an interesting photo. I'd look into it in greater detail, but I had a scare of a lifetime when Rutoon's secretary made a secret appearance. I'm leaving now. I promised to meet with President Spendorf later today."

"He's supposed to be on bed rest. Shouldn't you talk to Acting President Harris?" Cordy asked.

"I'm on official business for Zac, but I will if Zac asks me. Listen to that message and let me know what you think. Share it with Acting President Harris if you must. I really don't have an in with the man. He treats me like I'm only a geek."

"Well, you are." Cordy laughed. "Now, get out of the Pentagon before someone sees you."

"Girlfriend, I'm scared." Quint's voice trembled with obvious fear. "Our nation is at risk. Listen to that message I sent you."

"Do you think this is a nuclear threat or another biological attack on the U.S.?" Cordy gasped.

"Worse." Quint's voice cracked. "Multiple nations?"

"Which ones?" Cordy asked.

"If I had to guess, they will hit main cities," Quint said. "London, Paris, Rome, and the U.S., maybe more, but I don't have any proof yet."

"When will they strike?" Cordy asked. "We must be prepared. You're my go-to geek, and I need your help."

"I can't crack this." His whisper made her blood run cold. "Check in with Usher. He must find Okueva. He's top dog in this fight, and time is running out!"

FALSE ALARM

Sept. 18 – 3:04 a.m. CDT, Wichita, Kansas/
4:04 a.m. EDT, Cincinnati, Ohio

A little after 3 a.m., Tattoo man's phone rang. He was already pissed off at the driver, who had called him out of the lab in a panic. It ended up that the only lights the driver had seen were reflections of the moon on scraps of metal. Tattoo man signaled to the driver to wait up and stepped behind a bush to answer the call, "Da."

"This is Smith. I have some concerns about Termine. Act swiftly and make it look like an accident, but make sure everything and everybody inside that lab vanishes. Understood?"

"Da. Vill do," Tattoo man said, "Count on me."

"I've doubled your funds, and I'm leaving the country now," Smith said, disconnecting the call.

Tattoo man beamed and was making mental plans on how he'd spend $2 million. He was startled when the driver came up behind him. "Who was that?"

"Smith called. Termine and boys are history. Smith's leaving now."

"Good. We should leave, too. Set up those explosives before sunrise," the driver said. "Then I'm out of here before all hell breaks loose. The timer will go off at noon as planned. You're flying to Dallas, right?"

"None of your business," Tattoo man scowled.

The driver burst out, "Da. Don't take it so personally." Tattoo man's glare made the driver break out in a cold sweat, and he backed away, whispering, "You know where to place the C-4 packets?"

"I know plan," Tattoo man snapped. "Can do in my sleep." The darkness in him had blocked out all personal connections. "I set bombs and leave with you."

"Good thinking," the driver said.

Tattoo man had no plans to let the driver survive. "You stand guard." *See what other lights you can panic over.*

When the driver grabbed his M-16 and high-powered scope, Tattoo man set to work. First, he attached a light over his forehead. This was a delicate task, and any mistake would be his last.

His nimble fingers never trembled or touched anything without intent. He loved to use his hands, whether to break a neck or body parts. Inflicting an injury meant second-guessing another's action. In contrast, a bomb was simple. The only moving part was the switch that ran from the power source and back.

He had designed each part with precision to reassemble in exact order. Nothing was at risk if he kept the switch open while adding each unit. It only became deadly the instant he engaged the switch. Then the detonator would send a charge through the cords to the blasting caps, and kaboom!

Two C-4 packs should be placed on each corner of the lab and in the middle, taking care of all evidence. He moved with silent haste, so Termine and the students had no clue of his plan. He'd run a tripwire by the door, so if any of the students, or more than likely, Termine, tried to leave before the timer went off, the explosives would detonate—one *regret. I won't be here to see my results.* There was a little surprise waiting for Smith, too. He wouldn't be leaving the country unless someone scooped up his ashes.

SNIPERS

Sept. 18 – 4:10 a.m. CDT, Wichita, Kansas/
5:10 a.m. EDT, Cincinnati, Ohio

Russ Bracken and his six team members landed outside of Wichita, Kansas, in the dark of a private landing strip known only to a privileged few. The night was eerily silent, with only the distant sound of crickets breaking the stillness. Already ten minutes late, the team gathered their gear. Two gray ballistic armored tactical transport units awaited as pre-arranged. "Chico, take the larger unit. George set up for surveillance. Guy promised to have it decked out with the latest technical equipment. We'll use that BATT as temporary headquarters while on site."

"Roger." George grabbed his medical equipment and laptop and darted for the larger transport unit.

Bracken's second in command, Poncho, motioned to Kayman and Chico, "Load our SWAT gear. Foley and Desmond, organize your bomb equipment, and meet me in the BATT while Bracken calls his boss in Washington, D.C." The team, well-prepared and focused, carried out their tasks with practiced ease.

"This is Homeland Security, Guy Weimer speaking."

Bracken was shocked at how strong the connection between the two phones was, even out here in the middle of nowhere. "We're headed for Joyland Park now. Where are my FBI negotiators?"

"Meet our agent at the entrance to the park," Guy said. "He'll be in uniform and will join you for the rest of the mission. His name is Orin House. Do you know him?"

"No, I've never met him. Is there only one negotiator?" Bracken asked. "Usually, there are three."

"He's the best, and with such short notice, it's all I could do," Guy said. "Besides, you have worked both SWAT and as a negotiator. Use your skills as you see fit."

"I don't need to tell you, but SWAT is trained to take the bad guys out swiftly," Bracken said. "As a negotiator, I aimed to get everyone out —a huge difference in outcomes."

"Try not to butt heads, Bracken," Guy warned. "Orin knows his stuff. Include him in briefings, and set expectations right up front."

"Will do," Bracken said.

"I'll send the latest drone photos. Text me when you've arrived at Joyland." Guy disconnected the call.

Bracken pulled his credentials from his pocket and nearly raced over two uniforms standing guard in the front and rear of the larger vehicle. Their insignias identified them as members of the Evidence Response Team (ERT), but following protocol, the two men set aside their machine guns and handed him their own IDs. One man was tall and thin as a beanstalk. The other was older and a head shorter.

Preliminaries were completed, and reporting began. "We believe at least two guards are posted outside the lab," the older man added. "They're armed."

Beanstalk reported, "Drones with infra-red cameras sent up within the last hour also show five people inside the lab. I presume one inside is also a guard and may be armed."

A muscular man dashed forward, holding his ID. "Sorry I'm late, Joint Terrorism Task Force. The drone doesn't have a bomb sniffer, so we don't know if there are any explosives on the property. One sniper was on top of the Whacky Shack but may have moved by now."

"How long ago?" Bracken asked.

Muscles checked his watch, "Reported to me nine minutes ago. We'll let you take it from here. You might meet up with the locals. They want in on the action, so I hope there's no turf war. I tried to quell their unrest. They're not happy that the FBI is running the show."

"It happens all the time," Bracken said. "Thanks for the update." Filled with adrenaline, he darted toward the larger BATT. This was finally it. They were going to have their standoff.

Bracken bounced through the door to update his men. "Dual teams as usual. Poncho, head up team two. As planned, you take Kayman and Desmond."

"Roger," Poncho said.

"Chico and Foley stay with me. One more thing—I got word that no bomb sniffer has been launched, so we'll send up ours before we make our move. Are we ready to roll?"

Each man raised their fist. "Roger!"

George's monitor pinged. "Great, we have photos! I'll download them as we drive so we can get going.

Bracken pointed. "Chico, you drive. team one will stay here. Poncho, take your team to the smaller BATT and follow close behind us."

Team two moved with haste, and soon, the headlights of the smaller BATT blinked. Poncho was ready to roll.

George manned the monitors in the upper left corner, following mission instructions. The engine roared to life, and a map on the far right showed a blue GPS location dot maneuvering toward the red blip of Joyland, their destination. The BATT raced to beat the twilight. "According to Google Maps, it takes seventeen minutes to Joyland. ETA is 4:08."

A black sedan was parked off the road leading to the park. As expected, a blond-haired man in a navy jacket with "FBI" in large gold letters stepped from the driver's side and waved.

Bracken spoke into his headphones, "Looks like that's our negotiator. He's coming with us. Poncho, bring your team up here for a briefing, and then we'll enter the park."

Chico put on the brakes, and the BATT came to a halt. Poncho and his team did the same.

Bracken opened the door for team two, followed by the FBI agent. "Good morning. I'm Russ Bracken. Welcome to our team."

"Agent Orin House. Glad to meet you. Call me, Orin. I hate using my last name. It's confusing when working in D.C. People think I'm talking about the House of Representatives, which is far from the truth and gets me in trouble more times than not." He shook hands.

Bracken noted a firm handshake, and Orin's smile reached his dark brown eyes. Bracken felt at ease in an instant—*an honest and genuine man. No wonder he has a reputation. I hope he is as good as he seems.*

Bracken introduced the other team members. "Did you wait long for our arrival?"

"I parked less than five minutes ago. What's the plan?" Orin asked.

"Foley will send up our modified bomb sniffer before we move forward," Bracken said. "We've muffled the sound so it won't warn our enemies. Once we determine bomb status, we'll walk around the fence to check for any breaches before moving through the barbed wire gate."

"Are you going to announce your arrival before entering?" Orin asked.

"Our usual rules of engagement are to search the perimeter before making any warning," Bracken said. "If we encounter anyone unarmed, we'll announce we're FBI. Depending on their response, you can step in as a negotiator, but if sniper activity occurs, my team will defend themselves and the hostages. Our main goal is to free these kids. We want them alive. Is that understood?"

"Yes, but what happens if you observe a suspect with a rifle carried in a non-offensive way or within reach?" Orin asked.

"My team will consider and make a judgment call whether they employ deadly force. They have the knowledge and experience to make the best call when it comes to using their weapons."

"But you agree that all efforts should be made to avoid confrontation with the students," Orin said.

"Of course, with the students, but they are being held hostage by armed guards," Bracken reminded him. "Any armed adult outside of the lab will be neutralized. Does that meet with your approval? Not that it matters because that's how I'm playing it."

Orin pursed his lips for a moment. "I guess, but let's chat after you walk the perimeter. Your bomb experts will deal with any explosives. I get that."

"It's now 4:20 a.m. Desmond, Foley, send up your sniffer drone," Bracken said. "George, let us know what your monitor reports."

It took less than ten minutes to get results from the launched drone. George called out, "Bracken, the whole lab is surrounded by C-4 explosives. I don't think they plan to let any students survive."

Bracken studied the monitor. C-4 packets were in each corner of the building. No one was in sight outside the door, but thermal images showed five people inside the lab.

Orin stepped up behind Bracken. "Crisis negotiation. My favorite."

"Before we announce that we're out here, we'll walk the perimeter as we discussed. Team one will go left 500 yards from the main gate and check for more explosives, tripwires, or obstacles before proceeding. Poncho will take team two right the same distance, and then we'll return to our starting point."

Bracken and Poncho's teams exited the vehicle, dressed in full gear. The extra weight added to the heat of the night. Night vision goggles made everything appear greenish-gray as they moved in a quiet trek in opposite directions. Foley, being team one's bomb man, led to the left. His moves were swift with silent grace. Like a hungry wolf hunting for prey, his footing was soundless.

Bracken followed a few steps behind with a rifle slung across his chest and a semi-automatic pistol held low, barrel toward the ground. His head constantly turned from side to side, alert and on the lookout for any potential hazards.

Desmond's bulky form led team two in the opposite direction. Despite his muscular mass, he walked in a soft, fluid, cat-like motion and was soon out of Bracken's sight.

As team one returned, nearly a quarter of the way to headquarters, night noises, crickets chirping, and squirrels' chattering became silent.

Foley stopped short and held up his hand. "Sniper, two o'clock," he whispered into his headphones.

Bracken's calm voice returned as he dropped to his belly. "Keep moving and watch for a second sniper." Rifle poised, he crawled forward behind a tree stump and caught the sniper in his scope.

The sniper had an M-16 poised at Desmond, who rolled forward, and the puff of dirt that absorbed the blast where he had been a second before flew into Bracken's face. Too close for comfort. Bracken lined up his sights and returned fire with a small pop from the silencer. The sniper flew backward and dropped from the tree he'd been hiding in. The shot was clean and deadly. "One down. Two to go," but a second guard didn't appear. Bracken gave the order to move forward.

The teams reconvened at headquarters at 5:15 a.m. Orin asked, "What happened? George said that you shot a guard. Was he armed?"

Bracken put down his weapons. "Armed, aimed, and fired at Desmond. Fortunately, he missed and didn't get a second chance."

Orin seemed to ponder the response. "Okay. Thermal images only picked up two people outside, plus a few animals in the woods. We've taken care of one guard, but there's at least one more outside and another inside. How do we free the students without getting them killed? And if we make it that far, do you think the students will cooperate if given a chance?"

"If they want to live," Bracken said. "I bet the hostages have been threatened with their own lives and probably the lives of friends and family. That is their usual MO."

Orin said, "Neutralize the outside sniper if you must, but let me negotiate terms with the one inside directly holding the students. I think I can reason with him."

"What makes you say that?" Bracken asked.

"Gut feeling," Orin said. "Frequently, if a hostage-taker gets to know their victims, they can be swayed. Let me at least try."

"Before getting inside that lab, we have to defuse the bombs," Desmond reminded the team.

"It might make a good negotiation point because there's no way anyone inside the building will make it out alive," Orin said.

Bracken added, "I'm sure there's a tripwire at the door. We're hoping our bomb squad can neutralize it, but we won't know until we get closer. There's no one else to call in for help, but Sgt. Foley and Desmond are the best at what they do and have a lot of experience."

Bracken squinted into the sky. Stars were rapidly disappearing as the darkness retreated. His voice became resolute. "Let's move."

PLOT TO ATTACK

Cracker sat at his table digesting Uncle Albert's good news that he'd tracked down General Okueva. It was time to strike. There was a shuffling sound outside the kitchen door. Cracker knew it was Rozalina. He had discovered Rozalina's cell phone had a secret linked to Cracker's new phone and computer system—a precaution, but he'd let her think it was her secret. After all, she wanted no harm to happen to him again. He chuckled at the ruse.

Before Rozalina entered the house, Cracker's phone rang again.

"Hello," Cracker's voice was low and hesitant.

"This is Special Agent Usher Hastings. Are we on a secure line?"

"One moment," Cracker moved to the back door and found Rozalina. "It's Usher Hastings. I need a secure line."

Rozalina pulled him outside. "Take my computer to our room and call him back on my darknet account. I haven't had time to set up yours. I'll unload the supplies."

Three minutes later, Cracker returned Usher's call. "So what did President Harris say?"

"He's in meetings all morning and will not be able to speak with you, but I spoke with Spendorf, and he agreed. I'll send you an email approving your pardon."

"How can I be sure?" Cracker asked.

Usher admitted, "You'll have to take the email as proof."

"Oh, right." Cracker sounded miffed. "You could have anyone send that to me. I want to hear President Harris' approval in person."

Usher blew out a deep breath. "We need to talk. I haven't been entirely honest with you."

"As I suspected!" Cracker's voice raised in pitch.

"Hear me out," Usher said. "This is not the best time. We are facing an emergency here. To put it bluntly, Harris is involved with bigger fish to fry than one man's pardon, so I contacted President Spendorf. He agrees to your terms. We must move quickly. Even you said an al Qaeda secret unit could attack our country. Thanks to you, we now have indisputable evidence that you are right, but we don't know when or where they'll hit. I haven't been able to get the current president's approval to pardon you, but at this point, we need your help more than ever."

"Why should I put my life in jeopardy again?" Cracker asked. "You could change your mind, and I have no recourse. You wouldn't even know where to start without me."

"Listen, we can make your life a living hell, and if anything happens because you don't help us, you can count on a very short Russian winter," Usher warned.

"So, the claws come out and if I do help you? Are you willing to put that in writing and sign it?"

Usher blew out a deep breath. "Yes! In blood, if I must. Look, I promise I'll find a way to let you stay in Russia, but we must stop Okueva. His forces will destroy us," Usher whispered. "If we work together, we can stop him, but we need to find him. I'm willing to work with you. Are you willing to work with me?"

"Send me a handwritten message, an email, and a text message." Cracker's text message and email pinged.

"The handwritten note will be e-faxed shortly," Usher said. "Where do we start?"

Cracker admitted, "Uncle Albert and I found Okueva."

"How did you track him down?" Usher asked.

"I followed his phone calls. Uncle Albert and I worked on a plan all night, and the resistance Army just located Okueva's headquarters, but I warn you, if you're working with us, you'll follow Albert's rules. This is a dangerous operation. We're all putting our lives on the line for your country and mine."

"Okueva has already caused extensive damage to New York City," Usher said. "Now he's threatening our financial and banking systems and preparing an attack in the U.S. We have to stop him."

"And I want revenge for killing my FBI contact and pinning the blame on me. I nearly spent my life in prison because of him. If we don't stop him, he could attack anywhere at any time."

"Okay," Usher said. "We're a team. Will your Uncle Albert agree?"

"Yes," Cracker said.

"How can I be sure?" Usher asked.

"I owe everything to Albert," Cracker said. "He cared for my family and is like a father to my children. He'll team up with you if I say to, but I repeat, you will follow his orders while you're here in Russia. Agreed?"

"Agreed," Usher said reluctantly.

"It's already getting late, so hurry." Cracker gave Usher directions to meet his Uncle and then filled him in on Okueva's hideaway.

Rozalina shot through the door like a bolt of lightning. "I'm going with you; nothing you say will stop me. Mama will care for our children, and I'm not losing you again."

Sept. 18 – 1:32 p.m. MSK, Moscow, Russia/
6:32 a.m. EDT, Cincinnati, Ohio

Zina stared at Usher as he pocketed his cell phone and asked, "What's the latest news?"

"They've located General Okueva and decrypted several email messages. I need to contact Braun. There's secret cell activity in the U.S., but I don't know where. Vlad, get whatever gear is available, and let's go. We meet Uncle Albert in two hours." Usher's agent phone chirped. "It's President Harris."

Zina slipped into a Kevlar vest, much too large for her body, and wrapped a black fleece over it. After gathering supplies from Perry's old stockpile, she dialed her sister Heather. "Sorry I didn't make it to your birthday party, but we've been busy—"

Heather's voice was barely a whisper, "Zina, don't come home! London discovered terrorist cells. We're on a red alert—all airports are closed, and they're diverting incoming airplanes to other countries. Special Armed Forces of the Crown are on a massive hunt. Rumor has it that Paris, France, may also be hit. All of Europe is on high alert. I can't tie up the cell lines. Gotta go. Stay safe. The family sends their love." The line went dead.

Zina's knees buckled, and she would have fallen if she hadn't braced herself against the couch. *My family could be killed. Is Okueva behind this? I thought he was some creep that Usher, with his need to be macho, had concocted to make me stay in Russia.*

Usher, wearing combat boots, a half size too small, and borrowed camo-fatigues that came to mid-calf, stood at the rear door ready to leave, a rifle slung over his shoulder. His face paled as he listened to President Harris. "Cordy says he's attacking multiple nations? Which ones?" "What about Canada, Spain, and Australia?" "…you sent who to London?"

Zina's ears perked up. "What about London?"

Usher glanced at her. "President Harris is sending Dr. Nat Ping to London. He's a good choice—a former CIA operative with decades of experience in counter-terrorism, but it may be too late."

Zina interjected, "London's under attack. The Prime Minister put the U.K. on red alert and is diverting all planes."

Usher relayed the message to Harris, "Good, he'll be on Air Force One, well it won't be called that, but he's traveling on a Stealth B-21. So, you're sending him to Rome instead… Yes, we've tracked Okueva and are on his trail. I'll report back to you as soon as I can." He pocketed the phone.

Zina asked, "Did Okueva plan the attack on London?"

Usher nodded. "I'm sure he did. He's dangerous, and we're going to stop him."

Oh my God! Zina couldn't believe she was on this mission. This was the most dangerous assignment she'd ever had, and she wasn't going to fail. It could save her family.

Usher stepped closer. "Where do you think you're going?"

"With you to capture General Okueva," Zina sat on the couch and pulled her laces tighter before retying her shoes.

"I've changed my mind," Usher said. "You can't go. I have Leo, Vlad, and Cracker's team, so you can stay safe."

Zina pulled herself upright. "My family is under attack. They are counting on me, and I'm going!"

"This is an order!" Usher said louder than he intended.

"And I'm defying that order, so get over it." Zina stepped around him. "I know you're worried about my safety, but this is my job! And nothing you can say will stop me from going—short of tying me up."

Usher pursed his lips and nodded his head. "If I must, that's exactly what I'll do."

"Bugger off!" Zina yelled. "We have less than two hours before we meet Albert."

"You have no military experience," Usher said.

Zina placed her hands on her hips. "More than you think. I'll hold my own. You'll see."

Leo opened the door. "Arguing again?"

"No, we're having a discussion," Zina smiled, "and I just settled it."

"That's debatable." Usher's gray eyes darkened.

Leo ignored the glare between the agents. "I found two other motorbikes. We'll load the gear in the Ural sidecar. Did Cracker say where to meet him?"

"Yes," Usher held up Google Maps with the location. "Albert has a prop jet and will be waiting for us. Then we have a ten-minute flight out into the country. It's hilly, and land cruisers are ready to take us to Cracker and his men. They have Okueva's hideaway in their sights, but getting to the man won't be easy. Armed guards protect him and his retreat, which is also his headquarters. Mountains surround the area, so it is nearly impregnable. We should be there in 30 minutes. I don't want to be late."

"Half an hour?" Leo said. "It would take that long on a good day. That's not today. It'll take at least two hours. I hope Albert has more ammo." He turned to Zina. "Have you driven a motorcycle?"

"I'll manage," but her voice had a tremor.

"No," Vlad said. "I'm going along. She can ride with me."

"If you're coming along, you'll ride with me," Usher snapped. "Let's go! We're wasting time."

Zina certainly wouldn't ride in that sidecar again, and Vlad's motorcycle was already underpowered. Reluctantly, she shoved a helmet over her head and climbed behind Usher.

"Hold on!" Usher revved the engine and took off. Leo stayed on his tail, but Vlad was nearly a mile behind them. The traffic was awful. The muddy roads were slick, and it took two hours and ten minutes before they arrived at the grassy strip—anything but a runway. But this plane was anything but a prop jet. It was an Aero-L 39 Albatross. The jet-powered trainer aircraft was perfect for a ground attack mission. One problem: it was only a two-seater.

"Sorry, we're late." Usher held out his hand as he met Albert. "Impressive. Where did you find this?"

"My team served in the military for many years. We have old equipment, but we keep it in fine shape. Do you fly?"

"Yes," Usher said. "I'd love to fly this jet."

"You'll get your chance, but not now. We have another two hours and twenty minutes to get to our headquarters."

"More than two hours?" Usher asked. "Where is this place?"

"Outside the small town of Pervouralsk, at the foot of the Central Ural Mountains."

Usher rubbed his chin. "How do we get the rest of our team—"

A military truck came from behind several trees a few meters away. A logo of a Russian bear was painted on the hood. "Does that answer your question?" Albert asked. "The team will be along in due time. I thought you and I would take the jet. We need to discuss tactical plans. Then we'll inform the ranks once they arrive."

"Where's Cracker?" Usher asked.

Albert bristled at Usher, obviously unhappy with an unknown and potentially dangerous U.S. agent included on his team—someone he barely trusted. Albert barked orders, "He's being briefed. We have only included your team at Cracker's request. He still believes the president will grant him a pardon. I'm not as convinced. Although, I'm glad to see you have Vlad and Leo on your side. They are good soldiers, but this is not your mission. You will do as I say. Do we agree?"

Usher knew that Vlad and Leo trusted Albert since they had served under him in the Army, but he didn't like taking orders from anyone. Glancing at the armed men, he agreed.

Zina came up behind Albert, "What is the plan?"

"We'll fill everyone in at headquarters." Albert motioned to one of his men. "Dimitri, come meet Agent Zina. She'll be your partner during this mission." Albert turned to Usher. "Don't frown so. He's my second Lieutenant."

Usher bit back a few swear words. He felt protective of Zina and wanted her where he could keep an eye out for her. But, giving in to conditions, he gave Zina the news. "I'm flying with Albert. We'll meet you soon. Make sure to load the motorbikes, too. We may need them."

Albert smiled. "Giving orders comes naturally for you. Okay, load the bikes, too." He motioned for Usher to board the jet, stepping aside to let him go up the steps first.

TARGET UNAWARE

Sept. 18 – 5:33-6:18 a.m. CDT, Wichita, Kansas/
6:33-7:18 a.m. EDT, Cincinnati, Ohio

While Usher hunted down General Okueva in Russia, Russ Bracken was in Wichita, Kansas, heading up one of his own ops to rescue students held as hostages at the abandoned Joyland Amusement Park. It was already 5:33 a.m. CDT. Bracken met Foley and Desmond for one last look after launching the drone before advancing. "Did the drone find any more explosives?"

"No, but our heat sensor located someone in the log ride area." Foley pulled out his cell phone and showed Bracken the latest photos, "See, there's a bridge where logs used to go underwater. Shrubs and log cars litter the path, making it a great hiding place."

Bracken considered his options. "We'll remove the guard first and then defuse the explosives. team one, go to the left. team two, to the right. We're heading through brambles, barbed wires, and the unknown, so be careful."

Foley led SWAT team one through the decaying park and along a barbed-wire fence until they reached a rusty, wobbly metal gate, which stood open—an uninviting sight. Crabgrass grew through cracks in the pavement.

Once everyone passed through the gate, Desmond led team two to the right toward the Log Jam rails. At one time, the tracks rose high overhead to let the cars slide up like a rollercoaster, then speed down a slope and splash through the water. Now, the rails were rickety and bowed, and some had fallen away from the track.

Team one went left toward the Log Jam waterway. Foley moved around several old log cars piled in the weeds. The watercourse comprised two parallel concrete slabs about four feet apart, creating a zigzagged trench through the forestland. Dense bramble grew rope-like vines, climbing treetops and looping along the ground.

Bracken followed Foley as they shoved through prickly pines and found a narrow, overgrown path that had been trodden upon recently. His senses were on full alert, his focus unwavering. Checking the thermal sensor, the sniper rushed along the channel directly into team two's path. He stepped over a dead stump, his concentration never faltering.

Bracken's voice, a mere whisper in the headphones, carried a weight of command, "Target three hundred feet, my one o'clock. Team two's, eleven o'clock, heading your way. Intercept." The team's coordination was seamless, a testament to their unity and trust in each other.

"Take him alive?" Poncho asked.

"If we can," Bracken said, "I don't think he's aware of us."

Sept. 18 – 5:45 a.m. CDT, Wichita, Kansas/
6:45 a.m. EDT, Cincinnati, Ohio

As the target rounded the trench's corner, his eyes flew open when he spotted Poncho. Whipping up his weapon, his finger squeezed the trigger. His bullet plowed into a wooden log that Poncho ducked behind.

Poncho leapt over the log, tackling the guard. The blow dislodged the pistol from the guard's hand, and Poncho was on him in a flash. He buried his knees into the man's back and grabbed the sniper by his hair, shoving his face into the dirt.

The sniper's nose cracked and spurted blood. He bucked, pulled a knife from his boot, and reached around, aiming for Poncho's gut.

Kayman launched forward, grabbed the sniper's arm, and twisted it until there was a loud snap. The knife clattered to the ground.

The sniper screamed and blood spewed from his mouth. His shoulder bulged with his right arm at an odd angle.

Kayman placed his boot over the sniper's upper back, yanked the arm high in the air, and pulled the shoulder back in alignment, causing another yelp from the man. Then Kayman stepped aside.

Poncho slipped zip ties over the sniper's wrists and rolled from the man's back. He flipped the man over, bent down over his face, and adjusted the man's nose with a crack. The sniper paled. His eyes rolled back into his head, and he fainted.

* * *

Bracken moved through the long grass, rushing to get to the sound of the shot and the screams. "Well done."

Poncho frisked the man and found a knife in his other boot.

He handed Bracken his canteen. "Want to do the honors?"

Bracken opened the flask and poured water over the sniper's face, bringing him back to consciousness. "FBI SWAT. Where are the students?"

"Nyet, Angliyskiy!" The man had a six-sided star tattoo with an odd inner circle of waves on each shoulder. Bracken suspected it was a Middle Eastern symbol but hadn't seen one like it before. The man spoke Russian or maybe Belarusian. He pulled the man up by his uninjured arm. "Who else is with you?"

The tattooed guy shook his head as if to clear it and then blew bloody snot from his nose.

"What's your name?" Bracken asked. "Take him to the lab," Bracken said when he still got no answer.

"Nyet," Tattoo said, "Boom!"

"Oh, so you know about the explosives," Bracken said, "Did you plant them?"

Tattoo guy jerked away from Bracken, "Nyet."

"For some reason, I don't believe you," Bracken said. "No English, but you sure seem to understand me. When are they scheduled to detonate?"

Tattoo guy spat at Bracken and launched forward with all his weight trying to knock him down.

Bracken grabbed Tattoo guy's hair, yanked up his head, and forced a pistol to his forehead. "When do they blow?"

Tattoo guy looked cross-eyed up at the gun held at his forehead.

"Or should I blow your brains out," Bracken said with a shake to the guy's injured shoulder.

"Mmm… Don't shoot. I talk."

"Then talk," Bracken said. "Are you the only guard?"

"No, driver here somewhere."

Bracken figured the driver had already been neutralized. "Where are the students?"

Tattoo guy hesitated once more.

Bracken bumped Tattoo guy's broken nose.

"Ahh!" Tattoo guy yelped. "Termine has students in lab."

"Is he armed?" Bracken asked.

Tattoo guy tried to move his head, but Bracken put a firm hold on his injured shoulder, and the pistol pressed closer to his forehead. Tattoo guy moaned, and his breath hitched. His words came out in short sentences. "Has gun. Like me, not good shot. I know bombs. He know noshing…but hacker."

"So, Termine is a hacker?" Bracken asked.

"He bad guard," Tattoo guy said, "Best hacker."

"When is the bomb going off?" Bracken cocked the pistol when Tattoo man refused to speak. "I'm only counting to three. Then I pull the trigger. One. Two—"

"N..noon," Tattoo man spat out. "Noon today."

"Any other surprises?" Bracken didn't ease up on the man's shoulder, causing Tattoo man to flinch.

"Door tripwire…blast sooner if triggered. Trap in tree."

"Move!" Bracken said.

"I'm moving." Tattoo guy shuffled forward, favoring his injured arm.

"Poncho, he's yours." Bracken holstered his gun and called Orin on the radio. "We have the Tattoo guy, our second guard. He's alive and probably their bomb expert. We're moving to the lab now. Care to join us?"

"Roger," Orin said. "Where's Tattoo guy?"

"Poncho's taking him to see George, our medic."

"Is he injured," Orin asked.

"I'd say he has a few medical issues—a dislocated shoulder, broken nose, and maybe a few torn ligaments."

"At least he's alive," Orin said.

"We'll meet you at the barbed wire gate," Bracken said. "How long before you arrive? Time is slipping away."

"George is driving me," Orin said.

They arrived at 6:18 a.m. Tattoo guy, still cuffed, was transferred to George's care.

Bracken speed-dialed Guy Weimer.

"Homeland Security."

"Hi, Guy, I don't have time to talk with President Harris and his security team. This is just a brief update from Wichita, Kansas. C-4 explosives surround the lab with the students inside. They are due to explode at noon. Our team plans to defuse it. I'll keep you informed."

WECHOLTZ TRIAL – PLAINTIFF

The courtroom was divided into two zones: a public and a litigation area with two long tables, one for the defendant and the other for the plaintiff. A low railing separated the two areas. Sophia sat at a table to the left of the room. Chief Jackson and her paralegal joined her to go over some last-minute details.

The courtroom was abuzz with whispers as an officer escorted Wecholtz into the room. Floyd sported a conservative black suit that was two sizes too large, a white cotton shirt, and a maroon striped tie. His slumped shoulders and sleeves reaching his fingertips made for an ill fit. Despite his baggy pants, the spit-shined toes of his shoes reflected the overhead lights. Floyd, clean-shaven with slicked-back dark hair, had hollowed cheekbones, a nose sticking out like a beak, and lips with a grayish hue. However, his bright eyes gleamed through thick spectacles and captivated Sophia's gaze as he seated himself at her side.

Sophia leaned over and whispered in Jackson's ear, "Is that the best you could do? He's drowning in that suit."

"It's the smallest one I have, and he didn't want to appear in an orange jumpsuit," Chief Jackson said.

"Get him another suit by this afternoon. That's an order." Sophia turned toward Floyd. "Ready?"

He nodded, but his fingers were folded so tightly that his knuckles turned white.

She placed her hand over his. "Relax."

It took until 9:00 a.m. to find a jury amenable to both sides. The person selected as a lead juror was a heavy-set black woman who went by the name Grezelda. She was barely thirty and had grown up in the slums of Queens, been a victim of gang rape at the age of fourteen, and saw her brother murdered when he tried to defend her.

She ended up pregnant, her parents abandoned her, and she dropped out of school. Her aunt gave Grezelda a roof over her head. Now, raising a teenage daughter, she vowed to keep her safe, so five years ago, she got her GED and socked away enough money to attend night school. She worked as a bank clerk. Because of her history, she usually wouldn't have been selected as even a juror, but something about her confidence and demeanor won her the position.

There were three other women, a nurse, a school teacher, a homemaker, and eight men on the jury. The men ranged from blue-collar workers: a bus driver and a sanitation worker to a jeweler, a rabbi, a French chef, a car salesman, an engineer, and a school principal. There were also two substitutes in case someone became ill or ineligible—women in their thirties. Grezelda was the only person of color, yet she sat up straight, proud, and clear-eyed. Nothing was going to get past her.

Sophia was pleased with the selection. Grezelda would make a solid lead juror whom others could look up to.

As a senior judge, Nif had a spacious courtroom lined with golden oak panel walls. The witness's chair had thick leather padding, making it comfortable enough for hours on the stand—not that anyone wanted to be exposed for any longer than necessary.

On the right side of the room, the Judge's left, sat the plaintiff's team. Ron Moore-Les chatted quietly with his paralegal, a young woman in a tight navy suit and red blouse.

The courtroom deputy swept up to the front of the room. "All rise. District Court of Manhattan County, State of New York is now in session, the Honorable Judge Nif presiding." The room came to life as everyone stood.

Judge Nif flowed up to the bench, stepped up to the mic, and could barely see over the podium. He glared at the deputy. "Where's my step?"

The deputy turned beet red. "Sorry, Your Honor. One moment, sir." He darted behind a curtain, came back with a wooden platform about ten inches high, and set it before the bench. "Is that all, sir?"

Nif grunted and adjusted his glasses.

"The court will now rehear the case of New York State vs. defendant Floyd Wecholtz." Judge Nif motioned to everyone, "Sit! We have work to do. I do hope you all will be brief. I hate minutia." He fluffed out his black robe with a great flare and sat in his chair. Two snaps of his fingers, "My papers."

The deputy darted to a stand beside the bench and hoisted up a file.

Judge Nif leafed through the pages and spread them out before him. "I have reviewed the written briefs submitted by each party, and I read every word. We'll start with opening statements from the prosecuting attorney, Ron Moore-Les, for the State of New York."

Mr. Moore-Les stepped forward. "Good morning, ladies, and gentlemen of the court." He began in lengthy detail. "Seven years ago, on July 5, Floyd Wecholtz was CFO for the OYZ Foundation. His partner and CEO, Andrew Madeim Edwardo Flinsh-Kedderton, founded the company and was a well-known philanthropist who went by his initials, AK. The company was extremely profitable until a few days before AK died in a hit-and-run motor vehicle incident. At 3:47 p.m., the Emergency Communications Center received a 911 call from Alexa Flinsh, reporting that her half-brother, AK, was run down in the company's parking garage by a car driven by Floyd Wecholtz. An onsite security camera caught the incident on videotape. According to the 911 recording, Alexa found her brother, the victim, unconscious and dead."

"Objection," Sophia said. "Alexa has no medical knowledge..."

"Sustained," Judge Nif said.

"I'll rephrase that. Alexa feared her brother was already dead," Moore-Les plowed forward without even taking a breath, "when paramedics arrived on the scene, the victim was not breathing, nor did he have a pulse. They initiated CPR immediately and continued throughout transportation to Belleview Hospital Center's Emergency Room. The victim was pronounced dead on arrival.

"Later that same day, it was also discovered that someone had embezzled $25 million in corporate funds invested by a Chinese firm. We have receipts of the investors' funds from five separate Chinese investors, and the funds have yet to be recovered. Floyd Wecholtz was the CFO. We also have a job description signed by the defendant detailing the role and responsibilities of this position. The CFO is responsible for receiving, depositing, and reporting all investment funds in this job description.

"In summary, count 1—We charge the defendant, Mr. Floyd Wecholtz, with embezzlement of corporate funds. When his boss, AK, discovered the deed, Mr. Wecholtz used his car to deliberately run down his boss, resulting in AK's death. Count 2—We intend to prove murder in the first degree.

"Today, you will hear from Alexa Klinedorf, AK's half-sister, who discovered the incident. We also have an expert witness, Dr. Horace Kiddash, New York's medical examiner, who completed an autopsy on the victim. Cause of death was a severed spinal cord at the level of C4, resulting in instant death." Moore-Les discussed other witnesses he would call to the stand.

Sophia jotted a few notes as Moore-Les summarized his case.

"I must warn you that the defendant claims that AK threatened Floyd Wecholtz with a gun when he ran down his boss, but there is no evidence of a gun on the videotape. Now, it is true that gunpowder residue was found on the victim's right hand and coat sleeve, but as you know, the residue can stay on one's hands for 30-40 minutes. The point here is that there was no gun found at the scene of the crime." Moore-Les wrapped up his case. "Ladies and gentlemen, this case is about a victim deliberately run down and murdered in cold blood. The murder was premeditated, and Mr. Wecholtz got away with $25 million of corporate funds."

Moore-Les strolled to his right and looked each juror in the eyes as he stated, "By examining the evidence, it is your job to bring justice for the murder of AK, a world-renowned philanthropist. Floyd Wecholtz is guilty of embezzling corporate funds, and when his boss discovered the deed, Wecholtz murdered his boss by running him down with a deadly weapon, his car. That's murder in the first degree. I am confident that when you hear all the evidence, you, the jurors, will have no doubt of Mr. Wecholtz's guilt." Moore-Les took his seat.

Sophia walked to a small podium and blew out a deep breath. "Good morning, ladies, and gentlemen of the court. I am Sophia Hendrum, and I represent the defendant, Floyd Wecholtz. As Mr. Moore-Les has already stated, on July 5, 2015, Floyd Wecholtz was CFO of the OYZ Foundation. On that same day, between 2 and 3:00 p.m., he received phone calls from five irate Chinese investors demanding the return of their investment funds totaling $25 million. That was Mr. Wecholtz's first awareness that anyone had submitted additional funds to the corporation. He researched corporate financial records to determine where the funds had been deposited. When there was no record to support the investors' claims, he reran a corporate financial analysis, discovering that the corporation's assets had dropped by over $23 million overnight.

"The office was hectic that day, causing many interruptions in his research. AK wasn't there when my client went to his boss's office. Mr. Wecholtz asked the corporate secretary, Maude Ingram, if she had seen AK. Maude told Mr. Wecholtz that AK hadn't been to the office all day. Mr. Wecholtz decided to do further research at home, where he wouldn't have any interruptions. He took several corporate files to his car and placed them on the front seat. AK must have arrived at the parking garage about that same time. Mr. Wecholtz climbed into the driver's side and started the engine. That's when

AK dashed in front of Mr. Wecholtz's car and yelled, 'How could you steal from our company!'

"Mr. Wecholtz rolled down his front window, leaned forward, and asked, 'What do you mean, steal from the company?' AK swung his arm up, holding a pistol in his right hand, and aimed the gun at Floyd's head. Mr. Wecholtz panicked and stepped on the gas. He heard a loud bang like a firecracker as the car bolted forward and knocked AK aside. Mr. Wecholtz saw from his rearview mirror that AK was on the ground, but he rolled to his side and continued yelling as Floyd drove away. My client was shocked to hear his boss died within an hour after being run over.

"As Dr. Kiddash will, no doubt, report, there was gunpowder residue on AK's right hand and coat sleeve, and there was a .38 shell casing found on the garage floor 200 ft. from the victim. Although there was no gun found at the scene, nor was a gun evident on the parking camera's videotape, we have proof that the videotape was tampered with, thus cutting out the sections showing AK approaching the car with a gun. Even the part where Floyd Wecholtz got into the car is missing from the tape, but it resumes in time to see Floyd run down AK. The tape is very blurry, and there is a loud sound like a car backfiring, which may have been gunfire."

Sophia described the discrepancies on the tape when comparing the same timeframe with the 911 audiotape as she had at the previous hearing. She wrapped up with, "So members of the jury, I will prove beyond any doubt that Floyd Wecholtz did not embezzle funds, nor did he murder his boss, AK." Sophia sat down.

"Mr. Moore-Les, you may call your first witness," Judge Nif said.

Alexa Klinedorf was called to the stand and sworn in.

"What do you remember on the day of your brother's death?" Moore-Les asked.

Alexa wrung her hands as she told her story. "That day was awful, but I didn't suffer the greatest hardship. No, not by far. His death gripped the poor orphans. You know it was all over the news— National and International news. Those poor children ended up back on the streets, homeless, starving, and dying. AK's money had been a God-sent to them. He put food on their tables, gave them a roof over their heads, and then that schmuck," she pointed to Floyd Wecholtz, "ran him down, and murdered the most kind, generous man on earth." Alexa put her head in her hands and wept.

Sophia said, "Objection. The defendant is innocent until proven guilty."

"Oh, he's guilty, all right. I saw it with my own eyes," Alexa said.

"Objection," Sophia raised her voice.

"Sustained," Nif warned. "Mr. Moore-Les, please explain to your client…"

"Yes, Your Honor," Moore-Les said. "I'll rephrase the question."

It took forty minutes for Alexa to answer the DA's questions. She sat up tall, grieving for her brother, with tears running down her cheeks.

Sophia had objected on two more occasions but was rapidly told to ask those questions upon her cross-examination of the eyewitness, so she jotted down several notes and waited for her turn.

When Moore-Les was done, Sophia rose and walked toward Alexa. "I am sorry for your loss. Did you observe your brother actually being run down by Floyd Wecholtz?"

"Of course I did," Alexa said.

"You saw your brother before he was hit by the car," Sophia clarified.

"Well, no," Alexa admitted.

"Did you find your brother after the incident?" Sophia stepped closer.

"Yes, ah, no…"

"Be sure. You're under oath," Sophia warned.

"I…I saw AK on the garage floor," Alexa sobbed. "There was blood everywhere."

"Did you see Mr. Wecholtz run down your brother?" Sophia repeated.

"No, but I heard the car racing away," Alexa said, "and it was Floyd's car on the tape."

"But you didn't actually see Mr. Wecholtz drive over your brother," Sophia said. "Perhaps seeing the tape made you think you saw the actual incident."

"I...I can't say for sure." Alexa's hands shook. "I was so upset at the time, and AK wouldn't shut up."

"Objection!" Moore-Les shouted.

But Alexa kept on. "...I had to push him back to the ground to stay still. He insisted on sitting up and shouting—"

"Objection," Moore-Les shouted even louder. "You mean he was breathing so hard because he was in pain? You tried to comfort him."

Alexa's eyes darted toward Moore-Les. Her mouth gaped open momentarily, then snapped shut, and she nodded.

"Objection," Sophia said. "You're leading the witness."

"Do you care to restate your comment?" Judge Nif glared down at Moore-Les.

The attorney opened his mouth, but Alexa jumped into the fray, "Yes, that's what I mean. AK was moaning, and his breathing wasn't normal." She broke into hysterics—sobbing and patting her chest as if she couldn't catch her breath. Gasping, she added, "My poor, poor darling. How could anyone do such a terrible thing? There was so much blood. I still have nightmares. AK reshaped my entire life and the lives of so many."

Sophia folded her arms. "Perhaps we should take a break and allow Mrs. Klinedorf time to compose herself."

Judge Nif banged his gavel. "Bring the lady some water," he directed the clerk. Turning to Alexa, he added, "Try to calm down. We don't have all day."

A murmur went through the courtroom as Alexa stepped down from the stand and whispered something into Mr. Moore-Les' ear. He shook his head, "Return to the witness stand," but Alexa walked to the back of the courtroom and argued with the bailiff to let her leave the room.

"Mrs. Klinedorf, you can't leave just yet," Sophia said. "You've been subpoenaed and agreed to testify. You are still under oath to tell the truth, and you've been called to the stand. You have not been released yet."

Alexa turned toward the Judge. "You're Honor. I have nothing further to say on this case."

"Take the stand," Judge Nif ordered. "If you refuse to answer any questions, that's your prerogative, which will be recorded accordingly."

"Must I?" Alexa asked.

Mr. Moore-Les got up from the table and escorted Alexa to the stand. "Plead the 5th amendment if you wish."

Judge Nif cleared his throat. "Let's get on with this. It's already 10:00 a.m."

Sophia stepped closer to Alexa. "Did you know Floyd Wecholtz personally?"

"Not really. He was my brother's CFO, so he was well-versed on the company's financial status. That's why it only makes sense that he embezzled the funds."

"Can you explain how the hidden files were entered under your user access code on the secretary's computer?"

Alexa glared at Sophia.

"Let's examine exhibits 1a, 1b, and 1c. Exhibit 1a confirms an offshore account opened at Geneva Bank in Switzerland on July 5, seven years ago, for $10.3 million under the name Alexa Klinedorf." Sophia placed the document in front of Alexa. "Did you open this account?"

Again, Alexa stayed silent. Sophia produced exhibit 1b, showing that the same account was closed ten days later, on July 15, and a copy of a check written to Alexa Klinedorf for $10.9 million was paid out by Geneva Bank. "Is that your signature on the back of the check?"

"I have no knowledge of that check," Alexa said. "I never received those funds."

"May I remind you that you are under oath to tell the truth," Sophia said. "Would you like to rephrase your answer?"

"No," Alexa glared at Sophia. "I never received those funds."

"Did you open that account using the secretary's computer?" Sophia asked.

Alexa turned right and stared at her husband, Victor, sitting in the back row. "I can't answer that, but I never received any funds from that bank, and that's the truth."

Sophia followed Alexa's gaze and saw Victor shake his head slightly. "Are you secretly communicating with your husband?" Sophia asked.

Alexa's eyes snapped back on Sophia. "No, I can talk to him directly. In case you hadn't noticed, we are in the same room."

Sophia ignored the barbed words. "Why was an account opened in Alexa Klinedorf's name when your name was Alexa Flinsh at that time?"

"As I already stated, I can't…I can't answer that, but I never received any funds from that bank."

"You can't answer that, or you won't?" Sophia asked.

"I've already answered your question two times," Alexa snapped.

Sophia moved on. "What can you tell me about exhibit 1c, which shows an investment of $15 million in a Chinese Magnesium Corporation on July 15, seven years ago? The name on the account is also Alexa Klinedorf."

Alexa took a deep breath. "I have nothing to say about any of these investments. My only guess is that Floyd Wecholtz is trying to frame me."

At that, Floyd shoved back his chair and stood. "I did not frame you. I didn't know about any investment funds, and I didn't murder your brother!"

Judge Nif slammed down the gavel. "Order! I will have order in the court! Mr. Wecholtz, sit down!"

Floyd said, "Sophia, I want to speak! I have the right to tell what happened."

"I'll call on you shortly," Sophia said. "For now, listen closely to what Alexa has to say."

"Exhibit 2a is a phone recording made by AK's secretary, Maude Ingram. We will hear from her later, but you're on the stand now, so play that recording, please," Sophia asked the clerk.

The clerk cued the recording of Alexa, saying, "...One problem is that AK started diversifying, making it more difficult to track. I created several accounts in Geneva, and the bankers set up real-time information so I can easily trade and conduct business with others in the industry. The funds are secure. Even my brother can't get access. I plan to simply cash in and disappear." The clerk shut off the recorder.

"Can you explain that call?"

"No, I don't recall any phone call. And if that is me, I certainly wasn't talking about AK's corporation. I'd never steal from my own brother. He was teaching me how to secure my money, so I made investments as he recommended."

"Where did you get those funds?" Sophia paged through her notes. "According to your financial statements, your net worth was only $380,000 at the time."

"Is that right?" Alexa asked. "I don't recall. A lot has happened over the past seven years."

Sophia switched to another line of questioning. "When did you meet your husband, Victor Klinedorf?"

"On the day of my brother's death, July 5," Alexa said with certainty.

Sophia glanced toward Victor, who was nodding. Pausing, Sophia asked. "Then did Victor open these accounts?"

"No!" Alexa shouted, took a few deep breaths, and calmed herself. "I mean, no. He didn't even know how to access a computer at that time. He was only a manager of the parking garage. It had to have been Floyd."

"As a manager, Victor worked with computers every day, so how can you say he didn't know how to access computers?" Sophia asked.

"I mean, he never had any access to AK's corporate computers," Alexa backpedaled. "Of course, he knew how to turn on a computer. He's not an idiot. As a matter of fact, he's the most intelligent man that I know."

"Was it Victor that you were speaking to on Maude's recording of your phone conversation at 6:48 a.m. on July 5?" Sophia said.

"There's some mistake," Alexa said. "That wasn't me on that recording."

"Very well, we could do a voice analysis," Sophia said.

"Whatever." Alexa shrugged.

Sophia repeated, "Why were these accounts in the name of Alexa Klinedorf when you had barely met Victor? You didn't get married for another four months."

"That proves it wasn't me who opened those accounts," Alexa said. "My name was Alexa Flinsh at the time. If it wasn't Floyd, then it had to have been Maude who opened that account."

Sophia squinted at Alexa. "Not likely. It was an encrypted file accessed by user code 10200, assigned to you weeks before AK's death. That leads me to ask again: where did you get $10.3 million to open an offshore account with Geneva Bank, and where did the $15 million investment in the Chinese Magnesium Company come from?"

"No comment," Alexa said.

Sophia asked, "Are you pleading the 5th amendment?"

"No." Alexa hesitated. "That was years ago. I can't remember any of this."

"Also, if you did cash out $10.9 million, it did not appear on your IRS statements," Sophia said.

"So there you have it," Alexa said. "I never received the cash."

"Did you reinvest those funds into the Chinese Magnesium Company?" Sophia asked. "Perhaps you never received a check but transferred the funds directly."

"I really have no answer for you," Alexa said.

Chief Jackson entered the courtroom with a broad smile. He crept around the side aisle to sit at the front table with Sophia and nodded.

"Yes," Sophia referred to the exhibit marked 1-g. "After several attempts, I finally accessed NBC's copy of the parking garage videotape showing my client running down his boss, AK, with his car."

Sophia continued, "Let's move on to exhibit 2b. A fire destroyed the original parking garage security tape, but I can still prove someone tampered with the evidence. We sent the NBC copy, which is a duplicate of the original, to Professor Seamore Hyde at MIT. He ran a digital analysis of the video and found several areas that have been cut and spliced throughout the tape. The professor's affidavit stating that the video had been tampered with is marked exhibit 1h. I offer the exhibit to the court. I've marked each area and will play it with your permission."

"The exhibit is received, but wait to submit this evidence during the defense presentation," Judge Nif said.

Sophia stepped up to the judge. "There are many questions concerning that recording that I must ask Alexa, so I'd like to address those issues while she is still on the stand."

Judge Nif blew out a deep breath and glanced at his watch. "It's 10:20 a.m. I suppose we have time now. Please, proceed."

The court clerk cued the recording.

Sophia added, "Before starting the video, I want each of you to listen and watch closely. Professor Hyde noted in his affidavit that there are abrupt changes in background sounds during the cuts. Lighting changed from dark to black, then pops back to the original colors, making the video appear jumpy. There are digital numbers hidden on the tape, which also advances from 15:45:12 to 15:47:38; another skip occurs from 15:48:16 to 15:49:07, and there are three more skips with the last one at 15:52:28 to 15:54:42. What happens during those missing time frames are of the greatest importance."

"Why?" Judge Nif asked.

"Mr. Wecholtz swears that AK had a gun pointed at him. He panicked and ran his partner down. Then AK shouted at my client as he drove away. The tape, on the other hand, shows AK, without a raised gun, standing in front of Floyd's car when he ran AK down. The next scene has AK unconscious and perhaps even dead—that's when you, Alexa, find him. You called 911, but your initial call is not on the tape, yet it picks up mid-sentence. Exhibit 1i is a copy of the audiotaped 911 phone call for comparison. When you play both tapes together, pieces are missing from the parking garage video."

"Turn down the lights so we can get a better view and play the video," Judge Nif ordered, "and then play the 911 audio." The room fell silent.

Sophia paused the recording at the cuts mentioned and pointed out the discrepancies. She asked Alexa several questions but got no further answers.

After hearing the 911 audiotape, Sophia asked Alexa, "On the 911 call, you said, 'No, you can't have that,' but it doesn't appear on the video when we match the audiotape with the video during the last three minutes. Why is that?"

Alexa shrugged her shoulders. "Play it again. I don't know what you're referring to."

"Watch closely," Sophia said.

When Alexa said, "You can't have that" on the 911 call, a rustling sound followed. At the same time on the video, Alexa was leaning over her brother. Something shiny glinted as she slid her hand into her purse, and a shadow fell over her. The purse then disappeared from the tape.

Sophia clarified, "I believe Alexa slid a gun into her purse—the same gun that AK used to threaten Floyd Wecholtz and sent him into a panic, causing my client to rundown his boss. Alexa covered her actions by leaning over her brother, but she definitely slipped something into that purse. A purse that disappeared on the tape, and there was no purse found at the scene when the police arrived. AK had gunpowder residue on his right hand and the right cuff of his coat. Can you explain how the parking garage tape was edited?"

"That, I definitely can't address," Alexa said.

"Maybe you can explain what happened to that beige leather purse that was on the tape at the 15:47:38 mark but disappeared at the 15:48:16 cut?"

"I don't think that was my purse," Alexa said.

"Then whose purse was it that you slipped that shiny object into?" Sophia asked.

"I don't think I slipped a shiny object into anything," Alexa said. "I just leaned over my brother."

Chief Jackson spoke softly to Sophia, "Mr. Hyde is waiting to be called. He can maybe clarify these questions." Jackson tapped his watch. "It's already 10:30 a.m."

"I can't call on him yet; he's a witness for the defense," Sophia whispered, took a deep breath, and turned to Alexa. "I have no more questions of this witness at this time, but I reserve the right to recall her. There are many unanswered questions."

Alexa nodded to her husband. "I'm leaving. I have nothing else to discuss." She bolted for the back door and left the courtroom.

"Call your next witness," Judge Nif said to Moore-Les.

Dr. Horace Kiddash raised his right hand, swore to tell the truth, and sat on the witness stand.

Moore-Les said, "I have an autopsy report marked as plaintiff evidence 1j before me. Do you recognize this report?"

The medical examiner briefly flipped through the three-page report. "Yes. I wrote this report."

"Can you tell us in layman's terms what you found during your forensic exam?" Moore-Les asked.

Kiddash tugged at the lapels of his gray suit jacket. "The victim died of a fractured C4. That means the 4th cervical vertebra broke, and a bone fragment sliced through the spinal cord, causing instant death."

Moore-Les continued, "Does the physical evidence corroborate with Alexa's testimony?"

"In some aspects, yes," Kiddash said. "He would have difficulty breathing, and perhaps he moaned, but only briefly, as once the air rushed from his lungs, he could no longer inhale. The brain stem was severed, so no brain activity could trigger the lungs to breathe. Witnessing the final moments would have been devastating, especially for a sister. It would be like watching someone drowning."

"What about Floyd's statement that AK rolled over and was yelling?" Moore-Les asked.

"Not very likely," Kiddash said.

"Thank you," Moore-Les nodded to the Judge. "I have no further questions of this witness."

"Do you wish to cross-examine?" Judge Nif asked.

Sophia stood. "Dr. Kiddash, could that cervical fracture have severed the spinal cord after AK rolled to his side and yelled at Mr. Wecholtz?"

"Yes, I suppose that could have happened."

"If there had been immediate medical care rendered, his spine and neck would have been restrained," Sophia said. "Thus, he could have survived the injury without moving. Yet, Alexa states that he wouldn't shut up. Her initial statement declared that he sat up yelling at my client. And she had to push him to stay still. Could her pushing him have severed the cord?"

"I couldn't say without being at the scene at the time of the incident," Kiddash said. "A spinal fracture is very ominous. Even a sneeze can cause the bone to sever the spinal cord. It's like dropping a quarter into warm Jell-O—that fragile. The quarter will sink."

"Also, did you find gunpowder residue on AK's right hand?" Sophia asked.

"Yes, it's in my report," Kiddash said. "That means he would have come within three feet of a firearm within the last 20-30 minutes of his death."

"That is consistent with my findings as well," Sophia said. "Alexa also stated there was a lot of blood. What other wounds did you find that would cause so much bleeding?"

"Facial and scalp wounds," Kiddash said, "little bleeders that create a bloody scene, but rarely are they extensive enough to be fatal."

"Thank you," Sophia said. "That is all for now."

Moore-Les also called the first responder to arrive on the scene, followed by two police officers who initially investigated the case. The interview ended with the emergency department physician who declared AK DOA. The interviews were straightforward, and Sophia had no further questions for the plaintiff's witnesses.

Judge Nif asked Moore-Les, "Do you have any more witnesses?"

"No, Your Honor." Moore-Les gathered his notes.

"It's now 11:10 a.m. Before we hear witnesses called by the defendant, we'll take an hour's break for lunch. Be back in this courtroom at 12:15 p.m." Nif banged his gavel.

Sophia noticed a Fed Ex package had been delivered during her cross-examination with Alexa. She tore open the envelope. A note and small pieces of videotape fell from the package. She whispered in Chief Jackson's ear, "I think we finally got a break. Victor's cellmate, Adolf Mandolf, sent these. That was a great idea Cordy had, to track him down." She glanced around the room. "We need Mandolf to testify this afternoon." Sophia sent her paralegal to track down Mandolf while Chief Jackson went to find a better-fitting suit for her client. She also delivered the videotape segments to Mr. Hyde, who was sitting in the back of the room.

Two officers arrived and escorted Floyd from the courtroom to return after the break.

HIDEAWAY EXPOSED

Sept. 18 – 2:00 p.m. MSK, Moscow, Russia/
7:00 a.m. EDT, Cincinnati, Ohio

Back in Russia, Usher felt as if he were up to his neck in a swamp full of alligators. No longer in control of the mission, he knew he'd have to be on the alert. During their flight, the men discussed a strategic plan to reach Okueva's hideaway. Fortunately, it soon became apparent how Marshal Albert had earned his status as a war hero. The man was courageous yet humble, open-minded to a point, but a decisive decision-maker.

After deplaning, Usher strained to hear the unmistakable rumble of the truck's motor, but as time passed, there was no sight of Zina or Dimitri. Usher's worry for Zina was obvious, and he didn't like the situation one bit. He half-listened as Albert laid out plans for the rest of his team. Leo, Vlad, and four of Albert's men stood on either side of Usher, taking notes.

"Where's Zina?" Usher whispered.

Leo shrugged and pointed to the man briefing the team. "Listen up. Albert knows what he's doing."

Albert pointed to a screen. "Okueva's cell phone activity touched two cell towers up that mountain. Drones have located his headquarters. We've mapped out a route and recorded the area using infrared cameras. This is only a brief look, so evaluate the wall heights, lighting, security posts, and the locations of each door and window. Cracker sent this information to each of your cell phones for later inspection. Our bomb sniffers have also located a whole warehouse filled with explosives and ammunition at the crest not far from the main house. A guardhouse sits to the east of the warehouse."

Usher studied the grainy maps, making plans for his own route once he arrived at the top. It would be a rugged venture, and he didn't like the odds. His concern for Zina kept gnawing at his mind. *Why weren't they here by now?*

"Are you listening?" Albert asked Usher. "There are at least five clusters of armed forces blocking our route to the mansion at the top of the mountain—four below and one at the gate. We could take out each of the teams below, but it will take time, and we don't know how many armed men are at headquarters or what type of weapons they have at their disposal. The largest problem is that our target is more sophisticated than most. If we attack any cluster, Okueva may have additional resources available. Plus, I only sent the drones along the main roads so other units could be hidden in the woods."

"Where are Agent Zina and Dimitri?" Usher finally blurted.

"Safe," Albert said.

That wasn't good enough for Usher. "Safe, where?"

"With Cracker and Rozalina, can we move on now?" Albert snapped. "We'll talk to them once they set up at their destination."

Usher was definitely unsatisfied with that answer but felt that he could get little more out of Albert at the moment, so he forced himself to focus on the screen showing the enlarged view of Okueva's headquarters. "Wait, I see two helicopters on that helipad in front of the warehouse. Aren't you afraid he will escape before we get there?"

Albert nodded his head. "I see you and I think alike."

Usher ran a finger over the map. "So, we attack from the top?"

"Yes, send in paratroopers, but we must keep the guards pinned below," Albert said with determination. "Let's check in with Cracker and Rozalina before dark and maybe talk with Agent Zina and Dimitri, who guard them."

"Where are they now?" Usher asked.

Albert placed his pudgy index finger on the drone's map. "Here. They are already on the mountain in an armored van supplied with the latest communication and electronic surveillance equipment." The van was far from any road, making it three-quarters up the mountain. "Hacking is their specialty, and they will cover our tracks and block Okueva's spyware. Dimitri and Zina are their guards. I need the best on that mission." Albert tapped his wrist radio. "Cracker, what do you have to report?"

"Twenty cameras dot the property that we've found so far—perhaps more en route. They swivel and scan the area every thirty seconds. Rozalina blocked the motion-sensor activation and freeze-framed the swivel images. Hopefully, the guards monitoring the screens won't notice since they rapidly rotate through each location."

Rozalina added, "Infra-red cameras show six people guarding headquarters—two at the front, two at the rear entrances, and two more at the main gate. A guardhouse about fifty yards from headquarters sits next to a warehouse filled with ammunition. There are probably another ten men in the guardhouse, but that's an estimate based on the number of men in each of the smaller teams stationed along the roadside below."

"Do you have access to radiofrequency devices to tell how many people are inside headquarters?" Usher asked.

Albert shifted his stance but didn't interfere with the question.

"We have Radar-R," Cracker said, "but the device must be closer than fifty feet. There are at least three people inside. We know because we saw them enter the building ten minutes ago."

"Okueva has been very busy," Rozalina said. "Our Stingray captured several more outgoing phone calls, but he doesn't know that our cell tower has intercepted those calls. We tapped into the phone numbers and recorded each conversation."

"Who has he called so far?" Usher asked.

Albert took a deep breath. His ears turned red, but again, he held his tongue. Usher caught the cue but focused on other data. He needed answers.

"Two calls to Syria, one each to London, Paris, Berlin, and Rome, and four to the U.S."

"Can you forward the numbers and recordings to our Security Agent Cordelia-Hastings?" Usher asked.

"Already done, I spoke with Cordy and have been forwarding additional information as we discover more facts," Cracker said. "She is forwarding our information to President Harris and his emergency council. Your Homeland Security and Department of Defense are working with Special Forces overseas to track each call location. Harris is in contact with the French president and German Chancellor, and they have teams hunting the terrorists down as we speak. Your president also sent Dr. Ping on to Rome."

"Are there any more questions?" Albert snapped.

"Is Zina there with you?" Usher asked.

"Yes, she's outside on patrol with Dimitri," Rozalina said. "She's safe."

Usher blew out a deep breath. "We have to keep her that way. She's my responsibility. Who's orchestrating the terrorist attacks?" Usher asked. "Okueva is here, but someone must oversee his operations in the U.S. and elsewhere."

"We don't know the answer yet, but we'll find whoever it is. They'll slip up sooner or later," Cracker said.

Albert cut in, "None of the men who planned the 9/11 attacks on New York City or the Pentagon were even in the U.S. at the time, yet the missions were successful." He glanced at the sky, checking the light. "It's time to move. We must land before twilight."

"Are any more members of your team on the mountain?" Usher asked, still worrying about Zina.

"Yessss," Albert hissed. "They'll keep the four lower teams pinned to their locations while we take the main headquarters. Our plane is too noisy to fly directly overhead, so we'll go in low, parachute to an open space near the woods, and hike in or maybe—"

"Who are we?" Usher asked.

"You, me, and the rest of this team you see standing before you," Albert said. "You do have jumping experience, yes?"

"Yes," Usher checked the map once more. "Where is the drop zone?"

Albert tapped the drone's map and clenched his teeth. "Behind that clump of trees." By now, his ears and cheeks were flushed as he held back his frustration with Usher's questions. "We'll fly in from east to west to accommodate prevailing winds." Albert grabbed a helmet and a gear pack from the table. "The key to success is to pull this off as quietly and quickly as possible. The terrorists will check in with Okueva, and they may panic if they don't get an answer. We must stay beneath the radar and not get caught. It's ten miles to headquarters. Every man, grab your gear. The terrain is rocky, so be careful." Albert gave a deliberate stare at Usher. "Any more questions?"

Usher smiled. "Not at the moment."

"Then we're good to go. Follow me." Albert stalked off toward the plane. Everyone grabbed a helmet and a pack and followed.

Leo grabbed the last pack and turned to Usher, "You'll be Albert's partner. Vlad and I are last to jump. A second plane will deliver additional equipment."

Usher checked out his gear.

Leo motioned Usher to follow. "Our parachutes are packed and by the plane. Check it before boarding."

Sept. 18 – 4:08 p.m. MSK, Moscow, Russia/
9:08 a.m. EDT, Cincinnati, Ohio

Usher followed Albert, the second man to jump out of the plane. The sun was setting, casting a warm glow over the rugged landscape below. The sky was painted with beautiful shades of orange and red, a stark contrast to the mission's seriousness. Their objective was to extract a high-value target, Okueva, from a hostile territory. Standing in the plane's side doorway, Usher felt the wind hit his face, causing his eyes to water. Despite this, his focus was solely on the jump. He took a leap of faith and freefell towards the ground, keeping his body tight. He gripped the gear tightly before dropping it on a string and counting to six. Once the count was up, he pulled the ripcord, and the parachute opened with a loud crack. The sudden jerk of the parachute swung him like a trapeze artist heading for the ground, less than a thousand feet away from him.

Usher kept his legs and feet together as he approached the drop zone. As he landed, he threw himself sideways and rolled to a stop. Quickly, he untangled the cords, flipped onto his back, released the harness, and deflated the canopy to prevent being dragged across the drop zone. After removing his gear, he retrieved his parachute.

Glad to be on land, he scanned the area and saw Leo, his trusted comrade, walking toward him. All four of Albert's men had also landed, and Vlad was in the air, the last man out. The plane veered off and was soon out of sight. Within two minutes, another plane flew low to the ground, scarcely visible in the twilight. A pallet rigged with parachutes dropped an Army vehicle, artillery, and additional supplies. Albert and his men were in place to receive the gear before the plane veered off and disappeared.

"It'll be dark soon enough. Suit up, and use your night vision goggles when the sun goes down. Fortunately, we don't have to hike in after all. So, maybe we'll luck out and complete our mission before sundown." Albert's instructions were clear and concise, a testament to the team's thorough preparation for the mission.

"What are you worried about?" Usher asked.

"Nothing. Why?" His question seemed to catch Albert off guard, adding a ripple of anxiety to the tension.

Usher backed off but would remain on hyperalert. *Something isn't right.* His eyes darted to Leo, who nodded. He had noticed the concern, too.

Leo mouthed, "Later."

Every second counted, and it was time to extract Okueva alive. Usher was determined, but was that also Albert's plan? To ensure they were aligned, Usher said, "I want Okueva alive." His voice was firm, reflecting his unwavering determination to see the mission through.

"We want Okueva! Dead or alive," Albert said. "My men are risking everything for this. If we get a chance to kill him, I won't stop my men from shooting. That goes for you, too, so don't get in my way. I wouldn't want you as a casualty."

Usher was pissed off and growing angrier by the moment. "That's good to know," Usher said. "What about Leo and Vlad? Will you kill them, too?"

A flash of anger crossed Albert's face. "They aren't stupid enough to disobey my orders. You, on the other hand, I don't trust."

"The feelings are mutual," Usher said, "but I promised Cracker, and I live by my word. I hope you are as honorable."

Albert climbed into the Jeep without another word.

Leo turned toward Usher. "You coming?" Usher grabbed his gear bag and got in the vehicle. It was crowded with eight men, gear, and ammo, but Vlad drove like a pro.

CRISIS NEGOTIATION

Sept. 18 – 6:23-9:00 a.m. CDT, Wichita, Kansas/
7:23-10:00 a.m. EDT, Cincinnati, Ohio

SWAT team leader Russ Bracken knew anything could happen during a rescue mission, and he was responsible for ensuring no glitches. The new negotiator, Orin House, was an unknown member of the team, so Bracken set down the rules he expected to be followed. "We have no idea what to expect when we reach the Wichita lab. I can't have you going off half-cocked trying to woo some terrorist hacker to release these students—especially when explosives surround the lab. So, you'll do as I say or stay behind!"

"I'm going with you," Orin insisted. "What do we know about the third guard?"

"Tattoo guy says that his name is Termine, and he's not a good guard but the best hacker he knows," Bracken said. "Termine oversees the students' activities, but he's one of the hostage-takers."

"Okay, so we'll announce our arrival and warn him not to harm the students," Orin said.

"You won't negotiate with anyone until the C-4 explosives are defused," Bracken warned. "That may take a while. In the meantime, we have to know that the students are safe and unharmed. We don't know Termine. He might kill the students, even if he doesn't like it."

"Can we enter the building without detonating the bombs?" Orin asked. "I'm willing to go inside while your team neutralizes the devices."

"Tattoo guy mentioned a tripwire and a tree trap," Bracken said. "That will be defused first. Desmond and Sergeant Foley are our bomb experts. No one enters without their approval."

"What kind of experience do they have?" Orin asked.

"Sergeant Foley has twelve years in the Army, worked EOD in Iraq and Afghanistan, and a few secret missions I'm not at liberty to discuss. He's been on our team for five years. Desmond has six years EOD and IEDD in the Army, four years on the Texas bomb squad, and joined us a year ago."

Foley didn't wait for formalities. "We need to assess the situation, and I'll confer with Desmond before we determine the status."

"According to the drone's image, there is a path we could use that allows access to the front of the lab without too much exposure," Bracken said. "I'm going to try that. Termine probably heard Tattoo man's gunfire and is already on alert." He held up his phone and drew a green line along the path. "Are we ready to proceed?"

"Roger," each man said.

"Let's go. Orin, you'll come with me." Bracken glanced at his watch. "It's 6:23 a.m. The sun rises at 7:01. The New York Stock Exchange opens in nearly two hours, and although Cordy hopes they've blocked any current hacked code, the students could have added more. Cordy is running out of time to stop this craziness. We don't know what they have planned or even who Mr. Smith is yet!"

It took seven minutes to trek through the plotted route to a path leading to the oyster-gray lab pre-fab building. Three steps led up to the door. The teams split as pre-planned and walked a wide path around the building. Each bomb man took mental notes of the explosives as they passed by C-4 packets.

When the teams met in front of the building, Foley turned to Bracken and said, "We're going to get these students out alive, so give Desmond and me a few minutes to see just what we're dealing with."

Bracken said. "We'll wait here until we hear from you."

Desmond followed Foley up the steps. Foley pointed to the tripwire and ran his finger upward—pointing at a large pine tree near the west corner of the lab. "Can't defuse this one without triggering log spikes," he whispered into his mic.

Eye-balling the tripwire's line, it led to a grenade in the tree's bottom branches. Foley absently rubbed the long scar running from his left eye down to his cheek. Memories of two years ago flashed through his mind. An explosive had nearly ended his life. He wouldn't let it happen again. Foley hopped from the stairs and knelt on the ground near the western corner of the lab, focusing on the explosive devices.

"What do you see?" Desmond asked.

"It's another grenade." Foley motioned for Desmond to join him.

Foley shone his flashlight on the detonation box, and followed another wire up to the same tree above him. "It's also connected to spiked log traps. If we cut the tripwire, it'll send a pulse and set off the traps like a stack of dominoes."

They carefully backed away, walked around the lab, and found two more trigger points.

"Problems?" Bracken asked. When he got no immediate answer, he advanced toward the lab and stood behind the two men. He knew better than to enter a live bomb area but was too impatient to stand by. These were his men.

Foley summarized the situation. "There are sixteen packets of C-4 explosives, four on each corner, and two in the middle of each side of the building. Each packet is 2" by 11", weighing about 1 ¼ pounds. Tripwires to log spikes and grenades—west corner prime target for the detonator, a clock timer, and another tripwire blocks the front door, which is also attached to a log spike and another grenade." He pointed overhead to the foot-long log covered in metallic spikes.

"But you can disarm it." Bracken knew his bomb squad was experienced.

Desmond added, "We'll need to disarm all of the modules before the timer is scheduled to go off at 12:01 p.m."

"What's going on out there?" a man shouted from inside the building.

"Leave this to me." Orin moved from behind Bracken and dashed to the front of the building, making sure to avoid the tripwire, and held the front door shut. "This is the FBI! I'm Agent Orin. Don't open the door!"

Bracken was shocked to see that the negotiator had followed him and yelled, "Orin, don't be stupid. This is not safe for you yet! Follow my orders! I'm responsible for you and the safety of these boys. He might shoot them."

"That's why I'm here!" The door jiggled in Orin's hand as he ignored Bracken's commands. "I repeat. This is the FBI! Termine, there's a bomb ready to explode as soon as you open the door! All of you will be blown to bits if you step out through the opening. We're here to save you and the students. I need you to listen to me closely."

The doorknob kept jiggling. Orin put forth his most commanding voice, "Step away from the door. Do you understand me?"

"No!" There was pounding on the door and muffled student voices in the background.

"Termine, listen to me." Orin repeated in a calm voice, "Do not harm the boys, and step away from the door."

One of the students called out, "Don't shoot." Barely understanding the words, Orin heard the defeat in the boy's voice. Squinting and leaning forward, he concentrated more carefully and understood, "We unarmed. Please, don't shoot us."

Sept. 18 – 6:50 a.m. CDT, Wichita, Kansas/
7:50 a.m. EDT, Cincinnati, Ohio

Panic grew inside the lab. Termine broke out in a cold sweat and cried out in alarm, "Go away or I'll…I'll—" His heart hammered in his chest as he scanned the room for a place to hide. Not finding any, he couldn't catch his breath. His mind raced. He didn't know which option was better. To take his chances with the Americans, after breaking the law, or with the Russians who had his family. Then, everything seemed to become clear. "Wait, there's no bomb. You're going to shoot me as soon as I step outside."

"No," Orin said. "That's not going to happen, but you are in danger. Explosives surround the whole lab. Please step away from the door and let us rescue you and the students. There is no reason for anyone to get hurt."

"That can't be," Termine insisted. "Smith promised we had until noon." His hands shook, and his legs wouldn't hold him up. *Could it be true? He hadn't seen any other guards in over an hour. They were supposed to check in hourly.* "Where are the guards?"

"He is in custody," Orin said. "He is safe, and we are here to free you, too."

"He who? There are two guards." Termine's voice quaked, "Why should I believe you?" But deep down, he did believe him, at least about the bomb.

"Because I'm telling you the truth, and you have no other choice," Orin said. "Let me talk to the students. I must know they are alive and unharmed."

Xander glanced at Termine. "We're safe from that terrible man." He paused and whispered to Cadden, "I know we have parents who are still hostages, and we have broken the law, but we have no choice." His eyes roamed the room and landed on the rifle propped against Termine's desk.

Termine caught the glimpse and made a bee-line for the rifle, but Cadden grabbed Termine's arms and held tight. "Stay here!"

"Let go of me!" Termine yelled.

"No!" Cadden spoke something in Punjabi, and Termine stopped fighting.

Xander grabbed the rifle. He cracked the gun barrel open with fingers flying into automatic mode as he removed the bullets, pocketed them, and left the weapon cracked open. "You have Termine?" he asked Cadden.

"Yes," Cadden said.

"Can anyone hear me?" Xander called out. His voice shook. "Don't shoot! We understand there are bombs outside, and we do not harm you. Just students." His thick Russian accent made t's sound like z's, h's like g's, and he gave a slight roll to his r's.

Termine slumped into a corner. "I've failed."

Cadden wrapped an arm around the defeated man. "No, you have not failed. We're safe now. Let them defuse the bombs. We're almost done with our projects, and you've done well. We all can go home. You can see your wife and children."

"It's not up to me," Termine said. "Smith will kill us all."

"I knew it!" Jabril grabbed Zev's arm and pulled him into the bathroom. The door slammed, and the lock clicked behind them.

Cadden lifted Termine's chin so they held a stare, eye-to-eye. "No. Smith is not here. You are. Everything that happens from here on is up to you. We need you to be strong. Let these men free us."

"Do you have guns?" Orin spoke close to the door, "Is Termine unarmed?"

Xander said, "Gun, no bullets."

"Kripa Karke…" Termine held his hands up, palms clasped. Tears filled his eyes, and his words rushed out in his native language.

Cadden interpreted. "Termine is very upset. He says, 'Please, Sir. Do not harm my boys. I am unarmed.' You are FBI, yes?"

"Yes," Orin said. "And you are students who bring harm to our country, yet we are risking our lives to save yours."

"No, you do not understand." Cadden's Urdu accent became more pronounced the more upset he became. His vowels shifted, accents fell in unusual places, w's sounded like v's, and v's sounded like b's. "That is not vhat ve vanted to do. Smith has our families. Dey threatens to keel our loved ones and us."

Termine spoke again in his native tongue.

Cadden said, "Our guard pleads forgiveness. They have our families!"

Xander moved between the door and Termine. Trying to be as calm as possible, he spoke slowly and clearly, "Please, do not harm him or my fellow students."

Orin repeated. "We will not harm you. What are your names?"

"I'm Xander, and Cadden is with Termine. Jabril and Zev are very afraid. They have locked themselves in the restroom at the far southeast corner of the building. Are they safe there?"

"No, be sure they do not jostle the flooring," Orin said. "The explosives are on every corner and in the middle of each side of the building."

"What about the windows?" Xander asked.

"Good idea," Orin said. "I'm going around to the back and will meet you. Is there a window in the restroom?"

"No," Xander said.

"Okay," Orin said. "I'm alone and unarmed. Can you open the window for me?"

There seemed to be some discussion before Xander said, "Southwest corner. Termine fears for his life. Can you guarantee he will come to no harm?"

"Is he armed?" Orin asked.

"No. I already told you we have a rifle, but it is not loaded," Xander said. "The bullets are in my pocket. I will give them to you."

"I promise not to harm him," Orin said.

Termine's voice trembled. Cadden translated for him once again, "What about the others?"

"One moment, I'll have our team leader speak to you. His name is Agent Bracken."

Bracken stepped over to the door. "Termine, my agents will not harm you or the others as long as you cooperate with Agent Orin. You must keep the students safe. Do you understand?"

Termine finally spoke clear English, "How can I be sure I can trust you?"

"You don't have any choice, Termine. We will all blow up if you don't follow my directions exactly. These bombs could go off at any minute."

"No, it's not supposed to blow until 12:01 p.m. Smith promised we could all leave before destroying the evidence."

"Did that include the students?" Bracken asked. There was no answer, but Termine listened intently. It was a shame that he failed this assignment, but he was relieved that he wouldn't be forced to kill the boys. This nightmare would end by some miracle, and they all might survive. He was now worried about the future. How would this failure affect his family? If they didn't shoot him, would he have to go to jail?

"Orin, we're still going to storm the door when they defuse the bomb, so be ready."

"Give me ten minutes. I'll frisk everyone for you. Give me a boost." Orin tapped the outside of the window.

"Again, I warn you," Bracken's eyes narrowed, "don't make any promises that we can't keep. These may be only students, but they are dangerous and have broken into our financial systems. I'm still responsible for their safety and plan to get them out alive. Do you hear me?"

"Loud and clear," Orin said. The window opened, and a lad passed over six bullets. "I'm Xander."

Orin handed the bullets to Bracken, then grabbed the window ledge, stepped into Bracken's folded hands, and boosted one leg over the windowsill. He glanced up to see Desmond climbing a tree. "Let me know when they defuse the bombs."

Bracken nodded his grudging assent.

Xander helped ease Orin's other leg through the narrow opening.

"Turn around with your hands in front of you. I need to check you for weapons." Orin said.

"I heard that Bracken man say you have to do that." Xander held up his hands and turned around so Orin could pat him down. "I have nothing to hide. Can I frisk you?"

"That sounds like something my son would say. He's about your age. His name is Ryan." Orin became serious and turned out his pockets. "See? I'm unarmed."

Xander asked, "Is he going to the University, too?"

Sept. 18 – 7:00 a.m. CDT, Wichita, Kansas/
8:00 a.m. EDT, Cincinnati, Ohio

Orin nodded, "But he's not as computer savvy as you." He scanned the room, which had four computer terminals in separate corners and a larger monitor in the front.

An older man, maybe in his mid-forties, wearing a camo turban and traditional Punjabi shirt and pants, stood about three feet from the front door. He stepped in front of a teenage boy. "I'm Termine, and I'm responsible for these boys. Are you going to frisk us, too?"

"Yes, I am," Orin said.

Termine grumbled but allowed Orin to pat him down. Orin cleared the man. "You've done a fine job guarding these boys and keeping them safe from the snipers."

Termine jolted, "Snipers?"

"The other two guards," Orin said.

"Oh, them," Termine said with disdain. "They want to hurt my boys."

Orin caught the man's concern for the students but watched Termine's every move.

"Xander, can you introduce me to your friends?"

"They aren't friends," Xander said. "Well, maybe, Cadden. I only met them yesterday, but we have a lot in common." He stepped closer to the door, introducing a golden-complexioned lad in his early twenties. "Cadden, this is Agent Orin. He's here to free us."

Cadden raised his arms for Orin to check for weapons.

"You're clear," Orin said. A second room appeared to be a break room. Three pizza boxes lay open with only crumbs. "Where are...," he turned to Xander.

"Jabril and Zev," Xander prompted. "Like I said, they're afraid. I will get them."

"Thank you," Orin said. "Once I talk to everyone, I'm going to lower each of you out of the window while the bomb squad works to defuse the explosives. We'll take you to a safe zone far enough away."

Cadden said, "You are all FBI? We asked for your help but didn't know there would be so many."

Termine whipped around. "What? When did you do this?"

Cadden put his hand on Termine's shoulder. "It is okay, Termine. If we hadn't called for help, we all would be dead."

"So this is your guard?" Orin asked.

"Well, yes, but he's been helping us, too." Cadden appeared confused.

"Helping you break into our financial systems," Orin said.

"It isn't what we wanted to do." A flash of fear crossed Cadden's face. "I know what we did was wrong. We will help you reverse our codes if that will make a difference. You are going to let us go free, aren't you?"

"You will be safe, but not free," Orin said. "You broke the law."

"But we didn't have a choice," Cadden said.

"You may think you didn't have a choice," Orin said, "but you did break the law."

"Y…yes, I guess we did," Cadden admitted.

Xander returned with two golden-skinned boys. "This is Jabril and his cousin Zev." They stood close together. "Agent Orin is here to rescue us, but first, he needs to check to be sure there are no weapons."

The two boys stood close together. Jabril stepped forward and held up his hands.

Zev held back. "Why do you need to pat us down? We are no threat to you." His thick Yiddish accent gave a guttural sound from the back of his throat.

Letting the comment slide for the moment, Orin had a job to do. "I'm with the FBI, and I need to know you have no weapons. Turn around and spread your legs."

Zev's eyes narrowed. He placed his fists on his hips. "What if I don't?"

Jabril whispered, "Do it, Zev!"

Orin reached for Zev's shoulder.

Zev backed away and huffed out a deep breath. "No! I've taken enough orders from other people and won't take any more."

Jabril turned to Zev, glaring into his eyes, and they never left Zev's face as he spoke to Orin. "We will do whatever you say. Zev will cooperate, and so will I. Just free us and save our families. My eema is ill." Jabril was near tears.

Orin nodded and reached out to Zev, forcing him into the stance, legs apart.

Zev's body was rigid with anger, but he stood still, accepting his cousin's advice.

"Let's get you all to safety." Orin held his wrist radio to his mouth.

Termine said, "No one is safe until Smith frees our families. We don't know where to find him or where they're keeping our families."

Orin paused before saying, "Agent Bracken will want to know those things."

Termine added, "Smith may have already left the country,"

Sept. 18 – 7:20 a.m. CDT, Wichita, Kansas/
8:20 a.m. EDT, Cincinnati, Ohio

The boys started talking at once. Cadden let go of Termine's arm as he darted forward.

Orin reflexively snatched Termine's elbow. "Where are you going?"

"I need my computer to go with me."

Cadden grabbed his other arm and held tight.

"We'll arrange that after everyone has escaped the lab." Orin spoke into his wrist radio, "Bracken, we're ready to evacuate. What is the bomb status?"

"Give them a few minutes, and we'll finish the last bit. Then I'll be at the door. Wait for my warning."

Outside, the bomb team eliminated each threat one by one. Bracken waited for his team's final okay. When it came, the relief was evident.

"Okay, Orin, we'll meet you at the front door." Bracken's voice echoed as the hostages could hear him outside the door, then a slight delay over Orin's wrist radio.

Sunlight nearly blinded the students as the door burst open. Then, four men filled the doorway, guns raised. Poncho and Kayman took the left side, Bracken and Chico the right.

At the sight of the armed and uniformed men, everything broke into chaos again. Jabril and Zev ran for the break room, shrieking in terror. Termine screamed and dropped to the floor, "You said no one would be hurt." Cadden and Xander looked on in horror.

Bracken shouted, "Freeze."

Jabril and Zev stopped in their tracks, hands raised. Jabril yelled, "Don't shoot."

Orin moved in front of the boys, arms outstretched, and said calmly. "We agreed to go peacefully."

Bracken lowered his gun. "Stand down." He turned toward Poncho. "Round up the computers and anything else of value. George has the vehicle waiting. Sorry, Termine, but I have to cuff you until we sort this out."

One cuff locked onto his wrist. Orin kept a hand on Termine as he climbed to his feet.

Chico clamped the wrists together so they were in front of Termine. It would be more comfortable for the man.

Cadden held up his hands. "Are you going to cuff us, too?"

"Yes, I'm afraid so," Chico said.

Orin called Jabril and Zev. "Come out here. Let's go."

Jabril obeyed. Xander and Jabril held up their hands and were cuffed, but Zev dashed for the front door. "No, we have to find Smith! Where's Tattoo man?"

Bracken managed to trip Zev. The lad tumbled down the steps and landed at Foley's feet.

"Not so fast." Bracken bounded down the steps and clamped zip ties on Zev's wrists. "We have a lot of questions before you go anywhere."

"But Smith has our families," Zev said. "He's the man you need to capture. He'll kill all of them."

Chico led Termine and the students from the lab. Cadden was at Termine's side.

Jabril paused by Zev. "For being so smart, you are an idiot. Come on. The only way we find our families is to help these men."

Zev hung his head and kicked at a rock. "I guess."

Jabril bumped his shoulder with his own. "Hey cousin, we are together, right?"

Zev bumped him back, although harder than expected. Jabril nearly fell.

Bracken caught the boy. "Let's move. We have a lot of work to do before we can find anyone's family, let alone save them. You've threatened all of ours, so don't think that you have much to say about this. We have to reverse the damage you boys have created before your code goes live."

Xander paused. "Mr. Bracken, you're in charge, right?"

Bracken nodded.

"There are two other men with guns. The driver and Tattoo man. That's not his real name. Orin said you have them in custody, but they know Smith better than us. Termine was waiting for us at the lab, but those men left Smith's office and forced us to come here. Have you talked to them?"

Bracken said, "Your Tattoo man is in our custody. The driver wasn't so lucky. We'll talk more soon."

Xander spoke rapidly, filled with fear, as they walked along the path to the BATT. "Our families are overseas but still in danger, and as you say, many people here in the U.S. will be too in a few hours. None of us wanted to be here, but they made us. Please help us, and I'll tell you everything we've been forced to do. I have a detailed record of everything I've done in the last year back at my apartment. And we deliberately entered a few flaws into the code to stall their efforts. We haven't finished testing, so I don't know if anything works as planned."

Bracken nodded. "Who sent the message asking for help?"

"Cadden came up with the plan, but we all worked on it while the guards were busy."

"Thank you for notifying us," Bracken said. "Do you know who is behind this terrorist attack?"

Xander flinched, "Terrorist attack? I never thought of it like that." He hesitated. "I guess you're right." His eyes widened as the consequences of his actions gelled in his mind. "What's going to happen to us?"

"That's not up to me," Bracken said, "but cooperation could improve your odds."

Xander added, "Mr. Smith was the one who gave us our orders. We got more assignments through Termine, but I think Smith got orders from higher up. I don't know who that would be."

Bracken held the BATT door open for Xander. Termine and the other students were already buckled into seats, ready for the ride. Xander sat in the rear. He turned and spied Tattoo man—one arm in a sling, a large bandage over his nose, and both of his eyes were bruised and swollen. The man's other arm was cuffed to a ring in the wall. His feet were in chains welded to the floor.

Even now, battered and cuffed, Tattoo man was an imposing figure, and Xander somehow feared he could get free. The brute stared at each of them in their seats, saying nothing, but oozing resentment and threat.

Xander turned toward the back of the BATT and was relieved to see the rest of the SWAT team lined up along the side benches facing one another. The computers lay on the floor in front of them. He raised his hand. "Mr. Bracken, sir. I remembered something important that might help you track our family's attackers. My father said a group of four armed men took my brother into custody. They had odd-looking tattoos on their shoulders. It sounded like the same six-sided star as he has." Xander pointed to Tattoo man. "What does it mean?"

The man only glared. "We'll find out soon," Bracken said. "Chico, drive us back to the smaller BATT. We'll use that as our interview room."

Chico nodded and moved to the driver's seat.

Bracken tapped the front seat to get everyone's attention. "It's already 7:20 a.m. CDT. We'll have a debriefing, but first, I need to call our IT expert. Her name is Agent Cordelia-Hastings, and she will be listening to the interviews with each of you about your projects or your role in the hostage situation. Please cooperate with her."

Interviewing and recording each student, Tattoo man, and Termine took another two hours.

EVERYTHING HAPPENS AT ONCE

Sept. 18 – 7:30 a.m. CDT, Wichita, Kansas/
8:30 a.m. EDT, Cincinnati, Ohio

Cordy-Hastings broke out in a sweat. The conference room in Ohio was too warm for comfort as time raced at an alarming pace. Her cell phone rang yet again. Between Usher, Guy, and Cracker, plus another update from Quint, she barely had time to think, and now the caller ID read, "Russ Bracken."

"This is Cordy."

"We've freed the students," Bracken said. "They are safe, and we're starting our interrogations." He gave a brief update.

"That's great news." Cordy motioned to her husband, Braun. "The students are safe and free!"

Svetlana and Perry hopped up from their terminals. "That's terrific!"

"Bracken's sending over all the hacked codes." Cordy balanced her cell phone between her shoulder and chin as she frantically opened a new darknet account. She hoped to get the codes reversed ASAP but couldn't seem to type fast enough while holding her cell at such an odd angle. "Let me plug in my earbuds."

Braun glanced at his watch. "It's already 8:30 a.m. in New York. The Stock Exchange opens in one hour. Bank of America and American Express open 30 minutes later."

Cordy felt her heart throb in her temples with every rapid beat, "I hope we caught the hacks early enough to reverse them. The last thing we need is a stock market crash. Send me everything."

"We want you in on the student interviews to be sure you get all the information you need," Bracken said.

"I don't have time, just send their code," Cordy said. "I need time to reverse them. Record the students' interviews to review later. If you run across something urgent, call me. Talk to you soon." She disconnected the call.

"Was anyone hurt?" Perry asked.

Cordy said, "The students are fine, but I don't know about their guards."

Svetlana beamed. "We'll help reverse the codes."

"No, I'm forwarding everything to our security team," Cordy said, "but thanks. We wouldn't have found the students without your help."

Braun also congratulated the teenagers. "What do you have so far on General Okueva?"

"I tracked down two bank accounts," Perry said, "one in Syria and the other in Moscow. They both were closed in the last twenty-four hours."

Svetlana added, "And I found a third for twenty-two million dollars collected in cash at 5:10 p.m. Moscow time."

"Okay, let's get back to work," Braun said. "See if you can narrow down what the funds are used for."

Cordy nodded, but she was still receiving the download of hacked codes. She sent them through her detection software. After isolating all the code the student hackers had written in the last twenty-four hours, she started an upload to her security team.

Sept. 18 – 7:55 a.m. CDT, Wichita, Kansas/
8:55 a.m. EDT, Cincinnati, Ohio

Cordy's cell phone rang again, and Bracken's ID popped up. "Now what?"

"This is Orin. I'm the SWAT FBI negotiator in Wichita. We're interviewing Termine, and you need to be on this call. I also want you to hear the other guard's debriefing. The students call him Tattoo man, but we found no ID. However, Xander says a group of armed men in his hometown of Pushkin kidnapped his brother. The men each had the same tattoo on their shoulders. We need to find out what it means and the location of each family member."

Cordy was juggling five things already and wasn't sure she could handle a sixth. "Is it urgent that I'm in the interview?"

"One of you needs to hear this," Orin insisted.

"Okay, one moment." Cordy tapped Braun's shoulder. "Orin has interviewed and recorded most of the students and is including us in Termine's interview. Can you handle that?"

"Okay, I'll do my best, but I may need to interrupt you at intervals." Braun took her cell phone.

Cordy added, before he took the call, "May I use your phone?"

"What for?" Braun asked.

"I forwarded the hacked codes through my Detection Software program," she said, "and I need to call my team to help reverse the codes quickly."

Braun handed her his personal phone and plugged his earbuds into Cordy's. "Orin, how do you want to handle the interviews?"

Cordy grabbed his phone and texted her team. "Vital information, I'm reprioritizing your assignments."

Her Solar Winds security team coordinator replied to her text, "Sorry, Cordy. Everyone is tied up with other projects. I'm the only one left in the office."

Cordy huffed out a deep breath, plugged in her headset, and dialed her coordinator directly. "This is urgent."

The coordinator apologized. "There's no way we can help you until we get more staff. Remember, our teams are following your orders to help Governor Hendrum 'to throw everything we have at the crisis.' Teams one and two are on-site upgrading New York's nuclear energy software."

Cordy slammed her fist on the table. "And the financial system could implode in the next hour!"

The coordinator continued, "The generator software goes live in fifteen minutes, the second and third launch at three-hour intervals, and I can't pull those teams—"

Cordy cut in, "We have hacks into the New York Stock Exchange, American Express, Wells Fargo, and the Pentagon. I need your help."

"Listen, Cordy, I would, but how can we? Another team is upgrading the water plant to reverse contamination. New York is running out of drinkable water, and we can't abort that project. More teams are getting temporary solar panels connected to the energy grid and upgrading the EMS systems. They all go live over the next four hours. The Pentagon is also in chaos. Major upsets with all branches of armed forces."

Cordy knew the team was overwhelmed. "We need to reprioritize. This is urgent."

"Didn't you hear me?" The coordinator plowed on, "On top of that, someone broke into General Rutoon's office. I sent the last two members to check out the problems—"

Cordy's teeth clenched as she listened to her coordinator rant. "I understand, but—"

"…the nuclear core could melt down. Call Quint. Get Crowd Strike to pick up the slack. We are doing our best here. Call anyone but me."

"Fine, I'll do that!" She disconnected the call and wanted to throw the phone across the room.

Svetlana glanced up. "What's wrong?"

"Nothing!" Cordy's temper rose another notch. She pulled an earbud from Braun's ear. "Is Guy on the line? I must speak to him immediately."

Braun checked. "No, he hasn't connected yet. What do you need?"

"Help to reverse these codes! I've run them through my forensic analysis and built an encrypted replacement, which must be tested. Everyone is tied up with other projects. This is a priority. I must—"

Braun stood up, stepped behind Cordy, and touched her shoulder. "Relax. We'll take care of it."

Cordy snapped, "I'll relax when I'm dead! Now shut up and help me save our nation!"

"Yup, that's more like you." Braun pulled out his Special Ops Agent phone and speed-dialed Guy Weimer, head of Homeland Security.

Cordy's DarkVid pinged with an urgent message from Quint. "Call me when Guy's on the line. Maybe he can pull some strings to delay opening at American Express and Wells Fargo." She rushed to her computer catching Quint mid-sentence, "...talking with our ailing President Spendorf."

Sept. 18 – 9:10 a.m. EDT, Cincinnati, Ohio

Quint hadn't waited for an answer, so he must have hit auto-send. "Have you read Rutoon's file I sent you? It's a transcript of a phone call from Damascus. Spendorf's concerned there's an Al Qaeda sleeper unit in Wichita Falls."

Cordy's mind spun, trying to grasp everything thrown at her. Since the DarkVid was live, she answered, "We successfully freed the students in Wichita. They are being questioned as we speak, and Braun is on the phone. He's debriefing and recording their interviews, and I'm working to reverse their hacks as fast as possible. It's almost 9:10 a.m. EDT. The NYSE opens in twenty minutes. Can you help?"

The line clicked as Quint picked up the line going live. "You're not listening to me, Girlfriend." Quint's voice grew louder.

Braun's cell phone, which she held in her other hand, rang. "One moment." She glanced at the caller ID. "It's Usher. He's calling from Russia. He's tracking down General Okueva. I need to take this."

"Listen to me," Quint said. "This is urgent."

"Isn't everything these days?" Cordy snapped. "Text me, and I'll read it as soon as I get off this call." She disconnected DarkVid to end the conversation and plugged in one earbud to keep Usher's call private. Using only one bud allowed her to hear everything going on around her. Svetlana and Perry had heard too much already, even though she isolated the two Russians at the other end of the conference room. She must be more careful. They shouldn't be listening to top-secret communication. "Hi, Usher. Give me a moment."

When she raised her head, Braun stood over her. "You need to be in this interview."

"Your brother is on the line," Cordy said, handing him the other earbud. "Do you want to switch places?"

Svetlana hopped up from her terminal. "Cordy, can we help reverse some of the hacker's codes? I know Perry and I can help, and time's running out." She blushed. "I admit it. We've been listening. If I take the hacks from American Express and Perry reverses the hacks from Wells Fargo, you can concentrate on the Pentagon. We have already reversed the NYSE hack."

I knew it. These teenagers have big ears and watchful eyes. Cordy shook her head. "Not now, Svetlana."

"What about the NYSE? Perry has locked out the hacked code, and…" The girl nodded at Cordy's glare. "Okay, I understand." She slowly walked away. Head low, shoulders slumped.

Sept. 18 – 4:14 p.m. MSK, Moscow, Russia/
9:14 a.m. EDT, Cincinnati, Ohio

"Usher, are you still there?" Cordy asked.

"Yes. Cracker's going through the general's emails and personal files, and he believes Okueva is behind the Wichita student caper, but that's just the beginning. There's a sleeper unit in the U.S. Cracker doesn't know where. He says he has some leads for you to check out. General Rutoon is at the top of his list. I told him Rutoon's dead, but Cracker insists there's a connection with Okueva."

Cordy nearly dropped the phone. "A sleeper unit? That's what Quint just said. I'm handing you over to Braun." She pulled the second bud from her ear and shoved the cell phone into Braun's hand.

Braun cleared his throat, "Wait, Cordy. Let Svetlana and Perry help reverse the hacked codes. You must focus on more important issues." He picked up the earbud. "One moment, Orin. Something just came up. Can I talk to Bracken?"

"I've been here all along," Bracken said. "Guy from Homeland Security just tapped in, and he wants to know why you called."

"Is Termine on the line?" Braun asked.

"No, Termine is in a separate room with Orin, and we'll continue to record his interview. My major concern is the hack into the Pentagon."

"Right, this is TS/SCI," Braun said. "I'll call Guy and President Harris from a private line, and sorry, Orin, but we need to bow out of this interview. Send over the transcripts as soon as the interviews are over."

Cordy's heart raced. *TS/SCI. Top-secret/sensitive compartmented information.* Her fingers shook as she copied the newly encrypted hacked codes for the banking systems to a thumb drive. "Are you having President Harris call in the National Security Council Team?"

"Yes, if he thinks it's appropriate." Braun got back on the line with Usher.

Cordy grabbed the thumb drive. "I must talk to Quint first, and then I want to be on that call." She stopped by to chat briefly with Svetlana and Perry and handed them the thumb drive she had just made. "Off the record, I still don't feel that this is appropriate, but I'm running out of time, so I approve of the plan you just proposed to reverse the banks' codes. These go live in less than one hour. This may keep you out of jail or put me in it."

She waved her hands in the air and then took a deep breath. "Sorry, I'm a nervous wreck. Reverse the codes ONLY on these accounts and ONLY on your terminals. When you finish, I'll send your revisions through my Detection Program before it goes live. Understand? I can't let you directly access any companies' software programs."

Svetlana nodded and pulled Perry aside. "You work on Wells Fargo. I'll work on American Express. Let's reverse these and encrypt the systems so they can't be hacked again."

Sept. 18 —9:57 a.m. EDT, Cincinnati, Ohio

Cordy walked to the opposite corner of the large conference room with her laptop so no one could hear her and read the transcript between General Rutoon and Gertie. She entered DarkVid. "Quint, sorry I cut you off a moment ago. Tell me exactly what transpired on that transcript."

Quint didn't hesitate. "Gertie told Rutoon that Risingsickle's on the prowl, and she wanted to know what Rutoon was waiting for?"

Cordy typed on her laptop as she listened. "Yes, I read that, and Rutoon wanted to know where Risingsickle was at the moment."

"Can we believe Risingsickle is General Okueva?" Quint asked.

"Yes, they are the same," Cordy admitted.

"Okueva stopped off at Libya, where orders to intercept Air Force One took place," Quint added, "and Agent Smirro just spoke to President Spendorf. Okueva met with Roland Kildeer and delivered the 5ᵗʰ Dimension malware. Then Kildeer headed to the U.S."

"Why did Smirro call President Spendorf?" Cordy asked.

"Smirro wanted to grant Kildeer a lighter sentence since he gave up information about the cyberattack."

Cordy's heart leapt at the news. "And, what did Spendorf say?"

"No way," Quint said.

"That's a relief. I wonder why Smirro didn't talk to Harris."

"I don't know," Quint said, "but Kildeer did give Smirro some vital information."

"A sleeper unit in Wichita, right?" Cordy asked. "That's what Usher is discussing with Braun and President Harris right now. Braun says this is top secret, and Harris called in the National Security Council. Fortunately, we're one step ahead and have intercepted the hackers, and after we reverse the code, we've put that issue to rest."

"No, Girlfriend! We have a much larger problem!" Quint nearly shouted. "Spendorf believes there's an Al Qaeda sleeper unit in Wichita Falls. You read the bit about seeds planted—"

"Yes, in Wichita, and as I just said, we've already freed that unit," Cordy insisted.

"Think again," Quint said. "Wichita FALLS, not Wichita. That's in Texas, not Kansas. Did you see that photo I sent of the six-sided star? A circle of eight waves intersecting in the middle was inside the star. I'm curious what it means. Those numbers may hold the key."

Braun tapped Cordy on the shoulder. "Orin insists that you listen to Termine's interview now."

Cordy blew out a deep breath. "Okay, just a moment, Quint. While I take this call, run those numbers through—"

"I've already done everything. There are no hidden bank account numbers that I can find, no phone numbers, military coordinates, or oh, wait. NASA satellites. They can't be hacked, or not that I've heard. But these numbers can be encrypted and sent all over the globe. Let me see if I can find a code. There are eight wavy lines, eight sets of numbers, five symbols in the upper left-hand corner, and the top and bottom of the star. Check it out, Girlfriend, and we'll compare notes."

"Keep me posted by text." Cordy grabbed an earbud from Braun's outstretched hand and placed it in her left ear. "Yeah, Orin, what's so important? We're—" A few moments later, she paled, "less than five hours? Braun, plug in your earphone. Orin, play that tape again so the president's team and I can hear Termine's debriefing."

Orin replayed a section of the interview tape. "Jabril broke into the Pentagon to eavesdrop." There was pause followed by, "The cell is due to activate during all this chaos."

"What time," Orin asked.

"Four o'clock today, Texas time. That would be five in Washington, D.C.," Termine said. "Smith bragged the U.S. is doomed."

"Jabril didn't mention this when he talked to me," Orin said.

"The poor lad hasn't a clue." Termine tsked. "They kept him in the dark. I had to step him through a complete process before he even grasped what to hack."

"How will Jabril's hack gather information?" Orin asked.

"When each person logs in this morning, they will be redirected to an update page requesting new user data and passwords," Termine said. "It will give Smith access to all information from the Department of Defense, the Army, Navy, Air Force, Marines, and National Security Systems."

"Do you know where this sleeper unit is located?" Orin asked.

"No," Termine said, "somewhere in Texas."

Cordy interrupted, "Pause, the playback. Quint says the unit's in Wichita Falls, Texas."

Guy said, "That's between Dallas and Oklahoma City. Where do you think they'll hit?"

"Good question." Harris asked, "Does anyone at the Pentagon know about this secret cell?"

"Not that I'm aware," Guy admitted.

Orin jumped in, "There's more. Listen to the rest of Termine's interview. He says that Jabril also downloaded an invisible camera eye and a recorder, so anything said in the Pentagon will be recorded."

"Get Loran on the line," Harris ordered. "As head of the FBI, he needs to know about this threat."

"Let's hear the rest of the interview," Cordy said. "Back up the tape so I remember where we left off."

The tape restarted with Termine saying, "No. Somewhere in Texas. I didn't know the full extent until my last message with Smith."

"When was that?" Orin asked.

"About a quarter to four this morning," Termine said.

"What type of attack are we looking at," Orin asked.

"Smith didn't say anything to me, but I overheard that he was leaving the country before any of this hit. We were to follow as soon as we completed our tasks. All except for Tattoo Man as the students call our explosives expert. He would fly directly to Dallas."

"Do you believe this is credible information?" Orin asked.

"Yes, why wouldn't I?" Termine asked.

"Are there any other sleeper units that you're aware of?" Orin asked.

"Anything is possible," Termine admitted, "but I don't think Smith is privy to the details."

"So Smith is not the top boss," Orin said.

"No, he gets his orders from higher up." Termine's voice quivered and dropped to a whisper as if he was afraid to speak. "Someone… in Russia."

Cordy strained to catch the words. She turned to Braun. "Is Orin still on the line?"

"I'm here, Cordy, and hearing everything you are."

"Good. Have you sent a photo of the bomb expert?" Cordy asked. "I need his real name to research his background, and I'll run the photo for an ID."

"I just sent it," Orin said. "You might track him down by the tattoos on his shoulders—a six-sided star in a circle. It's unusual."

Cordy flipped through her computer. "Actually, that star sounds familiar. Quint found one just like it in Rutoon's papers."

"President Harris, are you raising the national threat level?" Cordy asked.

"Not at this time," Harris said.

Cordy couldn't believe what she had heard. "You have an Al Qaeda sleeper unit in Wichita Falls, Texas, and you're not moving the country to a red alert?"

"That's right," Harris said. "I'm not going to send the public into a panic when we know so little. Dallas-Ft. Worth is the seventh-largest region in the U.S. Do you want to see nearly seven million people try to leave the area? It would be impossible in such a short timeframe. Roads would be blocked with traffic. The airport flooded with families and children, and who knows, that might be where the terrorists strike first."

Guy jumped in with, "We must have indisputable facts that a terrorist cell is about to strike, but that doesn't mean we aren't going to act. I assure you that the FBI, CIA, Homeland Security, and DoD will expend every available resource to find their location."

"So, this information isn't credible enough?" Cordy challenged.

"I didn't say that," Guy said. "We have the element of surprise on our side. The terrorists don't know we are looking for them, so we need to hold our activities closely and share on a need-to-know basis only."

Acting President Harris cut in. "Good news, Cordy. I just got word that the New York Stock Exchange opened without glitches. The Dow, NASDAQ, and S&P are on par with yesterday's prices, and General Rutoon's shares are blocked from trade. Let's pool our resources and reconvene at 11:00 a.m. EST. You get a lead. We chase it down and stop it, but we can NOT go on the record with this. It will cause a massive panic."

"Wait." Usher asked, "What are your plans for General Okueva if we capture him alive?"

"Keep him under wraps for a day, as it is probably as long as you can remain in the country," Harris said. "We can't extradite him, but get as much information from him as possible. Act fast. Time is running out. You have to get out of Russia, too, or risk international consequences."

"I plan to interrogate him as soon as we can," Usher said.

"Find out if he's aware of the six-sided star tattoo," Cordy said. "I'm forwarding a photo of what it looks like. One of the students in Wichita claims that his brother was kidnapped in Pushkin, Russia, by four men bearing this tattoo on their shoulders. If so, Okueva may be behind the kidnapping."

Usher's cell phone vibrated. He opened the text message. "Thanks, I got the photo. I'll see what I can find out."

"How will you get him to talk?" Harris asked.

"Respect, rapport, cunning, and deception," Usher said. "Unfortunately, we don't have much time to develop a rapport, but Uncle Albert has plans for Okueva. In the meantime, Cracker and Rozalina are searching his office for any hidden Intel, and they discovered that Okueva has Al Qaeda cells in other cities. We'll forward important info as he uncovers more data."

"Be sure it's encrypted," Cordy warned.

"Cracker knows what he's doing," Usher said.

Cordy cut in, "Have you heard from any of our allies?"

Harris said. "Terrorists already hit London's subway. The Prime Minister called me, and it's all over the news."

"What are the damages?" Cordy asked.

"Eight terrorists killed, forty-six fatalities, and over 100 injured," Harris said. "London police are on a massive hunt for the last four assassins. They've closed the airports, and NATO has sent in reinforcements."

"I already heard that terrorists hit London's subway system," Usher said. "Zina talked to her sister, but I haven't heard of any other sites."

"I have more information to forward—a recording of Rutoon's meeting nearly a year ago." Cordy tapped at her computer and uploaded an attachment to a secure site. "I don't recognize three members who attended, but Quint tracked down their names. Did you get this message?"

Harris paused. "Yes, and I'm reading it as you speak. I'm calling Dr. Nat Ping to update him. He's a man I trust. We're signing off." There was a click.

"Orin, are you still there?" Cordy's hands clenched and unclenched as she tried to calm down.

"Yes, but I know you're swamped," Orin said. "I need to go, too. We're bringing in the students' Tattoo man for another interview."

"Did the bomb expert have a cell phone?"

"We didn't find one on the man," Orin said. "I'll record his interview and send it to you when we're done. Since this man was to fly to Dallas, he may be joining the terrorists, and with no identification, he was probably flying there on a private jet. I suspect the attack will deal with explosives if that's the case. We'll get as much information as possible."

Cordy heard another click, and the call went silent as Orin signed off. "Usher, are you on the line?"

"Yes," Usher said. "Harris didn't give me a straight answer on Cracker's pardon, but we must move immediately. Cracker is helping us hunt down General Okueva. I'm willing to grant his wish to stay in Russia. What are your thoughts on the matter?"

Braun jumped in. "Whoa, big brother. You can't pardon Cracker without the president's approval."

"Got any better ideas?" Usher shouted, "Spendorf already agreed, but he's not currently on duty."

"Do you trust Cracker?" Cordy asked.

"I do, and Vlad and Leo trust his Uncle Albert, who headed up the manhunt." Usher paused. "I guess I would agree with them."

"I suppose you could accidentally lose Cracker's whereabouts just before your departure," Braun replied. "Russia won't allow you to stay longer than your initial visit without a major hassle."

Cordy said, "If Harris doesn't agree to a pardon, you'll need to wait until Spendorf he returns to the office to deal with a pardon."

"Gotta go," Usher said. "Okueva's lair is in sight."

THE HIT

Sept. 18 – 5:32 p.m. MSK, Moscow, Russia/
10:32 a.m. EDT, Cincinnati, Ohio

The Jeep traveled across rugged terrain, dodging trees, and running over scrubland until they reached a hilltop that gave a commanding view over the target compound. This was as far as the Jeep could take them. The rest of the way to Okueva's lair would be on foot.

Usher hopped from the vehicle and handed his radio to Albert for a brief Com check. "If you see Okueva, contact me directly." Usher grabbed his backpack, took out a few items, and pocketed them for rapid access if needed. Then he took a grappling hook launcher—a small gun-like apparatus attaching the hook to 20 feet of braided Kevlar line rated for up to 2,000 pounds, wound tightly inside the launcher. He placed a CO_2 cartridge into the pressure chamber and strapped the gun across his back.

"What's that for?" Albert asked.

"Backup. I never know when it will come in handy," Usher said. The rest of the team had unloaded their gear and were doing a last-minute equipment check.

"Where are you going?" Albert asked.

"I saw a drone among your equipment." He repositioned his night goggles. "Let's get it in the air. We could use some photos."

"It's too dark to see anything," Albert said.

"Not if we use an infrared camera and video feed to hear what's happening." Usher dug through his gear and put on a special helmet.

"Hover the drone over the property and circle the front gate. I want to know what to expect. I'll be able to see everything it spots with this helmet. You'll see the same images on your radio screen." Holding up a pair of bolt cutters, he added, "I'm going in with or without you. I want Okueva alive. You can remove any other guards as needed, but leave Okueva to me."

"I'm going with you," Albert said. "Leo, man Bear One with the grenade launcher and a mini machine gun." He tapped his wrist radio. "Cracker, we're sending up a drone. Lock onto it and send our men all your images."

Rozalina answered, "Cracker's talking with Dimitri. We're moving closer to you to minimize static and avoid any communication problems. What frequency on the drone?"

"Use 5.8 GHz.," Albert said. "We need speed, not distance."

As soon as Leo and Vlad had assembled Bear One and loaded the weapons, Albert asked Usher, "Are you ready?"

Usher nodded. "Launch it." The drone lifted and hovered overhead long enough for Usher to get an image through his helmet. Once he was satisfied with the picture quality, he swung his right arm forward and signaled to move the drone over the property.

"It's quieter than I expected," Albert said.

"We muffled the noise so the speaker can pick up a wider range," Usher said. The first images popped up on his radio screen. "Circle it twice over the entire complex and then the back fence."

The drone indicated the presence of an access road that led to the top of the mountain. Two men stood outside the front gate, while two other men were positioned by the headquarters' front door. As they observed the drone footage, suddenly, the front door burst open, and an armed guard rushed out, shouting something in Russian while heading towards the guardhouse. A group of men quickly followed him and headed towards the main headquarters.

Usher adjusted something on his helmet and then spoke. "Can you hear me, Cracker?"

"Loud and clear," Cracker came back.

"Any updates," Usher asked.

"We've captured Okueva's first two units along the road leading up the mountain," Cracker said. "His third unit merged with the fourth, and they're heading your way. Okueva must have gotten word of our team's ambush and is preparing for an attack. We lost two men. The enemy lost twelve. They refused to be taken as prisoners and fought to their deaths. So will Okueva."

"Thanks for the update," Albert said to Cracker. "We need to keep Okueva's teams three and four pinned to their location." He turned to his men. "Advance to the tree line, and then spread out. We'll walk the perimeter and find the best location to cut our way through the fence."

Usher grabbed his rifle. As they approached the fence, he noticed movement near the rear door of the headquarters building. He motioned to Albert. "We have company."

"There are two guards by the back door. You take the right guard," Albert said. "I'll take the left, and then we can go through the fence."

Usher lay in the grass and raised his rifle, but his target went down before he could pull the trigger. Albert was behind and fired with a loud pop. His designated target collapsed. Usher looked around to see who his protector was, but dazed by the suddenness, he didn't move until he was jolted into action by Albert yelling "Move! Move! Move!"

Albert contacted Cracker. "Cover rear cameras and any alarm panels. We're cutting through the fence."

Usher pulled a small copper pipe from his pocket and short-circuited the electrified fence, rendering it powerless. Relief flooded through him when no alarm sounded. Cracker had diverted the panel alarm. It took a few seconds to cut through the wires.

"Hurry," Cracker said. "If nothing changes, Okueva's reinforcements will arrive in four minutes. The drone, alone, won't be able to hold them. Is it time to send up your prop jet? Dimitri and Zina are ready to fly."

Usher's heart skipped a beat. "Zina? You're going to have Zina fly that for real?"

"We need to keep Okueva's backup team at bay," Albert said. "Dimitri is my best flyer, and he'll take them out."

"But, Zina? She has no flight experience," Usher objected.

"That's not what she says." Albert smiled at Usher's frown.

Zina patched in through the radio. "My grandmother flew a Spitfire during WW II. She was a WASP, and she made sure all of her children became pilots, as did my mom. I've flown since I was a teenager. Take care down there."

"Well, I'll be…" Usher said under his breath.

"Let's go," Albert said. "You have one chance to get Okueva out alive. He'll kill himself before he surrenders." The men dashed past the fence toward Okueva's headquarters. "The hardest part will be the last sixty yards out in the open."

The drone was a lifeline to the team and flew so quietly that one would have to actively search for it to spot it.

Ready for battle, Albert drew up his rifle. "Usher, Leo, and Vlad, you're team one and will accompany me. The rest of you are team two. Keep us covered until we're directly outside the building. Then go around to the front. I'll give you the sign." He bolted forward.

Usher was grateful that he brought along his super-scope with its long-range extended thermal weapon sight and suppressor since he couldn't see much in the dark without it. Each of Albert's men had a submachine gun. Team two covered his back.

Albert spoke into his wrist radio. "Cracker, have the drone drop a blast at the gate and the guardhouse to be sure no one escapes. The helicopters are in plain sight. Usher, once we get Okueva, head for one of them. That's our new getaway plan to bring Okueva out alive. Our jeep is too far away and will take too long to get back down the mountain." Albert raised his fist, calling, "Move it men."

Staying in the trees, Usher darted forward swiftly with purpose, but his footfalls were like a breeze over the fallen leaves—not even a rustle as he kept a constant vigil for any tripwires or traps.

Now that they were only ten yards from the back door, Albert used hand signals and motioned team two forward.

Albert quietly asked for an update from Cracker. That's when the drone blasted the front gate. Cracker's voice seemed muffled, then cleared after the blast. "…Dimitri made a direct hit on the two teams coming up the mountain, but now everyone is on the alert. Okueva will do everything in his power to escape. He always has a plan B."

Albert gave another hand signal. Team one dashed for the back of the building—Vlad was at Usher's side. Leo stood next to Albert. Loud voices came from inside but soon went silent as gunfire erupted out front. Albert's team two had positioned themselves in front. "Ready," the commander of team two radioed to Albert.

Leo stepped closer to the back door, which was ajar. Albert braced himself against the building and spoke to Usher's men, "We'll clear. You follow." He spoke into his radio. "Ready. On the count of three." He nodded and held up one finger, then two. When he flipped up the third finger, Usher slammed his boot against the door, which flew open. He took a right, and two bursts of gunfire greeted him. Usher quickly dispatched the men.

Albert moved at his back and took a left, then opened fire. Three more men down. "Clear," Usher said and moved to the hallway. Team two had gone through the front door. "Clear," echoed from the entry.

Usher and Albert headed down a long hall while Leo and Vlad moved in the opposite direction. "Kitchen clear," Leo shouted. "Heading upstairs," he said into his radio.

As Usher and Albert cleared the hallway, two enemy guards returned a fire round and ducked behind a partially opened door.

Usher could see a desk. "I think that's Okueva's office." He found a boot in the hallway, picked it up, threw it at eye level toward the door, and dropped to the floor. Shots from a semi-automatic rifle ripped the door from the hinges and shredded the boot. Usher's heart raced. That was too close. One deep breath washed calmness through him, and his training took over. He automatically returned fire. No thought, just reaction. Thinking would get him killed. He had a job to do, and today, his job was to get Okueva, alive if possible. When all went quiet in the office, Usher threw himself through the opening and rolled. "Clear."

"Where did they go?" Albert asked, still scanning the room, and then headed for the window. "Men are running for the helicopter."

How did Okueva escape? Usher's eyes roamed the room and fell upon a closed closet door. Usher fired two shots, but the door was metal, and the bullets ricocheted back at him, barely missing his head. The door was locked.

"Bet there's a tunnel through there," Albert said. "We'll have to go around." He contacted Cracker. "Do you see Okueva?"

"I think so. Four men crawled out from under the porch and headed for the helicopters. Dimitri has him in his sights and can cut him down, but I want him alive. Your team two has pinned down most of Okueva's men."

"Have Dimitri blow up the ammo warehouse. That'll get their attention," Albert said. "I'm going after Okueva."

Usher watched Albert break the panes from the front office window and hoist himself through the opening. "Are you coming?" Albert asked, but Usher had other plans.

"Meet you outside in a few minutes." Usher rummaged through Okueva's desk and found a cell phone, a computer, and a ring of keys. Probably a burner phone, Okueva wouldn't leave his cell behind. Usher pulled a small device from his pocket, plugged it into the computer, then attached the cell phone and keyed in a password. He spoke into his radio, "Cracker, download this hard drive and forward it to Cordy. I don't have time to finish running the app, so I'm leaving Intel in your hands. I gave you access to the files."

"Where are you going?" Cracker asked, but Usher didn't answer. He crashed through the back window and headed for the helicopter.

"Four men in a military vehicle just barreled through the open gate," Cracker warned. "Okueva's team four is heading your way." The drone hovered over the already destroyed gate and dropped a grenade. The Jeep rolled into the front yard end over end. Okueva's men bailed from the Jeep. Some continued to pummel the air and hit the ground, shooting in the search for a human target. Others scattered behind the destroyed Jeep, using it as cover, raised their weapons and kept firing round after round.

Usher hit the ground.

Albert was also returning fire while on the ground, hiding behind several boxes.

Usher hoped the boxes didn't contain explosives as gunfire surrounded them. Unsure of what direction to take, Usher rolled as a puff of dust blew up into his face. He scampered to his feet and zigzagged toward the helicopter.

Okueva was already on board. The blades roared to life. A guard next to him covered Okueva, shooting down in a continuous arc.

Usher took careful aim and hit the guard in the chest. The man fell from the chopper as Okueva hovered the bird overhead.

"I don't think we can take Okueva alive," Albert called out from behind him. That's when Dimitri flew the prop plane over the warehouse and dropped a grenade. The ammo exploded, causing a gust of wind to grab the helicopter blades slowing them.

Okueva fought to keep control and was nearly blinded by Usher's exploding flash grenade. The chopper headed for the ground. As it dipped low enough, Usher grabbed his grappling hook gun, launched the dart into the helicopter's hull, and hung on as Okueva pulled the bird back into the air. Usher dangled at the end of the rope, twisting round and round, struggling to untangle himself from the line. Once he freed his arm from the tangle, he hit the ascension device, which pulled him toward the helicopter. When his feet reached the runner, he grabbed the rear door frame and inched his way forward to the passenger's side. He pulled a small dart gun from his pocket, aimed, and fired. A drug-tipped dart flew into Okueva's neck.

Okueva swore, and then shouted, "You're too late! I couldn't stop the attacks even if I wanted to." His laugh was bitter. "Everything's set to blow! We've hit London already. Paris is next, then the Vatican. We'll hit the U.S. before anyone stops us." His speech slurred, but he wouldn't quit laughing. "It doesn't matter now. I can crash, and we're both dead."

Usher struggled to enter the chopper while Okueva tipped the bird from side to side, trying to shake off Usher's grip. At last, Usher reached inside the cockpit and hoisted himself aboard. They fought. It felt like hours, but it took less than two minutes for the drug to incapacitate Okueva.

The chopper weaved and rocked, but Usher finally wrestled control away from the unconscious Okueva. Lifting off fast, Usher banked and made several evasive maneuvers to avoid sniper fire near the gate.

Dimitri's jet came into view. Zina sat in the rear seat of the cockpit. "Usher has our target," she radioed to Cracker, Albert, and everyone on her frequency. The plane dipped low over the gated area, which lit up with another explosion. Sniper fire ceased.

Albert radioed, "Cracker and Rozalina are on their way to investigate headquarters. They'll forward any data to Cordy. Is the target alive?"

Usher radioed back. "He's incapacitated but alive. He says everything is set to blow. London's already been hit, followed by other major cities, and the U.S. Cracker is trying to locate the attack sites and will forward them to Guy Weimer at Homeland Security."

"Will it help Cracker get pardoned?" Albert asked.

"There are no guarantees," Usher said. "I need to land before Okueva wakes up."

"My team will stay with Cracker to keep him safe," Albert said. "I'll take Leo and Vlad with me in the other chopper. We'll meet you at our base at the bottom of the mountain. Dimitri and Zina will join us. Then we'll decide on what to do with our captive."

"Roger," Usher said.

SECRETS NO MORE

Sept. 18 – 6:00 p.m. MSK, Moscow, Russia/
11:00 a.m. EDT, Cincinnati, Ohio

Albert's Russian Rebel Army had rapidly set up their base in the foothills of the Ural Mountains near Pervouralsk, Russia. Agent Usher Hastings paced within the canvas walls, pondering his next steps. He had joined forces with Marshal Albert and captured General Sukho Okueva as he tried to flee his secret hideaway via helicopter and brought him here. The bitter wind threatened to uproot the army tent.

Albert ordered, "Leo, reinforce those stakes and bring us more coffee. We need this guy to give us critical information ASAP, and we don't have time to bother with minor details."

"Yes, sir," Leo motioned for Vlad to help with the tasks and went outside.

Usher checked his watch. "There's no time to waste. We have less than four hours before an attack in Texas. How are we going to get him to talk?"

"I have my ways, but with his background, I had to increase the dose." Albert pulled a chair closer to General Surko Okueva's cot. His wrists and feet were in leather restraints, but Okueva lay in calm repose.

"Where am I?" The captive spoke in Russian.

Albert replied, "Rebel Army camp. It seems you've been busy these past few days—an attack on London and the U.S."

Okueva chuckled. "So, we must have succheeded, but that's not all."

"I expected as much," Albert said. "Would you like to gloat a bit more?"

"Nooo, you'll shee…soooon," Okueva slurred and yawned. "Why am I so tired?"

Agent Zina entered the room with a cup of tea and pulled up a chair. "Drugs will do that."

Okueva turned his face toward her. An odd smile crossed his lips. His eyes roamed as if unable to focus. "Whaaat kinda…" He snored softly.

Albert checked Okueva's wrist. "He has a strong pulse. Do you think we waited long enough for the truth serum to take effect?"

Zina lifted Okueva's eyelid. "His pupils are dilated. Amobarbital works rapidly, but every person responds differently to the dose. We must monitor his heart rate and watch for pauses in breathing."

"Truth serum?" Usher asked. "Good idea. Let me test how well it works." He turned on his phone recorder and asked Okueva in Russian, "What is your full name?"

"My father named me Surko Piosenki Okueva. Some call me the Journalist or Risingsickle."

Usher needed current information. "Do you see General Rutoon?" Usher tried to put his words into Russian, but it was slow-going.

"Nyet, he's dead," Okueva said.

Usher rolled his eyes and spoke softly. "I didn't mean see. I meant know."

Okueva must have heard. "Da. I took over." Okueva replied in his native tongue. "We make many plans."

Running a tense hand through his hair, Usher wanted to scream. His limited knowledge of the language was taking too long. "My Russian isn't good enough. Zina, can I use your phone to call Braun? I'm using mine to record his answers. We must be sure to ask the right questions, and Braun speaks Russian fluently."

"I'll question him," Albert said. "Text me your questions, and I'll ask. Okueva should only be exposed to one voice so we don't confuse him."

"I need to know his plan to attack each country and the U.S.," Usher called Braun and whispered over the phone, "I'm putting you and Cordy on speaker. Text any questions to this number, and Albert will translate them."

Albert leaned forward close to Okueva's ear, speaking in Russian. "How did General Rutoon plan to attack each country and the U.S.?"

Okueva licked his lower lip. "He mastermind…bioterrorist attack…but died. He planned cyberattacks. I do his orders."

Usher opened his mouth, but Albert held up his hand to silence him. "What were Rutoon's orders?"

"Chaos." A smile came over Okueva's lips.

Cordy forwarded a list of questions to Albert. "Where will they strike?"

"London first, then Paris, Berlin…," Okueva paused, "tonight Rome." He chuckled.

"What was attacked in London?" Albert translated from Cordy's message.

"Subway."

"You also mentioned Paris, Berlin, and Rome. What will be attacked in those cities?"

Albert asked about each city, "What was attacked in Paris?"

"Eiffel Tower." That was new information for Cordy.

"What was attacked in Berlin?"

"Opera House." More new data.

"What was attacked in Rome?"

"Not time yet."

"Where in the U.S.?"

"Texas."

"Where in Texas?" Albert asked.

"Rutoon's location," Okueva said.

"Rutoon's dead!" Cordy interrupted.

Albert took over, "You said that you carried out his orders."

"Can't do everything," Okueva slurred.

"Who helped?" Albert asked.

"Students."

"What did the students do?"

"Wrote viruses."

Albert read Cordy's next question, "What were the viruses attached to?"

"Electronics, memory chips, motherboards, cameras."

"Why students?"

"Innocents. No one suspect."

"What did you do with these hacks?"

"Got data, firewalls, security programs..."

Cordy texted, "What can you do with this data?"

"Everything—transfer funds...bogus accounts...steal data," Okueva's speech became thick with a Chechen accent and more difficult to understand.

"Go back to Wichita Falls, Texas," Albert translated her question and added, "What will be attacked?"

"Rutoon knows. Not me," Okueva said.

"What was attacked in the U.S.?" Albert tried again.

"Rutoon knows," Okueva repeated.

"Where is the attack in Rome?" Albert tried to clarify.

"Vatican and more, but too early for big attack," Okueva said. "Too soon."

Cordy texted, "What does a six-sided star tattoo mean?"

Okueva didn't answer.

"What's so important about a tattoo?" Albert asked.

Cordy gasped. "It's a link. Quint found a symbol with letters and numbers in Rutoon's office. He took a photo and forwarded it to me. At first glance, I didn't think much of this drawing, but then the explosive expert captured at Joyland had a tattoo with that same symbol, and the men who captured Xander's brother also had that tattoo. Coincidence? I don't think so."

Cordy took a deep breath. "I must tell Harris about Paris and Berlin and check out Rutoon's star. Braun will stay on the line."

Cordy contacted President Harris. "Usher is interrogating General Okueva using truth serum."

"Does that work?" Harris asked.

"It seems to. At least we're getting some answers," Cordy said. "Okueva says they plan to attack the Eiffel Tower in Paris and the Berlin Opera House in Germany. We couldn't get any information about where the strike in the U.S. will occur, other than General Rutoon knows and it's in Wichita Falls, Texas, and it isn't time yet for an attack in Rome."

"I have Nat Ping in Rome," Harris said. "He'll keep us informed, and I'll contact the French president and German Chancellor to update them. Hopefully, we can abort any attacks in their countries. Let me know if you find out anything more." Harris signed off.

Cordy downloaded Quint's latest research at the Pentagon and brought up a photo of a six-sided star inside two circles. The star was tipped a bit to the left and had other odd symbols between each point and the rim of the circle.

Braun stepped behind her and peered over her shoulder. "Is that a Jewish star? Are we facing another attack on a synagogue?"

Cordy entered a hexagon into a Google search, and the six-sided star of Armenia came up. "It's not Jewish—look at the circle inside the star."

"The Armenian wheel of eternity," Braun read. "Armenians are renowned for their science and math skills, especially geometry."

"And astronomy," Cordy added. "My research shows the wheel of eternity, but it's not usually inside an eight-sided star. It's considered a powerful sign by many. My search also shows there is a group of Russian Armenians, Libya's hardline Islamists, who have been recruited. I'll need to investigate more, but in the meantime, maybe these numbers and letters will hint at where we'll find the terrorists." She uploaded the file into a second analysis program and texted Albert.

Sept. 18 – 6:36 p.m. MSK, Moscow, Russia/
11:36 a.m. EDT, Cincinnati, Ohio

"What does the Armenian Star mean?" Albert asked.

Okueva didn't answer.

Albert went on to say, "There's a circle inside—"

"Wheel of eternity," Okueva said.

"What does the wheel mean?"

"Loyalty. My men, loyal."

"How many men?"

"Maaany," Okueva slurred.

"Are they all from Russia?" Albert asked.

"Nyet," Okueva's eyelids fluttered briefly, and he inhaled a jagged breath. "Some …in Pakistan,…Israel, Europe,…U.S."

Albert glanced up at Usher, waiting for the next question, and asked, "What do they do?"

"My ooorders…Hooold hostages, plant fake…news, but… No crack…darknet." Okueva coughed.

Albert motioned to Usher. "I want to clear Cracker's record and find out if he killed that FBI agent."

Usher held his phone closer to be sure to capture every reply.

"Have you ever been to the U.S.?" Albert asked.

"Da."

"Did you know FBI Agent Crueger Yates?"

"Da."

"He was investigating your Middle Eastern activities, wasn't he?" Albert asked.

"Da," Okueva replied.

"What did he discover?" Albert asked.

"Selling Plu..to...ura...nium." Okueva managed to spit out.

"What happened to Agent Yates?" Usher asked.

"Dead," Okueva said.

"Did you murder Yates?" Albert asked.

There was a pause. "Da."

"So, you did murder Agent Yates?" Usher adjusted his cell phone to be sure to capture the confession. "How did he die?"

Okueva paused again. "Car got flat tire. I help...tire iron slipped." He seemed to give a slight chuckle.

Agent Yates had died of a massive head injury, but Usher hadn't heard it was from a tire iron. He'd have to pull old reports to see if he could verify Okueva's details.

Albert whispered, "Does that clear, Cracker?"

"I think so." Usher hoped President Harris would grant Cracker a pardon based on this recording. If not, Spendorf had already agreed to the pardon. Harris had more pressing issues. A snorty whistle came from Okueva's lungs as he exhaled, and his breathing ceased.

Zina grabbed his wrist. "His pulse is only 30 beats per minute." She shook Okueva. "Take a deep breath."

Okueva coughed. His lips paled.

Zina raised her fist and thumped his chest.

Usher grabbed her arm. "What are you doing?"

"He stopped breathing." Zina yanked her arm away from Usher's grasp. "We're going to lose him."

"Enough!" Albert said. "He's not going to talk."

Braun heaved a sigh. "I hope someone stops the attacks before it's too late."

"You tried your best and knew it was a long shot," Albert said.

"Keep me posted. Cordy has President Harris back on the line. Braun signed off."

"We can't just let him die!" Zina thumped Okueva's chest once more.

"We'll turn Okueva over to Moscow's chief of police." Albert disconnected the call.

"No!" For the first time, Okueva fought his restraints. "My kid brother…will kill me! He'll kill me…Kill me." His body jerked, rattling the bed. Froth bubbled from his lips.

"What's happening?" Albert asked.

"He's having a seizure!" Zina grabbed an arm. "Take off this restraint. We need to put him on his side. He'll choke and die."

Albert dug the key from his pocket and tried to insert it into the restraint's lock, but Okueva's wrist kept jerking. "Hold him down."

Usher grabbed his arm to steady it. The key engaged, and the restraint popped loose. Okueva's eyes snapped open. "Kill me." He became a wild man, wrestled his wrist free from Usher, and grabbed Albert's pistol nestled in a hip holster. Before anyone could stop him, Okueva aimed the gun at his own temple and fired.

Sept. 18 – 7:04 p.m. MSK, Moscow, Russia/
12:04 p.m. EDT, Cincinnati, Ohio

Zina threw her arms over her face and let out a scream as blood and brain splattered across her face. "How gross!" Her fingers shook as adrenaline pumped through her. Shaking like an unbalanced washing machine, she ran her wrist over her face. It came away bloody. The coppery stink clung to her hair as clumps of sticky, warm blood pooled and dripped down her neck. "Get this off me!" Her voice quivered in a loud shout as she tore off her jacket. A deafening roar washed over her. A scream built in her throat along with bile, but she kept swallowing, trying to make it go away.

Usher had seen several deaths in his career and knew the first time was especially hard to witness. He pulled a handkerchief from his pocket, dipped it into her cup of tea, which was the closest liquid, and dabbed it across her forehead—scrubbing away most of the gore from her face, but her hair was hopeless.

Zina, embarrassed to have anyone see her like this, grasped his fingers. "I'll do it." She was unsteady on her feet as she scrubbed her face. Usher didn't let her go, and she welcomed his support. An annoying buzz filled her senses. Swallowing back bile, she blurted, "I think I'm going to puke!" Her hand covered her mouth, and she gasped for air.

"Take some deep breaths." Usher looped his foot around the leg of a chair and pulled it closer. "Sit down and put your head between your knees." He eased her into the seat and supported her as she leaned forward, heaving shaky exhalations. When she sat up, he dabbed away a few leftover smudges.

Vlad raced into the tent, pausing to stare at Zina. The gulp he took could be heard throughout the tent. "What happened?"

"Okueva's dead!" Albert said.

Leo was right behind Vlad. When he saw Zina, he found his backpack. "You need to wash with soap and water. It's the only way to get rid of the stench."

Zina stared at her trembling fingers. Blood had nestled in the lines of her palms and her nail beds. "I need a shower."

"This is the best I can do." Leo fished through the bag and pulled out a towel, soap, and a mirror. "There's a kettle of water heating outside over the fire. I'll be right back." He grabbed her mug, left the tent, and returned with her cup filled with hot water. Leo handed her a mirror. "I always carry this so I can shave each morning."

"Thanks," Zina eked out.

Usher used the soap and hanky to wash her face as she held up the mirror, although she couldn't look at herself in this condition.

Usher got another cup of water and washed the largest clump of blood from her hair. "How are you feeling now?"

"My insides are churning, cold, shaky, but we have a job to do." Zina set down the mirror. She grabbed the soap and did a better job of washing both hands and then wiped them with the towel. "Thanks, Leo. I feel much better."

"Seeing your first kill is always the worst," Leo said.

"This isn't my first," Zina whispered. "It flooded my mind with the last time." Her eyes pooled with tears that threatened to spill.

"Do you want to talk about it?" Leo asked.

Zina shook her head, but her story spilled anyway. "I was in Iraq. An IED hit our Humvee—everyone inside was blown to bits. I hadn't boarded yet, but the impact sent me flying. I could see my team gone, unrecognizable hunks of flesh, before I hit the ground. I didn't wake up for almost two weeks. I don't want to talk about it." With a shudder, she handed him the towel, took a deep breath, stood, and deliberately walked back to Albert. "What do we do now?"

Albert politely turned his head. He had thrown a sheet over Okueva's body. "We better notify his next of kin."

"Who's that?" Leo asked.

"Moscow's chief of police," Albert said.

Vlad turned pale. "I don't want to be anywhere near him."

"Time for your revenge," Albert said.

Zina still felt queasy. "I'm going outside." No one stopped her as she dashed through the door. Tears streamed down her cheeks. Her eyes squinted as she tried to adjust to the bright lights of the camp outside. Blowing grit stung her face. Her brain was in a fog—an echo of the past with hazy memories crowded too close for comfort.

Sept. 18 – 7:44 p.m. MSK, Moscow, Russia/
12:44 p.m. EDT, Cincinnati, Ohio

"Need any help?" Usher called from the doorway.

"No! I don't want anyone to see me like this." Zina shouted and then darted for the bushes. Usher had been so kind. Damn him anyway. Why couldn't she get the man out of her thoughts? It scared the hell out of her, reminding her she was damaged.

"Usher, she'll be fine," Albert said. "I want to bounce an idea off you. Do you know enough Russian to make a phone call to the chief?"

"What do you have in mind?" Usher asked, but he continued to watch Zina to be sure she was okay.

"We're going to capture the chief in his own web, and Okueva will be our bait." Albert pointed to the body.

"Sure, I'll practice until I get it right," Usher said, "but why me?"

"He'll recognize your American accent and jump at the chance to meet you. Let me get Cracker down here." He tapped his wrist radio. "Cracker, I'm sending Dimitri up the mountain to fly you and Rozalina back to headquarters. General Okueva's dead."

"Did he confess to killing FBI Agent Yates?" Cracker sounded distressed.

"Yes," Albert said. "Usher recorded his confession on his cell phone. Bring all of Okueva's computer equipment and important files with you. Have the rest of our team head down the mountain."

"We're gathering everything as fast as possible," Cracker said. "Rozalina found a burner cell in Okueva's desk. She's been tracking his phone calls for several weeks, but she discovered new messages from Pakistan and Israel dated two days ago. This morning, he made calls to all the target cities. I'm sure we can locate his contacts."

"Good," Albert said.

Usher added, "There were student hackers from Pakistan and Israel in Wichita. Their families are being held hostage in their homelands."

"Rozalina, this involves you, too," Albert said. "Okueva's brother is the chief of police in Moscow. You know what that means."

Rozalina's voice shook. "Yes, he's a leader of one of Russia's most powerful underground organizations. He is behind several high-powered deaths. His most lethal weapon seems to be drinks laced with antifreeze. That's how General Urk died."

Vlad gasped, "Do you have proof? I thought Urk was beaten and hung up in Red Square."

"He suffered that, too," Rozalina said, "but I was at the morgue during Urk's autopsy. Urk met with the chief of police just before his capture by Denys Evanko. Antifreeze was in his bloodstream. I'm sure that prevented Urk from fighting off his attackers."

"Okueva must have been tracking his brother's activities," Cracker said. "He has hundreds of emails verifying the police are behind bribes, gang rapes, land grabs, and murder. Okueva is at the top of their hit list."

Vlad's hands clenched into fists as he raged, "Being a prisoner is hell. The guards do nothing to stop the infighting. In fact, they instigate beatings daily. I barely survived, and if Leo hadn't found my unconscious body and declared my death, I would be truly dead by now."

"We're putting an end to that." Albert turned to Usher. "We should inform your president." They huddled briefly to discuss a plan of attack.

"I'll check in with Harris." Usher speed-dialed the president on his agency cell phone.

"Hi, Usher, I have great news," Harris sounded exuberant. "Your warning came in time to stop the terrorist attacks in Paris and Berlin! How are things in Russia?"

"We still don't know where they'll attack in Texas," Usher said. "Okueva wouldn't give up the information. Everything was going as planned until Okueva shot himself. If it's okay with you, I'd like to put Marshal Albert on the speaker, and we can update you."

There was a pause and a few clicks. "Go ahead," Guy said. "I connected you to our security team."

Usher updated the president and his team on what had transpired during Okueva's interrogation. "He admitted killing FBI Agent Yates with a tire iron. I recorded his confession. Cracker was not guilty of Yate's murder, and he has fought by my side to track down the killer. I'm requesting that he be pardoned and free to remain in Russia."

Harris said, "Send me the recording, and I will draw up the legal documents. You did well getting any information out of General Okueva. It's more than I expected. Cordy and her team will have their hands full locating all that malware, but she'll be pleased to know that Cracker is tracking down the thugs holding Xander's family ransom. We must still locate the other students' families and work to free them. I'll be glad to have you come home."

"There are a few loose ends to wrap up in Russia before I leave," Usher said. "I'll let Albert fill you in on the details."

"What's the plan?" Harris asked.

"Okueva's brother is Moscow's chief of police and a leader of one of Russia's most powerful mafias," Marshal Albert said. "He's been gunning for Okueva for a long time, so we'll use his brother's body as bait. If we can capture the chief, it will stop his syndicate's activities."

"How will that affect the U.S.?" Harris asked.

Usher piped up, "No more interfering in U.S. elections, money laundering, or extortion of our business and financial systems."

"Anything we can do to help?" Harris asked.

"You may hear from Russia's president, and Albert needs to know where you stand if the Rebel Army wipes out this mafia," Usher said.

Albert added, "They are oligarchs who have fought the president on many issues. The insurgents control everything, but once their leader is out of the picture, his followers will disperse and fall in line under the president's rule."

"Thanks for the heads-up," President Harris said. "Usher, when will you be back in the States?"

"We'll wrap up here within the hour," Usher said. "Then Zina and I will head to Moscow to pick up our luggage. I plan to leave Russia tomorrow morning, barring any unforeseen obstacles."

"Report in when you arrive." Harris disconnected the phone call.

Sept. 18 – 8:00 p.m. MSK, Moscow, Russia/
1:00 p.m. EDT, Cincinnati, Ohio

Twenty minutes later, Cracker entered the tent. "Dimitri will fly Usher and Zina back to the outskirts of Moscow, where we met up originally. Do you want Vlad and Leo to accompany them?"

"We're all leaving for Moscow, including Okueva's body," Albert said. "That's where we'll find Chief Ignacio."

Rozalina filled Zina in on Chief Ignacio as they entered the tent.

"There are only the two-seater trainer plane and the Hawk jet," Leo said. "They'll carry all of us back to Moscow, but what about the equipment? Are you planning to leave that behind?"

"No, Larensky and Lukovich will load up the supplies, break down headquarters, and drive back with the equipment," Albert said. "We can't include them in our immediate plans."

"What are your plans?" Usher asked. "You mentioned you needed me to call Chief Ignacio and inform him of his brother's death."

"No, not of his death," Albert said. "I want you to tell him that we have captured General Okueva and know the police are giving a reward for any word of his whereabouts. Make sure you let him know you are only interested in the money and will gladly turn over your captive for no extra fee, no questions asked. I plan to see the chief in person."

"Where will you meet?" Usher asked.

"See if you can get him to agree to meet you at the rear of the jailhouse," Albert said. "I know he has a secret chamber where he wines and dines key officials, and I'm sure that's where he drugged General Urk. It should meet his needs as well as mine."

Leo piped up, "I know exactly where that is, and it's unsafe. He could ambush you without anyone noticing."

"Da, and I, too, can play his game," Albert said. "Usher, you make the call, set up a time when and where he'll meet you, and I'll take care of the rest."

Zina cleared her throat. "Rozalina and I were talking a few minutes ago, and I think it would be better if a woman made the call. I know a little Russian." She peered over at Usher for his response, but he only scowled. "I have to shower and say goodbye to my friends before leaving, but I could stand in as bait if you need my help."

"Oh, no," Usher jumped in. "You're not going anywhere near that jailhouse. Vlad can tell you what happens behind those prison walls."

"Well, you men aren't going to let him get his hands on me," Zina said. "I'm safe, and it might get his immediate attention. After all, what woman would be able to capture Okueva?"

"I hate the plan," Usher said at the same time as Albert said, "Love it. Let's make it happen."

"I'll need some clean clothes before tonight," Zina said.

Rozalina nodded. "I have a few skirts and blouses you can borrow, but I'm not quite as endowed as you, so it might be a tight fit."

"Thank you," Zina said. "The tighter, the better if I'm going to lure Chief Ignacio."

Usher let out a gasp. "Lure him? You better not. I'm going with you, and there'll be no debate about that."

"Are you going unarmed?" Zina asked.

"Yes, Albert will have our backs."

"How will we get Okueva's body inside," Zina asked. "He can't just walk along beside us."

Rozalina said, "I'll get the ambulance to take him to the station or maybe the morgue, and we can pretend to have Okueva in the next room."

"If we arrive early enough, the chief's butler can let us in," Leo said. "Butler duty is rotated through the police staff. I'll have my brother take that duty tonight. I'm sure he can trade with whoever is scheduled. The policemen feel it's beneath them to serve the chief, but they're too afraid to tell him face-to-face."

"Everything is coming together better than I thought," Albert said.

Leo poured everyone a cup of fresh coffee and a hot tea for Zina. "I've been thinking. I could ask Captain Boris to get his men to raid the jail and break out Marot and Xander's brother, plus a few good people down on their luck. That could cause a diversion and make it easier to get to the chief."

"I thought Boris was a Lieutenant," Vlad said. "Is he in charge of Urk's division now?"

"He was promoted after Captain Anton's death," Leo said. "I'm sure he'll help us, and since I was Urk's aide, I know all the men. They'll do anything to help retired Captain Marot escape. His hot-headed son would lead the way if Boris let him."

"Good plan," Albert said. "Drink up. It's mighty cold out there, and it will take another two hours before we're back in Moscow. We'll make the arrangements en route. Once we arrive, we'll meet at Cracker and Rozalina's."

Zina chugged her tea. "Let's go! I can't wait to take a shower."

WECHOLTZ TRIAL – DEFENDANT

Sept. 18 – 12:00 p.m. EDT, New York City, New York

When Sophia arrived in Judge Nif's courtroom at noon, the crowd had doubled since the morning session. She pushed through the overflow of reporters and sketch artists to reach the front table.

A breaking news report about the trial had already spread through the media. An interview with Alexa replayed on her cell phone at 11:30 a.m. revealed, "The murderer of AK is seeking a retrial. We will finally get justice. Wecholtz should receive the death penalty! Even better, he should face the same fate as my brother and be run down."

Sophia locked eyes with Chief Jackson as he entered the room.

His eyes narrowed. "It could get ugly." He dropped the local newspaper face up on the table. The headlines read, "AK's Sister Declares Wecholtz Deserves Death Penalty!"

The room erupted with boos as Floyd entered with a guard on either side, but the noise died down quickly when the bailiff stepped to the door. His strong stance and stern glare made it clear that this court would not tolerate such behavior.

Sophia whisked the paper from the table into her briefcase.

"Did you see the paper? I don't have a chance," Floyd muttered. At least this afternoon, he wore a better-fitting suit, thanks to Jackson's purchase at Salvation Army.

"I want to speak with Judge Nif," Sophia said. "He did not sequester the jurors during the break, and every one of them could have heard the news or read the paper."

"It's too late to meet before the trial starts," Jackson said. "Make a motion from the floor so all hear your concerns. In the meantime, our MIT professor has agreed to reveal what he found on the missing video splices. He'll be here shortly."

Ron Moore-Les, the DA, entered the room with a flurry of activity as three aids trailed behind him. They were serious, expensively suited, briefcase-carrying young attorneys hoping to curry favor and career prospects with the boss.

The courtroom buzzed with anticipation as the trial time approached, and the tension escalated.

Floyd sat forward on the edge of his chair. His hands folded, and fingers clenched so tightly that they shook. "Where's the judge?"

Sophia glanced at her watch. It was already 12:20 p.m. "Something is going on. Nif is never late."

A bailiff approached Moore-Les' table and whispered something in his ear. Moore-Les nodded and stood. Then, the bailiff came over to Sophia. "Judge Nif requests the presence of both of you in chambers." The unexpected summons added a new layer of intrigue to the already tense atmosphere.

They followed the bailiff and found Judge Nif pacing his office. His shirtsleeves were rolled up, his tie loosened at the neck, and beads of sweat sprinkled his forehead. He looked up as the two attorneys entered the room. His robe and suit jacket were draped over the back of an oversized leather chair.

Sophia halted when she saw a juror, Grezelda, wringing her hands behind him. "I'm not a liar. It's true. Just ask them."

"What a mess!" Nif said.

Grezelda stepped forward, "I came here with deep concerns. I overheard two other jurors discuss news about the trial, even after you ordered us to refrain from watching, talking to others about the case, or reading the news."

"What's going on?" Moore-Les asked.

"You tell me!" Nif shouted. "Did you see the news? How could you let your witness talk to reporters about this case? It's all over the papers. Half the jurors have heard—"

Grezelda placed her finger up to her lips. "Oh, no. Don't say anything. As you instructed, I haven't heard the news or read the papers. I just heard two members, not half of the jurors, discussing the news, and put a stop to it. They are behind closed doors with a bailiff. Your Honor instructed them all to keep their mouths shut, and I came directly to you."

"I was going to bring the same news to your attention as soon as we restarted the trial," Sophia said. "How many jurors are we talking about?"

"Two," Grezelda said. "Jurors five and seven were huddled in the corner, talking about what they heard on the news while on break. The other jurors denied hearing or seeing any news."

"How did this happen?" Nif yelled and glared at Moore-Les. Seething at this predicament, his face flushed clear to his eartips. "I distinctly told every juror not to listen to the news or read the papers."

"I heard you say that," Moore-Les said. "It's not my fault they didn't listen to you."

Nif placed a finger over his lips. "Grezelda, you can't be here while we're discussing this. Please sit in the jury room until you're called into court."

"Yes, Your Honor."

After she left the chambers, Nif added, "Did you know Alexa Klinedorf was holding a news conference when she left the courtroom?" Sophia asked Moore-Les.

Moore-Les stared at his shoes.

"You did know what she planned to do," Sophia said. "I can see it written all over you, clear down to your toes."

Moore-Les lifted his eyes and stared at her. "She didn't tell me any such thing."

"Get Mrs. Klinedorf in here on the double," Nif told the bailiff.

Nif stated the obvious. "We must ensure no one else overheard and remove jurors five and seven. There are only two substitutes, so there better not be anyone else who has broken the rules. Mrs. Klinedorf deliberately planned this, didn't she?" Nif moved toward the door and shouted at the bailiff. "What are you waiting for? I gave you an order. Get Mrs. Klinedorf, now!"

"Yes, sir!" the bailiff saluted, scurrying into the courtroom. He returned shortly, shuffling his feet. "She's not in the courtroom, sir."

Sophia and Judge Nif said in unison, "Where is she?" They both turned toward Moore-Les.

He shrugged his shoulders. "Didn't we finish up with Alexa this morning? You insisted on going through that blasted security tape with her."

"No!" Sophia said. "I reserved the right to recall her. You know that. Is Victor here?"

The bailiff shook his head.

You could have heard a snail breathe. It was so silent. The recorder looked as if she was ready to bolt.

"This is grounds for a mistrial, again," Sophia warned.

The air pulsed with unused energy and suffocated the small chamber. Moore-Les had miscalculated Alexa's actions and might be removed from the case, vied with Nif's need to make a quick, weighty decision. A ripple effect would hound Judge Nif for years if he made the wrong choice, and he knew it.

A murderer freed and on the streets would forever be tied to his name. What would the governor say? After all, he was the one who put Wecholtz in supermax. "How did I get stuck on this case? Elections are next month." Nif's eyes darted toward the court recorder. "Strike those last two sentences. They didn't happen."

"What's it going to be, Judge Nif?" Sophia finally asked. "The courtroom is busting at the seams."

"I know!" Nif flicked his wrist. "Leave me alone. I have to think for a few minutes."

Sophia kept pushing. "Are we going to interview jurors five and seven? You probably want to talk to them in here instead of in the courtroom, and I want to make sure they are the only ones who disobeyed your rules."

Nif walked over to his bookcase, staring at the volumes of leather-bound tombs before him as if one would fall at his feet and give him a ready answer. At last, he turned. "Bailiff, bring in juror five."

The aroma of garlic and basil filled the room before the French chef stepped into the chambers. A rotund man about 5'5" wedged sidewise through the door, nearly knocking the bailiff off his feet. "Excusez-Moi, we must talk?"

"I understand that you heard the news about this case before returning this afternoon," Nif said. "Is this true?"

"Oui, but I must defend myself. The TV was on at the restaurant. My boss, he say, 'I can no shut it off.' This Alexa person keep telling her story over and over again. So sad. She misses her frére."

"You were told not to listen," Judge Nif said.

"I didn't want to, but..." he shrugged his shoulders. "Life happens. Am I in trouble?"

"We will have to remove you from the jury," Nif said. "You are dismissed. You must not say anything to anyone about this conversation. Is that understood?"

"Yes, sir. Will I still get pay?" The chef paused.

"For the morning only," Nif said.

The chef left the office looking relieved at his sudden release.

"Call in Juror seven," Nif said to the bailiff.

After his interview with juror seven, Nif dismissed the sanitation worker and called in the two substitutes. "What have you heard about the trial so far?"

"Nothing," both said.

"If that is true, you are officially on the jury." Nif studied each juror's face. "I believe you're telling the truth. You will perform according to the guidelines discussed this morning." Nif briefly summarized the rules as he rolled down his shirt sleeves and shrugged into his suit jacket. Reaching for his robe, he flicked his other wrist. "We have a trial waiting. Go, go."

Sophia took it as a dismissal and headed back into the courtroom. As she left, she heard Nif call to the bailiff. "Escort these ladies to the jury room and announce me."

"What's going on?" Floyd asked when she approached the table.

"We'll soon find out." Sophia scanned the noisy room, but there was still no sign of Alexa or Victor Klinedorf.

The jury returned to the courtroom with replacement jurors, numbers five and seven. The spectators and the other jurors gawked at the two substitutes, wondering what had happened, and whispered curiously to each other.

Jackson glanced around the room. "Our MIT analyst is sitting in the back of the courtroom. I don't see Adolf Mandolf or your paralegal. Put Maude on the stand first, and I'll track them down."

Sophia nodded, "Thanks. I need Mandolf to explain how he edited the security tape. It's important."

The room held a noticeable silence. Each person barely breathed as the court bailiff entered. "All rise for the honorable Judge Nif." The bailiff darted around a curtain, grabbed a wooden step, and placed it with practiced deftness just before Judge Nif stepped up to the mic.

Nif announced, "The court will continue the New York State vs. defendant Floyd Wecholtz case. Take a seat. We haven't got all day. The defense may call your next witness." His voice carried a sense of urgency, adding to the tension in the room.

"Thank you, Your Honor." Sophia stayed standing while the rest of the courtroom took their seats.

Sophia called Maude Ingram, AK's secretary, to be her next witness.

Maude wore a navy pencil skirt and matching suit jacket. The skirt was narrow, hindering her normal stride as she walked to the witness stand and paused before stepping up. She gave a little chuckle at her dilemma. "These highfalutin' styles really are a pain." Without a flourish, she hiked the hem up a bit and climbed a step to the chair. Maude sat, gave her full name, and was sworn in.

Sophia asked, "What was your role as Secretary for the OYZ Foundation?"

Maude handed Sophia her job description. "AK relied on me to keep the office running smoothly, and on most days, it ran like clockwork. That is until a few weeks before AK's death. That's when Alexa Flinsh started working for the company."

"Let the record reflect that Alexa is AK's half-sister," Sophia said. "Was there any particular incident that caused you concern that you recall?"

"Yes, on July 1st, I came to work early to do a few last-minute details before leaving for the Fourth of July holiday. It was at about 5:40 a.m. I brought a pile of papers into AK's office for his signature and discovered a list of passwords lying on his desk."

"Was that unusual?" Sophia asked.

"Of course," Maude said. "AK always kept those top-secret codes locked up in his wall safe. No one in the company had the safe combination except AK. Not even our CFO, Floyd Wecholtz, had access."

"Who left the list on AK's desk?" Sophia asked.

Maude frowned. "The list wasn't there when I shut off his office lights at 8 p.m. just before I left the night before. The only person logged in before I arrived the next day was Alexa. She came to the office during the wee morning hours. Her badge opened the door at 3:12 a.m., and somehow, she opened the company's safe. Inside that safe were those passwords she left on the desk. My badge was the second arrival recorded for that day."

"Do you think Alexa's brother gave her the combination?" Sophia asked.

Maude shook her head. "No one got that combination! It was a written corporate policy."

"What did you do with the list?" Sophia asked.

"I put the passwords into the top drawer of AK's desk and told him what I found when he arrived at the office," Maude said. "AK was very upset and quickly checked his computer but found nothing unusual. I went about my work, and it wasn't until after AK's death that I discovered that user 10200 had opened some of those password-protected files using my computer and probably AK's. The files were well-hidden, so that may be why AK didn't catch it. I never had access to his computer, so I can't be sure, but I still have my computer at home. I made a copy of the hard drive, and Chief Jackson sent the data to an IT expert, FBI Special Agent Joshtine Cordelia-Hastings, who goes by Cordy. She found the hidden files, and her analysis was thorough."

Sophia held up Cordy's detailed report and handed it to the clerk. "I've marked this analysis report as defendant exhibit 3a." She turned back to Maude. "Who was assigned user access 10200?"

Maude didn't hesitate. "Alexa Flinsh, AK's sister." Maude went on to verify hidden accounts and opened files, as Sophia had described earlier. The files detailed the Geneva bank accounts and a record of investing in a Chinese Magnesium firm, all in the name of Alexa Klinedorf.

Sophia asked, "Can you tell us what happened when you arrived at work on July 5th, the day AK died?"

Maude noted a small thumb drive already placed as evidence. "That is a recording of Alexa Flinsh's phone call with someone. It's only one-sided, and I don't know who she was talking to. I wish I had thought to dig my cell phone out earlier, but I can summarize the first part of the conversation."

"Thank you, Maude," Sophia said. "What did you overhear that caused you to tape the conversation?"

Maude scooted forward. "AK's door was ajar, so I thought he'd come in early and hoped he'd signed the pile of papers I had left on his desk. Instead, Alexa was on his phone. Her back was to me. She said, 'AK's snoopy secretary, Maude, discovered I was sitting in AK's office typing on his computer. Word got out to AK, and he's livid, but I have already accessed several offshore accounts and siphoned off money in small amounts that will go unnoticed. Then I set up my own accounts.'"

"Are you sure you understood Alexa correctly?" Sophia asked.

"Close enough," Maude said. "Her plan was shrouded in secrecy, even kept from her brother. I know, to this point, it's only hearsay evidence, but that's when I turned on my cell recorder. As I said, I should have recorded the earlier conversation, but I didn't like being called a snoopy secretary."

Sophia replayed Alexa's recording, saying, "…One problem is that AK started diversifying, making it more difficult to track. I created several accounts in Geneva, and the bankers set up real-time information so I can easily trade and conduct business with others in the industry. The funds are secure. Even my brother can't get access. I plan to simply cash in and disappear." Sophia shut off the recording and removed the thumb drive.

"Were you able to track any of these accounts?" Sophia asked.

Maude continued, "As we discussed earlier, one account was opened that same day for over $10 million, and I found that account closed ten days later."

Maude also was a character witness for the defendant. "Floyd has a rational and scientific mind, excellent math skills, and is honest."

Sophia thanked Maude. She peered around the courtroom, but Chief Jackson hadn't returned, and Adolf Mandolf was nowhere in sight.

"Who do you call as your next witness?" Judge Nif asked.

"I have received the missing sections of the original security recording, and I want to play the tape in its entirety. I call an expert witness, Professor Seamore Hyde of MIT, to the stand. He evaluated the NBC videotape, a copy of the corporate parking garage camera feed we have already reviewed, and the additional missing sections."

Moore-Les jumped up from his seat. "Objection!"

"Overruled," Judge Nif said and turned to Sophia, "You may proceed, but it is the last time we'll view this videotape."

"Thank you," Sophia said.

A thin man with a receding hairline, framed by a silver fringe around his ears, stood and made his way to the stand. He removed his spectacles and wiped them on a handkerchief he took from his blue pin-striped jacket pocket. He seemed to clean them for an extended time before replacing the glasses on his face, looking every bit like a college professor.

The bailiff stepped forward. "Please raise your right hand. Do you swear to tell the truth, the whole truth, and nothing but the truth?"

"I solemnly affirm that the evidence I shall give will be the truth, the whole truth, and nothing but the truth." When Hyde spoke, a pleasant, mellow bass voice resounded. He sat in the witness chair.

Sophia took a deep breath and addressed the witness, "Professor Hyde, you received a few snippets of videotape for review earlier this morning. What did you find?"

"The tape from the original parking garage camera that I reviewed earlier, but I did not have these missing segments at that time, as I placed in my affidavit. These snippets of videotape provided to me this morning are from that original tape."

"The security recording you are referring to is marked as defense exhibit 1g," Sophia said. "How can you tell that these splices are from that tape?"

"There is a hidden timer noted on the background of the videotape, marking the time in hours, minutes, and seconds. The times on these splices match the missing segments from the original video." Hyde pulled a sticky note from his pocket. "I jotted down the times for each of the splices. The first runs from 15:45:13 to 15:47:37, another skip occurs from 15:48:17 to 15:49:06, and there are three more skips which I wrote down, and the last one at 15:49:28 to 15:50:42. My notes are on MIT's letterhead, and I have signed my results. I was able to make a single recording of the six splices."

"Thank you." Sophia took the note and the short video of the spliced snippets. I'll enter these as defense exhibits 2b and 2c."

Professor Hyde said, "If you play the original tape and pause where the splices have been cut from the NBC tape, and insert the missing pieces, the jury can see the recording in its entirety."

Sophia motioned to a clerk. "Please set up the NBC videotape copy for review again."

"I object." Moore-Les stood up and glared. "Judge Nif, must we? We already spent half the morning on this ridiculous recording."

"It is new evidence," Sophia insisted.

Nif muttered under his breath, "I'm aware of the time rushing by. We'll review this only once. The jury will have access to all evidence during their deliberations and can review any recording repeatedly."

Professor Hyde leaned forward. "Yes, the jury may want to see each again, but I want you to watch this closely. The tape starts with AK getting out of his car. You'll see the real scene unfold in detail and compare these to the 911 recording."

Sophia motioned. "Dim the lights, please."

The tape rolled. AK leapt from his red Rolls Royce convertible as Floyd Wecholtz opened the passenger door of his blue sedan and placed an armful of manila file folders onto the front seat. Floyd closed the door and walked around the car to the driver's side when AK dashed in front of Floyd's car.

Floyd entered the driver's side of his car and rolled down his front window.

"How could you steal from our company?" AK shouted.

Floyd leaned out of his passenger-side window. "What do you mean 'steal from our company?'"

AK swung his right arm up, held a pistol in his right hand, and aimed the gun at Floyd's head.

"Don't shoot!" Floyd pulled his head back inside the car. The car engine revved. A loud bang like a firecracker sounded as the blue sedan swerved and bolted forward. The tape jumped.

"Stop there," Hyde said. "If you picked up the camera feed from the original NBC tape here, you would see Floyd running over

AK." Hyde paused and studied each of the jurors' faces. "Do you understand what just happened?"

Grezelda nodded, but some of the juror's faces showed disbelief.

"AK was holding a gun on Mr. Wecholtz," Hyde said, "but there's more. Start the recording right where you stopped it."

The large screen in front of the courtroom lit up, showing AK on the ground. He rolled to his side and continued swearing and yelling, but it was difficult to determine the words being spoken. A yellow hatchback drove into the garage. Alexa Flinsh pulled up alongside AK, parked her car, leaving the engine still running, and bolted from the passenger door to AK's side. She was screaming, "AK, are you hurt? Don't get up. You might be hurt." She knelt beside him and shoved him back to the ground. Then she stood and put her hand over her forehead to shield her eyes as if she were straining to see who was driving away.

Alexa grabbed her cell phone from her beige purse. "I'm calling 911." She dropped her purse onto the floor and knelt beside her brother. Someone must have answered the call. Alexa yelled into the phone, "Help! My brother's..." She sobbed, and her words were garbled. "My brother's been ... Hit. The driver didn't even stop!"

"Stop the recorder," Hyde said. "I listened to the EMS audio tape and the parking garage camera feed several times a few weeks ago. Everything synched up at this point. The operator was online asking, 'Where are you calling from?' Alexa answers, 'I'm here. AK, AK, talk to me. What about the e... ac...?' The tape is muffled and then becomes clear again with, 'Where does it hurt? You can't die. Not today. Not now. What am I supposed to do? Where do I go? Where's the...' and the two tapes diverge at this statement. Start the spliced videotape. Watch how it jumps and restarts."

The screen lit up. AK sat up, yelling at the car that had knocked him down. Alexa reached over and shoved her brother aside. AK gasped, perhaps his last breath. Alexa said, "...No, you can't have that..." There was a rustling in the background.

"Pause, the video," Hyde said.

Sophia realized this was the proof she needed to free Floyd and jumped in. "Note that Alexa shoved her brother. He let out a gasp, and then he quit breathing. According to Dr. Kiddash, AK's death was due to a fractured C4 severing the spinal cord. Did that little shove cause AK's fractured cervical vertebra to cut through his spinal cord? Think about that." Sophia turned to her witness. "Professor Hyde, did you want to add anything?"

Hyde nodded. "On the original NBC videotape, Alexa says, 'What will happen to me? Our future…' Then the operator says, 'Ma'am, we've tracked your location. We have an ambulance on the way. Please stay on the line…' Now start the last segment of the videotape I brought in today."

The screen lit up. Alexa was still bent over AK. She exclaimed, "I found it!" Another jump was in the tape. Victor Klinedorf stepped up to Alexa as she retrieved a gun wedged under AK's shoulder.

"Stop here," Hyde said and spoke directly to the jurors. "If you recall, a shadow fell over Alexa and AK on the original NBC videotape. The shadow appeared to be a man in a ball cap. As you can see in the missing spliced tape we just played, Victor walked up to Alexa. He wore a red ball cap, matching the shadow you saw earlier in the original videotape."

Sophia chewed on her thumbnail as Hyde spoke. She didn't want to repeat his explanation and knew Jackson had prepped Professor Hyde to highlight these little details. She was proud of her team. *Floyd may be acquitted.* She sure hoped so. *This was his last chance.*

"Start the tape," Hyde said.

The videotaped jerked, and then Alexa shoved the gun into her beige purse and pushed it toward Victor. "Hurry!"

Victor glanced around the garage, ran her purse carrying the gun to her car, and put her bag inside the glove compartment. Alexa disconnected the 911 phone call. As sirens sounded in the background, Victor ran, and the videotape stopped.

Sophia stepped forward. "As you can see, Floyd Wecholtz was correct when he claimed that AK had a gun. He also shot at Mr.

Wecholtz, which explains the cartridge gunpowder residue on AK's hands and the .38 shell casing found on the floor 200 ft. from where AK fell. This videotape is the proof we've been missing all along. I have no further questions for this witness," Sophia said.

"Mr. Moore-Les, do you wish to cross-examine this witness," Nif asked.

"No, I have no further questions," Moore-Les said.

Sophia thanked Professor Seamore Hyde. "You may step down."

Hyde stepped down, spoke briefly to Chief Jackson, who had just returned to the courtroom and took his seat.

Sophia's paralegal entered behind Jackson and hurried to the front table.

"Did you find Mandolf?" Sophia whispered.

"Yes and no." The paralegal handed over a document.

Nervous, sweat beaded Floyd's forehead as he smoothed his suit lapels and rolled up the long sleeves of his suit jacket in preparation to go to the stand when Sophia handed over new evidence. "I have an email from Victor Klinedorf to his former Lincoln Correctional Facility cellmate, Adolf Mandolf."

Judge Nif nodded. "Please read it for the jury."

Sophia opened the email and read, "'Thanks for helping Alexa open AK's safe. Now I have another little job for you. A security videotape, dated July 5 at 5:58 p.m., needs to be modified to remove evidence of AK threatening Floyd Wecholtz with a gun.' There's also a second email dated July 4, at 10:20 p.m., that reads, 'Adolf, come by the garage office around midnight at the shift change. A videotape is lying on the desk. Check it out, retrieve, and doctor it.' It's signed by Victor. I submit this as evidence as 2d and 2e."

Moore-Les asked, "Why haven't you called Adolf to testify?"

"I did," Sophia admitted. "I even subpoenaed Adolf Mandolf to be here today. Unfortunately, when my paralegal checked to see why he hadn't appeared in court, she discovered Mr. Mandolf is in a hospital ICU in critical condition. The police say he was a victim of attempted murder last night. Fortunately, he sent copies of those emails and the missing bits of spliced videotape that we just reviewed."

Floyd was next up to go on the stand, but he was a nervous wreck. Sophia placed her hand on his. "Can you do this?"

"I'm not sure." Floyd licked his lips, sweat beading his brow. "I think that tape and those emails may have saved me, and I might mess everything up if I make a mistake on the stand. Please, close without my testimony."

Sophia nodded and stood. "Mr. Wecholtz feels the security tape has given the jury enough evidence of his innocence, and noted the late hour, he has declined to take the stand, so I have no further witnesses."

Judge Nif seemed relieved and glanced at his watch. "Okay, we still have time for final statements."

Ron Moore-Les gave his closing statement first.

Sophia watched the jurors' eyes follow Moore-Les as he paced to and fro before them, but in truth, she couldn't have repeated what he said. Instead, she had been rehearsing her summary in her mind.

Grezelda glanced toward Sophia and gave a slight nod of her head. It gave Sophia hope.

When Moore-Les wound down and finally sat, Sophia got up. "I want to remind you, the jury, of your job when considering murder in the first degree. Although we have no burden to establish Floyd Wecholtz's innocence, we have shown you overwhelming proof that he acted in self-defense. The State of New York has failed to prove beyond a reasonable doubt that he committed first-degree murder.

"AK did indeed wield a gun, fired it at the defendant, and although AK was knocked down by Wecholtz's car, it did not kill him outright. Nor did the injury incapacitate AK, as you saw for yourself on the videotape. AK was able to sit up. As pointed out earlier, it wasn't until his half-sister, Alexa Flinsh-Klinedorf, shoved him back to the ground and lifted his shoulder to remove the gun that he took his last breath. Dr. Kiddash isn't here this afternoon, but he did mention that a slight jar to his body could sever the spinal cord. As you saw, AK was no longer breathing at the end of the videotape."

Grezelda nodded ever so slightly.

"During our investigation, we found that Mr. Wecholtz did not embezzle the corporation's funds. Instead, Mrs. Klinedorf opened an offshore account in Geneva, Switzerland. A check in her name was cashed, and the money was used to invest in a magnesium firm in China. Since Alexa and her husband are not present this afternoon, I cannot cross-examine them, but you have the evidence from your earlier review. I request that you find Floyd Wecholtz not guilty of murder and of embezzling corporate funds."

Judge Nif turned toward the jurors. "The jury and all in the courtroom have heard the final arguments. I will remind the jury of your civic obligation to reach a decision and compel you to return to the courtroom with your verdict. In this case, you may take the exhibits introduced into the record for further review. No one is allowed to communicate with the jurors during deliberation. All communication will go through the bailiff. The jury may retire to the jury room to begin deliberating."

The jury members got up and filed out of the courtroom. Nif said, "The jury will be allowed to take as much time as necessary to come to a verdict. This court is now in recess until you are recalled." He slammed his gavel and left the courtroom.

"How long will this take?" Floyd asked Sophia. "Do I have to go back to jail while they deliberate?"

Sophia checked her watch. "It's only 3:10 p.m. We'll stay here for the rest of the day and hope the jury agrees on a verdict soon. If they need more time, they will be sequestered, and you will return to your cell for the night. For now, let's have coffee and wait."

Sept. 18 – 3:13 p.m. EDT, New York City, New York

The court bailiff escorted the jury to a private room. Boxed snacks, bottled water, sodas, tea, and coffee were already on the long table in the middle of the room. Several jurors headed straight for the refreshments. Some sat alone, not wanting to associate with the other members, tension pulsing as they nibbled at their food. Others chatted about the weather, work, family, or anything except the trial.

Grezelda was the last to enter the room. Her take-charge attitude kicked into gear. "Our first order of business is to select a foreperson," Grezelda reminded the jurors.

Juror three, the nurse, glanced up from pouring a cup of coffee. "You went before the judge earlier this morning. I think you should be our foreperson. Is there a show of hands in agreement?"

All hands went up except Grezelda's.

The nurse asked, "Do you want the position?"

Grezelda turned to each of the jurors. "I'll do it if you all agree to help me." People nodded their heads. "I'd prefer to make this more formal. All in favor, please raise your right hand." All hands went up, as did hers. "Thank you for your vote of confidence. I'll do my best."

Turning to the bailiff, Grezelda said, "Before you leave to stand guard, we need a copy of the NBC videotape, the additional video of the spliced tape segments, and the 911 EMS audiotape for review."

The bailiff nodded. "Anything else?"

"No, we'll set up the tapes while we have a snack." Grezelda turned to the room. "Does that meet with everyone's approval?" When she didn't get an immediate answer, she tapped a spoon against a glass and repeated that they would eat first and then review the tapes sequentially to include the segments removed from the original.

"Yes, I hoped we would see it again," the nurse said. The others agreed and turned back to munching.

The bailiff arranged for Grezelda's request.

The jury reviewed the tapes three times and debated their content. "Are we ready for a vote?" Grezelda asked. She handed each juror a small slip of paper and a pencil. "Write your answer and put it on this plate when you've voted regarding murder in the first degree."

When everyone had written their vote, Grezelda read off the results. "There are twelve votes, eleven not guilty, and one maybe.

I'm not going to ask who voted, maybe, but I'm going around the room and asking what the one question that needs to be answered for a maybe to turn into a definite verdict is. I'm juror one, and my vote is not guilty. Let's move on to juror two."

The jeweler said, "I've seen the videotapes. I'm convinced that AK pulled a gun on Mr. Wecholtz and fired. I voted not guilty."

The nurse was juror three, and she sipped her coffee. "I have a splitting headache, and I want this to be over. Come back to me."

They went around the room to juror eleven, the rabbi. "I know AK was run over, but he didn't die instantly. I'm concerned that AK sustained a critical injury, though. Dr. Kiddash said he had a fractured C4. That's the same fracture sustained from a hangman's noose. He would not be able to breathe, yet the video shows AK sat up after he was hit. Would this be manslaughter?"

The nurse jumped in with an answer. "No, we are judging if Floyd Wecholtz killed AK in the first degree. That means pre-meditated murder. If anything, this was a terrible accident. I believe Wecholtz panicked. How would you react if someone put a gun to your head?"

"I never thought of it that way," the rabbi said. "God bless this man. Let's have a revote."

Grezelda was still on task. "Everyone else has gotten to say what's on their mind. Let's hear from juror twelve before voting, and then we need to determine if Mr. Wecholtz is guilty of embezzlement."

Juror twelve, a local elementary school principal, said, "I'm ready to vote on both counts. The first vote can determine if guilty or not guilty of first-degree murder. The second vote guilty or not guilty of embezzlement."

"Can we all agree to those terms?" Grezelda asked. The members agreed and cast another vote in the same manner as the first. Grezelda collected the ballots, read them off, and said. "We are in unanimous agreement. Not guilty on both counts. I'll inform the bailiff. I appreciate your patience. You've done a great job."

Grezelda completed the form provided by the judge and also signed it. The paper felt like the weight of the world was in her hands as she carried it to the door and knocked gently.

The bailiff answered. "May I help you?"

Grezelda handed him the form. "We have a verdict. Notify the judge and the attorneys." Blowing out a deep breath, she returned to the table and finally took a bite of her uneaten turkey and provolone sandwich. She never wanted to experience such an ordeal again, but her responsibilities weren't done yet.

The bailiff returned. "Judge Nif wants you in the courtroom. Follow me."

Sept. 18 – 4:30 p.m. EDT, New York City, New York

After deliberation, the courtroom was back in session. The jurors filed in and took their places.

The courtroom fell silent. Judge Nif said, "Mr. Wecholtz, please rise."

He and his council stood in anticipation of his final verdict.

Judge Nif asked the jury, "How do you find the defendant in the charge of murder in the first degree?"

Grezelda stood. "Not guilty." The courtroom burst into small whispers.

"Silence," Nif ordered, banging his gavel. "How do you find the defendant in the charge of embezzlement of corporate funds?"

Grezelda stood tall, glanced at Floyd Wecholtz, and smiled. "Not guilty, Your Honor." The courtroom became a low buzz of activity.

Nif again said with more authority, "Silence."

The people in the courtroom obeyed.

The DA stood. "Your Honor, I wish to poll the jury."

Grezelda felt her heart leap into her throat. *What if one of the jury members changed their mind while walking from the jury room to the courtroom?*

Judge Nif wanted only the briefest replies, "Yes or No, do you agree with these verdicts?" After juror twelve agreed with the verdict, Grezelda breathed a sigh of relief.

"Members of the jury, this Court dismisses you. Thank you for a job well done. I will now release the Defendant. This court is adjourned." He banged his gavel.

The bailiff said, "All rise." The honorable Judge Nif hovered over the raised platform and hopped down. He flowed out of the courtroom as he had come in—distinguished, if not arrogant. He had done his job.

Floyd stood. "Am I free to go?"

"Not yet. You must return to jail to be processed and pick up your belongings, but then you're free." Sophia hugged him.

"Do you have a place to stay tonight?" Chief Jackson asked.

Maude came running up and flung her arms around Floyd. "You're free. I knew you couldn't have killed AK. I found you a job at the same place I'm working. They need a CFO, and I highly recommended you. We'll meet with the boss first thing in the morning, and there's a vacancy in my duplex. I put money down on a lease." She turned to Chief Jackson. "Can he keep the suit? He'll need it for his interview."

Jackson said, "Keep it. The suit will never fit me anyway."

Floyd had tears in his eyes. "You're a gem, Maude."

"Don't thank me," Maude said. "I know you'll pay me back. Let's go out for dinner, and I'll tell you all about this company. Do you need a ride to the station?"

Two officers walked up to Floyd. "We'll take you back to jail for processing."

Maude's smile never dipped. "I'll follow you out and meet you at the jail, and then we can eat at that little Italian restaurant we used to go to for lunch." They were still chatting as they walked arm-in-arm out of the courtroom with an officer on either side.

Sophia collected her notes and put them into her briefcase.

"How about that pizza I promised you and Mo?" Chief Jackson said. "It looks as if Floyd won't be joining us."

"I'll call Mo with the wonderful news," Sophia said. "Thanks for all of your help. Would you like to be my chief detective permanently? Cordy says there's a connection between AK and Russian General Okueva. We need further research on AK's involvement, but it has nothing to do with Floyd. I wonder where those funds ended up, maybe Russia."

Jackson kissed both her cheeks, as was their custom. "We'll talk about it over dinner."

FAST THINKING

Sept. 18 – 12:55 p.m. EDT, Cincinnati, Ohio/
11:55 a.m. CDT, Wichita Falls, Texas

Rubbing her throbbing forehead, Cordy paced the small conference room of Hyatt Regency in Cleveland, Ohio, as she spoke to Dr. Nat Ping. She stopped to slip into her burgundy fleece jacket hanging over her chair. It had been too hot when she was dealing with Quint, tracking down the students in Wichita, and trying to locate General Okueva. Now, the air conditioner blasted cold air, but the room still felt stuffy. Lack of sleep was robbing her of her senses. She tried to focus. Cordy knew of Ping's reputation as a former CIA agent, his experience with counter-terrorism, and the Senate Foreign Relations Committee before that, *but why is he calling me?* She stifled a yawn. "You're calling from Rome, and what did you just ask me?"

"President Harris mentioned the latest corporate hacks you are decoding, and we discovered a similar attack. I don't know all the details yet, but the Vatican has been hacked to the tune of €100 million.

I am asking for your help. After our talk with President Harris, we think these financial thefts are connected to students hacking into the Vatican. The Holy See needs time to find the culprits, but first, we must stop them. I am trying to assist their government and act as a liaison, but I need help tracking and shutting down any further illegal transfers quickly before more funds are stolen. This is an international financial catastrophe."

"My agenda's already full," Cordy said. "Will the Vatican even work with me on this? I can track down suspects and key data if they assist me with account numbers and…"

"Yes, yes," Ping said in haste, "but this gets even bigger. Although the money is a considerable theft, a Swiss Guard discovered an explosive device planted in the Sistine Chapel. There is no proof yet, but I suspect these events are connected in some diabolical way. We must keep people safe, and preventing public panic is critical. Will you help us? If we can avoid this attack, you will not read about it in the papers. We must work behind the scenes to prevent a total breakdown of services in Rome. The panic would cause great harm."

Cordy's thoughts spun at yet another threat falling into her lap. "How did a bomber enter without being caught?" Cordy gasped. "Are there signs of forced entry? Was there damage to the Chapel?"

"We don't know how they got inside," Ping said. "Interpol sent in a bomb disposal team."

Memories raced through her mind as she recalled the last time she visited Vatican City. *All that security and a terrorist still got through.* She shook her head to clear her head. Her adrenaline level soared with fear. She gulped a swig of lukewarm coffee to rid the dry lump in her throat and asked, "Is the Pope safe?"

"His guards moved His Holiness underground while the team defused the explosives," Ping said. "Several of us, including the Swiss guards and Italian Svizzera, are working with the Vatican staff around the clock. Without divulging the real reason officials closed the Vatican to the public, the media listed the Pope as ill with the flu. All officials are on alert, but the public and the usual visitors are under close observation. Our actions can't become a spectacle."

"Has the threat to the chapel been neutralized?" Cordy asked.

"The bomb inside the chapel was located, but it appears that the terrorists aren't done yet," Ping said.

Cordy gasped.

"According to a reliable source, the terrorist threatened to attack the Israeli Embassy. The ambassador is still inside the building, waiting for their security forces to arrive. President Harris is working behind the scenes to support them, and we will use our intelligence services to assist Amman, Shin-Bet, and Israeli Mossad. Only a few selected people are in the loop to contain this information to track down the terrorists and minimize the threat."

Cordy insisted, "Yes, we must act fast, but sending more boots on European soil isn't the answer." Organizing scattered ideas racing through her agile mind, she asked, "Have you thought about drones to track them down?"

"Drones are expensive," Ping said, "and they kill innocent civilians."

Cordy's stomach knotted with tension, but she argued. "True, but they also save lives and can track explosive devices."

"It would make more sense to station a few snipers on nearby apartment buildings," Ping said. "I've never trusted drones, and it seems like overkill."

"Snipers might find the target," Cordy said, "but drones can get a clearer picture. I'm not talking about drones as large as planes. I'm talking about small ones that carry cameras, gather data, and track terrorists. They can fly overhead, inconspicuously, zoom in to give us close-up shots, and if needed, they can fly low enough to hit the target with the highest precision without wiping out the surrounding city."

"I'll think about it," Ping said. "In the meantime, can you help track down the funds?"

"I'll do my best, but it's not my first priority," Cordy said. "Who do I contact at the Vatican?"

"I'm sending you a link as we speak, and they'll give you more information," Ping said.

Cordy jotted a note on a sticky and added it to four others stuck to her desk with reminders of little details she'd need to follow up on when she found a moment of free time. "Thanks. I'll keep you posted."

"Gotta go. Great news, I just got word the bomb was defused at the Vatican, and an Italian officer thinks he's located the terrorist unit," Ping said, "but they're on the move."

"Are there any drones available?" Cordy knew her persistence might offend Ping, but it only made sense. "Try Vatican City's Interpol National Central Bureau. I'm sending you a contact. He's always come through for me, and you can use my name as a reference, but I'm on overload. Wait, I have an idea. Just call my contact."

Ping blew out a deep breath. "Okay, I'll check."

Cordy heard clicks and noises in the background. She downed three Advil and then checked her messages while she waited. Knowing the vital threat to the Vatican's funds, she forwarded the contact information to Quint and asked him to follow up ASAP.

Sept. 18 – 1:15 p.m. EDT, Cincinnati, Ohio/
7:15 p.m. CET, Vatican, Rome

Quint had an automatic alert on all his accounts and answered immediately. Cordy informed him of the urgency of Ping's request to work with the Vatican to prevent any further hacks. Ping's caller ID flashed. "Sorry, Quint, gotta go. Ping's back on the line."

Ping said, "Interpol has two smaller drones, and they liked your idea, but we need a backup tracking system in case we lose power locally, and I'm moving to a new location."

"I'll call President Harris, and we'll work on a backup—" Cordy said, but Ping had already disconnected. In all the chaos and sheer exhaustion, her imagination ran wild for a few unbridled moments before something gelled. She snapped her fingers and hunted down Braun. "I have an idea, but I'll need your help. I just heard from Dr. Nat Ping."

"Harris sent him to track down terrorists in Europe," Braun said. "Why's he calling you?"

Cordy said, "He's in a quandary, but..."

Braun peered into her eyes. "I'm not sure what you have tucked away in that brilliant mind of yours, but it's sure to shock everyone."

"We need to act fast," Cordy said. "Ping's in Rome. They have a terrorist cell in their sights and are relocating headquarters to stay a step ahead of the attackers. Interpol is thinking about launching drones and needs a backup monitoring system. They could use your help."

"My help?" Braun's gray eyes widened. "What can I do from Ohio?"

"Get President Harris on the line." Cordy quickly laid out her plan, knowing a request from Braun would go farther with the security team than if it came from her. "You're with JSOC and have access to their latest tracking devices. Plus, you know drones. This is right up your alley. You can set up a satellite connection and log in using JSOC's monitoring system—"

"I get it. You're brilliant!" Braun smiled. "I've wanted to put that system into action for weeks now. You're right. I'll need President Harris' permission." He leaned over and gave her a peck on the cheek, then grabbed his agent's phone.

Sept. 18 – 1:22 p.m. EDT, Cincinnati, Ohio/
12:22 p.m. CDT, Wichita Falls, Texas

"Great. In the meantime, I'll check on Svetlana and Perry." Cordy stretched and walked across the conference room to where Svetlana and Perry silently tapped away on their keyboard set up on two other computer terminals.

A few Coke cans and empty paper plates cluttered their stations. Working steadily for the past twelve hours, these teenagers must be tired. Cordy was aware that a few questions had passed between them at intervals, but for the most part, they had been dedicated and worked diligently to reverse the Wichita student's hacked codes. "American Express agreed to delay opening their main offices in New York until 2 p.m., and Wells Fargo will open their main offices in California at noon. Both will soon open their California corporate databases for normal business. It'll take a few minutes to run your code through my OptiSnatch Analysis Program, but I must link your code reversals with their routine programs."

"I'm finished," Svetlana said. "Xander planted hidden encrypted code that tagged all funds removed from any American Express accounts. His code may not have prevented the embezzlers from transferring funds, but it would trace the money to its final destination. I reversed the hack so Okueva won't find any unauthorized funds, but Perry is having trouble with Cadden's code, and I've been trying to help him."

Perry continued typing. "I managed to trap the hack into Wells Fargo, but I need more time to make a complete reversal. The program has several convoluted fixes already in place. Maybe I could talk to Cadden."

"Trapped code is enough for now," Cordy said. "We'll start with that. Thanks for all your help."

"But their firewall is misconfigured," Perry said. "Cadden didn't attack that. It's been there since 2018. I see six patches to try to fix the problem, but they're incomplete."

"Okay, I'll look into it," Cordy said. "For now, you need to get some sleep, and you can tackle that tomorrow. You've only slept two in the last forty-eight hours."

"Will you let me tackle it tomorrow?" Perry asked, "Or do we have other pressing issues?"

"Good point." Cordy collected their codes and made a batch file to send to her OptiSnatch analysis program. "We'll wait and see what tomorrow brings. Why don't you go to your rooms and rest?"

"You haven't taken a turn napping yet," Svetlana said.

"I'll sleep after this is over," Cordy said, "and I know both of you are jet-lagged."

Perry yawned. "Thanks. Wake us in four hours." He took Svetlana's hand and led her toward the hallway.

"Call us sooner if you need us," Svetlana spoke over her shoulder.

Cordy nodded and processed their data. Svetlana's code transferred to her analysis program without a hitch, but Perry's kept stalling. With no time to waste, she linked the fix to American Express and took it live. Cordy opened the analysis feedback. It took fifteen minutes to discover the problem Perry was complaining about.

Cadden's hack had been reversed, but Wells Fargo had a much bigger problem and truly needed to clean house regarding their coding structure. This would take days to fix in its entirety. She dumbed down Perry's code to only Cadden's reversed code and sent it through her analysis program. It glitched twice and needed a slight modification, but it finally cleared all her analysis steps. Quickly transferring the revised code, she linked it to the Wells Fargo app at 11:36 a.m. PDT.

The program opened without a hitch, but Wells Fargo had tagged $78 million in transfers in those eight minutes. Cordy gasped at the amount.

Braun was having issues of his own. She could hear him talking to someone about getting access to three satellites.

Cordy felt herself drifting, "Focus!"

Sept. 18 – 1:38 p.m. EDT, Cincinnati, Ohio/
7:38 p.m. CET, Rome, Italy

"I am focusing," Braun snapped back. "Oh, you're talking to yourself again." Then they both laughed, and the tension seemed to break.

Cordy went through the Wells Fargo system's back door to determine the status of the corporate accounts. A request to transfer $14 million from a mutual fund and $40 million from an International account corresponded to the assigned numbers in Cadden's hack. They had been tagged, but the Russian bank hadn't confirmed the transfer yet, so the funds remained intact. Cordy immediately canceled the orders and searched for a request for the third account Cadden set up, a money market fund for $16 million.

Since there was no trigger so far, Cordy locked down the funds. To be safe, she required a second approval if requested, which would come to her directly.

"That was close…too close," she blew out on a deep breath. The Advil hadn't eased her headache one iota. She needed a break—if only for five minutes—with a fresh cup of hot coffee loaded with cream. Her mouth watered at the thought, and she entered the kitchenette to put on a fresh pot.

Cordy brought Braun a steaming cup of coffee and set it on his terminal table. "How's the project going?"

"I connected a satellite link to Rome, and with Guy's help, we also connected the JSOC monitor to Washington, D.C., so President Harris and his security team can also watch and give advice. Then I set up the recorder and called Dr. Ping."

"Thanks for tackling Rome's attack. I just didn't have enough bandwidth for one more task. Has Ping relocated yet?" Cordy asked.

Braun nodded. "They were setting up headquarters on the top floor of a building across the street from the Israeli Embassy. Ping's working with top-ranking Italian officials and the Embassy's personnel, including Mossad."

"I heard you have words with your computer," Cordy said.

"Yeah, the system isn't as easy to set up as it looks. It took a lot of discussions, tweaking of equipment, and help from a member of Interpol before we managed a three-way link—one in Rome, one in Washington, D.C., and here in Ohio."

"It's only the first trial of JSOC's monitoring system," Cordy said. "Each setup will get easier."

"I hope it doesn't fail the mission," Braun said. "Let's check it out." He flipped a switch. "President Harris and team, I have Cordy on our line."

"Hi, Cordy," Harris said. "Whatever you did, we're linked to the security team and Dr. Ping's associates."

Braun smiled at Cordy. "You made this happen. Let's make this test a success."

Without any warning, the large screen in front of Cordy lit up.

"They launched the drones," Dr. Ping sounded excited.

"Both of them?" Braun asked.

"Yes, both," Ping affirmed. "I hope this works."

"I'm splitting the screen so we can see what each camera captures." Cordy grabbed the keyboard and found the device manager on Braun's computer. She split the screen and found the mirror images, so the president's and Rome's screens also split for a better view of the action.

"What weapons are on the drones?" Braun asked.

"Rubber bullets, tear gas, and munitions if needed," Ping said.

The drones' cameras gave unobstructed views of the city. One flew higher than the other, so Cordy could see more detail. The lower drone kept a steady pace with the traffic.

Ping exclaimed, "There they are! Keep an eye on those two black vans traveling faster than the speed limit."

Braun warned, "The lower drone is alarming—there are explosives on board." Cars scattered everywhere to allow the vans to pass through the heavy traffic.

Cordy's heart raced as she pulled up a chair, getting a bird's eye view of the screen. "Why are some of those vehicles crashing into parked cars? Oh my, someone's shooting at the other drivers."

"Fly closer and zoom in," Braun said. "I want to know how many terrorists we are dealing with. Are they in two cars or one?"

"Looks like two," Ping said. "The drone indicates explosives are in both vans." Several orders were given in Italian in the background.

"The terrorists are heading for the bridge." Ping said, "Everyone is avoiding the area." The higher drone dove toward the vehicles. The first van's windows were open, and AK rifle stocks pointed toward the Embassy. It sounded like fireworks as bullets cut through tree leaves and shrubbery and bounced off the cement.

Braun's voice rose in a panic. "They're less than 200 yards from the embassy. Fire now, before it's too late!"

"Roger," Ping said.

Two loud blasts sounded, and the first vehicle disintegrated in the middle of the bridge on the main highway. The second van crashed into the first and burst into flames.

"There must have been many explosives," Cordy gasped.

The closer drone flew toward the flames. Cordy could see people inside the front of the second van. "They're toast," Cordy said. "Wait. The higher drone captured a view of one man who bolted from the rear door before the vehicle exploded. It appeared that the left leg of his pants was on fire." He patted it with his hat to get the flames out. Then he limped forward, dragging his injured leg.

Cordy pointed at the screen. "He's getting away! Catch him. Get him."

Break lights blinked as cars following the van scattered and screeched to a halt. The lone terrorist darted out of the way of an oncoming sedan. Four cars joined the incinerator pile. Passengers bailed from their vehicles and ran for cover amongst the flames and debris.

Braun shouted, "That terrorist just jumped over the bridge."

"Where?" Ping asked. "All I see is smoke."

"Over the east side of the bridge. His head went under briefly, but he's splashing to keep afloat."

"I see him," Ping said. "He won't get far." Orders spewed rapidly in Italian. Sirens sounded in the distance—a boat headed toward the terrorist, who was desperately treading water.

"Are there any casualties at the embassy?" Cordy asked.

"A few broken windows, but we haven't had a full report." Sirens grew louder, making it harder to hear Ping, but it sounded like, "Signing off for now."

President Harris said, "I'd declare this trial a great success. I wish we had more time to talk, but the threat to the U.S. still looms. We have less than two hours to discover where they plan to attack in Texas."

"I'm working on finding that location," Cordy said.

"Got any ideas where to start our search?" Harris asked.

"I'm running Quint's photo through my analysis program. It should be done shortly." Cordy signed off, and Braun disconnected the JSOC monitoring device from the call.

Sept. 18 – 1:55 p.m. EDT, Cincinnati, Ohio/
12:55 p.m. CDT, Wichita Falls, Texas

With the teenagers asleep and the New York Stock Exchange, Wells Fargo, and American Express hacks wrapped up for the moment, Cordy enlarged Quint's photo of the Armenian star, but nothing came up under her analysis. "We're running out of time—little over two hours until terrorists strike in Wichita Falls, Texas."

Braun stood behind her and pointed to յուղ above the top tip of the star. "What does this word mean?" Beneath it said նավթ. The bottom end had խողովակաշար written below it.

"I don't know what any of the symbols mean. The letters are ancient Cyrillic." Cordy ran the entire photo through another translation system, checking Armenian, Russian, and Qarahunj words, then added all Indo-European languages. It took a few minutes, but when her computer dinged, the revised photo emerged. The mysterious letters were replaced with oil and petroleum—the word beneath the bottom star point translated into pipeline. The numbers and letters at the top of the page, լայնություն, and երկայնություն, converted to latitude 32° 13' 19.9808" N and longitude -101° 49' 42.9907" W.

Upon further research, Cordy said, "That's Permian Basic Encampment in Martin County, Texas. I think the terrorists are targeting our oil reserves. According to Saudi Aramco, the world's largest oil company, Permian is currently the top oil producer We need to warn the oil crews working there."

"We can warn them and save a few lives today, but if terrorists succeed in hitting our reserves, it will devastate our country," Braun said. "That would weaken the economy and undermine the government by forcing the U.S. to buy Syrian oil, and I'm sure at inflated prices." Braun speed-dialed President Harris' security team and waited for the call to go through. He glanced at his watch, 12:15 p.m. CDT. "The terrorists are scheduled to attack in one hour and forty-five minutes."

Finally, the call went through, "Homeland Security, this is Guy Weimer."

"Cordy believes she knows where the terrorists will attack in the U.S.," Braun said. "Is President Harris available? We may need to pull some strings from high places."

"One moment, he's talking with the French president," Guy said. "Al Qaeda cells were captured in Paris and Berlin before they wreaked any havoc. Twelve men made up each cell, so that's how many we expect to hit Texas. Give me a minute…Okay, President Harris and the Security Council are online."

Sept. 18 – 2:20 p.m. EDT, Cincinnati, Ohio/
1:20 p.m. CDT, Wichita Falls, Texas

"Mr. President, we called to update everyone about the enemy cell in the U.S. I think they plan to hit our oil reserves near Permian Basic Encampment in Martin County, Texas. I forwarded an encrypted photo…" Cordy went on to explain. "Perhaps we should launch a drone to check the area and protect the reservoir."

Harris said, "Thanks, Cordy. We'll have drones over the Permian Basic Encampment within two hours. Braun, can you track the drones in Texas as you did in Rome?"

Braun jumped on the idea. "Give me the satellite coordinates, and I'll add Texas to the program."

Cordy interrupted, "Two hours is too late. Terrorists are scheduled to attack in ninety-four minutes. Don't you have an FBI team in Texas that could be on site before that?"

"I'll talk to Loran Sloan," Guy said. "He flew to Texas earlier this morning, and as head of the FBI, he knows who to contact. In the meantime, connect us to JSOC's program."

"Will do," Braun said.

BETRAYED AGAIN

Sept. 18 – 3:00 p.m. EDT, President Spendorf's apartment, Washington, D.C.

While recovering from the deadly Virus X infection, Spendorf moved from Camp David to spacious rooms near Vice President Harris' residence. It allowed him to be included in crucial decision-making. He enjoyed the secluded privacy, a vast improvement from the bunker below the White House, where he had spent his last few days as the U.S. president. The sunlight filtered through the upstairs windows, bringing peaceful rays of light into his bedroom. He spent hours reclining in the circular library, catching up on his reading. However, today had been a terrible day so far. After reviewing Quint's data, which was recovered from General Rutoon's office, he called Quint to return to the spacious apartment.

Quint raised his hand, poised to knock, when the front door flew open. Spendorf stood in the opening. Lean, maybe even gaunt, after his illness, he was still an able combat veteran despite the strands of silver in his jet-black hair. His face flushed, his breathing labored, and his fists clenched. "It's about time you got here!"

The door slammed behind Quint. "I came as soon as I received your message. What's wrong? You seem upset."

"I can't believe it! Twice in two months. First, I was betrayed by my closest ally and friend, who became a traitor to our country by launching a bioterrorist attack against us and nearly killed me with a lethal virus. Now this!"

"Now this, what?" Quint asked, totally confused as Spendorf paced the floor with his fists opening and closing. "Calm down. You're supposed to be on bed rest."

"My God, the whole country's falling apart," Spendorf snapped. "While the true commander-in-chief rests, poor Harris is fighting to prevent WW III. An Al Qaeda Secret Cell is poised to strike somewhere in Texas," he checked his watch, "in one hour. We're running out of time."

"Harris is working on that," Quint said. "How come you got so upset when I showed you the video I shot in Rutoon's office? What's that all about? Who is that man with Rutoon's secretary?"

"This is personal," Spendorf said. "Dora's plotting a coup to crash the stock market, but she isn't the real problem. Oh, she had access to Rutoon's databases. That's true, but the man she partnered with is the real sting."

"Who is he?" Quint asked again.

"Jed. My own brother!" Spendorf said. "Log onto my computer and do your magic. Catch that traitor ASAP!"

"Jed? He's your brother?" Quint asked. "I wondered who that was. Is your network secure?" Quint dashed for the desk. "It doesn't matter. I'll encrypt everything." His fingers tapped away as he spoke. "What are we looking for?"

"Find out if Jed's been working with Rutoon all along?" Spendorf said. "If so, he knows where the terrorist cell will attack in Texas."

"Do you have a photo of your brother?" Quint asked.

Spendorf pointed to a photo on the hearth. "That's our family Christmas feast in 2021. It's probably the latest picture I have of him."

Quint remembered the video of the men surrounding Okueva's conference table, then recalled Deen P. Fjord's name just above Zac Spendorf on Rutoon's phone contact list. Quint jotted something onto a scratch pad on the desk. "Of course, Deen P. Fjords is an anagram for Jed Spendorf. Rutoon's contact list even had an asterisk by his number. I can almost guarantee your brother was working with Rutoon."

Spendorf slammed his fist into the palm of his hand, "Get Jed before he leaves the country. He'll tell me where the terrorists are in Texas, or I'll wring his scrawny little neck to get the information out of him. And find Dora."

"Can do, sir." Quint logged into his encrypted search program, which linked to several security systems. "What have you done so far?"

"I sent agents to Dora's office, and they found nothing."

"Doesn't surprise me," Quint said.

"No, I suppose not," Spendorf agreed. "She was officially relieved of her position when Rutoon died two months ago, and her office was vacated within the first week. However, when the agents searched her home, they found nothing."

"Was she at home?"

"No, but she left in a hurry. A few bare hangers in her closet, drawers still left open, and clothes scattered."

"Any computers?" Quint asked.

"No, her laptop was missing," Spendorf said. "The apartment had no personal photos, scrapbooks, photo albums, or papers. Now I learn from our agents that Dora had no family. Both parents are deceased, and she had no siblings."

"It sounds like she's a spy." Quint typed in key search words. "How come this never came out during her security clearance?"

"Rutoon headed her security check." Spendorf blew out a deep breath. "I can't believe I allowed Rutoon to hire a spy. He even granted her access to the highest level of security. I've been surrounded by imposters my entire term in office."

"Bingo!" Quint said. "Dora boarded a plane to Vancouver, Canada, at 9:12 this morning."

"Is Jed with her?" Spendorf asked.

Quint tapped a few more keys. "Nope, only Dora's passport was located. I'm surprised she left the country even before the stock market opened. It's a five-and-a-half-hour flight. She should be landing soon."

Spendorf hit Guy's number on his speed dial.

"Department of Homeland Security, Guy Weimer speaking."

"Guy, this is Zac."

"Sorry, I didn't recognize the number," Guy said. "What do you need, Zac? Are you okay?"

"I'm fine," Spendorf said, "I know you're busy, but I need an agent at Vancouver International Airport to pick up Dora Pankerst on treason charges. She planned to overthrow the government by crashing the stock market."

"Are you sure?" Guy asked. "I thought General Rutoon was the culprit."

"She's Rutoon's secretary, and she's been hiding behind Rutoon's old privileges. Somehow, she slipped through the cracks. Bring her back to the States. We'll deal with her, and I want to hear everything she knows about my brother, Jed. Have your agent call me as soon as he apprehends her."

"Yes, sir." Guy disconnected the call.

"Did you find anything on Jed?" Spendorf asked.

"His plane is the Red Heron, right?" Quint asked.

"Yes, did he leave the country?" Spendorf asked.

Quint's fingers flew over the keyboard. "He filed flight plans with the FAA, which were excluded from the public database. Red Heron's set to leave Reagan Airport in forty minutes. He's heading for Dallas."

"Right where a secret cell is to attack," Spendorf said. "I could spit bullets!"

"He won't be going anywhere," Quint said. "I just put a work order on the jet's turbofan, aborted his flight plan, and grounded the plane. "Won't he be surprised?"

"He'll just get another jet," Spendorf said.

Quint beamed. "Nope, you sent an urgent message to Carl Wyller, who is in town. He and his team will bring Jed in."

"I did all that and stayed on bed rest, too?" Spendorf's smile reached his ice-blue eyes. His sunken cheeks became rosy. "I haven't felt this good in months, but I am ready for a nap. Have Carl call me when he tracks down Jed. I want a face-to-face talk with my brother before I lock him up and throw away the key."

LET'S LAUNCH

Sept. 18 – 3:10 p.m. EDT, Cincinnati, Ohio/
2:10 p.m. CDT, Wichita Falls, Texas

Cordy's cell phone rang. "This is Loran Sloan. It took thirty minutes for Guy to find a Texas SWAT team with six drones, but we're ready. Where do you need us?"

"We have land coordinates. Let's search there first. If that's not the location, we don't have enough drones to cover the whole area." Cordy's nervous energy flowed through her fingertips as she typed in Permian Basic Encampment GPS coordinates. "General Okueva planned to end his day of terror with the deadliest attack ever on U.S. soil, surpassing even the 9/11 attack on New York City's twin towers."

"What do you mean,'" Loran asked.

"Terrorists will strike the world's largest oil company, Permian Basic Encampment in Martin County, Texas." Cordy had set up the screens to accommodate six drone cameras. She studied photos hovering over the encampment. "Google search says the area covers over 500 wells producing more than 20 billion barrels of oil and 16 trillion cubic feet of associated natural gas. Look at all those railroad tanker cars. There must be hundreds lined up across that 300-mile route."

"It's anyone's guess where they'll attack," Braun said.

"We can launch directly over the coordinates you sent us," Loran said.

"Then let's launch." Cordy watched three drones fly directly over the coordinates while another three drones hovered higher, giving broader coverage. Hydraulic and horizontal drilling rigs used for fracking unreachable oil taps cluttered the area.

Braun zoomed in closer and pointed at the screen. "The coordinates are directly over a wellhead assembly. Blowing that up would be the worst scenario I can imagine. High-pressure gasses escaping from the earth's crust would create a sixty-foot blowtorch! Explosions and fires would erupt for months."

"Let's hope we can prevent that," Cordy said. "Do you see anything unusual?"

"I see crews working at several sites," Braun said. "Any one of them could be our terrorists."

"Let's focus intensively on a fifty-mile radius of these coordinates," Cordy said. "Each drone can cover fifteen miles with a slight overlap. Now, does anything look out of place?"

"I see five rig teams dressed in filthy coveralls," Braun said. "They seem to know what they're doing." Braun checked his watch. "If Termine is right, it's still fifteen minutes before the attack. Start wide and then narrow the search."

"If the terrorists plant a bomb, it could already be on sight and on a timer," Cordy warned.

"Good point," Braun said. "I wish we had control of the drones. I don't know if they have any bomb sniffers."

Cordy was already on the phone with Guy.

"Homeland Security, what did you find?" Guy asked.

"Are there bomb sniffers on the drones?" Cordy asked.

"Yes, on all of them," Guy said, "but they'll have to get closer."

"What other weapons and devices?" Cordy asked.

"There is a camera with interchangeable zoom, infrared, and full sunlight lenses on all of the drones," Guy said. "Two have video, sound, and tracking devices. Two weaponized drones have Tasers, munitions, and grenades."

"I hope there aren't any casualties," Cordy said, setting up the monitor, ready for the drones to carefully collect data. "Are there any FBI agents to send to the sight?" Cordy asked.

"Yes, the FBI SWAT is working with the Texas EMS system," Guy said. "EMS is to stay outside the gates on standby until the area is declared clear."

"Braun and I want access to the drone operators," Cordy said.

"I'll arrange it," Guy said. There was a blip on the screen, and then a face appeared in the lower left-hand corner.

Sept. 18 – 3:40 p.m. EDT, Cincinnati, Ohio/
2:40 p.m. CDT, Wichita Falls, Texas

"Hi, Cordy, it's been a while since I've seen you," Loran laughed since he had just disconnected her Vidcall moments earlier. "Connect directly using your satphone."

Cordy ran to her terminal to snatch the satphone from the charging unit and returned. "Braun is also on this call."

"Send in three drones with bomb sniffers first," Braun said. "Have them go low and search along the gravel road leading off the main highway. See what kind of traffic we have."

"Then, I want to concentrate one video drone and one weaponized drone directly over these coordinates." Cordy gave the location. "Hover low and go slow so I can put the video through my software detection. I know we don't have complete control, but we can openly communicate with you, and you'll need to direct the drones accordingly."

Within minutes, the photos zoomed in closer. The bomb sniffers were activated, but nothing was detected. Relief flooded through Cordy. The drone furthest away blasted a siren, nearly deafening Cordy. "Where's that coming from?"

A red light repeatedly blinked from the drone hovering over the main terminal just off the highway. A white van zoomed past the gate and continued speeding along the gravel road toward the principal coordinates, causing gravel to fly up.

"Is there only one van?" Braun asked. "They had two vehicles in Rome."

"I only see one, and they have explosives," Cordy said. "Raise at least one drone so the photos aren't blurred by dust. Then bring the second closer to the SUV."

The vehicles' windows slid down, and armed men shoved rifles through the openings.

Two men from the oil crew dashed forward and were cut down with gunfire. The rest of the oil team ran for cover.

Cordy's heart jolted. "They're firing on the men!"

Braun shouted, "Loran, fire. They're nearing the wellhead. Fire. Now!"

"Something metallic flew out from the SUV's window," but before Cordy finished her sentence, the drone shot it out of the air, and it exploded mid-air. She bit her lip, frustrated that she couldn't see clearly what was happening and couldn't do anything about it, even if she could see a perfect image.

"They're getting away," Braun said. "Stop them." His knuckles clenched in suspense. "Come on..."

A second drone dropped a grenade on the van, which erupted into flames as it raced away from an oil rig.

"Two men just dove out of the rear doors of that burning vehicle," Cordy shouted in excitement.

A second explosion blasted from the rear of the vehicle. Metal and glass flew twenty feet into the air and barely missed one of the terrorists as he darted behind a large metal shed.

Guy said, "Don't worry, we'll get them." The drone turned and hovered overhead for a split second, then hit each man with a Taser. They dropped in their tracks. "Okay, Agent Skaggs, they're all yours. Come clear the area. We have at least two casualties, maybe more."

"Which one is Skaggs?" Cordy asked.

"He's the driver of the first FBI BATT," Loran said.

Two FBI SWAT vehicles pulled through the gate and stopped a 100-feet distance from the van that continued to pop off small blasts of explosives as the fire raged.

Cordy watched two FBI agents, dressed in camo fatigues with "FBI" embroidered on their right shoulders and helmets over their heads, exit the BATT with their guns raised. They ducked behind their car doors and scanned the area before bolting forward toward the suspects. Skaggs covered his partner as he cuffed each of the tased men.

Team two arrived in a second FBI vehicle, which screeched to a halt behind the first. Two FBI agents stepped from the second BATT with guns raised. The driver had a fire extinguisher strapped to his left side. They advanced toward the van once the popping explosives had stopped. The FBI agent from team two's passenger side kept his gun raised and covered the driver as he fought back the flames with the extinguisher. The fire had raged throughout the burning car. The bodies inside were unmoving and charred beyond recognition.

The driver tried to open the front passenger van door using leather gloves, but it didn't budge.

Skaggs called out, "Any survivors?"

"Nope," the man with the extinguisher said.

"I'll call in the ambulance, surveillance team, and the medical examiner," Skaggs spoke into his radio.

The drone showed a shattered windshield. The roof was crushed and collapsed on top of the terrorists. Their driver had been thrown forward on impact. His body sliced as it launched over the steering wheel and through the windshield. Obviously, he had not worn any seatbelt, and the airbags were faulty or disengaged. The rear of the van was nothing but shredded debris.

The ambulance drove into the area and stopped behind BATT 2. The ambulance driver yelled from his window, "Are we clear?"

"Clear," Skaggs said.

An EMT and a paramedic ran from the ambulance to check on the two injured oil rig crew members.

"This one's dead," the paramedic said as he removed his hand from the man's pulseless neck.

The EMT knelt beside the second victim. "Chest wounds, broken leg, and is unconscious."

"Any other injuries?" the paramedic called out to the agents.

"None that requires medical assistance," Skaggs said. "We'll take our tased suspects in for questioning."

The paramedic started an IV in the chest-wound victim's arm. The EMT had started oxygen and connected a heart monitor. They lifted him onto a cart and put him into the back of the ambulance. "I'm rolling," the driver shouted to Skaggs as the paramedic radioed the hospital. They drove away, code 3, with red lights and sirens.

Cordy absently tucked a few loose curls into her French braid. "I want to know what the terrorists have to say—"

Guy interrupted her, "We'll fill you in on the details as we get them. We're collecting the drones and shutting down our operations. You okay with that?"

"Wait," Cordy said. "Did you track down Mr. Smith, who sent those students to Joyland, or did he manage to leave the country?"

"Rumor has it that he didn't even make it out of his parking lot," Guy said. "There was a bomb waiting for him when he started his car. Oh, yes, we also nabbed Rutoon's secretary as Dora got off the plane in Vancouver, and Spendorf's brother is in custody and on his way for questioning."

Cordy took a deep breath. Her adrenaline rush plummeted rapidly once the threat was over. "I'm exhausted."

Sept. 18 – 4:20 p.m. EDT, Cincinnati, Ohio/
3:20 p.m. CDT, Wichita Falls, Texas

Braun wrapped an arm around her shoulders. "We are on our honeymoon. Maybe we could spend the rest of the evening…" He raised his eyebrows. His lips curved into an uneven, boyish grin. "You know—after we eat and get some sleep."

Cordy said, "I should check in with Quint and see if he's reversed the hack into the Vatican's funds."

"You don't need to micro-manage everything," Guy said.

For some reason, his comment cut to the quick. "I don't micro-manage," flew from her mouth before she had fully considered his meaning. "I plan out loud; maybe I get caught up in the details, but…"

Braun took her hand and kissed her ring finger, admiring the wedding ring he had placed there a week ago. "Guy didn't mean anything by that. You're tired, ready to fall asleep standing up, and we're heading upstairs. Guy, we'll talk to you tomorrow."

"Sure. I'll call Quint," Guy said. "Thanks for all your help. I'm signing off now. Enjoy your evening, and you two get some rest."

Braun hit the disconnect button and pocketed the cell phone.

Cordy leaned her head into Braun's muscular chest. He was a good ten inches taller than her, but he gently cradled her, running his fingers through her hair as he loosened the French braid, letting her curls fall onto her shoulders. His long, strong fingers caressed the back of her neck until she tipped her face up to him. Braun leaned forward, gently teasing her lips to open with his tongue, and deepened the kiss.

Cordy knew he'd branded her as his own with that searing kiss, and she would never belong to anyone else. She handed him the key to the conference room. "Lock up, stud, I'm going to bed."

Braun laughed and grabbed her hand and the key. "Not without me." He scooped an arm under her legs and cradled her. It took only four long strides to reach the conference room door. He pressed the small knob on the inside door handle. Heading into the hallway, he nudged the door closed and checked to be sure it locked behind him. Then he walked to the elevator.

"You can put me down," Cordy murmured.

"Not on your life." Braun kissed her cheek. The elevator door opened, and he slid inside. His index knuckle hit the sixth floor, and before Cordy knew it, she was carried over the threshold and laid on the bed in their suite. She threw off her fleece jacket and curled into a ball.

Braun pulled a cover over her relaxed body. "Get some needed sleep." Braun kissed her and headed to the bathroom for a cold shower. Then he'd go back downstairs and make sure they had shut down all equipment. Tomorrow was another day.

CHEATING CHAOS

Sept. 19 – 1:00 a.m. MSK, Moscow, Russia/
6:00 p.m. EDT, Cincinnati, Ohio

Police Chief Ignacio stood in the shadows toward the back alley of the jailhouse. What a surprise to hear from Miss Muffet, a woman his brother had once been close to. But he believed the tale of her spider's web and that she had captured General Surko Okueva. What an idiot his brother had been to fall for a woman. Yet, it was the one thing that drove the two brothers apart.

A smile crossed his face. Creating havoc and mayhem delighted Ignacio to the core. Watching the city burn in raids, forcing the citizens to pay for protection or squirm under his thumb if unable to meet the demanded price, made his day. He would rise to the highest power and even take down the president of Russia. But first, he had to wipe out the one man who could stop him—his own brother, Surko. A pity. They had been so close at one time. Again, he chuckled, divided by a woman. But the thought of his brother's betrayal fueled his determination.

Gunfire erupted at the front of the prison, putting Ignacio on high alert. Believing it was his brother, General Okueva, who had managed to break away from Miss Muffet and attack the front checkpoint, the police chief bolted for the jail's back door. He weaved through a hidden opening near his office and descended into the underground secret chambers. Whoever raided the prison used automatic rifles that kept blasting away among the cries of agony. *Surko will never find me here.*

The rear chamber door flew open as Ignacio reached for the knob. "Quick," his butler called. "You have company. They arrived nearly an hour ago at the front gate along with your brother. Were you expecting them?" The unexpected arrival of the guests left Ignacio momentarily stunned.

"Quick lock up. Something is happening at the jail." Ignacio pushed past the butler. "Wait. Is Surko here?" He had mentioned to Miss Muffet that they would meet at the rear of the jail, *but how did they get down here?*

Ignacio grabbed the butler's arm. "Why did you let them inside?"

"The lady told me she had arranged a special meeting with you." The butler winked. "I know you have woman visitors on occasion, and—" The butler shrugged from Ignacio's grasp and moved into the living room.

That's when Ignacio saw the most beautiful woman he'd laid eyes on in ages walk past the living room door. *Must be Miss Muffet.* Ignacio was no longer interested in the butler. *Miss Muffet is talking to someone in the other room—probably Surko. The voices are friendly enough, but if Surko is here, who's raiding the jail? My men will deal with whoever it is. For now, I have other plans.*

Miss Muffet glanced his way and beamed a bright smile. "Good evening."

"So good to see you," Ignacio spoke in his deep baritone voice dripping with honey as he stepped forward. He spied a tall man walking from the living room into the foyer. *Miss Muffet is not alone, and where's my brother?*

"Good evening," the man said, his voice adding to the tension in the room.

Ignacio raised his gun, unwilling to take chances. "Who are you? No one comes in here without being frisked."

"Of course, I would expect as much. My name is Usher Hastings." The man raised his arms and turned in a circle. "I have no weapons. Zina and I brought your brother as we agreed. Where are the funds you promised in return?" Usher asked in a bastardized Russian accent, "You said to come late, and you would pay one million rubles in exchange for General Okueva."

Not seeing any visible sign of threat, he frisked Usher. Chief Ignacio straightened to his full height but didn't lower the gun. "So, you still have General Okueva?"

"We have him in the bedroom, but he's a bit incapacitated at the moment," Usher spoke as clearly as his Russian allowed. "He was a handful, and I admit, we had to drug him. He'll come to in an hour or so."

"Then, who's attacking the prison?" Ignacio asked.

"We had to make a diversion to smuggle him here," Usher said, "but no one's hurt."

Zina got up and followed the butler.

"So there's just the two of you?" the police chief asked. "Where is this Zina person going?"

Zina strolled back into the room with two glasses of vodka. Her teal rayon blouse was so tight around her bosom that she had to pin it to keep it closed. "Would you like to frisk me, too? As you can see, I have no gun." She held up the glasses, pivoted on her heels, and made a tantalizing 360° circle, wiggling her hips as she turned.

Ignacio holstered his pistol, but his hand rested on the butt of his gun, ready to use if needed.

"May I sit?" Usher sat on a wing-backed chair after the chief nodded.

"Sorry about the commotion," Zina said. "My friend and I brought your brother here, as you requested, but there are other men that I don't know, rioting outside the jail."

Usher leaned forward. "Your butler said the chambers were safe from outsiders, and these are comfortable quarters. Are you expecting an attack? Should we be concerned? Is there someone out there who plans to ambush us?"

"No, I have everything under control," Ignacio said, hoping he was right.

Zina blew out a breath. "That's a relief." She stepped up to Ignacio and handed him a glass. "I thought we should have a drink to celebrate Okueva's capture, but," she pointed to her friend, "Usher doesn't drink, but I'm not driving, so these are for just the two of us."

Usher leaned back with his hands in plain sight. Totally relaxed.

Chief Ignacio grinned. "How lovely, but I prefer whiskey. May I?" He reached out for her glass.

"Sure, but I think I'll take mine straight," Zina said.

"A splash won't hurt, and as you say, you're not driving."

"Maybe a little." She let him take the glass and turned her head for the briefest of moments, which allowed the chief to doctor the drinks as he saw fit.

Ignacio walked up to the bar and set down both glasses. A quick glance surprised Zina when he took a clean, cut glass identical to hers and splashed whiskey to two finger-widths. Then he added a splash to her drink and returned it to her. Ignacio scanned the room, keeping an eye on Usher.

Zina sat on the sofa and patted the cushion next to her. "Come sit by me. I don't bite." She held up her glass for a toast. "To your health."

Ignacio sat next to her and clinked the edge of his whiskey glass to hers. "Likewise." He took a large gulp, rolled it around in his mouth, and swallowed.

Zina tipped the glass to her lips, pretending to sip. Then she set the glass on the coffee table and fanned her mouth with her hand. "Whoa, that's strong." Her eyes filled with tears.

Ignacio set his glass next to hers, dug a tissue from his pocket, and handed it to her. "You don't drink much, do you?" He laughed. "Take a gulp. It goes down smoother."

She dabbed her eyes. "Thank you." She reached for the table and took his glass. "Like this?" She threw back her head and took a mouthful. The swallow burned her throat. Coughing, she tried to catch her breath.

He chuckled. It sounded much like Okueva's laugh. "Yes, but you need to swallow it all."

"Enough drinks," Usher said. "Let's get down to the payment. We need to leave."

As soon as the chief turned his head to look at Usher, she wiped her mouth with the tissue, still coughing, and held his glass between her palms—finally, able to speak. "Now, Usher, we are in no hurry." She smiled at Ignacio. "Drink up, then we'll check on your brother. The butler is keeping a keen eye on him for us."

Chief Ignacio didn't chug her drink, the only one left on the table. But he did take a couple of swallows. "Okay, no payment until I see General Okueva, and I don't have the cash on me, but I'll wire it first thing in the morning."

"Fair enough," Zina bounced from the couch. "Follow me." She walked toward the bedroom door, still holding her glass.

Usher mumbled under his breath, "Sure you will," but the chief dismissed him as if he were invisible.

Ignacio followed the pert brunette dressed in a tight navy skirt, playing his ego for all it was worth.

A young man dressed all in black flew through the bedroom door. Ignacio had seen this man before. "Vlad?"

The butt end of a pistol crashed over Ignacio's head. "Payback!"

Marshal Albert took over with a slash to the chief's throat.

Rozalina stepped from behind a curtain. "The ambulance is waiting outside. We'll take Chief Ignacio to his brother at the mortuary."

"Great job, you two," Albert said. "I guess this is goodbye for now. Vlad will take you back to Perry's apartment, and Leo says Zina will stay with her friend."

Usher clasped Albert's hand and thanked his team for all their help. "Can I treat you to dinner tonight?" Usher asked.

"Oh no, we're heading to Pushkin to free Xander's family," Albert said. "Cracker tracked them down. Armed forces have already freed Zev's and Jabril's families, and the Punjab police are freeing the hostages in India."

Zina handed Rozalina her glass. "The other one is on the coffee table. I'm unsure if there's antifreeze in either of these, but you can test them." She turned toward Usher. "Speaking of dinner. You could take me out before I see my friends."

Usher smiled, "It's a date."

"Not if you're including Vlad and Leo." Zina smiled. "And, of course, they'll want to chaperone, right?"

Vlad stared at his shoes.

Leo nudged Vlad, "Of course, but first, we must get out of here without anyone noticing our escape."

"At least Boris and his men broke Captain Marot out of prison," Vlad said. "Their timing couldn't have been better."

The butler stepped up to Albert. "Sir, I'm Leo's brother. It's an honor to be of service. You can follow me through the tunnel to the gates. Your vehicles are waiting."

HEARTFELT MESSAGE

Sept. 19 – 6:30 a.m. MSK, Moscow, Russia/
Sept. 18 – 11:30 p.m. EDT, Cincinnati, Ohio

Moscow's morning traffic was miserable, especially in the bitter wind and rain. "Hurry. I can't be late." Usher Hastings clung to Leo as the motorcycle swerved out of the way of an oncoming truck.

"We'll get to my uncle's with plenty of time to spare." Leo pulled back into his lane. "I'm sure your car is safe."

Usher adjusted his body with each turn. "Getting a rental was a waste of money. I hardly even drove it."

"Why are you leaving so early?" Leo asked. "Your flight isn't for another six hours."

"I want to say goodbye to Zina, and her flight leaves in four hours," Usher said. "After all, I did make her miss her original departure. It's the least I can do."

"After that dinner last night, I thought you might be planning a rendezvous." Leo turned off the highway and headed down a gravel road to his uncle's barn. The noise dropped several decibels. "You couldn't keep your eyes off one another. I swear sparks were flying between you. At one point, I feared the whole building would go up in flames." Leo laughed.

"She is special," Usher said. "Thanks for the lift and all you've done for Vlad. Do you think he'll be safe staying in Russia?"

"He's as safe as any of us." Leo drove to the barn, parked the motorcycle, and waited for Usher to climb off. "Uncle Albert was glad to have us join his Army, and now that the chief of police is out of the picture, Ignacio's men will disperse. It happens all the time. Rarely is there a strong enough second in command to take over, and if there's enough rivalry amongst his men, they'll soon assassinate one another."

"Marshal Albert is a good role model," Usher said.

"True, and you and Zina played your part perfectly," Leo said.

"When Zina called Chief Ignacio, I was surprised how quickly he wanted to meet her." He stepped away from the motorcycle. "Keep in touch. I'm not sure when I'll return to Russia, but I'll look you up when I do."

Leo clapped Usher on the back. "Better get going. You don't want to miss Zina."

Usher climbed into the car and returned the rental. He made it to terminal A of Vnukovo International Airport with thirty minutes to spare. He worried that his phone call would wake Braun and Cordy, but he needed to chat while he waited to check into the airline.

Braun answered, "Good morning, Usher. Are you on your way home?"

"My flight leaves in a few hours," Usher said. "How's Cordy?"

"She's terrific!" Braun said. "But you already know that. She's in the shower, and you made me climb out to catch this call."

"Oh, I don't want to think of that image." Usher laughed.

"Who's on the phone?" Cordy called out.

"It's Usher. He's leaving Russia." Braun asked, "Will we see you soon? We're planning on heading back to Fort Collins."

"I don't know for sure," Usher said. "I have something important to share with you as soon as I hear from a certain someone."

"Sounds like a girl," Braun said. "Anyone we know?"

"That's still up in the air," Usher said, "but you'll be the first to know. What have you decided about your two teenagers?"

Cordy came on the line, "I think we'll adopt them."

"What?" Braun shouted. "They're too old, and we just got married. I don't—"

"Not formally," Cordy said. "I talked with President Harris about getting U.S. citizenship for Perry and Svetlana. In the meantime, Svetlana needs to enroll in high school, and she'll move into our spare bedroom until we work things out. I thought we'd find an apartment for Perry in Fort Collins."

"Are you okay with that little brother?" Usher asked.

"I don't have a choice, but we'll see how it goes." The last few words sounded muffled.

"Are you smooching again?" Usher asked.

"Sorry," Cordy said, "but he's so—"

"Get serious," Usher teased.

"Okay, here's the scoop. Perry asked if he could work with me permanently, and I think it would be a good idea. Maybe he can tame Quint."

"Don't count on that," Braun said.

"What's happening in New York?" Usher asked. "Did they cool the nuclear reactors?"

"Yes, and Governor Hendrum is thrilled that they have clean water again," Cordy said. "Electricity capacity is now at 85%, and the airports are operating again."

Usher added, "Thanks to Cracker, all the students' families have been freed and reunited. I'll send you Okueva's recorded confession, and President Harris will write up a pardon for Cracker. You'll hear it all when I get home."

Braun said, "A final pardon for Cracker may need to come from President Spendorf as Harris is stepping back to Vice President soon."

"I've filed reports on consideration of good conduct for each of the boys since they were beneficial in reversing their hacked codes, and they feared for their families' lives," Cordy said.

Braun added, "We'll be glad to see you again."

Spying Zina, Usher rushed on, "I gotta go." He disconnected the call.

Zina rushed from the cab, and she was barely a blur as she dashed to the ticket counter. Dressed in a red wool jacket, she stood out among the crowd. A traditional black Ukrainian silk and wool fringed shawl with vibrant red was around her head and shoulders. She must not have noticed Usher standing off the side on alert for her arrival.

The crowd grew longer as she lined up at the baggage drop-off. Usher squeezed through a narrow opening while trying to text her cell and nearly tripped as a guard stepped before him. "You have a ticket? This is the line for ticketed passengers only," he said in Russian.

"I have to find someone before she leaves the country!" Feeling flushed and unnerved, Usher spoke in desperation. He'd never done anything like this before.

The guard waved him aside. "No ticket. No entry."

Many people moved between the guard and Usher as they exited the gate. Usher was shoved aside, jostled, and nearly trampled as he moved against the flow. Then he saw Zina.

She was now bag-free except for her purse and briefcase and walking rapidly away from him.

"Zina! Wait up." His moist hand grabbed the letter from his pocket, and his nerves shot up another notch. "Please, wait for one moment." He darted to her side.

She turned and gave a startled surprise. "Usher, what is it?" An involuntary smile crossed her lips. "Always in a hurry."

He shoved the now crumpled letter into her hand as the guard blew his whistle. "I have to go, but please read it before you board the plane. I'll be waiting at the baggage claim. I'll understand if your plane leaves, and you're on it."

The guard marched up to Usher. He was in no mood to discuss anything. "You are not allowed here without a ticket!"

Usher raised his hands in surrender. "I'm leaving," and made a last glance toward Zina. "Read it, please. It's your choice." Afraid he'd be hauled away, he said, "Have a safe flight. I've enjoyed working with you." Moving forward a few steps ahead of the guard, he had no wish to see her take his letter and stuff it in her pocket or throw it away.

The guard seemed satisfied and veered to the right. Usher turned to take a brief peek. Zina stood aside from the thinning crowd. She ripped open the envelope and started reading. Usher remembered every word verbatim. It had taken him several attempts to jot down his feelings.

My Dearest Zina: (May I call you that?)

I am afraid to say this, but if you leave now, I may never share with you what is in my heart. Perhaps this is too soon to tell you that first, I was pissed at everything you did, then I came to admire you, and something changed. Even after this short time, I feel incomplete without you in my life. I know that I love you—a heart-fluttering love. Could you be happy with a man like me, a man who eventually wants a family and children and a unique, fearless Celtic wife named Zina?

This may be a coward's way of asking for your hand in marriage, but I can't face a formal rejection. I'm writing this to give you time to consider before you reply. I'll ask for your father's approval if that is your preference. I have no reason to hope or no claim on you. Only my love pushes me to write this. You may find another more worthy man, but none who loves you more. Being your husband and lover would be my honor and greatest joy.

Usher

Standing amongst the crowd, he felt alone. The clamor around him faded to a distant din. He only had eyes for one petite, vivacious woman.

Zina folded the letter, placed it back in the envelope, and put it in her purse. She peered up and scanned the area. Spying Usher, she slowly shook her head, readjusted her briefcase, and walked toward her departure gate.

So that says everything. Usher didn't bother to wait at the baggage claim. *What is the point?*

Sept. 19 – 7:00 a.m. MSK, Moscow, Russia/
12:00 a.m. EDT, Cincinnati, Ohio

Zina stopped outside her gate. Oh, how she wished she could say yes to this handsome, courageous, strong man, but she was damaged material. He didn't deserve that. She set her bag on the floor and called Heather, hoping her sister might talk some sense into her about this stupid reaction.

"Hi, Zina. Are you heading home?" Heather asked.

Zina's words rushed from her mouth as if from a panicked baboon. She couldn't stop crying.

"Calm down," Heather said. "It can't be that bad. Do I need to fly to Russia to get you?"

"I messed up everything," Zina sobbed. "He'll never ask me again, and I know this is the last time any man will ever ask for my hand in marriage."

"Marriage!" Heather shouted so loudly that Zina nearly dropped the phone.

"I knew that would be your reaction. Of course, no one will ever marry me."

"Angel Face," Heather called her by her beloved nickname. "Stop! Listen to yourself. You're no more damaged than I am. Drop everything and find this man."

"But—"

"Three times is the charm. If you want him, go after him. Now! I won't let you come home. I won't be at the airport to get you. Go! Go, go." The phone call ended when her sister disconnected.

Zina clenched her fists. "Now, what should I do?" She pulled the crumpled letter from her purse and reread it. *He said that he'd meet me at the baggage claim.* She grabbed her bag and ran, first in the wrong direction. When she realized her error, she ran back to where she started and scanned the airport, but Usher was gone. *Why did I wear heels?* She kicked them off, tucked them into her bag, and ran. When she reached the baggage claim, Usher was nowhere to he found. *Okay, now what?* raced through her mind. *He's flying to Washington, D.C. Which gate?* She darted to information. Every bit of Russian had flown out of her mind. Finally, she found someone who spoke English. "I'm looking for the gate to Washington, D.C., I have to find someone."

"Shall I page her?" the clerk asked.

"Him," Zina hesitated. "Umm, maybe." *No, he wasn't waiting for me.* "No, I can't. Thank you." Her heart raced. It downright ached. *I'm such a fool, and a stupid fool* repeatedly chanted in her head. *I need a cup of tea.* She managed to find a coffee shop and sat down.

The waiter asked, "How may I help you?"

"Chai tea, please."

"Make it lukewarm with two sugars," came from behind her. Usher sat in the chair next to her. "Did you miss your plane?"

Zina's heart jolted. "Not yet. Did you mean what you said in that letter?"

"Every word," Usher blushed, took a clean hanky from his pocket, and dabbed away her tears.

"Then, the answer is yes." Zina flung her arms around his neck. "And my father would appreciate it if you asked for my hand in marriage, but I'll marry you without his prior approval if that's what you want."

"Oh no, Braun and Cordy would kill me if they couldn't attend," Usher said.

"What's our next step," Zina asked.

"Always planning ahead," Usher kissed her. "Let's fly to Dublin and get your father's permission. Then we'll plan as big a wedding as you want."

"Oh, no," Zina said. "I've been jilted twice already, abandoned both times at the altar. I think we better get hitched and then work out the details. And I know just the person to marry us. I'll call my friend, Pastor Gustav. He'll be glad to do the honors."

Sept. 19 – 8:00 a.m. MSK, Moscow, Russia/
1:00 a.m. EDT, Cincinnati, Ohio

An hour later, Pastor Gustav stood in a small room inside the airport before Zina and Usher. "Remember, you need a standard affidavit form completed in Russian and notarized at the Embassy for this to be considered legal," Gustav said.

"I know, and I don't care," Zina said.

"We'll make everything legal once we're in the States," Usher said. "You will be living in the U.S., won't you?"

"I'll live wherever you are," Zina said.

Cordy dialed into Usher's phone. "We're ready. I set up a large screen in the hotel conference room, and Svetlana and Perry are here. Braun linked you into a satellite over Dublin and connected Zina's family, too, so they can watch the wedding as it unfolds."

Braun said, "I upgraded your tickets, Usher, and booked Zina a first-class ticket on today's flight, so don't be late. It's our wedding present."

"Thanks," Usher said.

"Hello, Usher and Zina," President Harris said. "I couldn't miss this, so Cordy included your friends from Washington, D.C. Zac, Guy, and Carl's faces came into view."

"This is a wonderful surprise." Usher hesitated, then asked, "Is Zina's father on the line?"

"Ta, I am here for you, my boy," her father replied. "Am I getting myself a son at last?"

"I would be honored to wed your daughter, sir," Usher said. "I love her with all my heart."

"Zina, me darling, is this the man for you?" her father asked.

"Yes." Zina clung to Usher's arm, "My one and only."

"You have my blessings," her father said.

Her mother wept in the background, her tears a testament to the depth of her emotions. "Bring him home so we can see him in person. Then we'll have a wedding feast."

"Thank you," Usher turned to Zina, his eyes locked on hers, filled with love and determination. "I'm ready."

It seemed to happen in a blink of an eye, and then Pastor Gustav said, "I now pronounce you husband and wife. May I be the first to present Zina and Usher Hastings. You may now kiss the bride." The suddenness of the announcement left the audience in a pleasant shock.

Usher already had Zina in his arms. "You're mine—now and forever. Let's go home."

THE END
AND THIS IS JUST THE BEGINNING!

NOTE FROM AUTHOR

Thank you for reading *Combating Chaos.* I loved writing it, and hope you enjoyed reading it. If you did, please tell a friend and consider leaving a review on Amazon. Your sincere feedback means everything to me. There is nothing like a good mystery. Suspense novels get my juices flowing. Please visit me on my website and continue to read Cordy's next adventure. **https://jillflateland.com.**

The next book in this series is Caught Unaware. Check out the first chapter below.

PREVIEW OF CAUGHT UNAWARE – CHAPTER 1
CYBERSECURITY AGENCY

Jan. 27, 20?? – 7:20 a.m. EST, Washington, D.C.

It was a blustery winter morning in Washington, D.C. Unable to sleep, U.S. President Isaac Spendorf was on his usual prowl in the White House to fill his grandmother's old china teapot to brew his fifth cup of Morning Thunder tea. On his way back to the Oval Office, he stopped mid-stride, listening to a large-screen TV blaring from the conference room: "...Cozy Bear, a pro-Russia hacker group, rerouted a full bomb's worth of highly-enriched U.S. uranium to a nuclear plant in Iran."

"Oh my God!" Zac nearly dropped the teapot and set it down as his heart skipped a beat and then pounded like a jackhammer hitting his ribcage. Icy fear clutched his gut, while acid reflux caused a burning sensation in the back of his throat. He'd grown up hearing horrific war stories. His father, a paratrooper during WWII, had stormed Normandy on D-day and relived the nightmares every night for the rest of his life. *How did this slip by the Department of Defense?* The urgency of the situation bubbled to the surface, and Zac felt the weight of the responsibility fall heavily on his shoulders.

Eager to learn more, he stood outside the door as the news continued, "...a suspicious rock sample, weighing 95 kilograms, was obtained covertly by the University of New Mexico from a Texas laboratory that has been on the national watchlist. It turned out to be weapons-grade uranium."

How could this happen on my watch? He remembered visiting the Hiroshima Peace Museum, seeing the horrific photos from the raid, and watching testimonial videos of survivors of the first atomic bomb, Little Boy, which took only 65 kilograms to level Japan's city, killing 140,000 people. *This cyberattack could be the highest threat in our history.*

"...the rock, shielded to protect against radioactive exposure, was shipped back to Texas, but it never reached its destination. It arrived in Iran two hours ago. Cozy Bear also hacked four other countries, including the UK..."

Spendorf wasted no time. He dashed to his office, barking orders at his Chief of Staff Winston Willoughby, as he passed his desk. "Get Carl Wyller on the line immediately. Send it to VidChat—no security leaks." His determination was unwavering, and his resolve to tackle the crisis head-on was evident in every action he took.

The VidChat was already ringing when Spendorf entered his office. Recognizing Carl's image on the screen, he didn't bother with a greeting. "Why wasn't I notified of the missing uranium?"

"I was about to call you," Carl muttered. "I just got off the phone with Dr. Ping—"

Spendorf's temper flared as he exclaimed, "So our Director of National Intelligence knew about this, too, and I had to hear about it over the news? I hate being caught unaware!" The tension in the room went up a notch. Refusing to procrastinate, Zac was direct and to the point. Punctuality was a must in his world, pulling out all stops to complete the job. Perhaps he wanted too much of his team, but in his opinion, it was his job to be aware of small details and the large looming ones. "This is the fourth massive cyberattack in the last year. It's time to act. Cybersecurity falls under the Department of Defense. What are you doing about this?"

"Well, sir. We're working with SolarWinds, FireEye, and CrowdStrike to secure our networks with upgraded operating systems, and DoD is busy replacing outdated equipment." Carl sputtered. "You know my SUV has a better GPS—"

Spendorf snapped, "If you're too bogged down, I'll take action into my own hands," then bit back his anger. His eyes narrowed, jaw clenched, and he gave that familiar glare he was so well-known for.

Carl held up his hands. "Okay, Zac. I've seen that look before, and I'm not stupid enough to get in your way. Why, even you—Um, never mind, I'll get right on this," Carl hesitated before adding, "I'll have a word with the Russian president."

"No. If they are responsible, they'll be held accountable. Swift sanctions speak louder than words. We'll cut off all funding to Iranian and Russian banks and restrict their oil exports. Targeting personal assets will also impose severe financial burdens. I'm sure the EU will join us in imposing additional sanctions."

Carl cleared his throat. "I can—"

"You just get our military back on track, and I'll take care of the uranium crisis. As far as our cybersecurity, I have a better idea." As usual, Spendorf's innovative thinking blossomed. "I'm creating a new cabinet post. We'll call it the Cybersecurity Agency. It will be responsible for coordinating all cybersecurity efforts across different government departments, ensuring a unified and effective response to cyber threats. And I know the perfect person to run the department. I'm sure the Senate will agree."

Carl heaved a sigh. "That would be a relief, sir. Who do you have in mind?"

"I need someone to get this off the ground while launching at full speed." He added, "Dr. Joshtine Cordelia-Hastings has worked with me in the past. She's renowned for her IT and security skills, and I hear she just passed her board exam in forensic law."

"Cordy? She's well respected on the Hill, too." Carl sounded grateful. "You're right. I'm sure she can get Senate approval."

"Cordy will be perfect. She's brilliant, adventurous, quick-witted, and energetic. I'll keep you posted." He disconnected the call.

Zac needed this post now. This position will oversee all cybersecurity operations and strategies and carry enormous responsibility. I must find funding in the budget. Without hesitation, he called Cordy to ask if she'd accept the nomination for the new cabinet position.

Cordy was a lot like Spendorf—honest to her core, loyal, and would fight for what was right, refusing to admit defeat. "I'm deeply honored, Mr. President."

"Call me Zac. We've been on a first-name basis for years, and just because you're joining my Cabinet doesn't change how we address one another."

"Thanks, that means a lot. Tell me more. What will be my responsibilities?" Cordy tapped away on her keyboard in the background as Zac laid out his expectations.

"You'll report directly to me and work closely with Homeland Security, the Secretary of Defense, and the Director of National Security. You've worked with them in the past. We'll get input from you and the directors to draft a job description for all to review and revise as needed."

Cordy, a close friend and seasoned security data analyst at the FBI openly expressed her concerns, "It's not just about protecting the government's critical infrastructure. Our nation's businesses are ill-prepared for a cyber war. The DoD and Homeland Security lack the legal authority to enforce our strategies on private sectors. I'm skeptical that social media giants or private employers like Amazon, Microsoft, or Boeing have the necessary safeguards against cyberattacks."

Zac nodded. "We've made significant progress with the banking and financial industries, the Securities and Exchange Commission, and healthcare."

"True, but they still encounter breakthrough malware," Cordy said. "Spyware today is getting smaller, more complex, and easier to implant even when standard firewalls protect our systems. We would lose the battle if hit today. How can we unite everyone around a cyber defense system to combat current and future attacks? Even CrowdStrike, the leading cybersecurity firm, experienced a security breach that grounded planes worldwide, leaving families stranded in airports, either trying to get back home or traveling for business. The flawed update crashed Microsoft Windows, too, causing server outages and displaying the infamous 'blue screen of death' worldwide."

"You're right. Our nation is vulnerable to foreign cyber threats. We need an experienced team, and with your expertise, we can develop effective strategies to combat cybercrimes." Zac's plea was sincere, "I understand it's a lot to ask, and there may be no way to fully compensate you for your efforts, but I truly need you. We're navigating uncharted waters, and time is of the essence."

By the end of the call, Cordy said, "Yes, I accept the nomination. I'm anxious to start and have been jotting down ideas and questions as we speak."

Zac eagerly arranged a face-to-face meeting for the next day, ready to delve deeper into the cyber defense initiative.

Cordy gushed, "I can't wait to tell Braun. He's already in D.C., so I'll catch the earliest flight. Maybe he can meet me at the airport. See you tomorrow."

Zac said. "You and your husband make a good team, and we're lucky to have both of you working with us."

It could be weeks before the Senate would approve Cordy's nomination to head up the Cybersecurity Agency. In the meantime, Cordy had a lot to do.

* * *

Oh my, this is really happening! I need a top-notch team. Deep down, Cordy's goal was to make the U.S. the most secure cyber-superpower in the world. Challenged with concerns about fulfilling this enormous responsibility, Cordy spent a restless night, her stomach in turmoil, and by 4 a.m., she scrapped the whole idea of sleep. She brewed some tea and popped a slice of wheat bread into the toaster. After adding cream to her cup, she grabbed her phone and flipped through her contact list.

Cordy's first call was to Dr. Quint Altari, who had worked with her analysis team after getting his doctorate at her alma mater, MIT. His skills surpassed her expectations and would make him a strong team leader. She grabbed the phone while munching her toast—no time like now to gather talent. Between bites, she interviewed Quint and hired him on the spot.

Sept. 8 — 11:00 a.m. EDT, U.S. Cabinet Meeting, Washington, D.C.

At twenty-eight, Cordy was at the top of the world—married to the love of her life and ecstatic to be pregnant with twins. Her most challenging adjustment was that her husband, JSOC Commander Braun Hastings, was frequently away on special ops missions. She absolutely trusted him, but her greatest fear was for his safety—she never knew where he was stationed or how long he'd be away from home.

She also loved her new promotion, which took effect three weeks after Zac's proposal to the Senate. However, it meant frequent trips between her home base in Fort Collins, Colorado, and Washington, D.C. The job was challenging but didn't seem like work most days. It was fun. She used her ability to plot strategies like a three-dimensional chess game, staying a few steps ahead of most problems.

Her team updated security across various agencies during the last seven months. They analyzed, decrypted, and decoded complex applications, avoiding multiple foreign cyberattacks. Implementing an effective and efficient server-based backup system was critical to the network's security. All members were exceptional in their own rights, held accountable to one another, and carried their workloads with minimal complaints. They worked countless late hours and weekends to build a more robust and diverse network. She had every reason to be proud of their accomplishments.

Zac was also pleased with the team's endeavors and asked Cordy to give an update at tomorrow's cabinet meeting.

Cordy woke up early the next day, excited to update the Cabinet on the team's progress. Preparing for the meeting, she slipped into a navy blue pantsuit instead of her usual black jeans. One glance in the mirror made her sigh. It was essential to look her best. Makeup was a pain, but being a strawberry-blonde, her eyebrows appeared non-existent, and no one could see her long eyelashes, so she touched them up with an eyebrow pencil and a bit of mascara. After another assessment in the mirror, she pulled her shoulder-length hair into a French braid rather than her usual, casual ponytail. That was enough primping for one day, and she headed out the door.

When President Spendorf called for Cordy's report, she smiled. Despite the butterflies in her stomach, she was eager to share the team's results. "Thanks, Mr. President. With the help of many of you around this table, we managed to recover the uranium from Iran. The cybersecurity team worked tirelessly for the last seven months to cleanse our government systems of all traces of past cyberattacks."

Every eye was glued to her as she continued.

"Our internal network was riddled with challenges. The Pegasus worm had infiltrated our government's infrastructure, particularly our phones and emails. This spyware posed a significant threat, allowing adversaries to eavesdrop on conversations, read texts, and access data searches. It could even download photos and track GPS locations without the user's knowledge. Despite the difficulty in tracing the subtle footprint left by Pegasus, the cybersecurity team successfully plugged these leaks. All programs are now encrypted, and we are confident that we are fully shielded from future hacks, at least those known today."

President Spendorf and his senior team congratulated her on their significant achievement.

Sept. 9 — 9:14 a.m. EDT, U.S. Cabinet Meeting, Washington, D.C./ 7:14 a.m. MDT, Quint's Office, Fort Collins, Colorado

Cordy rushed to board a plane for Fort Collins, Colorado. It would be great to be home for the weekend. As she buckled her seatbelt, her cell phone rang. "Hi, Quint. I can't talk for long—the plane's about to take off."

"Glad to hear your Cabinet meeting went well, but I have some bad news." Quint sounded exasperated. "The Department of Justice has been calling for the past twenty minutes to complain that their screens froze after logging in this morning. Ten seconds later, the screens turned dark, and the system won't reboot. I thought it might be a hard drive issue, maybe the motherboard or an overheating CPU, but not all of them at the same time. Any ideas? We need to act fast."

Cordy's heart raced. Her cabinet report still echoed in her ears. *The potential threat is significant, as it could compromise the entire Department of Justice system, leading to data loss and potential disruption of operations. The implications are dire.*

Quint asked, "Do you think someone hacked into the DOJ? Were there any problems mentioned while you were on the hill?"

Cordy thought back to a major debate during the Cabinet meeting. "Yes, the Department of Justice is checking into possible illegal activities by traders who sell short."

"Why only those who sell short?" Quint asked.

"I don't have many details," Cordy wondered aloud, "but small investors are outraged over their losses, and Congress is demanding more government scrutiny. So far, the Securities and Trade Commission has tasked the DOJ with tracking how short sellers determine bets that stocks will fall. This investigation could have potentially angered certain parties who might want to disrupt the DOJ's operations."

Quint said, "Do you think there's a connection between the DOJ's investigation and today's computer glitch?"

"Good question. We need more research, but my main concern is that we just upgraded everything with new servers and modified security access. What if we missed something? We can't afford to overlook any detail in our investigation."

Quint heaved a sigh. "Hey, Girlfriend, you don't think China hid more of those microchips in their electronic devices, do you?"

Cordy's mouth felt bone-dry. "Quint, you're scaring the hell out of me. They could collect and alter data and jeopardize our justice system."

"Criminy, Cordy. What if they recoded those chips as we did at MIT?"

"Exactly," Cordy said. "Once activated, the screens go black, just like you described at the Justice Department. All files can disappear, and they don't even need to connect to the Internet. Low-frequency radio waves could trigger the malware—and easily take down the nearest power grid. Check for any sleeper surveillance components."

"Right. We found that old malware on the motherboards. I'll check into it."

There was a sudden commotion on the plane. The screens lit up with a video of safety rules, when, "Breaking news flashed across the screens. At first the plane became silent, then passengers began talking at once, and pointing to their TV screens. Cordy read the crawler scrolling below the newscast, "Intercity Future Transport, Inc. just made a bid to take over the Washington, D.C.'s Transit System." The screen flipped to the New York Stock Exchange floor, showing bidders waving their arms and shouting. The camera panned to a jagged line rising sharply, a visual representation of the stock prices soaring. The crawler read, "IYFTI stock has risen from $62/share to $280 and continues to rise."

A man sitting beside her pulled out his cell phone, his voice filled with excitement. "Nancy, buy 100 shares of IYFTI. Oh, why not? Make that 1,000 shares..."

A flight attendant tapped Cordy on the shoulder. "Please, turn off your phone." She glanced around. "Everyone, put your phones on airplane mode, now. We are about to take off."

"One second." Cordy rushed to disconnect. "Have the team backup all servers and do the same systems-wide upgrade we just completed on our network. I'll rerun everything through our analysis program when I get there. It should trap any spyware." The flight attendant's disapproving glare was unmistakable. "Sorry, Quint. Gotta go."

Sept. 10 — 9:00 p.m. MDT, Fort Collins, Colorado/ 11:00 p.m. EDT, Washington, D.C.

Home. At last. It had taken her entire team the rest of Friday and most of today to trap, quarantine, and backup data to new servers, but the Justice Department would be up and running smoothly when they returned to work.

Cordy was exhausted. Of course, fighting off dry heaves didn't help. Once again, she hugged the great white porcelain bowl with both arms. Her cell phone chirped as she was about to turn in for the night. She recognized the unique tone she'd assigned to her husband's texts.

Braun wrote, "Hope the twins let you get plenty of rest. I'm off to Maryland—testing a new weapon at Aberdeen Proving Ground early this a.m. I'll see you next weekend if all goes well. Miss you terribly. I can't wait to see you, and I'm counting the minutes until I can hold you again. LYA."

Cordy smiled at the initials—Love You Always. She wanted to talk to him in person, but he'd be heading for bed at this late hour, and with the two-hour time difference, he'd get up early.

As far as the twins letting her sleep, that was debatable. One moment, she felt ravishingly hungry and then nauseated the next. It's hard to believe she was already seven months pregnant. She'd lost her shapely waistline, had outgrown her jeans, and wore comfy maternity clothes. Resting her arms over her belly, she felt a ripple beneath her fingers. A warm glow rushed through her. *Twins.* She could hardly believe it.

It was dark when she stumbled to the kitchen in her stocking feet, grabbed a box of crackers, and went to her office. She made double-sure everything was locked behind a secure firewall before logging into her darknet account. Quint had sent the DOJ server files through her system's analyzer one last time. No hiccups so far, so she headed for bed. *Sleep at last. It will be nice to have a peaceful Sunday.*

Order *Caught Unaware* for the rest of the story.

ABOUT THE AUTHOR

Jill S. Flateland,
RN, BSN, CCRN, MBA

Although my background is over 40 years in healthcare as Supervisor of ICU, Director of MTU, and the CEO of an Urgent Care Corporation, I've been a writer all of my life. I've created 26 audio/video courses for nurses' continuing education and published 21 volumes of healthcare pathways for disease management throughout the U.S., Japan, Europe, and Australia. My husband and I live in Colorado, and we travel extensively.

I retired in 2006, and ventured into the wider writing world. In 2011, I published <u>A Lightning Slinger's Tales of the Rails</u>, which tells of Aunt Dr. Vera E. Williams' life as a female telegrapher during World War II. In 2014, I published <u>Ding Dong! The Rural Schools Are Gone</u>, a story of my two aunts, Vivian V. Lund (age 97 at the time, died at age 104 in 2022) and Dr. Vera E. Williams (age 88 at that time, died at age 90 in 2016), who were both teachers during the early twentieth century.

I entered my fifth novel, *Until We Meet Again,* in the 2014 Colorado Gold Contest at the Rocky Mountain Fiction Writer's Contest. Tobias McFitzroy's tombstone lay shattered in a cemetery outside a Colorado ghost town northeast of Fort Collins. The stonemason had carved his own epitaph. It read, "Until we meet again. 1830 – 1899." Unlike most people, it didn't mean when he'd meet them in heaven. He couldn't. He hadn't made it that far. The novel became a finalist in the suspense category.

Since then, I've continued writing action-packed thrillers in the Dr. Joshtine Cordelia-Hastings Crisis Series. The first novel, <u>Sweet Revenge</u>, introduces Cordy as she joins her ex-lover, JSOC Commander Braun Hastings, in a massive showdown with mafia members who seek revenge on the FBI agents who put the mob boss's son away in the federal penitenti`ary. Cordy's adventures continue in <u>Rapid Response</u>, where Cordy fights a bioterrorist attack when an astronaut unknowingly transports a potent virus, created without gravity on the space station, back to Earth. This virus is more deadly than our recent Covid pandemic. Not only does it devastate the lungs, but it also attacks the brain. Risking exposure, Cordy rushes to find a cure when U.S. President Spendorf, his key advisors, and many members of Congress become infected.

Next in the series, <u>Crashing The Grid</u>, sends Cordy and her team to reverse a cyber attack on NYC that shut down the power grid, water treatment plants, and more. Cordy's adventures continue in <u>Combating Chaos: All Systems Down</u>. Cordy and her new husband, JSOC Agent Braun Hastings, hunt down a Russian terrorist, General Okueva. He enlists student hackers to disrupt the New York Stock Exchange and major financial systems. Foreign forces have also attacked London and Rome. Cordy and her team risk their lives to stop the terrorists.

I'm currently writing *Caught Unaware,* where Cordy has been promoted to a new cabinet position at the Cybersecurity Agency. A massive cyber attack on Washington, D.C., challenges the team to pull out all stops to defend the president, especially when drones attack the White House. I hope you enjoy these fast-paced novels.

Sales Support a Worthy Cause

Byron and I are actively involved with two Non-Governmental Organizations (NGOs). The first is **Angel Covers**, who helped open Vill-Angel Medical Clinic in the center of a rural farming community in Endebess, Kenya, allowing poor families to receive high-quality healthcare.

As Director of Healthcare Services, my goal is to help expand the clinic to offer maternal-child care. Many families have no car to travel to a hospital, the nearest being 17 kilometers from the clinic. Some have a motorcycle, others have a cart pulled by a donkey, but many walk on foot.

Most women deliver babies at home, but the infant mortality rate in Kenya is six times higher than in the U.S. (Kenya has 30 infant deaths/1000 births compared to the U.S., which is 5 infant deaths/1000 births.) Some women travel up to two hours on foot while in labor to receive care during high-risk pregnancies. Plus, children are at the highest risk for death within the first 28 days. Most die of pneumonia, diarrhea, and sepsis. Our clinic can treat these ailments, and provide follow-up care as needed.

The second is Seeds of South Sudan, where donations help rescue refugees from Kakuma Refugee Camp in Kenya, allowing orphans to attend boarding school in Kenya. Once these students graduate, they plan to return to South Sudan to help rebuild its economy, infrastructure, and create a stabilized country.

You, too, can help. Part of the proceeds from the sales of these books help support these causes, and I thank you from the bottom of my heart. We know you have many choices for purchasing mystery novels and methods of donating to worthy causes, so I'm grateful that you chose to help support these charities.

OTHER BOOKS WRITTEN BY JILL S. FLATELAND

Thriller Series:

Sweet Revenge
Rapid Response
Crashing The Grid
Combating Chaos: All Systems Down
Caught Unaware

Suspense Series:

Until We Meet Again

Secret Series:

Secrets & Chandeliers
Family Secrets & Betrayals
Secrets Lost Among Forget-Me-Nots
Secrets of Grayson Mansion

Family Memoirs:

A Lightning Slinger's Tales of the Rails
Ding Dong! The Rural Schools Are Gone
Chugs & Hugs: Growing Up In A Train Station Vol 1
Chugs & Hugs: Growing Up In A Train Station Vol 2
Chugs & Hugs: Growing Up In A Train Station Vol 3

9 781966 012009